I0761952

IMMORTALILY

RISE

GE Beyers & JW Collins

A catalogue record for this book is available from the National Library of Australia

ISBN–13: 978-1-922343-72-7

Linellen Press
265 Boomerang Road
Oldbury, Western Australia
www.linellenpress.com.au

Dedication

For our beloved, blood-related or not

CONTENTS

Acknowledgements

With love and many thanks to my lovely husband, Leroux — for his unending patience and fabulous babysitting skills. And to Claude Carrello for your message of encouragement. Also, with love and thanks to Jak Collins, my son and co-author of this book — for the cover concept and design. You are a man of many talents, and I adore you – GE Beyers

To my beautiful wife Billy-Jo: thank you for your support and hours of creative editing. To my precious daughter Emerson — for being an angel child — allowing us to write and edit non–stop. And, for my mother, and co-author — for bringing my creative ideas to life. I love you all dearly – JW Collins

Finally, we would like to say a huge thank you to our amazing publisher, Helen Iles, who has burnt the candle many nights. Her dedication, final editing, and merchandise design will - we are sure - help our book to become a success. A wonderful person to work with: she has the patience of a saint, and we think she is simply fabulous – G E Beyers & J W Collins

NOTHING TO ME

'Your grandfather is right, Lily, you are a monster of sorts. It would have been far better if you had never been born.'

Twisting in his chair, Uncle Noah took a parcel from the shelf behind him. He spun back around to face me; shoved the parcel across the desk in front of him.

'I want you to have this; your mother asked me to give it to you on your eighteenth birthday. You're not to open it until then, not under any circumstances, okay?'

'Okay. But if I can't open it, why are you giving it to me now?'

'Because, Lily, I fear I may not be around on your eighteenth birthday.' He paused, and sat looking at me. 'Ah, Lily, I've kept you in the dark, but it's for your own good, your own safety. One more year won't hurt you.'

Every time we shared these conversations, this was all I got. It was useless pressing him for more because he was a sealed book. Whatever I had to fear was always going to be there. And yet, the only thing that worried me was that I'd never know exactly what it was until it was standing right in front of me. I was so mad at him. He could've told me what was likely to happen. He had no problem telling me that my grandad only saw me as a potential neck snap, but he wouldn't say more than that. He talked about the danger all the time, but never gave me answers to my questions. I was living on a knife's edge, but didn't have the faintest idea why.

Uncle Noah was always saying stuff to me like: 'Never go out in the garden alone, Lily, you know it's dangerous.'

Or 'No, Lily, you can't walk to school, don't be ridiculous — you know the streets are full of bad people.'

Or 'Don't go past the front gates, Lily. It's for your own safety.'

You'd think he was an occupational health and safety officer, not a fantasy fiction writer.

I often thought about running away. After all, nothing scared me, and I was sure someone would take me in. I also thought about the big wide world, what my life would be like outside of this house and even this village. But I just didn't have the heart to leave him. It made me feel better knowing he was old, and would probably be dead soon, and then I'd be free.

'I'm going to show you a secret tunnel, Lily,' Uncle Noah said as I sat deep in thought.

'Lily!' he shouted.

'Yeah? What?' I said, snapping out of it.

'On the bookshelf right there,' he said, pointing, '- on the third shelf down — there's a copy of the *Nocturnal Academy*.'

'Great book, that one,' I spurted out.

'Concentrate, Lily! This is important!'

'Sorry!' I muttered.

'Behind that book is a button. If you press the button, a panel to a corridor will open. At the end of the corridor is a ladder leading down to an underground tunnel that runs the length of our garden and comes up beside the big old oak tree on the other side of the back fence.'

'A secret tunnel? Seriously?' I said.

Uncle Noah stood and came around the desk to where I sat. He put his hands on my shoulders and said gravely, 'Now, Lily, if anything happens to me, I want you to take that parcel and disappear through the tunnel. Don't waste one second, do you hear? Do not stay in this house — do not call the police — and especially, not your grandad, not under any circumstances. Do you understand?'

I looked at him, confused. Said nothing. Was he losing the plot spending so many hours locked away up here writing? Had he written fantasy fiction for so long he was now lost in it? *Silly old bugger. Has the train left the station without him?*

'Listen, Lily! Your life is at stake here. If I'm not here to protect you, I don't know what might happen, but it will not be good. So, listen and do as I say!'

'Okay, okay, you're hurting me,' I said.

He let go of my shoulders.

'In truth, Lily, you mean nothing to me, but I promised your mother I would keep you safe. I've done so for seventeen years, with great difficulty, and now we are heading towards your eighteenth birthday everything is about to change. It's going to get much worse. The stress of keeping you safe is making me ill.'

His cold words, like a straight-shooting arrow, hit me in the heart.

'W-what?' I stuttered. 'Are you going crazy, Uncle Noah?'

'No, I'm not crazy — just stupid to have made a promise to my sister when I knew I would be unable to see it through. And you, Lily, you don't seem to have a care in the world. You should be scared for your life, but you are not taking this seriously at all. Over the years, I have tried to warn you; tried to prepare you for the worst. But all I see is a smile and a shrug of the shoulders. Honestly, what's wrong with you?'

'Well, I don't know, do I? Because you won't bloody tell me,' I blurted out.

Grabbing the parcel, I ran from the room.

This anger was overtaking me. Oh yes, this was an emotion I couldn't shut out. It seemed to have just popped up in me over the last few months, and the more pissed off I got, the more it seemed to grow.

Up in my room, I shoved the parcel on top of my wardrobe then sat in the triangular window space that jutted from the brickwork over the front porch. I sat in there a lot, and this time I closed the curtains behind me. With a window either side of me, I could see up and down the road — not a busy road — just the usual leafy avenue with rows of detached Victorian houses. All of them had high walls at the front and huge gardens at the back: a great place to play with friends. But I didn't have any. As a kid, I was pretty much a loner. Most summers were boring; birthdays and Christmas's were pretty shitty too. In truth, I had no one, and now I knew he didn't love me, the loneliness threatened to crush me like a bug.

It felt strange hearing him say I meant nothing to him. It made me feel something, somewhere deep inside. Was this sadness or despair? Was this how my uncle and grandad felt when my mum died? Was this why they thought I was a monster? Because they thought I was the reason she died.

For a moment, I felt their pain, and I got it — got why they couldn't love me? There was a picture on the wall that I'd been given for one of my birthdays. It was a drawing of a little girl cuddling a grown man — I suppose her dad — and underneath, in curly writing, it said *'A promise is a promise, and I promise to love you always'*.

Had he loved me when he'd bought that for me?

I guess he must have, but now I meant nothing to him. How was that possible? What had changed since then? Maybe I simply hadn't noticed that he was growing to hate me.

I glared at the picture. It made me feel crazy inside, crazier than usual. Suddenly the picture burst into flames. I gasped and jumped down from the window space; threw a glass of water at the canvas, which put out the flames but knocked everything on my tallboy to the floor, including a lit candle.

'Shit, shit, shit,' I said, stamping out the flames on the rug.

Crap, what just happened? I've burnt the rug. Uncle Noah will be so pissed.

I pulled a box of vinyls onto the corner of the rug to hide the burnt patch. The vinyls belonged to my mum, and I played them often on an old record player Uncle Noah had given me. I popped one onto the turntable — *Sunday Girl* by Blondie — and gently placed the arm down. The tiny needle scratched the record slightly as it touched the surface. Oh, how I loved the sound of old vinyl records. When I played them it was so ghostly, almost like the singer was there in the room with me. Sometimes the record would crackle lightly, showing its age. It made me think about the past and calmed me down when I was upset.

I sat back in the window space, opened my diary and started to write. A while later, when I was feeling better, I peeked through a gap in the curtains; stared up at the top of my wardrobe and wondered what was in the parcel. Could I ignore my uncle's rules and open it? *No, I'd better not.* I wanted to, but couldn't, even though I'd just found out that his love wasn't real. I grabbed a book instead and snuck into bed with a torch; read under the covers until I fell asleep.

In the morning, I left early for school before my uncle was up. I didn't want to risk eye contact with him after yesterday's moment of truth. I couldn't face him. Plus, I was still angry that I'd been forced to feel an emotion I hadn't felt before, something that left me feeling unsafe and totally alone for the first time in my life.

He wouldn't be happy with me leaving the house alone, but right then I didn't really care. I climbed over the front gates of the house because I didn't want to ask him for the key. Landing on the other side, I stopped and peered back through the bars, up to my uncle's study window. A hand pulled the curtain back slightly. He seemed to be watching me from the shadows for a moment, then the curtain dropped back into place, and I sprinted up the road as fast as I could, in case he decided to come after me. There was no way I was getting in a car with that pig this morning — absolutely no way!

I'd never been out alone; always had someone with me wherever I went. The rest of the time I was locked behind those gates and kept inside the house, except on warm summer days when I'd sometimes sit out the back under the trees watching the gardener, Tallis, mow the lawn. I loved the smell of freshly cut grass, and also liked Tallis because he was young like me — about twenty or so. Sometimes it was nice being around someone closer to my age, rather than my miserable old uncle.

Tallis was the youngest member of Uncle's staff. Standing about 6ft tall, he had stony brown hair, stormy blue eyes, and a body to die for. A tattooed sleeve of spirits entwined around his arm — not the usual skull and crossbones stuff — but a beautiful piece of artwork in a semi-pale grey that blended perfectly with his suntanned skin. He was eye candy for my soul. If my uncle knew I felt this way about Tallis, I'm sure he'd have me fitted with one of those chastity belts I'd read about in history books.

So, this freedom was a first for me. I kept looking back as the autumn leaves crunched beneath my feet, but no one followed. Surprised by this, I walked slower, which gave me a chance to catch my breath, and looked back again. Still no one followed.

Maybe because I'd just turned seventeen, he'd decided to let me out alone. But this was hard to believe. I also wasn't quite brave enough to go back and ask him.

Just then a familiar car started coming up the hill, and I dived behind a broken picket fence; crouched down; peeked through the gaps and the high grass growing between them. It was Grandad's car. As he passed by me, I could see three other men inside; they were all listening to what he said. They didn't even look my way, and I waited until they were well past the end of my road before I shot out from my hiding place and headed up the road as fast as I could. I wondered what they were doing in this neighbourhood. Maybe they'd been visiting my uncle. *Seems odd.* But I was glad I'd left the house before they saw me. Maybe Uncle Noah was expecting them, and that's why he didn't come after me? *Yeah, that would be why.* Even if I meant nothing to him, he had made a promise to my mum to keep me safe, and I'm sure he wouldn't go back on that.

Tallis had once said that my uncle was nothing, if not a man of his word.

Eventually, I reached my school. I wasn't used to walking that far, and I hadn't timed it right. I was at least half an hour late, and John Roan's bell had filled the classrooms when I was still a good mile down the road. After chucking my stuff into my locker, I made my way to class.

'Morning, Lily. It's not like you to be late,' said Mr Page. 'Don't get comfortable. You have to go to the office.'

'Why?'

'Your grandad was here looking for you about fifteen minutes ago. He said your uncle was ill and he needed to take you home. I assume that's why you're late, but you'd better get the all-clear from the office before you go.'

A sudden rush of emotion washed over me, so uncommon to me. What was happening? I'd spent years feeling absolutely nothing, then in a matter of just two days, all of this, all at once. Sadness, anger, bitterness, and now this one, the worst feeling of all. Fear!

I ran from the classroom, but instead of heading for the office or the front entrance, I bolted out the back doors and up the hill to the woods behind. I ran fast; scrambled through the mud and leaves. Twigs and branches tore my clothes. My eyes felt wet, and I looked up. *Is it raining? No. Overcast, but not raining.* I wiped my face with the palm of my hand. My eyes were definitely wet. *What is this?*

Then a lump formed in my throat. *I'm crying!* I had seen this in girls of my age, but had never experienced it: Me, Lily Du Plessis: insensitive, unemotional, and lately, perhaps a little irrational but never upset, Lily.

I'm crying real tears.

I needed to pull myself together; needed to think straight.

What should I do now? Run home to Uncle? What if he's in trouble? Will I be able to help? What if he isn't? Will he be able to protect me if those three guys and my grandad decide to get nasty? Shit! How will I reach the parcel and the tunnel if I can't go home? What if I'm safer at home than here in the woods?

So many questions filled my head, I couldn't think straight. So, for a little while, I sat under a big old tree and let my emotions get the better of me.

An hour later it started to rain, and I ran for cover behind the school sports shed. When it slowed to a drizzle, I made my way out the gates and along the heath road. It was an open area and possibly not safe, but I had no other option. The big church, with its tall spire, stood out like a sore thumb in the middle of the common. I rushed along as the autumn breeze whipped my face and made my eyes water as I tried to cross the heath as quickly as I could. My heart beat so fast at the thought of bumping into my grandad.

As soon as I reached the village and felt safer, less obvious, I ducked in and out of shop doorways, made my way along the pavement, past the music conservatory, and turned the corner into my road. I ran along the tree-lined avenue towards the high, moss-covered stone wall that surrounded our front garden. When I reached there, the black, wrought iron gates were not only unlocked but also stood wide open. *Strange!* But I guessed Uncle Noah knew I wasn't there — he'd seen me leave for school. Maybe this was how it was during the school day; maybe he only locked them when I was home to keep me safe.

Nevertheless, an awful feeling gnawed in the pit of my stomach. Call it second sense or something else, but deep inside, I knew something was wrong. The feeling crept up my skin; electrified the tips of my hair, which stood on end. My hair turned clammy against my face, and my breath shortened. As panic began to rise, I fought the urge to throw up.

Sneaking around the side of the house, staying clear of the front, I moved around to the back garden and looked through the downstairs window, then crept through the back door. Tiptoeing along the highly polished wooden floorboards, afraid they might creak under the weight of my sneakers, I silently ascended the stairs to the second floor. At the top of the second flight, I heard a car, and quickly checked — it was Grandad coming along the avenue again.

I scurried up the next flight, passing my uncle's study on the way up to my bedroom.

And there I froze.

Uncle Noah was slumped on his desk; a pool of blood from a wound in his neck spread out around him. He'd obviously been dead a while as the blood had turned thick and sticky, like plum sauce. This was definitely grounds for calling the police, even though I'd been told *not* to call them, or anyone else for that matter.

I hurried to my room; grabbed a backpack and stuffed everything important into it, including the parcel. Then I grabbed my jacket and rushed back down to the study. Moving the book on the third shelf down, I pressed the hidden button. The wall opened a crack. I pushed the book back into place and slipped in, closing the panel behind me.

Footsteps sounded on the stairs, then muffled voices. I froze; hardly dared to breathe. My gaze fixed on the ladder at the end of the corridor and, while I knew I should be making my escape I was too scared to move — too scared they'd hear me — too scared my grandad would snap my bloody neck! Then I heard Grandad talking to someone.

'Where is she?'

'We don't know. We went to the school, twice, and checked everywhere.'

'You're a pair of imbeciles. Can't you do anything right? She's just a defenseless kid, surely it shouldn't be too hard to trace her.'

'She's hardly defenseless, sir. I mean, if the story is true, you know — about her mum -'

'That's my daughter you're talking about so you watch your tongue! And if she'd lived, she'd have killed Lily herself. Instead, that horror of a kid killed her before she had the chance.'

The room fell silent.

I flinched behind the panel. Had I breathed in too sharply? Had they heard me gasp in shock? *Shit*!

My hands started trembling. I held my breath; leant against the wall to stop my legs from shaking.

'She's pure evil, that kid; has been since the day she was born. Don't let that prettiness fool you — those fiery brown eyes and that beautiful face. With her dark hair and porcelain skin, she looks just like her old man, and her soul is as black as coal. She killed my daughter, and now she's killed my son. I want her dead!' He brought his fist down hard on the desk.

I couldn't believe my ears. Grandad thought I'd killed Uncle Noah? He actually thought I could do such a thing? And how wrong was I to think that he'd killed his own son? But this left a nagging question: If I didn't kill Uncle Noah, and Grandad didn't kill Uncle Noah, then who did?

Maybe the person at the study window this morning wasn't uncle at all. Maybe he was already dead when I left the house. Perhaps he was already dead when Grandad drove into our street. So, who the hell drew back the curtain and watched me leave? And why didn't he come after me?

'Try the school again. She has to be somewhere. I'll wait here for the police. She has no family and nowhere to go. Wherever she is, she has to come home sometime, and when she does -'

He must have made a comment I didn't hear because the two other men laughed. I heard their footsteps as they left the room and hurried down the stairs; heard the car start up and reverse out of the driveway. Then the floorboards creaked as Grandad walked across the room to the door. There he stopped. He must have turned around, because I heard his footsteps again, coming closer to the bookshelf. He was checking the shelf of the panel I stood behind. Moving books. Lifting them out. Putting them back. I seriously could have pissed myself right then I was so scared. I shouldn't have stayed to listen. I should've been long gone. *Shit!*

If he just touched the wrong book, I'd be discovered. *Run for it!*

Panic beat like a drum in my chest.

Panic makes you react in the wrong way sometimes.

The thought calmed me down; helped me think straight. Accordingly, my breathing calmed; my pulse slowed. I closed my eyes, and it was like I wasn't there. I was on the other side of the panel; inside my grandad, controlling his every move. I imagined him putting the book he held back in place and turning away from the shelf. I imagined him walking towards the door and out into the hallway.

It was the weirdest feeling, yet felt strangely familiar.

I had complete control of him for just a few minutes. I opened my eyes, and the sound of him had gone. The room outside was quiet. Footsteps now echoed from the ground floor. A television turned on. Now was my chance to get the hell out of there while the television drowned out any noise.

Sidling along the dark corridor to its end, I descended the ladder, nearly tripping over something hard at the bottom. Groping around in the darkness, I found a tin — obviously left there by my uncle so I'd find it. I picked it up and stuffed it under my jacket; made my way along the tunnel to the exit beside the big old oak tree on the opposite side of the fence. Warily, I climbed out, looking both ways to check the coast was clear. Then I dashed across the road and up the hill to the woods, where I crept deep into the trees, hoping no-one would find me. I had to decide where to go and what to do next.

Finding a large hollow oak tree, I crawled in through the thick shrubbery around the base; sat within its shelter and waited for nightfall — waited until it was pitch black. *I'll be safe here for a while.* When the moon was huge in the sky, I'd make my move, to where I really didn't know, but it would be as far away from the house as I could get — that seemed the most sensible plan.

Then I thought about Uncle Noah. Dead — completely.

My emotions had been so up and down the last two days: I had bawled my eyes out for the first time ever in the woods behind the school, and yet, knowing Uncle was dead, didn't stir up any emotions at all.

Maybe he'd actually meant *nothing* to me. Like I'd meant *nothing* to him.

FINDING LILY DU PLESSIS

Sitting in that hollow oak I had plenty of time to think. I knew this wasn't about my Uncle Noah. I knew his murder must have been my fault. Whoever had killed him would have been after me. I just knew it.

I spent the next few hours thinking back on all the things that had happened to me as a kid and trying to figure out if I was right. I mean, who would want to hurt my uncle, except for my grandad. Not that that made any sense, because he obviously thought I did it.

I was shaking, though I wasn't cold. I sat wrapped in the darkness of the cramped hollow, feeling the damp earth seeping through the knees of my jeans. As the day turned into night, and with no light to see by, the woods around me were deathly quiet and creepy. I closed my eyes to block it all out then began remembering.

My grandad had once said to me: 'You, my girl, should never have been born. You're an abomination! The Du Plessis name is a curse.'

At the time, I didn't know what he meant. I just smiled and hugged his leg. He tried to push me away, but at five years old I was pretty tough. I hung on tightly until my uncle peeled me off of him.

I remember thinking about what my grandad had said when I

was working on a project in school about the myth of the abominable snowman. I learned this creature was mystical, magical, strong and brave, and I wondered whether this was how my grandad saw me. After all, he had used the same sort of word to describe me.

I couldn't have been more wrong.

Since I was born, I'd lived with my Uncle Noah on the outskirts of Blackheath village in south-east London, in a large four-storey Victorian house. We never had visitors, and I can only remember a few times seeing my grandad. The first time was when he called me an abomination, and every time after that, he treated me with the same amount of disdain.

Luckily, my Uncle Noah never left me alone with him.

My mum had died giving birth to me, and my grandad had always held a grudge. My uncle didn't. He had loved me with all the love he had to give, or so I'd thought. As I was growing up, he talked a lot about my mum. He told me stories about when they were kids; how much he'd loved his little sister, and other intricate details of their lives. It was hard to imagine him loving someone other than me, but that was because, however hard I tried, I just couldn't feel anything for her. I'd never known her; only seen pictures. She was pale and freckly, with strawberry blonde hair and sky-blue eyes. She had an almost otherworldly beauty about her.

Lilith Montague was my complete opposite. I had dark-brown hair, and almost black-brown eyes. My small size was the only thing the same. I couldn't feel a connection, and it was hard to know how to react when he talked about her. I felt like he was talking about a complete stranger.

My mum's death was the reason my grandad felt the way he did about me: he hated my guts! I couldn't understand it. After all, it wasn't my fault. I didn't kill her. So it wasn't something I was going to feel guilty about. How could a newborn baby be blamed for its mum dying in childbirth?

Anyway, life was good with Uncle Noah. He was overprotective, but I guess after losing my mum, I was all he had to remind him of her. That possibly made me a bit precious. I tried hard, but couldn't remember any more of my early years. In fact, I couldn't remember anything before the age of five. All I remember was, our house was big and dark, and my earliest memory of grandad's words, which were as clear as if he said them yesterday.

The air became chilly, and I dragged my jacket around me and pulled it closer. Yet I remained cold, and confused, but not sad. I did feel something though — it was a need to get away — to make it to another day. This helped me keep my shit together, enough to decide what to do next.

Time to check the tin.

Inside was a small torch. *I wish I'd known that a few hours ago.* I used it to check the contents of the tin. There was a whole stack of cash, all tied in little bundles with elastic bands, and on the top of it, a note in Uncle's messy scrawled writing. It said: 'Get out of England!' and a scribbled phone number with the name Tallis underneath. There was nothing else to the message — no 'Goodbye, Lily'; no 'Love, Uncle Noah'; no 'Hugs & Kisses'. No nothing like that. Just straightforward instructions to leave this country and the only life I'd ever known.

Where to go now though?

The first person to come to mind was my best friend, Olive Briggs, from school. While my uncle's instruction was to contact Tallis and leave the country, I first had to understand why I should call the gardener. How could he help me?

Secondly, the only person I really felt comfortable with was

Olive, because she would demand nothing of me. No details. No explanations. She would just be happy to have me around. So I decided to head to her house.

I'd never been allowed to visit her before, and the thought that I could now do just that made me want to do it, much more than doing what my uncle said.

I guess I was giving Uncle Noah the middle finger. *Boy, once he's buried, I bet he'll turn in his grave.*

As night closed in, I crept quietly out of the hollow on my knees. The moon reflected brightly in a puddle on the forest floor. I didn't need to look up to see it was full and round, it provided enough light to see by as I made my way warily through the woods. Olive's house wasn't far, and I could go in via the back without being seen. Luckily, a Fair was in town. The streets were full of people on their way to and from the heath; the only open stretch being from the traffic lights on the edge of the heath, to the pond on the far side, halfway between the school and my house. So, I ran, shrouded by crowds of loud and happy fairgoers much of the way.

I arrived at Olive's without any problems; stood outside under the streetlamp, looking up at her house, which I recognised from her description of it in class. Her mum's Kombi van was in the driveway, and bright lights shone from the windows in almost every room. I stepped out of the lamplight and crossed the road; knocked on the door. I wasn't sure if I'd be welcome.

Olive's mum opened the door and immediately recognised me. 'Lily, my love, how are you? Come in, girl, come in.' She dragged me into the hall and gave me a huge hug. 'Olive. Lily's here,' she shouted.

Olive stood in the hallway, looking shocked to see me.

'Lily,' she said, 'what the hell are you doing here?'

'That's a rude question. Invite Lily in,' said Olive's mum, nudging her with her elbow.

'Oh, I'm sorry,' said Olive. 'It's just that you never come here — like ever!'

We walked through to the kitchen with its orange benches and purple walls. Olive had told me her kitchen gave her headaches, which I thought was a bit odd. But she was right: this was definitely migraine territory! A little dog yapped and ran in and out of the kitchen, the small space otherwise filled with people. Olive's dad stood by the sink, talking on his mobile. Olive's twin brother Frankie sat at the table playing Monopoly with a friend. Her younger sister, Angel, chased the dog in and out of the room, teasing it with a ball. The dog tugged and tugged at the ball, but Angel kept a tight grip on it and laughed. The dog shook his head wildly from side to side, trying to get the ball out of her hand. I felt something around my ankles and looked down at a big shaggy, ragdoll cat that wound its body around my legs. It purred loudly and looked up at me. I bent down to stroke it, and it looked up at me again snobbishly, as if to say, 'How dare you touch me'. Then it disappeared into another room.

'Oh, that's Pippa. Take no notice of her, she's always trying to get attention but doesn't actually want it. She's an odd creature,' said Frankie.

'What's the dog called?' I asked.

'Smith,' said Frankie.

'Strange name,' I replied.

'Strange dog,' said Frankie.

On the table where the boys played Monopoly, a little furry creature grunted and waddled around, occasionally stopping to nibble on a game piece or chew the edge of a card. It looked like a miniature punk rocker with its hair standing up like a Mohawk.

Olive's mum said it was a guinea pig — I'd never seen anything like it. But then, so overwhelmed by the activity and madness in this kitchen, I wasn't surprised by anything.

'What brings you here this time of night, little Miss,' Olive's dad said once he'd finished his call.

'Oh, well … umm … my uncle's gone out of town, and I was a bit freaked out at home all alone … and well, he's gone for a few days, maybe more. So, I thought I'd ask Olive if I could stay here? Only if it's okay with you though.'

'Of course. Sure you can. No problem. We've always got a houseful. Just squeeze in where you can.'

Grinning, he patted me on the back and wandered to the other room; sat next to Olive's grandad.

'Are you hungry, Lily? We're just about to dish up beans on toast. Would you like some?' said Olive's mum.

'Love some,' I said. I'd been a *meat-and-three-veg* girl all the years I'd lived with Uncle Noah, and something as simple as beans on toast sounded great! I was also starving, my stomach rumbling all evening.

Good job it was a large dining table. It was crammed into the small kitchen with hardly any room around the edge to get around. But when it came time to eat, the whole family, including Frankie's friend and I, squeezed in wherever we could — just like Olive's dad had said.

We all ate our beans on toast elbow to elbow.

After tea, we sat in the lounge. Some sat on sofas, some on the floor, as there wasn't room for everyone. But nobody seemed to care. The television roared in the background, the boys still chatted loudly, and not one adult told them to shut up. It's as if they were used to listening to the television over the noise of the yapping dog, the purring cat, the grunting guinea pig, and in the corner high up in a cage even a budgie tweeted. The bird contributed to the racket with 'Hello birdie' and 'Give us a chip'. It was great. I'd never heard a budgie talk before - just one more strange attraction to this amazing circus of a household that felt firmly built on love.

Olive and I said goodnight and her parents, grandparents and brother all stood and hugged me and wished me a goodnight. I felt as stiff as an ironing board, and they were all gooey and soft, like marshmallows. I'd have to learn to do this hugging thing ... to kind of melt into it like they did. It was nice. Not something I'd ever experienced before, as Uncle Noah hardly ever touched me, other than the rub of an arm if he was happy with me, or a pat on the head if I'd been a good girl. But no, the hugging phenomena was a new experience, and I kind of liked it.

Olive's room was tiny but interesting: lots of little trinket boxes sat around; a dressing table in the corner had all sorts of fake jewellery, hair bobbles, mini notepads, collectable erasers in all shapes and sizes, and little glass pots filled with tiny beads and coloured glitter. A bowl full of different coloured nail varnishes sat on one end of the dressing table, on the other, a tall figurine of a ballerina with arms outstretched. The ballerina was beautiful, but for Olive, it simply served as a spare hanger for necklaces and bracelets. All around the edge of the dressing table mirror were photographs — mostly selfies, or pictures of Smith and Pippa. A couple of Frankie. And just one of Angel dressed up as a fairy. It was weird: how long I had known Olive, how close I felt to her, she really knew little about me. She was my best friend in the world, yet there wasn't one picture of me amongst all the photos.

'We'll have to get a photo of us together to add to your mirror,' I said, smiling at her while skimming my hand across her stuff on the dressing table.

'Sure,' she said, looking up from the floor where she was pulling a trundle bed out from beneath her bed.

'What a cool idea. I was actually wondering where I was going to sleep?'

'Yeah, we don't have a lot of room here, but it works well. We work well.'

Olive was so right.

Being Friday night, we stayed up late, Olive doing most of the talking, as usual, while I silently considered what to do next? What should I tell her, and how much did she actually need to know? She was my only friend, in a place where I now had no one. And nowhere was safe for me. *How am I going to explain this without scaring the crap out of her?* I couldn't just stay with her without saying anything, because if I stuck to the big fat lie I'd told her dad in the kitchen, I'd soon be caught out.

So how long can I stay without questions being asked?

With Uncle Noah dead, it wasn't safe to leave Olive's house, or go to school, church, or home. How would I explain this to Olive unless I told her the truth?

'You're so quiet, Lily. Are you feeling okay?'

'Yeah … well no … not really, but I don't know what to say.'

'Well, if you don't want to say anything, that's fine by me. You know our D&M's have always been pretty one-sided.' Olive giggled and looked at me. 'Seriously, Lily, you can tell me anything, and I won't tell a soul, or you can keep it to yourself — it's entirely up to you.'

'Thanks, Olive. I know I've never really opened up much, but that's because my life is either really rat shit boring or really bloody complicated. I'm in a bit of a mess right now, and I need to tell you the truth, but I'm scared it's going to shock you.'

Olive sat bolt upright. 'Well … what? Come on, share.'

'My Uncle Noah's dead, Olive.'

'What!' Her beautiful chestnut eyes grew big as golf balls.

'He's dead as a doornail, and I don't know who murdered him, but it wasn't my grandad, and it wasn't me.'

'Well, thank God for that! I mean, thank God it wasn't you,' she said, aghast.

'I couldn't call the police. My uncle told me not to.'

'His corpse talked to you?' She looked completely shocked now.

'No, of course not. He told me before he died. He said that, if he died, I shouldn't call anyone, especially not my grandad. I just had to take the parcel he'd given me and escape through a tunnel under the house.'

'No way!'

'No shit, Olive! Honestly! And I've been hiding in the woods nearly all day and night wondering where to go; what to do. My uncle left me a tin with instructions, but what he wants me to do just seems stupid ... Then I thought of you.'

'Why me, Lily?'

'Because you're the only friend I have, Olive. You're the only one who knows me ... without really knowing me of course.' I smiled and winced.

'Oh, Lordy. What do we do? We can't tell the police. We can't tell my parents. You cannot go home — like ever! And we need to keep you away from your crazy grandad too.'

'Yep, that's about right.'

'Mmm ... this could suck.'

'I know, but I need your help. I've got nowhere else to go.'

'Don't worry, Lily. You've got it. It'll work out fine. Just you wait and see.'

Olive folded her arms around me and hugged me, and for the second time that day I balled my eyes out. But this time it didn't feel so terrible: telling her the truth made me feel a whole lot better; I wasn't alone in the woods anymore but in my-best-friend-in-all-the-world's bedroom. Somehow I felt she was right, and everything would work out fine.

Olive paced back and forth across the room, thinking, plotting, planning. Her ten-step traverse made me feel claustrophobic. 'Mum and dad both leave for work before we go to school, and us kids are always home before them, so neither of them will notice if you're not going to school,' she finally said.

'Okay, that's a plus.'

'If mum invites you to church, I suggest we say you're not feeling up to it. Got a tummy ache or something,' Olive added.

'Yeah ... good idea.'

'And we better tell them you don't get on well with your grandad; that your uncle wants you to stay out of his way while he's out of town. Just in case he asks about you at the school. We can't have my mum blabbing her mouth off that you're staying here.'

'Yeah. Totally.'

'You'll be okay to stay here for at least a week or so I'd say. If we tell them your uncle decided to stay longer. Any longer than that and they might get suspicious and think you've run away and all.'

'True.'

'They might try to fix something that can't be fixed, being the hippy, peacemaking, do-gooders they are.'

'Well, if things get difficult, I can phone our gardener Tallis. My uncle must have sorted out some kind of plan with him, so that's an option if I get desperate.'

'Okay. All sorted then,' said Olive.

'All sorted.' I replied.

We slipped into our beds and Olive whispered to me for a while, telling more stories about her crazy family until I fell asleep. I awoke late on Saturday morning, with something warm and fluffy snuggled up beside me under the covers: Pippa, the ragdoll cat. I could feel her little rumbling purr — it sounded so nice, so comforting. I'd never had a pet — never been allowed — and I swore right then that when I settled again, I'd get myself a cat.

I stayed at Olive's house for another week, and she was right. Her mum and dad started to question where my uncle had gone. Why was he so long coming back? And how irresponsible he was to leave me alone at home for over a week. Luckily, nothing was said by Olive's mum at the school, or at church, because my grandad had been to both places a few times asking where I'd gone? Of course, Olive had told the teachers and the church pastor that I'd gone out of town with my uncle on business, on a book tour or something.

The school headmaster was not happy that my uncle hadn't told him about the vacation during school times, but what could he do? So, when my grandad asked for information at the school, all they could tell him was that my Uncle Noah had gone out of town on a book tour and taken me with him.

Of course, my grandad knew this wasn't true because my Uncle Noah was only fit for lying in a cold grave.

He couldn't pressure them for any more information, as they obviously didn't know anything. My grandad approached Olive too, and she acted like she hadn't heard a thing; hadn't seen or heard from me in at least a week. I guess my grandad then thought I'd skipped town because he stopped coming into the school the week after that. Still, I couldn't go there, because the headmaster had promised to give my grandad a call when I returned. I was stuck between a rock and a hard place. Not that I really wanted to go to school. Who in their right mind does? But I was bored shitless sitting in Olive's room all day. My grandad was still looking for me, so I couldn't go out. I had gone from one prison to another, or rather a prison to a looney bin! There were no locks on the doors, nor bars at the windows at either place, but the inmates were much friendlier here. Indeed, I loved Olive's family, and they had all grown close to me in the short time I'd been here, but it was time to move on. I would miss Olive dearly, maybe not as much as I'd miss Pippa, but once things were safe and I was settled, I could always come back. I mean, this craziness couldn't go on forever, surely. It had to end sometime. I wondered then if I would ever truly be free

That night as we all sat in the kitchen, as usual, Angel came to me with a dead budgie in her hand. 'Look at poor Bernard. He fell off his perch and died today, coz he's really, really old,' she said tearfully.

I smiled and stroked the bird. 'How lovely,' I said.

Everyone at the table raised an eyebrow and frowned.

I looked up, a flash of a childhood memory racing to my mind, filling my vision. Something had happened at Uncle's house. I was ten years old, and Uncle Noah was dating a woman called Juliette. They'd been seeing each other for about six months and I was excited about having another female in the house.

She moved in, and life was good. She was kind and helpful, and I loved watching her; loved the smell of the kitchen when she cooked, all cozy and warm like a real family home. I hoped Uncle would marry her so she could be my new mum. Watching the two of them made me think that this was entirely possible. I could tell he was truly in love by the way he looked at her; by the way he touched her.

I loved Juliette too; felt almost the same way about her as I did about Uncle Noah. I felt possessive, like I wanted them to belong to me. Like, if someone tried to take them from me, I'd stab them through the heart with a bread knife.

I guess you'd call that love.

I guess Juliet loved me too. Like I was her very own kid. Like I belonged to her. This feeling didn't last long though, because, within weeks of moving in, she slipped and lost her balance, fell over the banister from the top of the fourth flight of stairs, right outside my room. She lay dead at the base of the stairwell.

I knew she'd fallen the full four storeys because there were nail marks in the wood of the banister where she'd tried to hang on for dear life. I must've slept through the whole horrendous incident. She might've been on her way to tuck me in. Not that she ever had before, but who's to know, hey? There's a first time for everything.

It took a long time for Uncle Noah to get over her. But not me. I wasn't sad. After all, these things happened in life, and everyone is replaceable, right? Tragedies seemed to happen more in my life than anyone's, but I wasn't going to dwell on it. Uncle Noah stopped going out after she died; started to spend more time at home with me, which I thought was a super bonus to the whole Juliette dying situation.

'There's no point in getting involved with anyone. Nothing lasts forever, Lily,' he said to me one day, manufacturing a smile. I guess he was hurting. I guess he missed Juliette.

Her sudden death seemed odd though. I'd been going up and down those stairs for a couple of years without any problem, and Juliette came up once and *POW!* I couldn't imagine how it had happened. I mean, there was nothing on the floor for her to trip over. The clumsy woman must have fallen over her own two feet.

After the funeral, Uncle Noah sat me down and angrily lectured me about singing *Don't worry, be happy* at the graveside. I'd sung it for Juliette. I thought she might like it, and all the people there sure looked like they could do with a happy tune to cheer them up. But he was not impressed! He said:

'Your behavior is so inappropriate, Lily! You need to learn how to act in social gatherings so that you don't draw attention to yourself with your lack of good social manners!'

What a load of rubbish! I thought I'd been pretty well behaved, so I didn't get why he was so upset with me. But I agreed, and nodded, and promised to try harder to behave better, even though inside I thought he was a miserable old git who would look better lying in the coffin next to Juliette.

He mourned Juliette for a long time after that, and something seemed to change between us. The closeness was slipping away.

Juliette was the closest I'd come to having a mum in my life ... A tear fell, and I wiped my eye on the edge of my sleeve.

When I focused on the now again, everyone in Olive's house was still looking at me; still waiting for me to fix the look of shock on Angel's face. I quickly made a sad face to match my tears and said, 'God bless poor Bernard,' just like the good people at church would do.

I thought about Uncle's lecture after the funeral and knew this was what he was talking about, so I let the tears fall and hugged Angel closely. This time everyone made a sad face with me and said nice things to try to cheer us both up.

An hour later, we buried Bernard in a decorated shoebox filled with glitter and fairy dust, a packet of his favourite birdseed, and his favourite little rope ladder and bell. We all said goodbye, and Angel said a little prayer and covered the shoebox over with the loose earth. She cried real tears and I couldn't really understand why? After all, it was just a bloody bird. But then I saw Pippa in the distance waiting behind a bush, probably marking the spot where we buried Bernard so she could dig him up at some point. I'd heard cats did that.

As I looked at her and imagined her dead, a lump rose in my throat. And the tears came again. Angel hugged me as if we were sharing the same sadness for Bernard when really, I was crying at the thought of Pippa dying. It was definitely a heartfelt moment, and, as we all made our way back to the kitchen, I felt almost proud that, for the first time in my life, I had actually shed a tear for the death of another living being — even though it was only a cat that wasn't actually dead. It still felt like I'd climbed a mountain in the empathy stakes.

But that moment didn't linger.

FEEL IT IN MY BONES

When a heavy pounding rattled the front door in its frame, Olive's dad opened it. My grandad stood sternly on the porch, his henchmen behind him. We could hear them in the hall. Olive's mum pushed me into the pantry and quickly sat down. But I heard them coming closer; heard Olive's mum gasp. Peeking out through a gap, I saw Grandad holding a gun to Olive's dad's head. I held my breath, swallowed it down, but deep down inside I could feel the anger building.

Who does he think he is? How dare he barge into my best friend's house and threaten her dad with a weapon!

'Where is my granddaughter?' Grandad demanded. 'Where the hell is she?' He rammed the gun harder into the side of Olive's dad's head.

The poor man looked terrified.

Everybody in the room fell silent, except for Smith who yapped at the strangers like any good dog should.

'We don't know what you're on about?' Olive protested. 'She's not here! I only see her at school or church, and she hasn't been at either place for over a week. I think she went away with her uncle. At least that's what I heard.'

'Shut your mouth, liar,' said one of Grandad's men, grabbing her by the hair. 'Tell the truth, or we'll put a bullet in his head.'

'We don't know anything!' Olive's mum squealed. 'Don't you

think we'd tell you if we did.'

Grandad paused, as if considering she might be telling the truth.

Inside the pantry, I struggled with what was happening. My hands had grown hot and sweat poured from my brow. I felt hot and clammy all over. Peering through the gap again, I tried to stem the anger; tried to slow my breathing, to keep my cool. I wanted to rip my grandad's guts out, and my anger was building fast.

'Get outside and check the garden,' he ordered two of his men. 'Check upstairs,' he growled at the other. 'You lot move!' he shouted to everyone else. '... up that end of the table so I can keep an eye on you.'

The whole family moved to the other end of the table, away from the pantry door. Grandad pushed Olive's dad down into a chair, the gun still held to his head. Pippa entered the room and wrapped herself around my grandad's legs. I hoped she didn't try to find me.

I tried to stay calm, but I was boiling up inside, this rage scaring me: it was another emotion I'd never felt before. I felt like I was going to explode.

Then the worst thing happened. Grandad, pissed off by Pippa, swiped at her with his gun, but couldn't reach her, so he kicked her across the room. She hit the wall with a loud thud, fell to the floor and didn't move. I lost it!

I'm not exactly sure what happened next, but the door of the pantry flew off! I can remember everyone screaming; running for the back door. Then furniture flew everywhere, and a vicious gust of wind whipped through the kitchen, like the middle of tornado alley in Texas — not like a quiet, sleepy, little road in Blackheath, England.

Everything in the kitchen whirled — chairs, pots, plates, knives

— and through all the madness, Grandad shot at me. Everywhere I looked there were flames … And when I glared at my grandad, his jumper caught fire, then his hands.

A few bullets stopped in front of me, spinning, everything moving in slow motion. My force had frozen the bullets. They exploded, shrapnel flying backward and hitting my grandad in the face, ripping off little strips of flesh that floated out into the chaos. He dropped the gun and ran screaming from the house, his men racing after him.

The kitchen bench caught fire and pretty soon the walls too. Smoke filled the kitchen. I heaved air in and out, trying to calm the rage before any more damage was done. Olive's dad rushed back into the kitchen with the garden hose; started spraying the fire. It soon died down to a smoulder. He shouted at me to get into the garden as smoke billowed around me. I bent down and scooped up Pippa's lifeless body; carried her out with me, my heart thudding … then she stirred in my arms … she was going to be alright.

Olive's family stood stunned.

Olive's brow creased with worry, then her eyes widened in disbelief. Then her arms wrapped around me, hugging me tightly.

'I'm so sorry,' I muttered. 'I can pay for the damage. My uncle gave me plenty of money before he left.' I trembled, not believing what had happened.

'Don't be silly. We have insurance. Your grandad is a bad man. This is his mess, not yours,' Olive's mum said.

'But … but … you don't know who you're dealing with. He's a nutter! That's why my uncle and I steer clear of him. He's got a screw loose.'

'Yeah. Well the police will deal with him, don't you worry. You and your uncle will be fine.'

Olive stared at me, and I looked back, feeling guilty.

'Well, I have to leave tonight anyway. My uncle wants me to meet him in London for the next leg of his book tour. I promised I'd join him. I'll leave you the money for the repairs, and I'll be in touch.'

'We don't want money from you, Lily. This wasn't your fault. You just need to be somewhere safe with your uncle, where your grandad won't go looking for you,' Olive's mum impressed.

I felt terrible lying to Olive's mum, but I couldn't stay here any longer; was fooling myself that Grandad wouldn't find me. And if I didn't leave, I'd be putting this wonderful family in peril. I just couldn't stand the thought that any of them would be hurt because of me. Especially Pippa.

Olive's mum let me borrow the phone to call my uncle. I pretended to do just that then told her I was going to get the train to London from Westcombe Hill. She offered to drive me down to the station in her Kombi van. It was a lovely offer considering I had just wrecked her kitchen and everything in it. Or maybe she was just so scared of what she'd seen she wanted me out of her house as quickly as possible. That was a huge possibility.

Terrified that we'd be followed, that something bad would happen to Olive's mum and I'd be to blame, I said 'No' in the nicest possible way; told her the short walk would be good for me after what had occurred.

When it was time to leave, I hugged them all and Olive thanked me for burning up the kitchen. The insurance money would buy a new kitchen, she said, this time she'd ask for one of a fashionable, non-headache-inducing colour with walls to match. I smiled but secretly hoped the old orange bench and purple walls could be fixed up. I just couldn't imagine that crazy house looking any different from how it did the day I arrived.

Before I left, Olive packed me some spare clothes and some sandwiches to eat on the journey. She made me promise to text when I reached somewhere safe. I promised I would, and we hugged and said goodbye.

I chucked my jacket on; slung my backpack over my shoulder; gave Pippa a huge unwelcomed hug and wandered into the night. Darkness fell, and the stars twinkled through the overhead branches as I walked down the tree-lined hill, the low-laying, lazy moon lighting the pavement like a lamp. When I reached the train station, I dug some change out of my jacket pocket and headed for the payphone near the ticket office. I dialled the number.

'Hi Tallis, it's Lily — Lily Du Plessis.'

'Where are you calling from, Lily?'

I sensed the urgency in his voice.

'I'm at the train station at the bottom of Westcombe Hill. Something bad has happened, Tallis … I … um …'

'Yeah, I know,' he cut in. 'We weren't there when the intruder broke in, Lily. We were at the markets. The police said there were signs of forced entry at the back of the house, and the muddy impression of size ten shoe prints on the stairs and in the study.'

'So you know I didn't do it.'

'You, Lily? Why on earth would I think that? It was definitely your grandfather.'

'No. It was definitely not Grandad, because he thinks I did it. I was hiding in the woods and snuck back into the house to get some stuff, and I heard him blaming me.'

'It's okay. Stay where you are, but stay out of sight. I'm coming to get you. I've been searching everywhere for you for over a week. I was scared your grandfather had taken you, Lily. Thank God you're okay.'

'Yeah, I'm okay. I'm sorry I worried you. I was staying with a friend, and I didn't get Uncle Noah's note with your number on it till today,' I lied. 'I'm going to hide behind the trees near the ticket office, okay? Hurry up and come get me, Tallis.'

The phone clicked, the money running out before he could answer, but I was sure Tallis would come as soon as he could. I crept across the small cement yard by the ticket office and hid behind the trees. The moon slipped behind the clouds, and the silence closed in around me as I waited for him in the dark.

Half an hour later, Tallis's dark-blue, soft-top Jeep turned the bend at the bottom of the road.

'Quickly get in!' he shouted through the window as he braked.

'Where are we going?' I asked, jumping in.

'My house ... It's not far.'

I'd never thought about Tallis having his own place. I mean, he came and went all the time from my uncle's house but growing up I'd never thought about where he might actually live. Under a rock for all I knew or cared. I was hardly a nosy kid.

The silence in the car soon became deafening — I didn't know what to say, so said nothing. Tallis drove on, staring at the road ahead, no time for idle chit chat apparently, then he said, looking sad, 'I'm sorry about your uncle's death, Lily.'

'Yeah,' I said, feeling flushed and awkward. *What else can I say to that without sounding cold-hearted?*

'He was a good man. He was always good to me. I'll sure miss him,' he said, looking at me for a reaction.

I didn't know how to react to that either. I thought about Bernard, the budgie, and how I'd dealt with that. 'God bless poor Uncle Noah,' I said.

Tallis felt sorry for me, I could tell, which let me off the hook. We were quiet again for a while, then he said, 'Where were you when your uncle was murdered, Lily?'

'Out of the house,' I said, feeling suddenly guilty.

'On your own?' He looked shocked.

'Yeah. We'd had a bit of a fight the night before, and I didn't want him to take me to school.'

'Bit foolish leaving the property without your uncle or one of us though.'

'Yes and no ...' I shrugged. 'It was a bit reckless, but it's probably the only reason I'm still alive.'

'True.' He nodded and looked at me as if he hadn't quite thought of that. 'I guess whoever killed your uncle would most likely have been after you too.'

'Yeah.' I recalled the hand that had drawn the curtain back in Uncle's study. Whoever it was had definitely seen me standing there, and I wondered once more why my uncle's murderer had let me slip away.

Twenty minutes later, I unloaded my backpack into a small wardrobe in a tiny room in the basement of Tallis's flat in Chislehurst.

'Get some rest, Lily, but there's no time to sleep. We'll be leaving here in a couple of hours. Mica is arranging the flights, and Slater will meet us at the airport.'

'Airport? Is that really necessary? I know the note Uncle Noah left said 'Get out of England', but now, tonight? ... Why?'

'Yes. Now. Tonight. Your safety is the only thing that matters.'

He started throwing stuff into a backpack, and I giggled because I'd only just unpacked mine.

He cast me a dark glare. 'What's so funny?'

'Oh, I don't know. You packing — the gardener — why would my uncle send me to you? I don't get it.

'And why is Mica arranging flights, and Slater meeting us at the airport? You're my uncle's employees. Why would you be doing this for me when my uncle's dead? Sorry, but I find this all a bit confusing.'

He straightened his back, turned away from me and carried on packing. A muscle in his jaw flexed — I could see he felt tense.

'I can't explain now, Lily. There's no time, and there are some things you don't need to know.'

'Oh, great, here we go again! I thought I'd just got off that roundabout when my uncle died!' My anger started to rise. I could feel it.

'All you need to know, Lily, is that we don't work for your uncle. We work for a private concern. I'm not a gardener any more than Mica is a personal trainer or Slater a publicist. We are contracted to keep you safe, Lily, so shut up and pack!'

His jaw muscle flexed again and, as angry as I was, I knew I'd pushed him too far. Not wanting to push my luck any further, I disappeared into my small room, repacked my backpack and lay on the bed trying to calm down. It took a lot of effort to stop the flow of heat building up inside me.

Breathing deeply in and out, I closed my eyes; tried to remove the thoughts of the damage I wanted to do to Tallis for keeping me in the dark — like Uncle Noah had done all my life. Another minute and I felt I would erupt. Heat poured into my hands again, like they were on fire, and sweat dripped from my brow. I tried harder to stop this horrible urge to hurt him. *Breathe in. Breathe out. ... Breathe in. ... Breathe out.*

My body trembled with rage as I lay there. Then a thought struck me. *Tallis is on my side. He's on my side.*

I forced this thought through my head over and over.

The anger started to dwindle.

Then it rose again. Tallis was going to force me to leave the country!

But that's what Uncle Noah wants. Leave and I'll be safe from Grandad. I guess Tallis is right. Nobody will ever think a seventeen-year-old girl would board a plane alone. Grandad wouldn't think it.

Where will he take me though? Will I have a choice in the matter?

I guessed I'd have to count the money in the box I'd found at the bottom of the ladder and figure out what to do next!

When the heat within me cooled, I disappeared into the bathroom and sat on the edge of the bath, counting the cash — it was more money than I'd ever laid eyes on. And there was something else I hadn't noticed. Underneath everything else, was a passport, and a cashbook for a bank account in the name of Lily Du Plessis. I'd never seen this before.

Opening it, my mouth dropped open. I stopped breathing; nearly choked at the figures on the page in front of me.

It was a while before I could breathe; had to cough to force a breath out and in. My eyes watered, and my throat stung. *Shit! … Double shit!*

There was more than five and a half million bucks in this account. *Five and a half bloody million!* Somewhere, someone, for whatever reason, was making sure I had a comfortable life. With this amount of money, I would never be hungry or homeless.

It can't be Uncle Noah. No way.

I'd seen the publisher's cheque that came in quarterly for his books. The bank letters demanding late payment of his bills outweighed the royalties. This much I knew for sure: he was not my benefactor, but someone very, very rich was. Maybe it was a family member on my dad's side or a close friend of my mum and dad.

When I was a kid, I had only asked once about my dad, and my uncle had said he was dead.

'How?' I'd asked, and he became angry and said, 'He's dead, okay. Don't ask me about him again. He ruined your mother, and I will not have him mentioned in this house!'

So I never mentioned him again.

I thought about him a lot though and wondered how he'd died. But I never mentioned his name again in front of my uncle. I thought maybe this could be another reason why my grandad wanted me dead ... for the money ... if he knew about it.

'Tallis,' I called.

'Yes, Lily.'

'Do you know where we're flying to?'

'America, I think. New York. Why?'

'Is that anywhere near New Orleans?'

'Near enough,' he said, popping his head around the door with a smile. 'Are you ready to go?'

'Sure,' I said, stuffing everything back into the tin. I grabbed my backpack, and we headed up and out of the basement and jumped back into the Jeep. Three hours later, I was sitting on a plane next to Tallis bound for America. Mica and Slater sat to our left. We were heading to New York City, and I knew from there I could possibly talk Tallis into taking me to New Orleans.

Why?

Because on the back of my bankbook was the address of Whitney Bank, in the French quarter of New Orleans, on a street called Chartres. I knew I'd need this money to survive, but found it really interesting that the bank was in such a strange place, so far away from England. Did it just happen to be in the French quarter? Could it be a coincidence that my last name was French? — Du Plessis was as French as you could get. And me, with my dark hair and dark eyes, made it far more likely that I had my roots in a place like New Orleans than in England … because, although I was fair-skinned, I was hardly an English rose.

Armed with this information, a full bank account, Tallis, Mica and Slater by my side, what did I have to lose? My old life was gone, except for Olive. I had no family in England, except for a grandad who wanted me six feet under. Something exciting was waiting for me in New Orleans. I could feel it in my bones. There was absolutely no way I couldn't go there. And it felt like I was going home.

TRUE COLOURS

After stopping for a while in Dubai and transferring to another flight, the following thirteen hours dragged by; the USA was a long way away and flying this route the only option at such short notice. When waiting to take off, I sat staring out the window at the tarmac, feeling weird knowing I was leaving my country for good. When we were in the air, I pressed my head against the window and stared down at the greenery through the clouds, wondering where my house was. I felt suddenly sick and ... ugh, my eyes were leaking again — not quite as bad as the time in the woods behind the school, but I could feel the tears falling. I kept my head turned to the glass so Tallis wouldn't see.

Images of Uncle Noah slumped on his desk in a pool of blood swam in my head. I didn't want that to be my last memory of him. Especially now I was leaving him behind. Even though he was dead, it didn't seem right, so I searched for fonder memories; thought back to when I was six years old. Uncle Noah and I were preparing for a trip to the seaside town of Folkestone. I stood in his study watching him through the window; could see him talking to a man, but I couldn't see who it was. They started to scuffle, and Mica, uncle's personal trainer, came rushing to his side. There was shouting, shoving and pushing going on. I knew now - it had been my grandad, because every time he came, it always ended the same. Uncle Noah said *Trouble* was grandad's middle name.

We left the house later than planned, and Uncle Noah kept checking his mirrors and was silent all the way there. I thought he must have been feeling sick or something.

'Stay close to me today, Lily,' he said with a smile.

Our destination was wet and windy when we arrived, and we headed for the markets, where he bought me delicious pink candy floss. After, we walked along the little café strip, Uncle Noah walking slightly ahead of me. I stopped at a coffee shop and spoke to a lady sitting at an outside table with her little white, fluffy dog.

'What a beautiful dog. Can I pat him? Does he bite?' I said.

'Go ahead, honey, he won't bite you,' she'd replied with a huge grin.

I'd bent down to pat her dog, and when I stood up again, she was dead! That's right ... dead ... shot in the head. There was blood everywhere. Some had splattered on my face and clothes. I stood confused, and Uncle Noah ran to me and scooped me up in his arms. Of course, that cut that little trip short and, within five minutes, we were back in the car and heading back to London and home.

On the way, I went on at Uncle Noah: 'Who will take care of her dog?'

'Quiet now, Lily. It's really none of our business. She's probably got family that will take care of the dog.'

I thought about that for a minute — she had a family. I tried to feel sad for her, but the emotion wasn't there. No. All I could think about was the pink candy floss I'd just had at the markets, and how amazing it had tasted. I kept bringing my thoughts back to the woman, to the blood, to the little whining dog. But no, there I was again, back with the candy floss.

'Can I have a dog, Uncle Noah?'

'No, Lily, we've had this conversation before, and it's not going to end any differently this time, madam. A little dog lives a good fourteen years. Who would look after it if something happened to you?'

I sat quietly looking out of the window for the rest of the journey home. Why did he always say things like that to me? Like I was a living time bomb waiting to go off. Like my days were already numbered. He made me feel so angry I wanted to slit his throat.

Uncle Noah was indeed a strange man.

Okay, so maybe that memory isn't such a good choice after all. When I first thought of it, being six and going on a trip, it seemed like a happy memory, so I'd gone with it … but what really happened pretty much sucked, and I'd forgotten the day had ended like that.

I was still crying, and unsure how to stop. I mean, I hadn't had a lot of practice at it, this only being my third time. I tried to switch off and not think any more about Uncle Noah or England, and soon my eyes stopped leaking. Thank God! I leant on Tallis's shoulder, and pretty soon we were both asleep.

We slept like the dead.

It was a nice feeling, falling asleep without that new sensation, fear, and we slept most of the way, waking up only a few hours before the plane touched down. A limo was waiting to take us to Times Square, and when we pulled up outside our hotel, all I could think about was how long we'd have to stay here before I could persuade the guys to move us on to New Orleans.

The hotel was comfortable and modern, and Times Square was like nothing I'd ever seen. It buzzed with lights and action, and so many people, more than I'd ever seen in one place before, milled around. Looking out of my hotel window was like looking at a poster or a picture in a magazine. It felt unreal. Yet it was nice to be somewhere different, in a new place where perhaps the threat that had hung over me all my life didn't exist. I mean, who could possibly find me here? My excitement chased away sleep; I wanted to go out on the streets and investigate this amazing place. I called Slater's room and asked him if he could take me.

'No way, Lily. We've just flown halfway around the world, and you want to party? Get some sleep, girl.'

That wasn't what I wanted to hear. The nightlife through my window was pumping. The noise coming from the street below was crazy. It stirred me up inside. I called Mica.

'No, Lily,' he said as soon as he picked up the phone. Slater must have been filled him in on my call.

'Oh, you guys are so old ... and bloody boring! What about Tallis? Is he up for it?'

I hung up and almost instantly a knock came on the door. It was Tallis, but not the Tallis I knew. Gone were the ripped jeans and baggy t-shirt: he looked ... nice, and I was drawn to his scent — it was intoxicating. Clearly, he had made an effort.

'So, where do you want to go, Lily? Want to eat?'

'Yeah, but let's walk around a bit first, hey? It's all so new.'

'Okay.'

I slipped my arm through his as we made our way out into Times Square. We walked in and out of all the stores then back onto the main street; turned into Broadway. Further on, we wandered down a side road and came across the Jekyll & Hyde Club.

'Wow! This place looks brilliant! Let's check it out,' I beamed.

'Okay, you first — in you go,' he said as we unlinked arms.

It was so cool inside, the walls lined with books, skulls, skeletons and weird props. A huge elephant head above a large fireplace spoke and moved. An experimental chamber for

Frankenstein sat on a stage. Upstairs was a talking elephant man, a freaky mermaid, Siamese double-headed twins, a ventriloquist dummy and a sweet doll that turned into some kind of Chucky monster. It was the freakiest place I'd ever seen.

Tallis surprised me by pulling out my chair as we arrived at the table. I sat down, and he pushed it in for me. We sat, waiting to be served. It felt strange to have a conversation with someone who'd been a part of my life for such a long time, but who I knew nothing about. I sensed he knew plenty about me because he never asked me anything about me — like he already had all the information he needed. Just then, the waiter arrived and placed a bottle of water at the table; handed us menus.

'I'll be your waiter this evening. If you need anything at all, don't hesitate to ask,' he said pleasantly, tilting his top hat to one side.

'Thanks,' Tallis said.

We sat checking out the menu and Tallis made small talk with me — asked me stuff about books I'd read and poets I liked. But he avoided any questions I asked that crossed the line from boring to interesting.

'Tell me something about yourself ... before you joined Uncle's household.'

'Like what?' he said and laughed.

'Oh, I don't know. Just stuff. Tell me about your family or something.'

Tallis stiffened and looked away. His jaw flexed slightly and I wondered why my question would make him feel tense.

'Got no family,' he said, still looking across the room.

Well, that was short and sweet. I wondered if I had the guts to pry further.

'Really? No family ... whatsoever?'

'Nope,' he said stiffly.

This is like drawing blood from a stone. 'There must be someone,' I prompted quietly.

'My mum died when I was small. I don't even remember her. I don't know who my dad was. I grew up with my grandparents, and they both died a long time ago.'

'Oh,' I said.

'Satisfied?' he replied.

'Yeah, I guess.'

He looked sullen, so I fell quiet. Then the waiter returned to take our order.

'Have you decided what you'd like?' he said, focusing on Tallis.

'Ladies first,' said Tallis, gesturing towards me.

I felt kind of special. Tallis was such a gentleman. At least that's what Uncle Noah would've called him, and so thoughtful. Even though there was a barrier up, or maybe a very secretive side to him, I still felt I could trust him.

'I'll have the nachos please, and a coke, thanks.'

'I'll have the BBQ ribs and large fries with a coke too,' said Tallis.

The waiter took our order and walked away. Tallis's eyes met mine and for a moment an awkward silence filled the space between us. He looked at me so intently the hairs on the back of my neck stood up. I shivered.

'You cold?' he asked.

'Mm, no not really ... well maybe a bit.'

'Here, have this.' He slipped his arms out of his jacket, stood up and put it around my shoulders. Sitting back down, he poured us both a glass of water.

'Thanks,' I said. 'So, what did you do before you were a gardener?' I asked.

He snorted, and in his laughter, nearly choked on his water.

'What? What's funny?'

'I told you before, I'm not a gardener. Never have been. I think it's funny that you still have that thought in your head.' He smiled a cute lopsided smile that made my tummy flutter.

'Well, it's all I've ever known. I mean, I grew up in a house with a personal trainer, a publicist and a gardener. All my life I believed this was true.' Then I laughed too, seeing the funny side of it. We both laughed a while longer, and I found it hard to stop. His laughter was infectious, and we seemed to enjoy it for way longer than we should.

'Okay,' I said, finally stopping, but still smiling. 'So … you have no family and you're not a gardener. So what did you do before?'

'Before what?'

'Before … me?'

He'd said he was contracted to keep me safe and if this was true, this is what he'd been doing since he became part of our household.

'I was in the army before, but it feels like a lifetime ago, and I don't really want to talk about that either.'

'Okay, so basically you're a closed book.'

'Basically,' he said. Then we both lost it again. It wasn't funny, and yet it seemed to be.

I watched him laughing and running his hand through his hair. His eyes smiled as much as his mouth did, and I wondered why I'd never noticed that before. I guess when I was young and didn't have any feelings, I didn't notice a lot of things. I can't actually remember Tallis being any younger than he was now, and yet he'd been with us for such a long while. Still, my memories of being a kid could be a bit blurred sometimes. It was only now that my emotions were kicking in that I seemed to be taking in everything around me … like suddenly I could see.

'Well, just tell me your last name?'

'It's Summers, but I don't see why you need to know?'

'Well, you know my last name. I'm just trying to even the playing field,' I said with a cute smile.

'Okay, enough of the really personal questions,' he said.

'Alright, then what music do you like? Is that a safe question?'

'Safe enough.' He smiled shyly, and my heart beat slightly faster. 'I actually love old school stuff; don't laugh but I love Motown, Frank Sinatra, Queen, Prince & The Revolution, Blondie, the Bee Gee's, but also some of today's stuff.'

At last, something he was willing to talk about. I loved the same kind of music.

The waiter arrived with our food and time seemed endless, we were so comfortable now.

'What's your favourite colour?' I asked.

'Mmm ... brown, I guess.'

'Brown? That's not a colour,' I laughed.

'Well, I don't know. I just like nature. Forests, rivers, earth. It's a colour that reminds me of that ... getting back to basics, you know.'

'Okay,' I said, suddenly feeling stupid. He had such a cool reason to like brown. Me, I liked red, because it reminded me of wet candy floss, Olive's hair, my favourite nail polish ... and blood, a pretty lame reason to like a colour.

Tallis tucked into his ribs like a starving animal. I was a bit shocked that the ribs were so large and yet they seemed to be scoffed down in mere minutes.

'Hungry?' I asked.

'Oh yeah. Sorry ... I'm always starving,' he said, dropping his ribs and trying to slow down. It was like he had to force himself to take it slowly, for me. He looked a bit embarrassed, and I wished I hadn't said anything. Pretty soon his plate was empty, and I had to hurry up eating mine to catch up to him. I was so full I felt I would pop.

'Want something for dessert?' he asked with a lovely smile.

'No thanks, I couldn't eat another thing, but you go ahead.'

He ordered apple pie and ice cream, and when it came, he looked like an excited kid at a birthday party. Boy, this man really loved his food. If he ate like this all the time, he should really look like a whale, but no, he was fit, like a Roman god. We finished up, and Tallis paid the bill. Outside we headed left and back up towards Times Square. In the distance, we heard shouting, and a man came sprinting towards us. Fear gripped me momentarily until I realised he was staring at something behind us. I turned on my heels to see him chasing a large black dog that was zig-zagging as fast as it could along the road, in and out of the cars, bringing everything to a stop. He suddenly changed direction and headed back towards us. The man was shouting at people not to touch the dog, so I guess it wasn't user-friendly. And he was shouting at the dog, trying to get it to come to him. It came racing along the pathway like a juggernaut, knocking a lady over on its way. She screamed, and it stopped and growled at her.

'Don't touch him — he bites,' the man shouted, rushing forward.

Tallis pushed me to the wall and stepped into the middle of the pathway, swinging around to face the dog as it bolted towards him. But, as it reached Tallis, something in its frantic manner changed. It stood still a few yards from him. Creeping slowly forward, it ended up at Tallis's feet.

It looked up at him, and they seemed to be staring each other down. Eyes locked. The large black dog's aggression suddenly calmed, and its ears drew back against its head like it was intimidated. It bowed its head and cowered down, and when it was calm, Tallis brushed his hand along its head and back, and the big black beast went tummy up. The man was beside Tallis in seconds and looked on amazed. This dog that only moments before had been in a wildly hysterical state, now lay on the pavement at Tallis's feet, completely in submission.

'How'd you do that?' the man said, looking shocked. He swiftly slipped the collar back onto the dog's neck.

Tallis continued stroking the dog. 'Oh I don't know, animals love me,' he said with a wide, confidant smile.

'Well, thanks,' said the man, looking relieved. He pulled the dog to its feet and started to walk away. But the dog just sat on its haunches, refusing to budge and staring after Tallis. It was a funny sight to see, as the man struggled to pull this huge, black, immoveable dog along the pavement on its butt because it desperately wanted to stay with Tallis.

'Always have that effect on animals, do you?' I asked puzzled.

'Yeah, kind of,' he said. 'Some animals tend to like me. Especially dogs.'

'Yeah. I can totally see that,' I said.

WHERE I'VE NEVER BEEN

As we made our way back to the hotel it started to rain. So we dashed along, sticking to the edge of the sidewalk, as far under the lip of the buildings as we could get. It didn't help much, and by the time we reached our hotel, our clothes were drenched through, and we were chilled to the bone.

'I'll run you a bath, Lily, then we should get some shuteye. We move onto Chicago tomorrow. Best not to stay in one place too long.'

'Chicago?' I protested as the lift stopped on the fortieth floor. 'Any reason for that?'

'Just following directions. By Friday we'll be in New Orleans. That's where we'll be based, according to instructions.'

I knew it! Someone in New Orleans was looking out for me. These guys were obviously working for whoever that was.

Tallis ran me a bath while I peeled off my wet clothes and pulled on a robe. Through the crack in the bathroom door, I caught a glimpse of him sitting on the edge of the bath looking in the mirror, but not at his own reflection … at me. He noticed me, noticing him, noticing me, and he quickly looked away. Pushing his wet hair up out of his eyes, he looked flushed.

'Bath's ready,' he shouted, ignoring the two minutes of awkwardness that passed between us.

I grabbed my pyjamas, and as I entered the bathroom, he rose and brushed past me. For a mere moment, our eyes met. I hadn't noticed how blue his eyes were. His wet fringe hung down, and in the next moment my heart felt like it was outside of my chest, beating loudly in my ears. It was a strange and fleeting feeling, which left me reeling.

This new emotion was one I had no word for: the tingling sensation was indescribable yet the nicest feeling I'd ever felt in my short life.

'I'll be off now, Lily,' he said as he headed to the door. 'I'm just next door if you need me.' And with that, he was gone.

I slipped off my robe, dragged my hair up into a bun and hopped into the hot bath. I lay for the next twenty minutes down under the bubbles, thinking about that new sensation I'd felt when I'd looked into Tallis's eyes, and when his body brushed against me.

I slept well that night and, even though the hustle and bustle of the city carried on into the early hours, and police sirens screamed intermittently in the background, the craziness was comforting. It reminded me of the chaos at Olive's house.

The following day we headed back to the airport and boarded a smaller plane to Chicago. At the Chicago end, another limo waited, and we made our way to another hotel in the heart of the city. Outside, rain poured down and added to the sound of sirens and traffic that similarly had flooded the New York City. But that was where the comparison ended. Here, outside my window, the streets were bare; empty like a deserted city. Not one car or person graced the streets. It was not at all what I had imagined. The excitement I'd felt in New York was nowhere to be found in me now.

I called Tallis's room. 'I'm lonely ... want to do something? Go down to the bar maybe?'

'I don't think so, Lily. You're seventeen. I don't think it's appropriate. Just order some room service and get some rest, hey.'

'Oh, come on! I'm so bloody bored. Can you keep me company at least? Play cards or something?'

He was dead quiet on the other end of the phone like he was deep in thought or caught between a *yes* and a *no.* He said nothing.

'Well?' I said impatiently.

'I don't think so, Lily. Get some rest, okay? We're here for three days. We'll do something tomorrow.'

Something in his tone said we wouldn't. Something in his tone said he was avoiding me. The last thing I wanted was for him to feel uncomfortable around me. I went to bed and lay trying to sleep, but sleep wouldn't come. I was too wound up. All I could think of was Tallis.

Then suddenly a knock came on the door.

I jumped out of bed, flicked on the light, peeped through the peephole. Tallis stood there. *Shit!*

'One minute,' I shouted, quickly checking myself in the mirror before letting him in.

He walked in wearing stripy pyjama bottoms and a baggy superman T-shirt, and he carried a pack of cards. I giggled and shut the door.

'What's so funny?'

'Oh, I don't know ... I've just never seen you in your PJ's before.'

He looked down at his T-shirt and stripy bottoms and grinned that cute lopsided grin.

'You hardly look a picture yourself,' he said with a shrug.

I loved my cookie monster pyjamas, but I guessed he had a point.

'Okay. Truce.' I said with a huge smile, and we both sat down on the bed.

'So, what made you change your mind?'

'Guilt,' he said.

'Guilt?'

'Yeah. I guess you've just been through a pretty rough time, hey. And me avoiding you ... well, that's not really going to work, is it?'

'Why do you want to avoid me, anyway?' I said, looking down at the bedcover and feeling a bit awkward.

'Because I like you, Lily, more than I should.'

'Well, that's okay. I like you too. What's wrong with that?'

'*Everything* is wrong with that, Lily.' He rose and wandered to the window; looked down at the empty street below. 'This is a serious position for me, and your safety is the only thing that matters. I can't let anything interfere with that. If I get sloppy, it could get us both killed. I've got to have my wits about me, Lily, and if I let myself feel anything for you, it could jeopardise everything.'

'Okay. I understand.'

I didn't. Not really. I didn't understand at all. What difference would it make if we liked each other? It would just mean we'd probably be together more. Surely that would increase the safety aspect.

We played cards until the early hours and joked and messed about and talked. Small talk as usual, and then he hit me with a pillow because I called him pedantic. Well, my cards were all over the shop, and his were all in neat little rows. I threw the pillow back, and a tussle began. He got me in a vice-like grip and tried to restrain my arms as I reached out trying to ruin his neat little piles. His grip tightened and I squealed and struggled ... Then it happened. Our eyes met again, and the room fell silent. The feeling was electric as we froze to the spot, our intense heavy breathing the only noise in the room. Then he kissed me. Just a slight kiss. Just a brushing of lips really, but it swept me up and away to another place. Another world. To a place I had never been before. And in that moment, I didn't want to come back.

'Stop. We can't do this,' he said in a whisper, and he drew away from me. 'I can't take care of you if my guard is down. I'm so sorry, Lily. I think its best that we aren't alone anymore, at least not until you turn eighteen.'

'Why eighteen?' I said.

'Because then you'll be safe. When you turn eighteen, nothing can hurt you, Lily.'

He stood, stroked my hair and walked to the door. It was such a serious conversation, but all I could think about was how cute he looked; how I had just felt when he held me in his arms. I had never been embraced. Never been kissed. This was all so new to me, and I liked it. I liked it a lot.

'Why? What happens when I'm eighteen?'

Tallis looked at me sadly, as if he'd said too much already.

'Just wait and see, Lily. Just wait and see.' He stroked my face and closed the door firmly behind him, leaving me puzzled.

The following day at breakfast, Tallis ignored me. Slater sat beside me, Mica opposite, and Tallis sat at the end, not making eye contact at all.

'Movies tonight, Lily? The Great Gatsby is showing. We'll all go, shall we?' Slater said.

'Whatever,' I said and played with my food.

'Don't play with your food, Lily,' said Mica.

'Ugh, piss off, Mica!' I said and stormed from the dining room.

I don't know why I'd said that. I really liked Mica. He'd always been there for me ... ever since I could remember ... as long as

Uncle Noah had been. But I was fed up and angry. I was fed up with being kept in the dark. I wanted to know what the secret was. What did everyone know except me?

And I wanted Tallis — more than anything I'd ever wanted before.

That night we watched The Great Gatsby. It was an awesome movie that blew me away. In the moment that Daisy Buchanan and Jay Gatsby locked eyes, like Tallis and I had, I realised what I'd been feeling. This unclear emotion, this overwhelming, electrifying otherworldliness was possibly what I'd read about in books — a thing called ... *love*.

I reached to the left of me in the darkness and found Tallis's hand; slipped my fingers into his. There was no resistance as he linked his fingers through mine, and we sat for the rest of the movie in silence.

The following day we drove to Wisconsin. Mica and Slater told Tallis there was no need for us all to go, that he should maybe take me shopping, but he talked his way out of that.

'I think the drive would be good for her. We've been cramped in hotels for days now and, anyway, we can't come this far and not try the Milwaukee frozen custard.'

On the way, I sat in the back of the car with Tallis, but he sat half turned away from me, head against the window checking his phone. His body language clearly said, 'Don't get too close' and as the day went on, I felt more uncomfortable, more pissed off, and more alone than I had since leaving England. But this was a familiar feeling, this isolation. This was the old Lily. Blackheath Lily. I could handle this. I'd known this all my life.

When we arrived, Slater took a package from the boot of the car and disappeared into a local elementary school. He was away for quite a while. I wondered why, but Tallis wasn't talking to me so I couldn't ask.

Two hours later, we were on our way back and, after trudging through heavy traffic, we arrived back in Chicago. As soon as we reached the hotel, I disappeared into my room. *Only one more day in the windy city.* I felt we could have done more, but I think all the guys were jet-lagged due to the vast time difference and were trying to recharge for the next leg of the journey. So, my last day in Chicago was spent tucked up in bed with a book, ordering room service and texting Olive, filling her in on all the excitement.

Early the next morning, we headed back to the airport, ready for the trip to New Orleans. I was excited about going there, more than any place we'd been so far. This felt like the only right thing about this whole trip ... well, except for Tallis ... but although it felt right to me, apparently I was wrong about him.

I sat in the airport lounge, reading. Four hours to wait and not much else to do. Occasionally I looked up and caught Tallis looking at me, but if I caught his eye, he'd quickly look away. I wondered why this was happening. In some ways, I preferred the old me that was never bothered by anything. I could sure use that lack of emotion right now because this feeling for Tallis was overwhelming. I wished I could just switch it off. I didn't want to feel this way, not if he didn't feel the same way about me. Then I caught him looking again, and this time instead of looking away, he smiled that incredible smile and all was right with the world!

We boarded the plane, and two hours later, touched down in New Orleans. Home of Creole food, Voodoo, Mardi gras, festivals and tiny shops filled with antiquities. Midnight was nearly upon us, and it took about forty minutes to drive from the airport to the French quarter. I fell asleep on the journey, and when I woke up, we were just passing a sign that said *Welcome to New Orleans.* The further we went, the cuter it became. The streets narrowed, and the buildings became more Spanish and French-inspired. Trees and pretty landscaped areas dotted throughout the little city and, within a short distance, we entered the long narrow streets of the French quarter. I rolled the window down, and the heat wafted in. It felt tropical and absolutely wonderful! My skin felt warm and clammy and, for the first time since I was born, I felt like my body was in the right climate. I'd always hated the cold and growing up in England there was plenty of that. My lips were always chapped in the winter, my skin always so dry. Here my skin felt suddenly infused with water, I plumped out slightly and almost glowed. I felt alive!

We drove into Chartres Street and headed for another little hotel just ahead on the right. This hotel was the best so far. Obviously Spanish in its build, the detail seemed more French; the old buildings in the central courtyard incredibly majestic and all lit up at night. We unpacked and went out walking. It was 2am, but in the French quarter, things were still buzzing. We looked for somewhere to eat and ended up at a little café — Daisy Dukes — that was open 24 hours a day. I had my first taste of New Orleans popcorn shrimp and chilli cheese fries, and the guys all tried something Creole and spicy, then raved about the food as we walked along Bourbon Street. It was now 3am, but the streets were still filled with people. The bars were packed to brimming, and New Orleans style jazz flowed out the doors of the bars onto the streets, making me feel more alive than ever. *What is this music? Why have I never heard it before? Why does it have this effect on me?*

It was like it was a very part of my soul that had been missing for years and was now re-entering my soul. We walked almost the length of Bourbon Street then turned around and made our way back through the partying crowds to our hotel.

On the corner of Chartres Street, I spotted Whitney Bank. To think that behind those doors was a fortune in my name. I wished I could share that information with someone, but was too scared I'd be in danger again if someone thought they could get their hands on that little mint. So, I kept it under wraps; pretended that all I had to live on was the money in the tin.

'Trust no one, Lily, not even me,' Uncle Noah had said, and he'd said that to me all my life.

We stayed at the hotel for two more days, and I was allowed to explore the French quarter, always with someone, of course, although I didn't see the need. Nobody knew me here. This felt like a place I could totally blend in without being noticed and finally have the freedom I'd always craved. On our fourth day in the French quarter, we moved to a townhouse. When we arrived, I was shocked, because when the door was opened, who should be standing there, but Mylo, the janitor from my old secondary school in Blackheath. My chin nearly hit the floor. He was not 'the janitor' ... obviously! Just like Tallis wasn't the gardener, Slater wasn't the publicist, and Mica wasn't the personal trainer. Boy, I'd been living a damn conspiracy all my life. I had actually started to wonder if Uncle Noah was really my uncle; was Mum really my mum; whether Grandad was really my grandad? Maybe none of them was actually related to me. Perhaps that was the real reason they hated me — Lily Du Plessis — who so very obviously didn't belong in their world.

Mylo hugged me and said, 'Welcome home, Miss Lily.' A strange comment, but I took it, and in we went, closing the door behind us.

The new house was huge — absolutely beautiful with fancy, black, French filigree, wrought iron balconies all around the front, sides and back of the second floor. The one at the back ran the length of the house and looked down into the gardens below. The balcony was all grown over with creeping vines of honeysuckle and magnolia, which looked and smelled so pretty. The garden was not as big as the one at home in Blackheath, and the walls were so high all the way around, and trees grew thickly all around the edge hiding the garden from prying eyes and other buildings. I was allowed to use the garden freely — and alone! — whenever I wanted to, and that meant everything to me. This house had plenty of long windows, floor to ceiling almost, and so many of them there were almost more windows than bricks. The tall windows filled the rooms with light. It was so different from Uncle's house. The air was warm and clammy, the atmosphere light and refreshing. Uplifting even. The house had a familiar smell I just couldn't place, and I felt unbelievably and overwhelmingly at home, and happy for the first time in my life. This was where I truly belonged.

GLIMPSES OF CHILDHOOD

That night in bed I lay with just a sheet over me, the night so humid I was unable to sleep. I felt so far away from my past now, yet felt safe, and it seemed strange that, as a kid, I'd been in constant danger, not that I'd noticed back then. But now I was older, I could look back clearly at some of the stuff I'd seen. Indeed, I was far from safe in England: a few things had happened that, at the time, I had taken with a pinch of salt, but now I knew my uncle was right. I should have been living in fear.

I lay there realising that, while I never thought I had any bad memories, actually, bad memories were all I had. I wanted to box them all up. I wanted a completely fresh start. This was the first time in years I had felt happy, and safe, and I wanted to hang on to this feeling for as long as possible. Tonight I'd allow myself to reflect on the past, then in the morning, with the lid firmly on the box, I'd move on.

I recalled my eighth birthday party, which was held at the ice-skating rink. A few friends from school attended and the party was fun. Olive and I were racing across the ice with Mica and Slater either side of us. Suddenly a chubby, bearded man bumped into Mica and sent him flying. Slater grabbed hold of me and swept me to the side of the rink, while Mica turned and skated swiftly after the man.

'Stay here, Lily, and don't you move,' Slater said, skating off in the same direction.

He swept the man's legs out from behind, and the man landed with a thud on the ice. Mica, going too fast to stop, skated straight into the man, the blade of his skate wedging itself deep into the man's skull. Blood spilled out onto the pure white ice and looked like red nail polish, shining and glistening under the bright lights. It spread out into the watery slush; lost its bright redness and turned almost dark auburn, like the colour of Olive's beautiful curly hair. Some kids started crying, and parents rushed them off the ice. The police came, then an ambulance, though a little too late for the chubby, bearded man who'd taken his last breath about fifteen minutes before. Of course, that ended the party early and put a bit of a damper on the occasion, but still, I was happy. After all, I had a new diary from my best friend Olive, and I couldn't wait to get home to write in it.

On the drive home, I said, 'Well that went well. I think everyone had a great time, don't you, Uncle Noah?'

He didn't answer, just stared at me blankly as if he hadn't quite heard what I'd said.

I shifted slightly in my new bed, trying to get more comfortable, though I didn't know whether it was the heat or my memories that made me so fidgety.

I pictured the house I grew up in. It seemed like a lifetime had passed since I'd been there even though I'd only left England a few short weeks ago. The house spanned four upper floors, and a basement, but this was never counted as a floor. When Uncle Noah was alive, he kept his wine down there. The kitchen was above it on the first floor, with an adjoining dining room, separate casual lounge and drawing-room. The whole house had a museum-like feel to it with dark, long corridors, old Victorian fittings, and massive fireplaces you could fit a claw-foot bath into.

Heavy woven Victorian curtains hung at the windows, with cushions to match on all the bay windows seats. Glass display cabinets dotted throughout the house. Most rooms had two or three, displaying antiquities, rocks, crystals, and old weapons my grandad had collected over the years and passed down to Uncle Noah. Upstairs on the second floor were three guest bedrooms and two bathrooms, all used by the household staff as we never had guests to stay. Then up another flight of stairs to the third floor where Uncle Noah had his bedroom, a large bathroom, and a huge study at the very end of the hall.

Up another flight of stairs to the fourth and last floor was my bedroom. I had my own bathroom too, and a small playroom. Here I kept all my books, an old Victorian pram and doll that had belonged to my mum, and a handful of old teddies that were all so old they'd probably pass as antiques. This included Tilly who'd been my favourite bear as a kid.

My bedroom had a domed ceiling, and panelling that had not very child-friendly paintings in each quarter. I don't know who painted them, but they were pictures of witches, vampires, werewolves, and rather large wolf-like animals hidden amongst tree branches. Graves were drawn all around the bottom under the trees, all the graves above-ground — which I thought odd — they were more like tombs than the usual underground graves with headstones. I was intrigued and wondered whether there was anywhere in the world that actually buried their dead above ground. It seemed a strange thing to do because it gave more importance to the dead. Because headstones were generally so small you never really thought about the body underneath — just the name engraved on the stone. With a tomb-like grave above ground, it made me think about who was in the tomb? Who was buried there? Did they die a natural death, or were they murdered? I thought about the many ways the person in each tomb could have died, and if it was murder. What would their last bloodcurdling scream have sounded like to someone nearby?

Uncle Noah thought it morbid that I wanted the loft as my room and couldn't understand why the paintings didn't frighten me. But they didn't. Not at all. Actually, I found them strangely comforting, like carrying around an old picture of a familiar place or person in your purse. The room may have been a bit creepy for Uncle Noah, but beneath the ceiling, he made sure almost everything else was pretty. The walls were eggshell pink; my bedspread, a fine china-blue check, with pastel-coloured cushions. The heavy curtains were powder blue corduroy with a very faint floral pattern in the material. On the door, a beautiful wooden plaque bore my name in large curly letters. It didn't look much like I would have liked it: black painted walls, and punk posters were more my thing. But Uncle Noah was fussy about his décor and everything had to be perfect.

I hadn't told Olive any of this. She shared a lot, and I usually just listened to the one-sided conversation. Still, she didn't seem to mind ... and I really felt I had nothing to tell. The only exciting things that ever happened to me were outside the house when Uncle Noah and I went on trips. And nearly every time something exciting happened, it always seemed to be a pretty gruesome something with lots of blood, and more often than not either broken bones or a dead body. *Not the sort of thing you would share with your best friend in the library at lunchtime.*

My house was the only place that seemed an incident-free zone, somewhere I had always felt safe and untouchable. Even as a small child, I knew the whole security set up was to keep Grandad out because he wanted to hurt me. And, according to Uncle Noah, there were many others out there who felt the same way. But at least in Uncle's house, behind closed doors, I'd felt almost invincible.

Sitting up in bed, I sipped water from the glass on my bedside table; kicked the sheet off so the overhead fan could be more effective. Then I leant comfortably on my pillow.

This time when my eyes closed, there was a distinct aroma of Italy, the balmy heat, freshly baked panini and a lingering taste of salty olives. This was a memory of mixed emotions because it was one of the happiest and saddest times of my life, and as a kid I hadn't even known it. But I knew it now.

In the year I turned twelve we'd travelled to Italy for the holidays. Uncle Noah was the most relaxed I'd seen him. Mica and Slater came along, and we all had the most amazing fun that long, hot summer. I made friends at the resort and I spent the whole six weeks with kids my own age. I enjoyed it, but at the same time realised how different I was to other girls. There were three girls: twins of twelve named Susie and Lucy, and a nine-year-old sister called Claire. Between them, they had the IQ of a mosquito. Sounds bitchy, but all they talked about were Barbie dolls and fairytales, the kind Uncle Noah had read to me when I was five or six. At that time, I was reading *The Nocturnal Academy*, a series of books by Ethan Somerville — 'Alice malice', the vampire, was one of my favourite characters. I loved reading complex tales, and when I tried to join in on the Barbie sisters' conversation about books, they all just stared at me with open mouths — and nothing … absolutely nothing came out.

Near the end of the six weeks holiday, my friends and I were playing in the sand beneath the cliff-face. Above us, a shelf poked out like a turtle's neck and sheltered us from the harsh midday sun. We built a tall sandcastle and brought buckets of water in from the sea to fill up our moat. I remember a loud bang, like a bomb going off, and a huge crack appeared in the shelf that protruded above us. I stared up, following the sound of the noise as the turtleneck broke in two. The left side came hurtling down towards us. Towards me. We all looked up, and the girls started screaming. I could see the rock falling; could see the horrified looks on the twins' faces; could hear their screams. It all happened so suddenly yet, in that moment, in seeming slow motion. Adults ran at us from all directions. Yet I felt calm. Somebody grabbed me from behind, and within a minute, I was away from the danger, standing on safe ground, surrounded by Uncle Noah, Mica and Slater. In front of me sat a mound of rubble, where a few adults frantically dug into the rock, trying to reach whatever was at the bottom of the pile. I could see the twins in the distance on the other side of the mound, both crying, hands over their mouths. Shocked. Then a body was pulled from the rubble — the younger sister Claire, bruised, battered, bloody, and very much lifeless.

That incident ended my summer adventure. I remember thinking it was a good job we were leaving in two days because the twins were so bloody miserable, and were no longer any fun to play with. We returned home, and Uncle Noah sat next to me on the plane and asked me how I felt about the incident, and whether I was okay.

'Yeah, I'm okay … a bit peed off really coz that sandcastle took us so long to build.'

'Don't swear, Lily. It's not cool.'

'I didn't say pissed … I said peed.'

'Same meaning and said with the same intent,' he said sternly.

Afterwards, while driving home from the airport, I didn't give a second thought to what I had witnessed. It had completely slipped from my mind and, back in Blackheath, life went back to normal. I read a lot of books, and summer turned to autumn. The leaves began to fall, and my mood became as sombre as the season. Stuck indoors with only Uncle Noah for company and the odd diary entry to keep me amused, I felt like I was going insane. I had asked if Olive could visit but always got a flat-out '*No!*' in reply.

'It's not safe for her, Lily. You know what can happen to people when they are around you.'

Wow, Thanks, Uncle Noah. Don't hold back with the sensitivity. Give it to me straight, why don't you!

I would have loved to have said this, but of course, I didn't.

Uncle Noah smiled sweetly and turned away from me, and the irony of that had made me want to rip his head off.

'There are a lot of bad people in this world, Lily, and most of them are out to get you. Believe me, you are better off never letting anyone get close. Because, if the bad guys can't get you, they'll get the ones you love.'

Uncle Noah was always talking about people being out to get me. Not just Grandad, but complete strangers apparently wanted me dead. Why? I never knew. And he wouldn't tell me, so when I was a kid, I thought that, maybe him being a writer, made him a bit of a nutter. Maybe it was all in his imagination.

The heat now bothersome, I rose and slipped down to the kitchen for some ice, Uncle Noah still on my mind. Back in my room, I sat chewing on an ice cube, my frown deepening. *Why was I a target for anyone other than Grandad?* Then other thoughts filtered in.

My only escape from boredom at home was school or church on Sundays. I hated both, but anything was better than being stuck at home with a load of old farts for company. So, I joined the hockey team. Uncle Noah wouldn't let me play at inter-school carnivals, or visit hockey centres, but letting me play in the school hall was a compromise of sorts, I guess. He could have said no altogether. I'd been in the school hockey team for a year, and the month I turned fourteen there was a terrible accident. A relief sports teacher told me I needed some after-school coaching, and that I should meet him outside the sports shed on the field after school. I said my uncle wouldn't let me meet him alone. Especially not outside.

'We most certainly won't be alone — what are you thinking? Of course, there will be other students there too,' he said, but he smirked and gave me a wink.

What was I thinking? What was he *thinking? The dirty old pervert must have thought I fancied him ... ugh!*

I remember feeling awkward and, blushing, agreed quickly and walked away. That afternoon, I ran across the field to the shed. I'd been talking to my form teacher, asking her whether she thought Uncle Noah might let me pop across to the sports shed for some coaching instead of going to the hall.

'I guess what he doesn't know won't hurt him,' she'd said with an understanding nod. She had dealt with Uncle Noah on a few occasions and knew just how ridiculously overprotective he was.

When I reached the shed, later than planned, there was a lot of commotion there. Kids hung around the entrance, and as I squeezed in further, I saw a group of paramedics lifting a body onto a stretcher. While waiting for me to arrive, the relief teacher had been practising his weights. He'd overloaded the bar, and on lifting it, he'd lost his grip and dropped it on his chest, crushing his heart. *Poor perverted old thing.* Mylo, the school gardener, had seen everything through the window of the ride on tractor-mower but was too far away to save him. I couldn't help wondering what would've happened if I'd got there on time.

There were other incidents, too many to mention. I think I witnessed maybe four deaths a year growing up, apart from my fifteenth year, which was totally uneventful — boring even — with absolutely no deaths at all. But of course, you can see why, up to that point, I'd felt I was a bad omen. Also, thinking back on all those occasions, not one of them had stirred me emotionally. People would be panicking all around me, and I wouldn't think twice about what'd happened, even more so once it was over. I didn't have one ounce of empathy back then. Uncle Noah would say, 'It's a self-protection mechanism, Lily. The way your brain processes these awful happenings is to shut your feelings off from the agony of them so you can cope with everyday life.'

That was a nice theory. But maybe this was why my grandad had called me an abomination. Maybe I *was* a monster, after all.

I pulled the sheet up around me again as the coolness of the fan suddenly chilled me. I thought about the year I turned sixteen and some of the stuff my uncle had told me.

'Lily,' he'd said, 'you should never be alone with your grandad. If you ever find yourself in that situation, get out of it as soon as you can. Okay?'

And things like: 'Lily, never trust your grandad. If I'm not around, he'll snap your neck as soon as look at you.'

This had shocked me. I mean, how screwed up was that. I had friends at school who all came from different backgrounds, with all sorts of family issues. Some had divorced parents, brothers or sisters on drugs, grandparents with dementia, that kind of thing. But did I know anyone with a grandad who wanted to snap their neck?

Shit no.

It just didn't seem right. I must have been the only teenager I knew with a twisted git for a grandad. Then on my seventeenth birthday, Uncle Noah had called me into his study for a serious talk.

'Lily,' he said, 'I'm not a well man. I'm worried about how much time I may have left, and I'm terrified for your safety should anything happen to me.'

'Okay. Perhaps now is an *excellent* time to tell me why,' I said with a heavy hint of sarcasm, given Uncle Noah had been pointing out the dangers almost my whole life, without actually giving me any good reason. Why would anyone want to hurt me — other than my grandad, of course? Often though, when Uncle Noah talked about the danger, I knew his warnings weren't just about Grandad.

How absolutely awesome it was that I had such a thick skin back then. I don't know why, but I rarely felt any emotion about anything — I just didn't seem to give a shit. But maybe that was a good thing. Maybe it was because I grew up without a mum, or with a reclusive writer for an uncle, or a grandad that wanted me dead. I don't know what it was, but I definitely didn't feel like other kids my age felt. All the girls I knew were neurotic in some way — stressed about life — pissed off about their weight, or spots, or greasy hair. They were full to the brim with low self-esteem, so desperate for love, and looking for it in all the wrong places. Most were already shagging boys, sneaking beer or using drugs behind the school sheds to cope with their apparently screwed up lives.

None, of course, were more screwed up than mine.

And yet I was a totally different breed. My self-esteem was through the roof. Still is. I thought I was rather funny and pretty, with my dark brown eyes that looked almost auburn in the moonlight, and long brown hair falling almost to my waist. I was pretty much perfect … and loved … and very much wanted. I guess Uncle Noah had done a good job of bringing me up without any hang-ups. When I really thought about it though, this just wasn't so. I had lived my whole life with a crazy recluse, without a mum; in a dark old house with hardly any toys — other than the original doll, pram and teddies that once belonged to my mum. No visitors ever came, and no friends were ever welcome. Uncle Noah had been strict, and although I *thought* he had loved me, he'd never said so. *No. Not ever. Not even once.* So, when he said I meant nothing to him, it shouldn't have come as such a shock. I should have been scared of a grandad like mine. I should have felt guilty that I was the reason for my mum's death. I should have felt unloved with nobody to turn to — no brothers, no sisters — no family that cared. I grew up without hugs and was never *ever* told I was special, or pretty, or anyone's darling … And of course, there was also the built-in factor that death seemed to follow me wherever I went.

I had so many memories as a kid that had led me over the years to believe that maybe I was as bad as Grandad said. But back then this didn't bother me, not in the slightest. I should have been a complete screwup, as screwed up as my life, but … no … I was fine: happy, resilient, unemotional Lily.

These memories though were now painful, and I had lost hours in my bed tossing and turning, unable to sleep, haunted by those dark times from my past. I heaved a breath in, blew it out, realising only I knew what had happened between entering Uncle Noah's study at the sweet age of seventeen — a shamelessly naïve, slightly ignorant, absolutely feelingless girl — and now being here, about to start my new life in New Orleans.

Outside, the sun was up, and I swung out of bed and ambled to the window. In the garden below leaves hustled and bristled across the lawn, fallen from their safe branches. They seemed so alive with the wind pushing at their back, scattering them in all directions as they danced to a silent song beneath the bluing sky.

I sighed. I loved it here, living in a town where nobody knew the old me. I could start again … make some friends and finally be happy and safe.

AN UNWELCOME VISITOR

On a chilly Sunday morning I sat out on the balcony with a book, snuggled in a blanket. The sweet smell of New Orleans drifted around me; a scent definitely original to this amazing place yet a scent so familiar to me. What was it about the French quarter that made me feel I belonged? I couldn't understand it. There was no logic to this feeling as I'd never walked these streets before, yet I felt like I'd been here all my life — not just three months. I'd been doing a bit of research in the time I'd been here, trying to find out more about the Du Plessis family name. In the local library archives there was little information, but apparently, this house we were staying in belonged to the Monsanto family. I didn't know who they were, and why we were allowed to stay here, but the local people were full of tales. Sometimes I felt like I was getting somewhere with my research, and then one story would contradict another, and I'd be right back to square one. One story was totally batshit crazy.

I was out to breakfast one morning with Mica and Slater. Even though it was a bit chilly, we sat outside *The Gumbo Pot,* eating Eggs Creole and listening to the steamboat puff its way out of its bay on the Mississippi River. The steamboat was full of tourists enjoying the onboard jazz that blared out across the rippling water. The waiter served us our coffees and asked if we were visiting.

'No. We're living in the old Monsanto townhouse,' Mica said.

'No way,' he said, staring at us with wide eyes. 'That place has been empty for years! You do know they were vampires, right?'

'Oh really,' said Mica, laughing aloud. '... and where'd you get that piece of information?'

'It's a well-known legend around these parts. The Monsanto family came here on a boat and settled in the early 1800s. They brought all their stuff in coffin-shaped trunks.'

'That's ridiculous!' said Slater. 'Just like all the other tales of New Orleans ghosts and curses. There's only one truth here, and that's that the people of New Orleans believe their own tales ... and everyone has a different version of the same tale to tell.'

Mica laughed again and Slater joined in and made a face like he was baring fangs. The waiter just smiled and said, 'Well, you wouldn't get me anywhere near that house, and I'd stay well away from the loft if I were you. That loft has been sealed since 1842. God knows what's sealed in there?'

That was quite funny really. I mean Mica and Slater were right. I'd been here three months and during that time, I'd heard so many different versions of the same tale. But in each tale the people of New Orleans, and especially the students at my new school, definitely believed the Monsanto and Du Plessis families were of vampire origin. Slater said the Du Plessis were one of the original settler families, and that they were a very distinguished and private bunch. So of course, these rumours started because the family members were hardly ever seen on the streets. Wild parties were held almost every weekend in the Monsanto townhouse, but, although the house was always full, none of the locals were ever invited. Guests would turn up from out of town, and on a Monday, the house would be silent again, leaving the locals wondering what had happened to the guests.

At the town's main library, I searched through the archives and newspaper articles, and there was certainly a lot of speculation surrounding my family. In their time in this city, there were deaths by the score, yet for centuries there didn't seem to be a single death registered in my family line.

This was really interesting.

I didn't believe in vampires, or any other supernatural creature, but I still wanted to find out where the rumours came from. I'd heard of a graveyard on the outskirts of the French quarter and decided to go there and check the graves out for myself. If the Du Plessis family had lived here since the 1700s, there would have to be headstones bearing the names of those who had died. I'd been warned not to go near the graveyard at night, as Voodoo was still practised here, and it wasn't safe to go there alone in the dark. Then again, I'd also been told that Storyville was right next door to the cemetery, and that this was where all the curious tales of ghosts, voodoo and vampires came from. It was therefore hard to tell if there was really anything to be afraid of, other than the wild imaginations of the people who lived here.

One day at the library, the librarian came to me with some information, having seen I was researching myths and legends of New Orleans. She told me that, at one time, the French quarter had been a pretty outrageous place, with partying 24/7 and illegal drinking and prostitution. Apparently, the governor at the time created Storyville as a legal area for prostitution, to keep the business of the ladies-of-the night separate from the respectable gentry of the city. She said that these tales of ghosts, voodoo and vampires and the like may have sprung up around that time, to keep respectable people away from the outskirts of the French quarter that housed the graveyard and lurid streets of Storyville.

The only safe way to check out the graveyard would be on a

day tour, I decided. Maybe once I was there, I could sneak off and check out the headstones and then join the group again right at the end. Slater agreed to take me although he couldn't see why I'd be interested. He tried to talk me out of it, but I insisted, and we booked the tour for the following day.

When it came time to leave the house, I sulked, because Slater, Mica, Tallis and Mylo were all waiting to take me to the graveyard. *Total overkill — treating me like a bloody baby!*

The mild winter sun was still quite warm, and as we arrived outside the graveyard, Mica popped up a sun umbrella to shade me and bought me a bottle of water from a guy at the curbside. The graveyard had high walls all around, beside which a long queue waited to go in through the entrance. The guys surrounded me as we edged our way through the front gates. The crowds in front of me moved off in all directions, and for the first time, I could see clearly around me. A sudden rush of goosebumps popped up on both my arms, and the hairs on the back of my neck stood up. My eyes widened as I stared straight in front of me. To my left and right, was row after row of *not* gravestones, but actual above-ground tombs!

So, this was that place in the world where they buried their dead above the ground. This was the place in the paintings on my bedroom ceiling in Uncle Noah's house. This was the old familiar postcard I'd been carrying around in my purse all these years.

Suddenly Tallis's voice brought me back to reality.

'Come on, Lily, move on. You are losing the group. Or are you looking for something in particular?'

'Well yeah, I was looking for the Du Plessis family tomb.'

'Oh ... well you won't find them here, Lily. I think they had their own plot somewhere. However, your mum's tomb is here.'

He walked me across the middle of the graveyard to a tomb

right in the middle, 'This is where your mum's buried, Lily,' he said, pointing to a large grey tomb. A statue of a beautiful woman swathed from her head to her bare feet in flowing robes that clung silk-like to her tiny frame adorned the top of the tomb. Her face resembled my mum's; maybe it was meant to be her. Carved from the same grey stone as the tomb, she looked kind of creepy, yet was such a masterpiece of feminine art that I couldn't help but stare in the silence. My bedroom ceiling came to mind: this was one of the scenes in those paintings, except the painting was dark and eerie, the tomb in total darkness other than the glow from the full moon, but, in the painting, there was also a candle alight, and a wolf laying at the base of the tomb guarding its mistress. It felt strange to stand in front of the actual tomb, as if the painting had come to life in a French quarter graveyard.

Anyway, it looked well-tended compared to the others around it. A bunch of almost fresh flowers lay on the top — they must have been put there recently because, while they were struggling to survive in the heat, they were certainly not dead or even that old.

On the tomb the inscription read,

Here lies Lilith Montague — Taken too soon — much beloved in life and death — 1980 -2003

It stood out amongst the other tombs because it was a single level. The other tombs were tall and seemed to have room for two or more bodies.

'The layers are so other family members can be added as they die,' Tallis explained. 'The older corpses move down levels until they end up as scraped out dust, which is poured into chambers at the bottom of the tomb to make room for more family members over the years.'

My mum's grave was only a single tomb. I guessed because

they were not expecting anyone to join her; guessed that if I died I'd be added to the Du Plessis family tomb — if anyone knew where it was.

'Who looks after her tomb? Why are there flowers here? Why is she even buried here?'

Here it was again, confusion. Another set of questions I was unlikely to get answers to. *Why, oh why is my life such a puzzle?*

'I don't know, Lily, but we need to leave now. This place is supposed to be out of bounds to us.'

'Why?'

'I don't know, Lily. We are just following instructions, and one of them was to stay out of the graveyards.'

I didn't get it ... couldn't wrap my head around all of it. I thought I was finally safe here. But it seemed that I would never be truly safe anywhere. My mum was twenty-three when she had given birth to me and died. And someone had loved her enough to fly her body back here for burial. And that someone obviously loved her enough to still be visiting her tomb. *Do they know about me? If they do, why has there been no contact? Could it be my benefactor, the supplier of my full bank account?*

'It's pointless asking questions, Lily, because we know about as much as you do. We know you are different ... special. We are contracted to guard you with our lives until you're eighteen; we are well supplied with all our needs, but beyond that we know nothing — all part of the plan to keep you safe, I think. We just follow the rules, Lily, that's it,'

Then he looked at me slightly guilty, as if he'd just lied, and I suspected he knew far more than he was saying.

'Even if we did know anything, Lily, we're sworn to secrecy, so I can't answer any of your questions.'

'Well that's just great, isn't it! But it's just not bloody good enough!' I scowled. 'I need more, Tallis. I need to know so much more. Why is she buried here? Who visits her grave? Why is there not a Du Plessis family tomb here? Where is it? Who do I have to be scared of? Do I have to spend the rest of my life running from an invisible monster? I need to find out what I'm up against and I need to find out now!'

Tallis stared at me sadly; obviously felt sorry for me, but he had limitations just like Mica, Slater and Mylo. They were all under strict orders to keep me safe, but from what? I believe they also had absolutely no idea.

There was only one thing for it: I would have to disobey my dead uncle and open the parcel. Although there was still another eight and a half months till my eighteenth birthday, I had a strong feeling that if I didn't find out the truth, I probably wouldn't make it that far, whether in Blackheath or here in New Orleans. Both places seemed just as dangerous for me.

So, what should I do? ... live the next few months under lock and key? I couldn't go back to England, not with my grandad still after me, but I knew now that I had a false sense of security here in New Orleans. I had to find out what I needed to do to be free.

Back at the house, I hurried to my room and pulled up the loose floorboard under my bed where I'd hidden the parcel then sat on the bed staring at it ... for a long time ... worrying about what my Uncle Noah would think. Silly I know, but he had instilled in me such a need to *do as I was told* that it was hard to kick that feeling even though he was dead. I turned the parcel over, and over, wondering what to do. *Should I open it or not?*

I hated indecision but I knew I'd feel so guilty if I peeled that paper back!

I started picking at it, lifting the edges carefully with my nails, as if my Uncle Noah's ghost would stir at the sound of it being unwrapped, but ... if there was no sound ...

But, as I peeled the paper away and moved on to the next bit, the paper sealed itself back up again, as if I hadn't just peeled it right open. Instantly, I pushed the parcel away, freaked out by what had happened right before my eyes.

I sat staring at it ... then pulled it towards me and starting tearing at it again. But as quickly as I unwrapped it, the parcel re-wrapped itself. And it didn't matter how hard I tried, this parcel and whatever was protecting the contents was not going to open for me. I raged. And my hands heated up as I envisaged setting the blasted parcel alight.

But, of course, even that didn't work. My little outburst only singed the cover on the bed around the parcel. And the parcel remained unscathed. I pulled the anger back in; breathed deeply; tried to stay calm because it was pointless. The house could burn down around me and the parcel would stay in one piece.

Screaming, I stood and threw the parcel at the wall. It landed with a thud on the floor. I grabbed it and shoved it back under the floorboard, thumping it down with my fist.

Slater banged on the bedroom door. 'Everything okay in there, Lily? What's the commotion?'

'Oh nothing. Just my bloody temper getting the better of me again.'

'Okay. Well, you need to try to keep that under control. It could be dangerous if you don't learn to control your outbursts. And there's been a lot of them lately. If you want to talk you know where I am.'

'It's okay, I'm practising keeping my cool,' I lied. Although in some way, I was telling the truth — I had, this time, drawn it back in at will. It had been hard in the beginning: something would just trigger my anger and I would struggle hard to control it. Now I could kind of control it. Of course, there was always the fear that someday something — or someone — would piss me off so much I would just explode; have absolutely no control at all … and some idiot would end up cremated before their time because this new talent of mine was more in control of me than me of it.

That night we all dressed up and went out on the town, ending up in an old jazz bar on the far side of town. In this small cozy bar packed with people, we sat inside and listened to the piano player and all the Sunday night chatter. A waitress with Barbie pink hair, bright red lipstick, tattooed limbs, and a yellow fifties dress served us. I ordered the usual coke. Mica and Slater sat talking to an old man by the door and Tallis and I stood close to the bar. Mylo played a pokie machine and Tallis left to go to the men's room.

Someone stroked my neck and whispered in my ear, 'You smell delicious.'

I turned to the tall, dark, handsome stranger standing beside me. He was dressed all in black; was about the same age as Tallis and had the most gorgeous striking green eyes. But his cold touch sent a shiver down my spine, and I quickly scanned the room for Tallis.

'I'm Alex,' he whispered, leaning in again. 'And let me guess … you are Lily Du Plessis? No?'

He smiled, and for the first time, I saw his fangs. I didn't answer; simply stared at him, at his pointed teeth, and relived the chill of him touching my neck; coming so close to me to whisper.

Then Tallis reappeared and Alex disappeared as quickly as he came.

'Did you see him? Did you see that, Tallis?' I said, my gaze darting around the room looking for him.

'Who? What?' Tallis said wearily.

He obviously had no idea *who* or *what* I was talking about, and how could I explain? *'Oh, the guy with the fangs' — yeah right, he'd buy that — not!* So, I fell silent.

We returned to sit with Mica, Slater and Mylo and ate some tasty popcorn shrimp in mustard, and more of those sweet chili cheese fries I was becoming addicted to. The guys chatted and the piano man played on. The pink-haired waitress scurried around serving everyone plates of delectable bites with a bright smile. I gazed out of the window; wondered who the hell my visitor had been? How did he know my name? Was he a friend or an enemy? *And are those teeth for real? Shit!*

Were these vampire stories I'd been hearing true? And if they were could this visitor possibly have been a Du Plessis too. It seemed a bit crazy, but at the same time not so unbelievable to someone with the ability to set the world on fire.

A conversation about the tombs brought my attention back to the room. I listened to the old man who had joined our table telling more tales of why New Orleans tombs were above ground. Apparently, when the first settlers came in the 1700s, the New Orleans graveyard was pretty much a flat swampland. When the towns' folk died, they were buried six foot under, but the water levels were so high that it only had to rain heavily, and the coffins would pop to the top. If a flood happened, the coffins would not only rise to the top but occasionally float down the streets, pop their lids and scared the shit out of all the suspicious townsfolk, who were sure magic and demons had something to do with the floating coffin phenomena. Eventually, they worked out what had occurred and decided above-ground tombs were the go, and they built them using cement rather than wood. Occasionally a heavy three-level tomb would sink into the ground over time, and the bottom level would end up below ground anyway, so at least one body would get buried! But the weight of the tomb above stopped it rising to the surface in heavy rains or floods. This was a great story and possibly the only tale I'd heard so far that actually sounded true. I wondered again why there were paintings of New Orleans tombs in a Blackheath Victorian house. But there was nobody alive who was able to tell me the reason. So, I guessed there was no point in thinking about it.

'And the Du Plessis?' I asked the old man. 'Would you know where their family tomb is?' He looked at me, shocked, then said, 'Why would the undead need tombs, Miss? The undead are free to roam the earth. Not lie still beneath it.'

Everyone sat silent, me included. I mean, what answer could I possibly have for that?

As the bar emptied out onto the street, we all walked home in silence, the hush drowned out by the sounds pouring out of every door and window along the way. Jazz and blues drifted into the air, and the streets still buzzed with life. People walked around aimlessly, drinking, smoking, holding hands and kissing in the cool night air. The atmosphere was full of romance, and the fear I'd felt earlier was snuggled up tightly now in this nice, warm fuzzy feeling that filled the French quarter streets.

When we turned into our street, Tallis stopped us walking. Up on the balcony, the windows were fully open, and the long curtains flew about outside in the breeze, brushing against the balcony railings. Slater rushed to the front door as Mylo swiftly climbed the outer brick with monkey-like agility and amazing speed. Mica jumped the high wall into the back garden and disappeared. Tallis pushed me up against the wall, his whole body in front of me, shielding me. We were in the middle of a seemingly dangerous situation, and yet all I could think about was this was the closest Tallis and I had been for months. I could feel his muscular body pressing up against mine. Then, when he leant in even closer and sniffed my hair, I felt his heart beating faster than usual and he breathed heavily, unnaturally, as if trying to control himself.

'Are you scared, Tallis?' I said, staring up at him.

'Not scared, Lily, not scared of anything but how you make me feel,' he whispered.

'Me?' I said innocently.

'Yeah, you know what you do to me?'

'Really. What the heck do I do to you? Please explain … because you haven't shown any interest in me for a long while now, Tallis Summers,' I said sarcastically.

'It's complicated, Lily. I have to keep you safe, and me loving you is probably not the best way to do that.'

'Loving me?' I said. A rush of warmth suddenly stirred in the pit of my stomach. *Had he just admitted that he loved me?*

'Yeah, Lily, loving you is very easy.' He looked at me, yearning in his eyes, and I could almost feel that yearning spreading through his body as I leaned in to kiss him, unable to stop myself. Our lips met, and he sighed as if realising he had no control, as if giving in to the temptation I was placing on his lips.

Suddenly Mylo appeared on the balcony, shouting down to us, and we swiftly drew apart. Averting our eyes from each other, we quickly put space between us.

'We've had visitors, but it's all clear now,' shouted Mylo.

Slater reappeared at the front door and hurried Tallis and me inside; he locked the big doors behind us.

'Someone's been here searching for something. Stuff's all over the place.'

'What could they possibly have been searching for?' Tallis frowned.

'I have no idea. The only thing of value here is Lily, so why empty all the drawers? It must be an object they're looking for. Maybe paperwork or a book or something?' said Slater.

'Anything in the instructions to warn us what it might be?' Mylo asked.

Slater shook his head. 'Not that I recall.'

Mica walked in from the garden scratching his chin. 'There's no sign of forced entry. I don't see how they got in. It's very strange coz I'm sure we locked up before leaving.'

'Do you mean someone had a key?' I piped up.

'No way … well I wouldn't think so. Only a Monsanto would have access, and I don't believe any of them still live here in New Orleans.'

'Could have been a Du Plessis,' added Slater. 'Lily's family would be the only others with free access to this house.'

'Family? You mean I *do* have family? Are they here in New Orleans?'

'Well, we didn't think so — but possibly,' said Mica, 'possibly.'

'We'll take extra special care locking up tonight in case this was our mistake,' said Mica. 'Come on, let's all get some shut-eye.'

Mylo checked the back perimeter and locked up downstairs. Mica and Slater checked upstairs and locked up tightly. The loft was still chained up and hadn't been touched, the hefty chain still tightly in place, so whatever the thief had been looking for certainly couldn't have been up there. Or maybe the legend had even reached the burglar community that the Monsanto sealed loft was not an area to be messed with.

I let Tallis check my room and double-check and lock the windows before I entered. As he brushed past me in the doorway, I closed my eyes and held my breath, so as not to let myself feel anything. This seemed to work quite well at keeping my infatuation with him at bay. He wandered off to his room without so much as a nod.

Closing my door, I waited a few moments before checking under the floorboard beneath my bed. They were still there, both my tin, with my money and bankbook in — and my parcel that refused to be opened. I was thankful I'd decided to hide them there, initially because I didn't know if I could trust the guys with my parcel or my fortune. But it seems it was the best decision I'd made, because obviously the thief had been after the money. I didn't think anyone would be interested in an impenetrable birthday present for an eighteen-year-old girl. But the money I was quite sure would be a drawcard for anyone.

That night I slept lightly, thinking about the possibility of meeting some of my family, if they were really in these parts. At one point I woke abruptly with a vision of Alex at the side of my bed, smiling at me, those pointed teeth glistening white in the darkness. When I rubbed my eyes, the vision was gone, and I realised it was just a subconscious thought entering my dreams because of how scared I'd felt at the bar.

It was, however, hard to fall back to sleep as Alex's face kept popping into my mind — such a familiar face, and those teeth, those vampire teeth. *Had I imagined them? Was all this talk of vampires affecting my mind? Maybe I'm going crazy.* I mean, it had been a pretty strange year with some pretty screwed up crap happening. Maybe my mind was playing games with me.

I dozed off again and the next thing I knew it was morning. My alarm for school buzzed in my ear and the weak winter sun streamed through the open window.

The open window! reeled through my brain.

I looked to the right at my bedroom door — it was still firmly shut — then back towards the window, which I had seen Tallis firmly lock from the inside before I entered the room last night. I hopped out of bed; grabbed my robe and crept carefully to the window; stood there nervously as the curtains fluttered in the breeze. Then I stepped out onto the balcony, not knowing what I would find. The balcony was empty, but on the little table at the end was a single red rose with a small note attached, saying, *'You smell delicious!'* and I knew in that moment that my vision of Alex was not a dream. He was there in my room, in the middle of the night, baring his fangs in the darkness. I sniffed the rose, and my answer came to me — he was my friend, not my enemy, and he might possibly hold the answer to all the questions I ever wanted to know.

THE GIRL WHO CRIED WOLF

The following three months we hardly went out. Winter left and spring arrived but other than going to school I spent most of my time at home. My nightly visits from Alex had become a regular thing, with a rose left on my balcony table with a cute little note every morning. It was like a love affair, without the lover! He never once made himself visible to me, but in my sleeping hours, I could feel his presence, and in the morning his aroma still lingered in my room. It was a nice feeling — someone watching over me whilst I slept. I didn't know why but I knew he was there to protect me. Not to hurt me.

Occasionally I tried my hardest to stay awake, but the night terrors that kept me from sleeping since my uncle had died had disappeared now. I guess because I felt safe knowing Alex was there in the darkness. Sometimes I struggled to read until 2am hoping to catch a glimpse of him, but then I'd fall asleep and wake to the familiar feeling that my night watchman had been by my side until the early hours, keeping me safe. Tallis locked my French doors from the inside every night before going to bed, and in the morning, they were always wide open, with the breeze sweeping softly against my skin as I slept. The single red rose was Alex's calling card, and I had so many of them now, that I had tied them in a bunch and hung them upside down to dry on a little hook beside my bed.

I was happy yet disappointed. I thought Alex was going to be the answer to all the mysteries I'd been unable to unravel in my life. My mother, the Du Plessis family, and of course, my fate. But other than the odd blurry night vision of him I never achieved the closeness I craved.

I'd been in New Orleans for six months now, going on seven. Although the security had been stepped up, and going out was rare, I still felt comfortable and very much at home — not imprisoned like I'd felt in Blackheath. Here, at least in the daytime, I was still allowed to use the balcony and the garden. And the house was filled with such light that I felt the sunshine was on the inside.

One warm Saturday afternoon, I wrapped a thin cardigan around my shoulders and sat out in the garden reading another book — a gory tale of attempted murder, and I wished the main character — poor Katy — had been as protected as I was, because those bad guys wouldn't have attacked her. Sometimes I felt way overprotected, but I also felt extremely lucky to have such a great team looking out for me. I missed Olive and having another girl to chat with, but on the whole, I was happy with life. I lifted my sunglasses and glanced to the left as I heard a rustle in the bushes behind me.

'Don't turn around, Lily. Just carry on reading,' a familiar voice said. 'It's just me ... Alex. Don't be alarmed.'

'Alex, what are you doing here?'

'I had to see you. I have some news that may interest you.'

'What? What news?' I shifted slightly to the left, trying to look into the bushes.

Slater popped his head out of the back door of the kitchen. 'Everything okay, Lily? Need a drink or anything?'

'No thanks, Slater. I'm fine. I'm reading. I've got a stiff neck and just trying to get comfortable.' I smiled, and he went back in and closed the door.

'See, Lily. They watch your every move. Your body language tells a lot so just relax and pretend to read.'

'Okay,' I said.

'I think you are at risk, Lily.'

I snorted and almost laughed. 'Tell me about it,' I whispered. 'I've been hearing that my whole bloody life.'

'I mean immediate danger. There's an English man here in the quarter, Lily, asking questions about you. He's well-known amongst vampires as an immortal child hunter.'

'Well, how does that affect me?'

'There's a legend, Lily. It tells that a vampire that bears a child with a mortal witch will produce an immortal child, but that immortality doesn't kick in until the child's eighteenth birthday. If the immortal child reaches adulthood, it will be one of the most powerful immortal beings on the earth. These hunters are sent to track and kill these children before they turn eighteen. So far it's just a legend because no immortal child has ever lived long enough to reach its immortality.'

'I've never heard of the legend, and I don't think it applies to me. The only English man I know that wants me dead is my grandad. If he has followed me here, I guess I'm in big trouble. I'll have to tell my guardians.'

'I think the legend does apply to you, Lily.'

'Look, I don't know who my dad was. But I do know that he's dead, and my mum was just a normal human being who died in childbirth.'

'Who gave you this information?'

'My uncle.'

'Did he tell you anything of any true relevance about your

mother, about your father, about how they met? Did he tell you why you felt no emotions as a child? Why your life was constantly under threat? Do you know why you are a mess of emotions now that you are soon to turn eighteen?'

'No, not really. My life is pretty much a mystery. How do you know so much?'

'Your father is dead, Lily. Your uncle told you the truth, but he is not dead and buried. He is part of the eternal undead … he is a vampire, just like me.'

I shot bolt upright; dropped my book and knocked my glass over with my foot. The back door flew open, and Slater and Mica were beside me in seconds. Alex was right. They watched my every move. Always.

'What's wrong, Lily?' Slater said.

'Nothing. Nothing at all. I'm sorry. I just thought a bee was going to land on me. I'm shit scared of bees.' I laughed.

'Oh okay, you had us worried there for a minute. We thought maybe something was coming at you.'

'Yes, but just a nasty insect. I'm so sorry.'

'It's okay. I'll grab you another drink.'

'Thanks, Slater.'

Mica and Slater went back in. Slater brought me out a glass of lemonade and went in, closing the door behind him.

'Alex,' I whispered, but there was no answer. He'd left me mid-conversation, just when it was getting interesting, and now I was left hanging, thinking about everything he'd just said.

My dad was a vampire — my mum, possibly a mortal witch. And me … an immortal child. The dodgy catch to that being, while I was still a *child* I could actually be killed! So, the description was a little deceptive. False advertising, I'd say! Well, I'd wanted answers. Now I guess I had them.

There were so many more questions I wanted to ask, and I wondered whether Alex would come back so we could talk again. If my dad was a vampire, part of the eternal undead, why didn't he appear to me like Alex had? If my mum was a mortal witch, why did she die in childbirth? Surely, her powers could've protected her. This was obviously why I had spent my whole life hiding in plain sight; why I'd witnessed so much death as a kid. Obviously, all those people who had died were after me, and my Uncle Noah and his employees had taken them out of the game to protect me. It all started to make sense now, all of those deaths.

But there were a lot of innocents killed along the way too, I guess caught in the crossfire: the lady in Folkstone with the little white fluffy dog — was that bullet meant for me? The rockfall in Rome when Claire was crushed — also meant for me? The chubby, bearded man on the ice, sent to take me out maybe? … but Mica and Slater took him out instead? The teacher in the sports shed … was he out to get me too? Did Mylo step in to keep me safe? And Juliette? Uncle's one true love, was she an assassin? Had they killed her to protect me? Is that what had changed my uncle's feelings for me? Because he loved her, but I had to be his first priority.

It felt like suddenly some of the pieces to a giant jigsaw puzzle had started to come together. And the strangest thing was, I'd actually started crying. Were these tears for those poor souls that had been lost in the battle along the way? Or for me, finally knowing the truth … that I, Lily Du Plessis, was the sole reason for so much carnage. I felt horrified, and for a moment, longed for the nonchalance I'd felt as a kid.

Then a thought suddenly came to mind. *If my grandad is here, how does he know my whereabouts? Has he gotten to Olive?* She was the only person I was in contact with. *Has my texting her put her in danger?* I thought leaving England would keep her safe. My grandad only wanted me. I thought with me gone the danger would be gone. What if I was wrong? What if she was in trouble? What if my stupid actions had caused problems for her after I'd left? My stomach knotted, and I felt nauseous. I ran to the kitchen to find Slater.

'Slater, I think my grandad is here. Don't ask me how I know, I just do. I've been texting Olive in England, and now I'm worried sick something might have happened to her.'

'I know, Lily. The word around town is that there is an Englishman asking questions about you. We are planning a move. I was going to talk to you about this.'

'Planning a move? No. I love it here. I don't want to move!'

'It's just temporary, Lily, until we've dealt with your grandad. We're not going far. Just to the Oaks plantation thirty minutes away. It's owned by your father's family.'

'Family! You mean I may get to finally meet the Du Plessis, my dad's family?'

'I guess so.'

'But what about school?'

I didn't know why I said that. School wasn't exactly my happy place. Most of the people there ignored me. Other than one girl with an English accent, with short blonde and big blue eyes, called Charlotte Rittal. She often sat with me but hardly ever spoke. And one cute looking guy with shoulder-length, dark-blonde hair that he tied back in a ponytail. Briff liked to show off his feathers, and not in a nice way. He'd write nasty notes and stick them to my locker and pour water into my backpack occasionally when I wasn't looking. Once he had tripped me up in the lunch hall, sending the contents of my tray flying across the black and white chequered floor. I didn't know what I'd done to offend him, but I felt like burning him to ashes. It took so much self-control not to.

In some ways, I guess he was good for me though, because he was an extracurricular lesson at school in 'How not to lose it'. I didn't think the principal of the school would be very impressed if I burnt Benjamin Franklin High to the ground just because of a shaggy-haired, beef burger eating brute, with less than two brain cells to rub together.

'You can still go to school; we'll drive you there, and anyway end of term is coming up. It'll be school holidays soon enough,' said Slater.

'And what about Olive? How can I find out if she's safe? She hasn't answered my text in over a week. I thought she might just be busy, but now I just don't know.'

'She's fine. We have some people there looking out for them. Your grandad's men broke into their house and stole Olive's phone. That's why there's no answer to your text. But it was a silly thing you did, Lily. Now your grandad knows your every move.'

'I'm sorry. It's just that she's the only normality I have in my life. She makes me feel like I can handle anything. I need to have contact with her. She keeps me grounded.'

Tears started falling again, and Slater wrapped his arms around me. I was over this bloody crying thing, but on the other hand, I enjoyed the attention that came from it. This was the third time in as many months that Slater had hugged me when I cried; it felt magical. Hugs were definitely food for my soul. This last year had shown me that these people I was surrounded by were not just bodyguards, but the family I'd never known. Over time we had become close-knit, like we had a true bond.

'You can't be expected to know the repercussions of all your actions, Lily, but in future, it would help for you to be upfront. No secrets, especially secrets that could get one of us killed … okay?'

'Okay.'

'By the way, Olive has sent you a little something. Mylo has gone to collect it from quarantine.'

'Quarantine? What the heck did she send me, a vile of the black plague to use on Grandad?'

'No. She sent you a damned cat of all things! Probably not the best thing to be dragging around with us at the moment, coz we may have to move about a bit over the next few months. But, oh well, it's here now. I guess we'll just have to make it work.'

At that moment, I felt like my heart would explode. I burst into tears again. But this time they were tears of joy. Slater gave me one last hug, and I decided that tonight's entry in my diary would state this day was possibly one of the happiest days of my life!

'I wish your uncle had known you like this, Lily. He only ever saw a monster, but *this* Lily … *this* Lily he would have truly loved.' He smiled and I smiled back; thought then about my uncle and how he'd treated me as a child; thought about how difficult it must have been for him to love me. For the first time in my life, I saw what Grandad saw, and what he had truly meant when he'd called me an abomination. It almost seemed reasonable that he wanted me dead.

That night we locked up as usual. I locked my bedroom door and sat in my room writing long after everyone had gone to bed. Pippa snuggled up next to me. I was much too excited to sleep, and so happy to have Pippa right here beside me that I continued writing late into the night. At exactly 2.30, the bolts on the French doors started to slide down by themselves, and the doors creaked slowly open. A gentle breeze wafted in and ruffled Pippa's fur. Alex was coming, and for once I had managed to stay awake. He appeared in the doorway and looked a bit confused that I was up, but he smiled a gorgeous smile and drifted in; sat on the end of the bed. Pippa looked up at him but didn't move. She was too warm and cozy beside me and obviously felt Alex was no threat.

'I'm sorry about today,' I said. 'I was a bit shocked by your last comment.'

'That fine, Lily. I just want you to know the truth. To be prepared.'

'Can you tell me anything else?'

'If there's anything you want to know. I'll try to answer your questions.'

'Okay. Well, if my mum was a witch, why did she die having me?'

'All mortal witches die in childbirth if the child is an immortal. It's just the way of the world. Vampire blood which courses through an immortal's veins is not compatible with mortal blood. And there is no mortal witch known that has ever successfully given birth to a vampire's child without losing their life.'

'So why get pregnant? Seems ridiculously stupid if you ask me. I mean if she knew the risks ...'

'Some mortal witches believe in the legend of the immortal child, and the good it could possibly do in the future. And some vampires believe in the legend and the possibility of harnessing the power of an immortal child for their own selfish uses. Both have an agenda and are, therefore, willing to take the risk. And sometimes, well ... it's just an accident, unplanned, poor birth control, or pure ignorance. I don't know what you were, Lily ... wanted for whatever reason, or a mistake ... that I cannot tell you.'

'Geez, thanks, Alex. Hit me in the feels, why don't you! You really know how to make a girl feel special!'

Alex laughed. And I laughed too.

'I have to ask you a question, Lily. Were you given anything special by anyone growing up? Something left by your father or mother maybe?'

As this question left his lips, I felt Pippa stiffen beside me. My heart started to beat a little faster. I knew exactly what he wanted to hear but something in me screamed *No.* So that's just what I said.

'No. Not that I can recall. My uncle looked after me when I lived with him, and now his employees take care of me and provide everything I need. I've never received anything special from anyone, and not anything from my mum or dad.'

'Okay. Well I need to tell you something.' He edged closer to me on the bed and started whispering. 'I think this gift is still to come. I don't think you'll receive it until your eighteenth birthday, but if you do, can you make me a promise? Can you promise to tell me when you receive it?'

He smiled an endearing smile that made me want to kiss him. I eagerly said, 'Yeah, sure,' wanting him to like me.

When he was this close, he felt almost like a second skin, almost like I belonged to him, or was a part of his very being. Something about him made my skin prickle; made my blood pulse madly beneath my skin. I needed to reach out to him, desperate to belong.

All of a sudden Pippa scowled and arched her back, her wide-open stare looking directly at the open window. On the balcony stood an enormous wolf, its eyes piercing blue. I reeled backwards onto my pillow, screaming; grabbed Pippa as the wolf stepped inside.

Alex flew at it with lightning speed and the two grappled with each other. I was frozen on the bed, too afraid to move. Pippa hissed wildly; tried to free herself, but I held on tight to her as furniture toppled all over the place. One minute Alex was on top of the wolf, the next the wolf was on top of Alex. Their struggle ended outside on the balcony where, with great force — and I'm not sure whose — they both tumbled over the balcony to the street below. I cowered into my pillows!

Hearing the commotion Slater, Mica and Mylo came running up to my room; they banged loudly on the door and I leapt up and unlocked it, letting them in.

'A wolf!' I shouted, pointing to the balcony. I couldn't get another word out as Slater dashed to the balcony and looked down below. He jumped over the edge and Mica ran straight after him and dived over the edge as well. Mylo rushed to the windows and banged them shut, locking them and closing the curtains. He ran from the room, shutting my door as he went, shouting at me to lock it and stay inside. I locked my door and stood with my ear against it, listening. I could hear a commotion going on in the hallway and was scared for Alex. What if they caught him?

I snuck out onto the landing and crouched behind the spindles of the staircase from where I could clearly see the hallway through to the kitchen.

'Bring him in quickly.'

I heard Slater's voice as the big front door banged shut.

Oh no, they've got Alex, I thought.

'Quickly, into the kitchen — bring the elixir. Hurry, Mica.'

The elixir? What is that? Shit! What are they going to do to him?

I crouched further down till I could see more clearly, and what I saw made me flinch. They were carrying the wolf! — the biggest wolf I'd ever seen — through to the kitchen and onto the table. *Since when were there wolves in New Orleans?* All those years I'd spent avoiding death, and he could've killed me with one fell swoop.

But why are they bringing him in? Is he dead? Did Alex kill him to save my life? And Alex, is he okay?

I couldn't take my eyes off the scene in front of me, Mica, Slater and Mylo all attending to the wolf; feeding it some kind of fluid from a small test tube and stroking its head like it was the good guy.

I shook my head and scowled, confused. Then gasped as the wolf took a deep breath and began to squirm on the table. I felt like shouting to them to get out of there, to escape quickly, but I couldn't speak. Unable to move, I continued watching as the fur started to diminish from the wolf's body, as it sat up like a man. Then its ears withdrew into its head; its snout shortened until its face was almost human. I gasped again — it was human! When it stretched its limbs, everything popped back into shape, and there, right before my eyes, sitting on our kitchen table where I ate breakfast every morning, was Tallis. Once wolf ... now man!

Rushing back to my room, I shut the door. *Oh, my God, what did I just witness? This is absolutely batshit crazy!* I locked the door, unlocked the window and ran out on the balcony; looked over the edge for any sign of Alex. But there was none. At the end of the balcony lay another single rose on the table and a little note that simply said, *'I know whose side I want to be on'.* I tucked it in my bedside drawer, tied the rose up with the rest and sat on the bed stroking Pippa, who was now calm and back to her old self. I, however, was totally confused.

If Alex isn't a threat, why did he fight with Tallis? And Tallis, a wolf! He is obviously here with one purpose only, and that is to protect me, so wolf or not, he is totally on my side.

I thought back to the paintings on my ceiling at home in Blackheath. There were wolves in the pictures, one sitting at the side of a single level tomb. *Was that my mother's tomb? And why did Alex want to know about my parcel? And why had I lied about it?*

It was almost instinctive that I keep it hidden. Maybe Alex's motives were not as pure as I'd thought. One thing was certain, and that was that Tallis would tell everyone about Alex's visit, and Mica would be pissed off at me, especially after our conversation about being upfront and not keeping secrets. I felt an idiot, like I'd been caught with my hands in the cookie jar. But I so loved knowing all the things Alex had to tell, finding out everything I'd never known. It was revelatory.

I wondered then if all the team were wolves. In some ways, this scared me shitless, but in others, it didn't, because I knew I was safe in their company. I was still reeling from this discovery — mortal witches, vampires, wolves, unopenable packages. This was turning into one whirlwind of a life where things I'd only ever read about in books were appearing right before my eyes, as real as the blood that pumped through my veins, part vampire blood at that!

The whole setting-stuff-on-fire thing made some sense now, and the ability I had to enter another body and make it do my will also. Was I actually half vampire and half witch, or was being an immortal different? Would I have the powers of both? Would I crave blood at some point, or ever want to feed on a human being?

I bloody well hoped not.

Maybe I was just the creation of two supernatural beings whose powers I would inherit, but hopefully not their tendencies. Not that I knew what a mortal witch's tendencies were. But the vampire side of me, well I knew what that entailed, and I didn't like the idea of that at all. At the moment, the only qualities I could see in me were Mum's. The powers I had already seemed to be those of a witch — setting stuff alight; entering bodies; feeling a strong connection to things around me, more so than usual, as if the world and everything in it were in every fibre of my being. In this year, I think I must have inherited my mum's whole range of emotions. But as to inheriting anything of my dad ... was there anything remotely vampiric about me?

No, I didn't think so, other than having no empathy, and no emotions from birth until my seventeenth year. That might very well have been a vampiric trait. But there was little else I could think of. After all, I slept like a log, ate proper food, and there had never been any sign of any pointy incisors, not at all. So, I guessed I must have just got some of the benefits of being their child without all of the horrible, nasty bits that made them what they were. Of course, not knowing my true identity until now, I couldn't say I really knew what my true capabilities were or potentially could be. I mean, how do you know you can ride a bike until you have actually ridden one.

I figured, with time, I would find out what Alex meant when he said: — *'If the immortal child reaches adulthood it will be one of the most powerful immortal beings on the earth.'*

Right now, I felt pretty pathetic; useless and vulnerable even. And I wasn't sure who I should trust.

I made my way downstairs to the kitchen. It was time to come clean, to confess to Mica about my meetings with Alex. If I was going to make it to my eighteenth birthday Mica was right, I needed to be honest, upfront and totally put my life in their hands. They had done an impressive job of keeping me alive so far. If there was one thing I knew for sure, it was that I could depend on these guys. I could totally trust them. Always.

MEETING MARCHELLA

Mica had given me a dreadful lecture when I told him about my visits from Alex.

'You don't realise the danger you put us all in, do you, Lily?'

'Well … he was so nice to me,' I squirmed under his angry gaze.

'You put us all at risk Lily, and nearly cost Tallis his life. If he wasn't a wolfling, he'd be dead now. That poxy vampire snapped his neck. We're just lucky that we have an elixir your mother created that brings us back from the dead.'

'Well, maybe if you'd been upfront with me about the whole bloody vampire-wolfling thing I might not have messed up so badly. It's hard to see the light when you're living under a stone.' I snapped.

'We were bound to secrecy, Lily. We were not supposed to reveal anything to you.'

'So … the tales here about the Monsanto and the Du Plessis … they're all true, right?'

'Yes, Lily. The vampire tales are true.' Mica hung his head, slightly ashamed I guess that he'd been withholding the truth, even making a joke out of the stories, and now I knew the truth he felt like a fool.

'Well, you can't blame me for this then. I couldn't have known Alex would be a threat to Tallis. But I am sorry …' I said, looking across the table at Tallis. He didn't look at me — just looked at the floor.

I was in everybody's bad books. I knew that full well. And I felt so bad for what I nearly caused. But how was I to know? Alex seemed harmless to me, and I guess the truth was, I had fallen hard for him and would have lied to anyone to have him close to me. When he was around, I craved everything about him. His smile. His eyes. Even his touch. He made my pulse race and my blood prickle under my skin — similar to what I felt for Tallis. But I knew it wasn't love. I'd felt that with Tallis, and it was a very different feeling. This was more of an intense desire that only seemed to affect me when Alex was near. When he wasn't around, he didn't cross my mind. Love was different. I knew I loved Tallis because I thought about him all the time, whether he was near me or not. I went to sleep thinking about him most nights, and he was my first thought in the morning. Trying not to love him was the most difficult thing I'd ever done, but I did it because I couldn't stand the thought of anything bad happening to him.

But my fascination with Alex had nearly ended Tallis's life. He was the one I was trying to protect by switching off to him and switching on to Alex. But it had nearly wrecked everything. Mica said I felt the way I did when Alex was around because some vampires had a connection that was so pure, a rare connection that was so intense, it could be mistaken for love. It created a strange and often misplaced loyalty. It was like being under a spell, but it most certainly wasn't love. Not at all.

'Well, of course, he was nice to you, Lily. He wants something. I don't know what exactly, but he's definitely after something. I wouldn't be surprised if he was the intruder who ransacked the house that time,' said Mica.

'Well, he did ask me if I'd ever been given anything from

anybody, that might have come from either my mum or dad. He said I'd get this gift when I turned eighteen, if I hadn't already. He said that I should be sure to let him know about it when it came.' I looked uncomfortably at the floor, not wanting to lie to Mica's face should he ask me if I'd actually been given anything. But he didn't ask.

'See, he has an agenda. Well, whatever he's after, you obviously don't have it in your possession yet, but when the day comes that you do have it, you had better steer well clear of him ... although I can't imagine what you could possibly receive that would be of any interest to him or his kind.' Mica scratched his chin and paced agitatedly up and down the kitchen.

Tallis looked up at me and my heart missed a beat as he smiled a weak but forgiving smile. I promised Mica I'd stay away from Alex, and if ever he came around, I'd tell him straight away so he could deal with it.

In an hour we were leaving for the Oaks plantation. I had decided to leave my belongings where they'd be safe. It was another five months until my birthday, and I'd already proven that the parcel would be of no use to me before then. Also, we were obviously not short of cash or a roof over our heads, or anything we wanted, so there was no point dragging the tin around with me either. It would be safe here until we came back. If we didn't come back as soon as I hoped ... well it would be safe here until my birthday, then I'd come back for it. Until then, I felt the tale around town of the sealed Monsanto loft would be enough to stop anyone entering the house while we were gone.

Leaving my parcel and tin under the floorboards here in the French quarter townhouse might turn out to be one of the most ridiculous things I'd ever done. But I had a thought, that if somebody had already searched this house and not found what they were looking for, then they weren't likely to come back. And if they did, they were just as unlikely to find it this time as last time. It made sense to leave it here. This move was only temporary according to Mica, and we'd probably be back here before we knew it.

Then we were off again, cars packed to the hilt with stuff; Pippa tucked safely under my arm. We drove through the French quarter and pulled up at another townhouse. I frowned as we pulled into the garage and the doors closed behind us, but no sooner had the garage door closed behind us than another opened on the other side, and we drove off again up a very long alleyway with high walls on either side, then out onto a desolate country road. A short while later we pulled into a long oak-lined driveway on a sprawling property with grassy fields all around. Up ahead I could see the enormous house in the distance, pretty vines growing all over the front, and all around the tall white pillars that ran the length of the front porch. It was a truly gorgeous sight, so magnificent. Simple and grand mixed into one. On the front porch, green shutters covered all the long windows floor to ceiling, and out on the porch sat a bunch of women who looked pretty much like they were still living in the 1800s when the house was originally built. They wore long dresses and bonnets, and I felt like I'd stepped back in time. We drove around the side of the mansion and into an undercover barn at the back. The doors were swiftly closed behind us. A back entrance led from the barn to the house, and we unpacked and carried everything in, helped by ten or so people who'd been waiting for our arrival. Inside, the house was a hive of busyness, so many people, all so welcoming, and seeming to know me immediately.

'Welcome, Miss Lily,' must have been said twenty times between the back door and the door to my bedroom.

I was so excited to think that there were women in the house, and the girl leading the way to my room would have been no older than me. *Female company at last,* I thought. And the sadness I'd felt at having to leave the French quarter townhouse behind for the plantation didn't feel so bad anymore.

My room was huge, much bigger than my bedroom in the townhouse. The walls were adorned with heavy flock wallpaper and had a grand open fireplace with intricate ornate tiles all around the edge. In the middle of the room, against one wall, stood a massive four-poster bed that was so high I thought I'd need a ladder to climb on it. I hoped Pippa would be able to hop on and off as easily as she could on my old bed. The décor was opulent, and one wall was lined with bookshelves filled to the brim with old books that looked like they belonged to some long-ago era. I decided I might've died on the way to the plantation, and this was my first glimpse of heaven. Attached to my room was my own private bathroom, with a large claw-foot bath with shiny gold fittings. It was filled ready for me and full of bubbles. On a tall stand beside the bath sat a bowl of fruit. A silk robe was draped neatly over a chair on the other side, and a pair of satin slippers sat just underneath.

'We'll leave you now, Miss Lily, so you can freshen up.'

The ladies left the room and closed the door. I could hear them in the bedroom unpacking my suitcases, and I checked the door was locked before slipping into the nice hot bath. *I think I'm going to like it here.* And I smiled deliriously as I disappeared under the bubbles that popped against my skin as I totally relaxed into the Louisiana lifestyle.

Later that evening, a knock came on my door.

'Dinner time, Miss Lily, on the first floor, in the dining room.'

I opened the door, but no one was there, the dark hallway

completely empty. I shut Pippa in my room and headed downstairs to dinner.

In the dining room, a long table seated maybe twenty people, each chair filled except mine. I sat down and pulled my chair in. Tallis sat to the left of me, and to the right a beautiful woman who smiled at me knowingly. Next to her sat Mica, and on the other side of him an old man who chatted away without a break, not allowing Mica to get a word in. Everyone chatted except Tallis, who sat in silence staring at me.

'Your hair looks lovely tonight, Lily.'

'Thank you, Tallis,' I said, blushing.

'So beautiful,' said the woman to my right. 'The photographs I have from your uncle don't do you justice.'

Photographs? Why would uncle have sent this woman photos of me?

'Lily, I'd like you to meet Marchella, your grandmother,' Tallis said, looking directly at her.

'My grandmother?' I said, suddenly shocked. *A real live family member — a Du Plessis?*

'Your father is my son,' she said, smiling at me.

'But you're so … so young.'

She laughed and patted my hand. 'Nearly all of us look younger than our years, Lily. That is something you will have to get used to. And there is not one of us here under one hundred years old.'

'Oh,' was all I could think to say. I scanned the table for proof of her last comment.

'So can vampires have kids then?' It was such a stupid question to ask, but I just couldn't work out the dynamics of this whole vampire family thing.

'Some of us can. The pureblood Du Plessis family line will continue to grow, but a vampire childhood is short and sweet. Our children grow at an alarming rate and reach the age of sixteen within their first eight years of life. Of course, they are not introduced to the hunt until they are sixteen and then only to hunt animals for food, not for sport. And certainly not to kill for fun, but only for necessity.'

'So, when does a pureblood stop ageing?'

'Purebloods remain the age they are when they taste their first human blood. I guess it depends on how long one can resist that temptation as to how old one will remain.'

'Oh,' I said yet again.

'Most of us here are pureblood. Josiah is my father. Melissa next to him is his second wife. She was once human, but turned ... although his first wife, my mother, was a pureblood. All the men and women who are married into the family have been turned. But your father is a pureblood, and so are you, Lily, because it is Du Plessis blood that runs through your veins.'

'Okay, so everyone here is related to me?'

'Whether they are pureblood or humans that have been turned; if they are Du Plessis, they are your family.'

'So, what about my dad? Is he here?'

'Not yet, but he will be. You'll get to meet him soon enough.'

This thought excited me yet scared the shit out of me all at the same time. I would finally get to meet my real dad — vampire or not, he was my only link to my humanity, if that's what you could call it? Or maybe *not*. Perhaps I should be calling it my *inhumanity*. But whatever it was, the same blood that pumped through his veins pumped through mine, and that made me feel a part of something I never thought I would know. I finally belonged to a real family.

'So, Grandmother, are they all vampires in this house?'

'Oh, Grandmother' is so stuffy, darling. Call me Marchella.'

'Okay … Marchella.'

'But to answer your question, yes … mostly. Other than a few human servants and the wolfling that are with you, we are all vampires in this house,' said Marchella.

'So, am I safe here then?'

'Yes, child. You are safer here than anywhere. I could never understand why your father left you in England with your uncle.'

'But at the moment I'm human. I don't become immortal until I turn eighteen.'

'Well, yes it's true. You can most certainly be killed by just about anyone up to that point, but you're not human, Lily. You do not have human blood.'

Her statement shocked me. Because I'd never thought of myself as … *not* human! All those Sundays I had spent in church thinking God created me. Mere flesh and blood. How wrong was I!

'No vampire will be interested in you, Lily, and surrounded by your family here at the Oaks, I don't think anyone else will be interested either, if they have any good sense.' She laughed and Tallis laughed too. I felt a bit pissed off that they were taking the possibility of my death so lightly.

'You are right to be confused, dear. You are not human because you have immortal blood, but you are not truly immortal until you turn eighteen. You are not all vampire, even though you are a Du Plessis. And you are not all witch, like your mother. You are indeed a strange creature … but trust me when I say that 'one day', Lily, you will truly know *who* and *what* you are, when you become one of the most powerful immortal beings to ever walk the earth.'

The whole room had fallen silent, all listening to Marchella.

'Here, here!' shouted Josiah, banging his glass on the table.

Within minutes, the room was in uproars with cheering and

the tinkling chink of glasses. Everyone stood and raised their glasses in a toast — to me.

'Welcome, Lily. Welcome home, Miss.'

Then everyone sat down again, and the room went back to its maddening chatter and laughter and rolling of eyes. I could hear some New Orleans tales being told. I sat in silence and watched them all. They seemed such a friendly lot, and there didn't seem to be one unattractive gene between them.

'One more thing … are you guys able to go out in the daylight?'

'Yes, because we're purebloods, Lily. We've always been day walkers, and the turned — well, sunlight has the same effect on them as it does on us.'

'Okay, it's just that I've read about vampires in books and they all burn up in the sunlight.'

Marchella chuckled. 'Purely myth, my darling; myth and a little bit of human speculation. We become weak in strong sunlight; it dims our strength, but it doesn't burn us up. That's utter nonsense, my girl.'

'I guess it all comes from the old stories of Count Dracula?' I said.

'Oh no,' said Marchella confidently. 'Vlad Dracul and his son, Vlad Tepes Dracula, are the original purebloods. Our family bloodline comes directly from them. All purebloods come from the Dracula family line, and their qualities are much the same as ours. They are day walkers too, the sunlight merely weakens them, reducing their strength.'

'When you say all pureblood vampires are from the Dracula family line … does that mean the Monsantos too. Are they purebloods?'

'Yes, darling. They are purebloods, other than the turned who joined them. There are different clans all over the world, and most are at war with each other, yet we all grew from the same vine.'

'Enough now,' said Josiah. 'I feel like I'm back at school … all this history!'

Everyone at the table went quiet at my great grandfather's command, and a tray of fresh baby rabbits was brought in and placed in the centre of the table.

That was my cue to leave.

'Oh, one more thing,' said Marchella. 'Watch the cat. The newly turned do like a snack before bedtime, most are bored with home-bred rabbit, and sometimes they can't be bothered with the hunt. If you value the cat, keep it locked away, Lily.'

'Yeah,' I said. 'I sure will.'

Then a guy sitting next to Tallis turned to me. 'You may as well say goodbye to the wretched rat now coz it's on my snack list this week,' he said.

He said this so flippantly I could feel my blood boil and my temper rise. My hands started to heat up, and I felt that, if I looked at him a minute longer, he'd burst into flames.

Indeed, in a matter of seconds, my calmness turned to rage. And it scared the crap out of me. I stood quickly and left the table, worried about what I might do.

'I'm going to my room now, and you'd better watch your mouth, whoever you are?' I snapped, glaring at him. 'If anything happens to my cat, I'll burn you to a cinder and add your stinking ashes to her litter box!'

He fell silent.

Marchella grinned. 'That's the spirit, Lily. That's the spirit,' she said.

And off I went to bed.

The following morning there was a note under my door. It read:

My apologies Cousin Lily for riling you yesterday about your cat, it was not my intention to cause offence. Cousin Dominic.

A nice note, I thought. But I still didn't like him — he was a nasty piece of work.

I wasn't sure why, but Pippa brought out the protective instinct in me. I felt I would kill for her, literally. And I was actually terribly afraid at the thought of somebody hurting her because I didn't know what I might do. But I did know it would be bad.

Early next morning, a bunch of girls sat out on the front porch, so I joined them. I took a book and sat in a comfy old chair.

'Watcha reading, Miss Lily?' one of the girls asked. She looked to be about my age.

'*The Boomerang Effect*. It's a suspense thriller. You can read it after me if you want. I'm nearly finished.'

'Oh, thanks, Miss Lily, thanks.' Then she went back to swinging her legs on the rope swing that hung off the front porch. Another younger girl came and sat down next to me. She leant on the arm of my chair and, with a goofy smile, looked up at me adoringly.

'Miss Lily, you are so pretty — you look like your daddy, Eli. I bet you're excited to see him, hey?' she drawled in her lovely southern accent.

'Yeah, you bet I am,' I said and smiled back. *So, his name is Eli.* 'What's your name?'

'Elisabeth, Miss. Just plain old Elisabeth. But you can call me Beth, if you like.'

She shot a glance up at the open doorway, jumped up and skipped off across the porch. I turned to see who she'd looked at.

Marchella stood there, listening. She smiled at me and asked another of the young maids to bring me some tea out on the porch, then she sat down next to me. 'Do you enjoy reading, Lily? Do you read a lot?'

'Yeah, I read a lot; have done all my life. Can't beat a good book.'

'I think I have a book you may be ready for, Lily. It belonged to your mother. I was not sure whether to save it until you were older, but after your little 'cat protection' outburst last night I would say you can handle it.'

"Handle it. What the hell. I thought you said it was a book?'

'A book of sorts,' said Marchella. 'It is a grimoire, Lily, it belonged to your mother.'

'A grimoire? What's that?'

'A witch's manual. A book of spells. A book of magic.'

'Shit!' I thought. 'Oh, I don't know if I'm ready for something like that.'

'Oh, I think you are, and I can help you, Lily. I'll help you understand it; help you learn to use it. This plantation is the best place for you. If you stay here until you are eighteen, I think you have a good chance of blowing the candles out on your birthday cake. If you use this time to listen and learn, you will be able to protect yourself against those that may come. The next five months are not going to be easy, Lily, but you are in the best place, with the best people, and I can teach you so much while you are here.'

This was my very own grandma looking at me so lovingly, and I knew that whatever she wanted from me, I would do, just to make her happy.

'Whatever you think, I'm not going anywhere any time soon.' I smiled.

'First a little chat then, Lily, because there are some things you need to know.'

'Okay,' I said.

'Last night when cousin Dominic was winding you up about the cat.'

'Yeah?'

'You rose to anger very, very quickly. I do believe if you hadn't left right then, things could have turned out entirely badly for him. Am I right?'

'Yeah … it was scary. I mean, it's happened plenty of times before and I'm learning to draw it back in. But last night it was like a switch on a lamp. He pressed the button, and the light came on. I very nearly burned that sucker up right where he sat.'

'It's the house, Lily, okay? It's the house. This house holds a lot of history. It's almost as if the rooms are alive with the past. I swear the walls are drenched in magic. Your mother used to practice magic here, and she was so powerful. Drawing on the house is a benefit to all who live here as it makes us stronger … but it also enhances our powers, almost to a point of no return. This is something we all have to live with and learn to control. Emotions run high here. And for us vampires who have very little feeling, that's fine, but for your mother, it was very difficult. I fear it will be the same for you, if not far worse.'

I nodded as Marchella continued talking.

'Every emotion you are capable of feeling will be felt tenfold. When someone holds the power within them that you do, Lily, this can be a dangerous thing. Not just for you, but for everyone around you. I'm going to help you to control it. I'm going to show you a safe zone your father built for your mother. It's away from the house just out through the oaks, towards the Mississippi River. I want you to make your way there whenever your emotions start to get the better of you, for your own safety, and for ours.'

'Okay, whatever you say. I mean, I didn't feel totally out of control last night. I managed to stop it by leaving. I've been practising controlling my anger for seven months now, and I'm getting pretty good at it,' I smiled at Marchella proudly.

'Yes, but as you get closer to your eighteenth birthday your powers will get stronger. I don't believe you have the use of half the powers you are capable of harnessing yet. Your mother's emotions will have started to work in you, and with great emotion comes great power. The two are very closely linked.'

'My mum's emotions?' I questioned.

'Yes, an immortal child inherits its mother's emotions as it draws near to its eighteenth year. It's a great trait to have, Lily, especially for you, as a mortal witch's emotions are strong. Stronger than any other being that walks the earth. Your emotions will supercharge your powers. They'll be harder to control, but they'll make you more powerful than any other immortal you may come across in your life.'

'Are there others then?'

'No. Not that we know of. And the immortal hunters do a pretty good job of killing any that are born before they reach their immortality. You will be the first immortal child to survive that I know of … in this century anyway. But in the future who knows, one may be born that survives and lives to challenge you. If that ever happens, you just better hope that its mother wasn't a mortal witch, because at this moment your powers would be unmatchable. But if another one of you were born with the same qualities … my, you would have a battle on your hands.'

'But I thought once I turned eighteen, nothing could hurt me. Doesn't 'Immortal' mean exactly that?' I said, a little confused.

'Well as far as we know only another immortal can kill an immortal — it's your only weakness. You will basically be immune to any other kind of death, but an immortal that has stronger emotions, and therefore stronger power than you, could wipe out your existence.'

'Great! Well, that sucks,' I said.

'Well, just be thankful that at this point in life, there is nothing to challenge you. You are one of a kind.' Marchella smiled and stroked my hair. 'So, any questions, Lily?'

'Yeah, sorry for asking stupid questions, but I'm trying to keep up ... so it's the mum's emotions that make immortal kids powerful right?'

'Well, yes, I guess you could say that — it is the depth of emotion in the mother that determines the depth of power in the immortal, if you understand what I mean?'

'Okay, so my emotions are strong because my mum's emotions were strong. But they're also even stronger because I'm half-vampire. And I should be careful not to feel too emotional around the house because it makes my powers extremely hard to control and I don't want to burn all you sucker's up. I get it.'

'Mmm, suckers. What do you mean by that?'

'Oh, nothing — just a cute term for vampires.' My cheeks flushed slightly, and Marchella shot me a confused glance but added a quirky smile.

'The house will draw you in, Lily, into the walls, into its heart and soul. You are a Du Plessis, and your roots are here deep down in the earth, on every inch of land this plantation stands on. This property will fill you with the power you need to survive, but it will also take a little bit of you to add to its archives. We are all about history here, girl.' Marchella nodded as if I should understand every crazy word she'd just said to me. And of course, I didn't. But I was getting used to these southern tales and I simply nodded back as I basked in the Louisiana sunshine.

HER MEMORIES WITHIN

The following day Marchella joined me on the porch again. 'Just a few more days and your father will be here, Lily.'

I nodded. The air was clammy, and I didn't feel much like chatting, but Marchella didn't seem to care; she just sat there quietly and started humming a tune.

'I know that tune, Marchella. Where have I heard that before?'

'Oh, probably from your father when you were a baby. I sang it to him, and I guess he would have sung it to you.' She carried on humming.

'Are you sure I was born in England? I wasn't just taken there as a kid?'

'No, Lily, you were definitely born there. What makes you ask?'

'I just feel like this is where I belong. I mean, everything is so familiar here ... the sounds ... the music ... the people ... the streets ... the smell of magnolia, even the Monsanto townhouse. This place ... it's like it's always been a part of me. I never felt like this in England, not in my whole darn life.'

'Actually, there is an explanation for that.'

'Really? What is it?

'They are your mother's memories. When a mortal witch has a child, every memory is passed on to them. Everything you will ever feel you know for yourself is an experience your mother has had. Everywhere you go that you have never been, you will feel at home if your mother has felt at home there in her lifetime. Like the Monsanto townhouse, because she lived there for a time. People she has felt close to, you will feel that also. And you may not feel the actual love for yourself, but anyone your mother has ever truly loved will be instantly recognisable to you as someone very important in your life. It's a kind of compass, passed on to you from her, to guide you in the right direction, towards the safe, towards the love of good people, and away from where you should not go. Because along with the good memories come the bad, and this will show up instinctively. If something or someone feels wrong, Lily, trust it. Trust the feeling and come to know it as your mother's guiding compass.'

'You know what? That's kind of cool because I never knew her. If how I feel about all these places and people are her memories, well it's kind of like knowing her, in a way. In fact, probably better than I know anyone.'

Marchella nodded and stroked my hair; smiled sympathetically at me, which of course was an act, because although I knew she adored me, she couldn't possibly feel much sympathy, being a vampire and all.

'Come and walk with me, Lily. I want to show you something.' Marchella rose and took my hand, coaxing me out of my seat. So it wasn't a request exactly. I followed aimlessly along through the woods trying to stay focused, my mind though still mulling over mum's memories, and my connection to them and her.

We came to a clearing in the woods amongst the tall oaks that ran all the way to the edge of the Mississippi, and forever along its banks until the eye could see no more than a green blur in the distance. It was so beautiful and peaceful here in the woods and the air smelt likely freshly mowed grass — probably someone mowing close by and the breeze bringing the scent my way.

Marchella knelt down. Clearing away some leaves, she pulled a trap door up and open, and disappeared down some stairs. I followed after pulling the trap door closed on top of us; down a few more steps; around a bend, we came to an underground cavern. The rocky wall smelt of moss and a small underground stream wrangled its way along a dark path and meandered off to the left somewhere. Marchella disappeared and I called her.

'Marchella!'

'This way, Lily, to the right. Follow the stream and then turn right as it turns left.'

I struggled to see in the darkness, then a bright light struck my eyes. Marchella had opened a large wooden door, and the light beamed out from a huge vault like room. Its stone walls were lined with shelves full of all sorts: books, bottles, candles, feathers, stones, sealed jars — jars upon jars filled with all sorts of weird stuff: toads, ants, beetles, hair of all things, and something that looked like tiny blue tongues. There were jars of lizards and then, in another jar, just their legs. *Poor things*. It was a freaky place, one that would take a week or more to check out, so much cool stuff, it might take forever to look at it all.

'Eli built this ... I mean your father built this, for your mother.'

'Cool,' I said.

'Well, your mother used to work in the house to begin with, but the house ... it got to her, I think. She would get very emotional when practising magic, too emotional sometimes, and she argued a lot with everyone. Sometimes the magic could not be contained, and it overflowed causing damage to property and sometimes to people in its path. Your mother couldn't control her power if she used it in the house. It became too magnified. So, this was the answer: your father built her this place to keep the magic contained, to keep her safe and to protect the house, and all the people in it.'

'Great idea!'

'It's yours now, Lily. This is your safe place. If your emotions get the better of you, this is where to come. In here, you can bounce off the walls and never hurt a soul.'

I smiled and put my arms around Marchella's waist — it was like hugging an ironing board, like I used to be with people before my emotions kicked in. It was quite funny really because she looked a bit shocked and was so obviously uncomfortable. But she tried so hard not to show it, and eventually she wrapped her arms about me stiffly and tried to hug me back.

'Walk over here, Lily,' she said, giving her an excuse to let go and remove herself from my hug.

'This is the book I was telling you about: your mother's grimoire. It's down here because this is where she used it most, but it's yours to do whatever you want with. I mean, you can read it in the house if you like. Just don't practise there, okay.'

'Sure,' I said, not really knowing what I'd practise.

I picked up the heavy brown leather book, which looked and smelt ancient, and we made our way out of the cavern. Marchella locked the heavy wooden door behind us and handed me the key.

'Yours now, Lily,' she said with a smile, then she blew out the wall torch and we made our way along in the darkness, towards the trap door, and the oak filled woods above.

A week passed by and Friday night came, the darkness filtering through the trees, where earlier there'd been sunlight. I'd been sitting on the porch and hadn't even noticed the lightness creep into darkness, my head buried in my mum's grimoire. It was so interesting because it didn't just hold magic and spells, but regular diary entries of my mum's time spent in the craft. It was like reading her thoughts, like being there with her, even though these entries were written long before I was born. One entry caught my eye, because it was written the year I was born, actually six months before.

February 18th, 2003

I was talking to Sassy today; we were talking about the fact that it seems an impossible task to find the other side of the coin. We are brewing this beautiful creation, but it will all fall flat if we cannot find the perfect companion to complete the union. Sassy was excited today at a file she read for a body brought into the morgue. It was a soldier killed in action and his record was exemplary. Although he was young, he was decorated for bravery, and prior to going to war, he was an acclaimed student with a university degree in history and politics. This could be the perfect specimen. Maybe our search will finally be over. I pray this is true as my time is drawing near.

These entries were so weird and confusing: there were so many entries that hinted at exciting stuff, but I couldn't make any sense of them. I closed the book, and my mind wandered to Tallis. He was stretched out asleep on a long lounge at the end of the porch, his tattooed arm draping lazily over the edge. As he slept, his T-shirt rose up, slightly revealing his lower back as it curved up towards his strong muscular shoulders. His face was turned towards me, and I longed to touch him, longed to feel his lips brush mine again. I had truly never felt this way about another person, and it made my heart ache because I just couldn't work out where I stood with him. One day he said he loved me, and the next he ignored me. He was so confusing, and it messed with my head. I found myself staring at him with a lustful feeling that was so hard to fight when he was this close. In the distance, a car pulled into the driveway and rumbled up the uneven dirt road. Running ahead of the car after opening the tall gates, Elisabeth shouted excitedly.

'Miss Lily, Miss Lily, your father's here ... he's here!'

I could hear her muffled words, and Tallis stirred as I stood and walked to the edge of the porch. As I waited for the car to come to a stop, excitement and fear churned in my stomach. The car stopped, engine turned off, the door opened and out stepped a young, good-looking man, maybe in his late twenties. *Freaky, this is my dad, but he looks more like an older brother.* He walked towards me, his arms outstretched as he gazed at me with gorgeous dark eyes. 'Lily ...' he whispered, coming closer.

'Dad?' I said, tears rising in my eyes, and in his. He wrapped his arms around me; held me for the longest time. Only minutes passed, but it felt like forever, and this hug was never-ending. The strongest hug I'd ever felt. It was like we were one and the same. Our heartbeats stood out in the silence, so much so that my ears felt like they would burst. *This is my dad, my very own dad* — a man who had loved my mum, who had given me up to protect me. Now we were together again. I could feel his feelings for me, as if he had just poured them straight out of a jar, right into the palm of my hand. There was no mistaking this love — it was strong and true, and all mine.

Marchella appeared in the doorway just behind us and smiled lovingly at our father-daughter embrace, 'She has her father's eyes.'

'Yeah, she certainly does,' said Tallis.

The contents of my dad's car was emptied into the hallway, and

I followed him like a lamb into the house.

'This is nice … all together again, all under one roof, just like it should be,' said Marchella, grinning widely.

The whole family gathered in the dining room around the large table, chatting, catching up on old times, talking about my dad's journey and where it had taken him. It felt crazy and yet comforting to be here like this, surrounded by so many people all related to me. I'd been alone most of my life, and now this was all mine. I knew right then that I'd never let anything destroy this; never let us come apart again. *No bloody way! No matter what, I will protect the Du Plessis family with my life.*

Later on, I lay in bed unable to sleep. Pippa couldn't settle either and her fidgeting increased my tension. My grandad kept springing to mind, and I wondered where he was; whether he'd give up and go home if he couldn't find me. But something told me it wasn't going to be as simple as that.

The following day, my dad — with Mica, Slater and Tallis tagging along — took me into town shopping. Everywhere we went, the people knew my dad and welcomed him with open arms. However, it felt like a covert operation: most places we entered via the front door then left by the back door. Still, it was a very successful day. When I opened all my bags at home, I realised my dad had bought me almost a whole new wardrobe of clothes!

'When your done unpacking, Lily, come walking with me,' my dad said, his head poking in through the doorway.

Half an hour later, we were walking through the woods amongst the tall old oaks heading to the place Marchella had brought me the day before. We were close to the underground cavern. Then we arrived, and Dad pulled up the trap door, and down we went into my mum's sacred place that was now mine.

'You like this place, Lily?'

'Love it,' I said with a smile.

'It reminds me so much of your mother down here. It's cold and lightless but so filled with her warmth. It's like a layer of her soul still exists upon these walls,' he said, stroking the hard rock as he walked along.

'Tell me about her,' I said.

'Do you have a year?' He laughed lightly.

'I have all the time in the world, apparently,' I said seriously.

'Your mother was twenty-two when I met her. It wasn't exactly a romantic tale ... not to start with. She was working for the Monsanto family.'

'Who are they exactly?' I asked. 'They own the townhouse I've been living in, right?'

'Yes. That's right. They're another vampire clan, of equal standing here in Louisiana. They had offended a Voodoo queen called Anastasia Du Preez in New Orleans in the 1800s, and many years later, your mother was brought in to remove a curse that was plaguing the Monsanto family.'

'Voodoo?'

'Yes, Lily, dark magic mostly, built on superstitions — very strong and still very much alive here, even today.'

'Mmm, but different to my mum's magic, right?'

'Yes, completely.' He fell quiet for a while, just walked around touching my mum's things.

'And?'

'Well, the Du Plessis had a longstanding feud going on with the Monsantos, branching back to the early1800s. I think they thought they'd kill two birds with one stone, and they sent your mother after Josiah to kill him.'

'Wow! How did that pan out?'

'Well, that's a long story, but basically, she came across my path and well … the rest is history. Josiah survived and your mother and I … we fell in love.' He smiled as if remembering a wonderful far-off time.

'Meeting your mother for the first time was like being hit by a bolt of lightning. She was incredibly beautiful, and her good soul shone out for all to see. I should have killed her right then and there. I should have, but I couldn't. When I looked at her, I felt something I had never felt before, and even though Josiah's life was at stake, I knew I would never be able to protect him, not if it meant hurting her.'

'You make it sounds so simple.'

'Far from it, there was so much resistance to start with. She knew what I was, and she knew it was impossible to love me. But I guess in the end what she felt with her heart was more important than what she thought with her head. What I felt was like an immediate and almost blinding feeling of overpowering love. I can't explain it any more than that really.'

'I get it,' I said quietly, thinking about Tallis's kiss and where it had taken me.

'When immortals fall, we fall hard, Lily. You'll have to watch that because you can just as easily fall for the wrong man as the right man.'

I nodded, thinking about the feelings I had for Alex. I hadn't been a good judge of character there. Even now when I thought about him, it sent a pleasant tingle up my spine, although I knew it was wrong to feel anything for him, anything at all.

'When your mother's third attempt at taking Josiah's life failed, Josiah's men had her locked in the cellar. There are metal walls down there. It's always been used for holding rogue vampires and werewolves that trespass on our land, but it served the same purpose for us with your mother, and that was to dim her powers. She was at her weakest point down there, vulnerable and scared. I started to visit her and filled her in on a few home truths,'

'Home truths? ... Like what?'

'Well, she was working for the wrong side for one.'

'So, they were the bad guys?'

'The Monsanto was the family who caused all the problems for us when they chose to settle here in the early 1800s. We had lived here peacefully for many years, almost a century, bringing no attention to ourselves. We lived out here at The Oaks in cabins before the house was ever built, and only ever fed on animals. It was a very small settlement then, and we had great relationships with the locals. We were just trying to live a normal life ... well, as normal as possible for a vampire clan.

'But the Monsanto's moved in and by the early 1840s the death toll; both supernatural and human, had gone through the roof, and the vampire hunters came. Somehow, they were alerted to our presence here, and they came after us. One afternoon the vampire hunters came out of nowhere, taking us by surprise. My father and grandmother were killed. Quite a few Du Plessis fought and lost, and quite a few fought and turned that day. That was the day my mother, your grandmother stopped ageing; she killed the man who killed your grandfather. That is the day most of us stopped ageing. We had to fight for our lives, for the first time in our lives. We slaughtered a lot of humans that day.'

He turned his back to me and walked around head hung low, deep in thought.

'Josiah never forgave the Monsanto for the death of my father and grandmother, and for the fact that we were all forced to take human lives, to taste human blood, to change the way we were forever. He knew they had betrayed us to the vampire hunters to save their own skin.'

'But didn't you just go back to the same lifestyle afterwards?'

'Some did, but most, no. Once a vampire has tasted human blood, it becomes an overwhelming obsession. It's a hard road trying not to … to … well, you know.'

'Yeah, I can imagine.'

My dad came close and stroked my hair.

'Your great grandfather Josiah had spent years causing trouble for the Monsanto. Whenever he had a chance to do them wrong, he would, and I think at some point they'd just had enough, so taking him out seemed a good option.'

'So that's when my mum came?'

'Yes, and everything changed. She was a mortal witch, but there was also something very 'green peace' about her if you understand the term? She always wanted to right the wrongs of the world. There was so much feuding going on between the clans, between one coven and another, between werewolves and witches, and witches and vampires, and vampires and werewolves. It was a vicious circle, which she despised. She started to believe there would always be unrest because all of them wanted the power. She simply wanted us all to live in harmony.'

I nodded and continued to listen intently.

'Anyway, when she was locked in the cellar, I used to visit her often. Firstly, because Josiah said he would never release her until she fully understood that she was on the wrong side. And secondly, because I had fallen madly for her, and my side was the only side I wanted her to be on.'

'And obviously it worked,' I said, pointing to myself as proof of evidence, and winked.

'Yes,' he said, smiling at my cheekiness. 'Your mother had heard from the Monsantos about the legend of the immortal child … do you know it, Lily?'

'Well, kind of. I've heard a few things from Marchella. I know so far I'm the only immortal kid to have lived this long.'

'It is written that an immortal child born to a vampire and a mortal witch will grow to be one of the most powerful supernatural beings on earth. The child will possess the strength and agility of the vampire and the powers of the mortal witch, including her natural powers of emotion and empathy. A witch draws upon this for her craft. Being half-vampire magnifies these qualities tenfold. It is said that the immortal child will form a new race, and this new race will lead the supernatural world into peace. But also, the personality and upbringing of the immortal child can change the outcome of the prophecy. You see, Lily, an immortal child has the potential to be both good and bad. Bad to the degree they could be responsible for ending the world as we know it. Or good to the degree they could be the bringer of eternal peace.'

'Holy crap, that's a lot of weight to put on one set of shoulders!' I sighed.

'So, with you being the only immortal child alive, you can see why your death is such a priority for some. There were others, but the path they chose was the wrong path. Those who want you dead are either the good guys, who are scared of your potential for pure evil. Or the bad guys, who are scared of your potential for innate goodness. Of course, there are others, who don't want you dead — but they would bring you in as one of their own and use you up; harness your powers to enhance their standing in the supernatural world.'

'Okay, so basically, I should be wary of just about everyone,' I said with another huge sigh.

'It's a lot to take in, Lily, I know, but it's good for you to know it all, just in case.'

'Yeah, well, I've gotten this far. I guess I can handle four more months.'

'You should be safe here, Lily. Nobody knows your whereabouts, and there are enough of us here to rally round if trouble brews. I felt you were safer in England when you were a child, and I'm so sorry I missed out on you growing up. But at least there, all you had to deal with was your grandfather and his men — amateur immortal child hunters at best. Here there is so much more you may have to come up against — witches, werewolves and vampires.'

'The Monsantos?'

'No, not the Monsantos ... although maybe? I don't think they are a threat as such. I don't think they would want you dead. But I think they'd want to use you, as a weapon against all the other supernaturals ... to make them stronger than the rest. We are at peace with them now, and they have sworn allegiance with us to protect you, but I don't know if they can be entirely trusted.'

'Great!' I said with another huge sigh.

My dad laughed and patted my back, 'It'll be okay, kid. Do you think I'm going to let anyone get within ten feet of you?' He smiled reassuringly, but I knew it was just an act. I think he was just as worried as I was.

'Just do your dad a favour, Lily,' he said. 'Make your mum and I proud. Use what you have for good, and not for evil, hey. I quite like this world of ours, and don't really want to see the end of it.'

We headed back to the house, locking the cavern behind us. 'Oh, one more thing,' he said, handing me a box as we blew the torch light out. 'Your mum would have wanted you to have these'.

Back in my room, I opened the box and inside were a few bits and pieces: a bracelet, a ring, a necklace, a bunch of photos tied with a ribbon, a small notebook with a picture of forget-me-nots on the front, a small folded piece of paper with a poem written on it, and a letter addressed to my mum. Nothing meant for me, just personal items of hers. I thought if I'd known her, I could've held them, and they would've meant something to me like they probably did for my dad. He could probably smell her scent on them, and when he felt them, it might've been like it had been in the cavern when he touched the walls and seemed to connect with something long gone.

I pulled the ribbon from the photos and looked through them. One of her and the Du Plessis family, one of her with a bunch of women I didn't recognise — *maybe her coven*. Two or three lovely pictures of her and my dad — they looked so good together; such a cute couple. I singled these out and placed them on my bedside table. Then I pulled out one of her and my grandad. She was very young and smiling, being carried by him with her arms around his neck, face close to his. He smiled proudly for the photo as he held his little girl. *Probably his greatest treasure*. It was becoming easier to see where his hostility came from. I wondered whether he was an actual immortal child hunter, or just an angry parent dealing with the loss of his kid. Perhaps wanting to take his revenge out on me.

That night I slept well, with my mum's box by my side and Pippa beneath the covers entwined in my feet. I remember falling asleep dreaming about the photo of my mum when she was a kid, but then, at some time in the night, I just couldn't breathe. I dreamed I was suffocating, that the walls were closing in, the air disappearing. I woke with a shock, to find a man standing in my room next to me, his hand tightly pressed over my mouth and nose. I struggled, but he was so strong. I tore at his arms, but he wouldn't release me, and I started to panic. But in the middle of that panic, all I could think was, *Don't lose it, Lily. Don't burn this beautiful place down. Do something — but not that.* And then I had it.

I couldn't breathe, but I let myself go limp, felt my chest drop, my heartbeat slow. My racing pulse filtered out to a fine hum, and I closed my eyes. Just as before, it felt like I was no longer there, and suddenly I could breathe freely again as I entered his body and released his grip on my mouth. He struggled as if he didn't know what was happening. He tried to fight it, but I turned and walked to the door. Out to the hallway. Down through the house to the back. Out into the dark. I could actually feel his fear, feel his sweat beads running down his forehead. His hands were shaking, his legs were weak, but I carried on walking towards the rear sheds. Once there, I pulled up a stool, collected some long thick rope from the corner basket. He was crying now and saying, '*No, Please, no!*' as he tied the rope in a noose, climbed the side ladder and tied the other end to the beam.

I felt awful and really evil, but it had to be done. It was my life or his.

I stood on the stool. His head shook from side to side, protesting at his own hands work as he placed the noose around his neck. I could feel the horror he was feeling, but I felt calm.

I wanted this.

I wanted this to end.

Wanted him to end.

After all, he was the bad guy … not me. I felt him kick the stool and felt the weight of his body as it fell, snapping his spinal cord in two at the neck. I smelt the burn of the rope as it tore into his flesh. *Unpleasant.* And the twitching of his limbs as the last breath drained from him, the last flicker of his muscles coming to a halt as he left the land of the living, while trespassing on the land of the undead. I opened my eyes and gasped for air; felt my throat and cleared it, as though I had breathed for the first time in ages. I was lying in bed, Mum's box still next to me, Pippa still curled up in the same spot. *Bloody hell, that was a pretty screwed up nightmare*. I lay, wondering what it had meant, whether it was significant. I had just killed a complete stranger in a dream. It was so upsetting but, no sooner had I cleared my mind and drank a glass of water, I fell back to sleep.

When I woke the next morning, I felt well-rested, and the sun shone through a crack in the curtains. Pippa was curled up tightly behind my knees, purring loudly in her sleep. I moved carefully so as not to disturb her. I eased out of bed and strolled to the window that overlooked the back paddocks and the rear shed; pulled the curtains open and blinked at the brightness. Rubbing my eyes so I could see more clearly, I noted in the distance a commotion going on. A bunch of people stood outside the shed. My dad was looking up at my window and shaking his head. Marchella seemed to be shouting at him. Mica stood next to my dad, shaking his hands in the air as if in disbelief. Then I saw a few men carrying something from the shed and placing it into the back of an old yard truck.

I squinted to see better in the sun. It was a body. *Shit! It was a body!*

Suddenly my dream came flooding back to me. A chill ran up my spine as I shook my head in dismay. *No, this wasn't possible. It was only a dream. A nightmare. How could this be real?*

Surely, I wasn't capable of killing someone in cold blood like that …

Or was I?

MONSANTO MASQUERADE

My dad, Marchella, and the guys sat around the kitchen table and, as I came along the hall, I could hear their raised voices. My dad seemed particularly angry as he banged his fist on the table. I stood outside the kitchen looking through the slightly opened door, trying not to be noticed.

'We have to take him out; there's no doubt about it. How her own grandfather; her own flesh and blood can be such a danger to her, I'll never understand! Plus, we have no idea how many men Montague has with him,' my dad said.

'More to the point, we need to up the ante. How on earth did that creep get within ten feet of her with all of us here in the house? I dread to think what might have happened,' said Mica, raking his hand through his hair, obviously still on edge.

'We can't leave her alone, not for a minute. Post me outside her door, and Mylo outside the window. We have to make sure this never happens again ... never!' said Tallis.

'Well, I guess we can be thankful she handled it herself, poor baby. Who knew she had it in her?' Marchella added.

They all nodded as I walked in, then they all glanced up at me. An uncomfortable silence fell on the room. I shuffled my feet, hands in my hoody pockets as I looked down at the floor, unsure how they felt about me. I was used to being hated, but the thought of these guys feeling that way about me was almost too much to handle. My dad stood up and walked over to me; stood in front of me, but he didn't touch me. I was scared to look him in the eye. But when I looked up the genuine look of concern and caring on his face melted all my fears. I moved closer to him, tears in my eyes as he wrapped his arms around me.

'Never feel bad about yourself, Lily, never! You have these abilities for a reason, and it's all about survival, kid. There are a lot of people, both human and supernatural, who would love to see you dead. It's you or them. Taking them out of the game is a necessary move, and it may feel harsh to you, but you have to trust your instincts. You'll never hurt someone who doesn't deserve it. And he deserved it.'

I sobbed and leant into him, feeling comforted. For the first time, I was not loathed for my evilness.

'We're shocked he got past us all, and we've decided much more vigilance is needed. You may feel smothered for a while, Lily, but it's not long now until you turn eighteen. We just have to make sure you make it. Hopefully, this death will send a warning to your grandfather to back off but, whatever happens, we need to eliminate the risk of his men getting anywhere near you again,' Slater said.

I looked across at my loved ones all sitting at the table, and, as I met each one's gaze, they smiled acceptingly. Although a battle still brewed inside me about my actions, I knew it was with myself and not with them. I sat at the table, and Tallis moved closer to me and rubbed my back.

'I'm so sorry I wasn't there for you, Lily. It'll never happen again.' He looked so disappointed with himself, guilty almost.

'It's okay, Tallis, honestly. I'm obviously more capable than I think, and that's a shock to me, but something I'll have to get used to.'

'But I should have sensed something was wrong. I should have …'

He hung his head and breathed in heavily, then he rose and left the kitchen. I felt so sorry for him. I almost cried again.

'Don't stress, Lily,' said Marchella. 'You have to realise that Tallis was created for the very purpose of protection. To keep you safe is his only mission in life. Nothing else matters to him, and at the moment he feels like a failure.'

'But it's not his fault. Marchella. It's nobody else's fault but mine. I'm the one who should feel like shit, not him. I murdered someone last night.'

'Yes. Well one good thing in all of this is that he will be on his guard now, more so than ever, and that can only be a good thing. I don't want you to consider yourself a murderer, Lily. It was self-defence. Remember that.'

Marchella smiled and slipped two fried eggs onto my plate as I buttered my toast.

'Eat up, young lady,' she said, 'and then we will measure you up for your ball gown. I thought you would like to wear one of your mother's, but it may need a little tweaking here and there.'

'Ball gown?'

'Yes. The annual Monsanto masquerade ball is this weekend, and now the feuding is over we will be expected to attend.'

'I thought the Monsanto were the bad guys?'

'Yes, well they are in vampire terms, but we have called a truce with them. There is so much trouble from the Lestrange Lair at the moment that we thought it was best for us vampires to stick together. You know the old saying: There's strength in numbers.'

'The Lestrange Lair. What's that?' My dad hadn't mentioned this to me, not that I could remember.

'A Louisiana werewolf pack — most deadly when turned,

although relatively civil when not.' Marchella said this with such matter-of-factness it was almost funny. We were obviously talking about deadly werewolves, yet she'd said it as blandly as reading her weekly shopping list.

'So, werewolves ... like Tallis and the guys then?' I said.

'No, no,' said Marchella. 'Werewolves are nothing like the wolfling. Werewolves are bad, Lily. They would rip you to shreds as soon as they saw you. When turned, they have no manners.'

I giggled, and Marchella smiled.

'The wolflings are completely different, Lily. They have extremely high morals; they are built to serve and protect; created by witches for one task only, and that is to keep immortals safe. They would die for you, Lily.'

"Well, I guess by now I should know that. Tallis already has once. Thank God for the elixir.'

'Yes, thank goodness,' said Marchella. 'Anyway, the ball is fast approaching and in the name of unity — for you, Lily — we will be attending.'

'Cool. I've never been to a vampire ball. Let's hope none of them want to suck the blood out of me!' I said, smirking.

'The Monsantos are not our real worry, Lily, and at the moment, we are unsure about the covens. But one thing we are sure of is that the Lestrange Lair somehow learned of your existence, and they want your head on a plate. To keep you safe, we have no option but to trust the Monsantos, of course only so far, but they have sworn to defend you.

Later in the day, Marchella measured me up for my ball gown, and Elisabeth came to my room carrying the most beautiful dress I'd ever laid eyes on. It was scarlet red, full and flowing at the bottom with ruffled layers and a strapless bustier top. Absolutely stunning, and when I tried it on it fitted me almost like a glove.

'No alterations needed here then,' said Marchella.

'Lily, you are so petite like your mum, and oh-so-pretty,' Elisabeth gushed.

I gazed at myself in the mirror and swirled the dress a little, feeling like a princess. Elisabeth's nimble fingers swept my long curly hair up into a bun on my head, allowing a few curls to fall around my face. It showed off my bare shoulders. I felt too grown up, but Marchella looked so proud, and I figured I could drop the slouchy teenager look for one occasion if it made her happy.

The night of the ball came around too fast, and the butterflies in my stomach were clearly on overdrive. I felt sick at the thought of the night ahead, but gradually calmed down knowing my family and the wolfling would be right beside me. There were at least twenty of us going, and I was sure it would be a memorable night.

Exactly an hour later, a knock came on my door. Elisabeth had finished my hair and makeup and helped me into my gown. She opened the door and in walked my dad.

'Wow, Lily, you look amazing,' he said as he came towards me. He carried a corsage, a small wrist band with a blood-red rose surrounded by baby's breath. *Totally beautiful.* He fitted it on for me, and this one small detail seemed to complete the picture. Then he offered me his arm, and we walked to the car together. In the hallway, we passed the guys who were all suited up. I glanced at Tallis who looked so smart in his slim-fitting dark suit, white shirt and black tie, all neat and clean-shaven. He looked so sexy, my heart skipped a beat as I passed him. I wanted to be on his arm, and I could tell from the way his eyes followed me that he was thinking exactly the same thing.

As we pulled up outside the Monsanto's huge antebellum mansion in the Mississippi River valley, I had a strange feeling of déjà vu … like I'd been here once before … like I was coming back.

But I remembered my mum had worked for the Monsantos before, so it seemed obvious I was feeling one of her memories. I was happy that I felt comfortable coming here — I didn't feel scared at all. My mum must have liked it here; must have been treated well by these people, because as we walked in, it felt like a second home. We were met by a group of seemingly genetically perfect people, who led us through to the extravagant ballroom, where twelve huge chandeliers hung from the ceiling, and floor to ceiling mirrors graced every wall. Tables were set around the large ballroom floor, and along one wall a stage with a band was set up ready to play. Butlers walked around with trays of champagne and small nibbles; the atmosphere was so grand it was overwhelming.

'Lily,' my dad said, guiding me by the elbow, 'I'd like you to meet Emmanuelle Monsanto, head of the Monsanto clan.'

An extremely good-looking man, much older than my dad, took my hand and planted a kiss on it.

'Welcome, Lily. We've been waiting a long time to meet you.'

I didn't know what to say, so just smiled, and eased my hand away. He looked at me intently as if his deep brown eyes stared into my very soul, a strange feeling but not too scary.

'How are you enjoying the southern hospitality? I hope they are treating you well.'

'Yeah, it's been great, really cool to be around so many people for a change, having grown up so alone. And they're all very good to me,' I said politely.

'Good. Good. I'd like to think that you could see us Monsantos as an extension of your own family, Lily. We knew your mother well, and any child of hers will always be welcome here. And safe ... especially safe.' He smiled at me, and I knew he spoke the truth, that he had really cared for my mum and that he felt the same way about me.

'Lily, I don't know if you've met my son?'

I turned around to see Alex standing behind me. *Shit!* I felt relieved as soon as I laid eyes on him, glad that he was alive, that he was safe. I hadn't seen or heard from him since the fight with Tallis, and I wasn't sure what had happened to him. I felt shocked at my reaction — I'd let myself fall for Alex in such a short time, and he, a Monsanto of all things.

From the corner of my eye, I saw Tallis standing over by the door, watching. The familiar clenching of his jaw let me know just how angry he was. To be in the same room as someone who had snapped his neck only a few weeks before. Alex leaned in and kissed me on the cheek, sending sparks of electricity coursing through me. My heart beat faster, and the familiar pulsing of the blood beneath my skin reaching out to him returned. I saw Tallis flinch and take a step in our direction, but Slater pulled him back. I flicked a reassuring glance at him, as if to say, *It's only you, Tallis. It's only ever going to be you.*

This seemed to calm him down. But standing here beside Alex, I couldn't be sure if I was lying to Tallis and myself. I wanted it to be true, but something about Alex made my heart race and my pulse quicken. And as hard as I tried, I couldn't fight this feeling when he was near.

'Shall we dance?' Alex said, holding out his hand.

I hesitated, glancing again at Tallis, but he'd left the room, and even if I wanted to say *no* I found myself nodding *yes,* and following Alex onto the dance floor. He drew me close, his arm sliding around my small waist, pulling me in. With the other hand, he slipped his fingers into mine and looked into my eyes. Not wavering for a second, he swung me softly round in time to the music. His dark wavy hair hung across his face, and his beautiful green eyes held me entranced.

'It's been a long time, Alex. How have you been?'

He looked at me, then quickly glanced to the side at another woman who had caught his eye; he smiled at her flirtatiously, and I think my question fell on deaf ears. He turned back to look at me.

'You look sexy in that dress, Lily. If we weren't surrounded by your family, I'd be overly tempted to take a bite,' he said with a cheeky grin. He pulled me even closer.

My face flushed crimson. I wanted to say something smart back at him but couldn't find the words.

'Or would that be too much in front of the boyfriend?' he said, looking across at Tallis who now stood in the open doorway again, watching me like a hawk.

'Oh, he's not my boyfriend,' I said boldly.

I looked at Tallis and suddenly felt an urge to make him jealous; leant my head back so Alex's mouth was close to my neck.

'Feel free ... bite me. I'm nobody's property.'

Alex suddenly spun me away like a puppet on a string and, bringing me back in, tilted me backward with full force; he leant over me so close he made my heart flutter. I almost couldn't breathe, the passion so intense.

'Later, Lily ... later,' he whispered in my ear. He pulled me back up to face him; brought me in so close I could feel his rippling muscles beneath his shirt as we danced on.

Then I remembered what Slater had told me about Alex; why I felt the way I did about him. I tried to look away; looked to the left to try to catch a glimpse of us dancing together. I looked across the crowded dance floor, into the tall mirrors. To my surprise, the only reflection was mine. I was dancing solo on an empty floor. The music played on, but the musicians played to an empty space. I could see waiters and waitresses carrying trays, and ushers at the door. But all the people in the crowded room, dancing all around me, were nowhere in the reflection. I suddenly realised … *of course!* The only reflections were of the wolflings, the human staff, and me because vampires had no reflection. And how clever … the room could be packed to the brim, yet every vampire here could see danger coming a mile off. The mirrors showed everyone who wasn't a vampire, everyone who was a threat. And the one who stood out most was me in my scarlet red dress, for all to see and all to protect.

The doors to the balcony were wide open, and on the far side of the balcony I could see two rows of stone gargoyles, sitting either side of a winding stone stairwell that led down to the forest floor below. Tall oaks spread thickly into the distance, and up above in the branches hung all sorts of crystal lanterns, sparkling like stars in the velvet blanket of the night. I could see the forest — it was like an extension of the ballroom with a large parquet wooden dance floor laid out beneath the trees. The song ended, and I looked across the room at Tallis, then at my dad. I smiled at Alex and went to walk away, but he wasn't going to let me go that easily.

'Follow me, Lily,' Alex said forcefully, offering me his arm.

He had such a charming manner, I found it hard to resist. While I felt I should be mingling with the other guests, I was drawn to him like a magnet. He pulled me along, looking at me so seductively my legs felt like jelly. He pulled me out onto the balcony and, as others spilled out, they passed us, heading for the steps. Alex led me to the side into a shaded corner under a tree, a private little area overlooking the dance floor. I smiled and followed as if I had no choice. My head said one thing, but my heart said another. The room we left was hot and stuffy, and as we stood out on the balcony, I breathed in the cool stillness of the night. The red moon hung so low it looked like it rested on the treetops. Its light spilled across the marble paving, bleeding into every crevice it touched. A few people remained on the dance floor, and the music that drifted through the warm breeze was soft, low and romantic, nothing like the lively dance music inside the ballroom. My mood seemed to change out here under the stars, alone with Alex, without the prying eyes of my dad and the guys. I was totally relaxed and this time when Alex stared into my eyes under the faint amber glow of the blood moon, it just made sense. I leant against the edge of the balcony, looking down to the dance floor. Alex turned my face to his. His dark hair fell across his beautiful green eyes as they stared into mine. Not for the first time, I looked at his face and thought how beautiful he was, most mesmerising.

'Finally, alone,' he whispered, sending a nervous shiver up my spine. It felt so dangerous being alone in his company.

His words about biting me and about telling me I smelled delicious came flooding back. I knew he didn't mean it literally, but fear and excitement filled me all at once.

Now was his *Later*.

He pulled me towards him with a playful look, and a sparkle in his eyes; he pulled my head back, his hand entwined in my hair, and leaned in close as if going in for the kill.

'Time for that taste,' he said wistfully.

Shit! The fear was electrifying. Every nerve in my body trembled with pleasure. He leant in even closer, his mouth so near to my flesh. *Bloody hell, is he actually going to bite me? Surely not. I'm not human. What good would it do?* I clenched my fists, alarmed, tense, and yet I wanted this so much. Then slowly, tenderly, he kissed my neck working his way up to my ear, then his soft lips touched mine, and I didn't resist. I melted into him, disappeared into a moment of pure ecstasy. He ran his fingers up my back and into the nape of my neck. I felt the goose bumps pop up on my arms as my body reacted to his touch. It was like fire and ice all at once. And when we stopped, and he smiled at me with those lips, those lips that had just been kissing mine, I felt as guilty as sin, guilty for loving Tallis but wanting Alex so much.

'Shall we?' Alex said, leading me towards the steps.

He led me down the winding stone stairs, past the gargoyles, onto the dance floor and we started to dance under the beautiful sparkling lanterns. Lots of people followed, and soon the forest floor was full of dancing couples, but it still felt like Alex and I were alone. We were so fixated on each other, so wrapped up in our feelings. Everything and everyone around us seemed to fade away until only we danced beneath the trees, only we danced to the music, touching, holding, moving as one. The guilt was still there, Tallis still in my thoughts, but I couldn't fight this. Every moment with Alex felt like a soft-centred chocolate in a box I was unable or unwilling to resist. It was like I was in a trance-like state, like the music had me under a spell. I wondered momentarily if this was a vampire trick. Was I being compelled to feel this way? Was it possible? Or was I falling for this dark-haired, porcelain-skinned Romeo?

I forced myself to turn away from Alex; searched the dance floor for my dad, for Marchella, for my own family. There was a mixture of Monsanto and Du Plessis all around me, and suddenly I relaxed again. I hadn't been spirited away by some kind of compulsion. So, my mind and heart had told no lie …

TO DIE FOR

Later in the night, as the ball was winding down, I danced slowly with Alex under the tall oak trees and the glittering lanterns. From the corner of my eye, I caught my father looking at me, not an admiring glance, more one of disappointment, and I wondered what I had done to upset him. He moved slowly across the dance floor towards me, and once by my side, he offered me his arm and Alex bowed out gracefully.

'Thank you, Alex,' said my dad. 'I feel the last dance should be mine.'

As he spoke, he smiled at Alex, but there seemed to be some animosity in his tone.

I watched longingly as Alex left the dance floor and went to stand at the bottom of the steps; he kept watching me.

'You know what I told you in the cavern, Lily … about falling for the wrong person?'

'Yeah, I remember.'

'Well, Alex is who I was talking about, figuratively.'

'Alex?' I said innocently.

'Yes, Lily, I'm not stupid. I can see the spark between you two. But you need to keep in your mind, at all times, that he is not for you. He's the bad guy. He's wrong in every sense of the word.'

'Oh,' was all I could say as I turned to look at Alex standing talking to a young girl.

My heart lurched with jealousy.

I knew my dad was right, that if I pursued this relationship, it would cause me problems. But I felt blinded by something … not love, surely not … but something strong and unexplainable, an unbreakable link seemed to have formed between Alex and I, and it was going to take a great deal of strength to fight it, even for my dad's sake. I had to cover my tracks, with my dad at least. He couldn't know this turmoil I felt inside.

'Oh, I'm just playing with him. He means nothing to me. I'm a girl — this is what girls do. There are many hats in the box, Dad, I'm just trying them on for size,' I laughed.

He laughed back, then we danced the last dance, dad and daughter for the first time.

From down on the dance floor, I could see the back of the house, the steps winding up to the balcony, the glass doors open from one end to the other revealing the mirrored walls of the interior ballroom. All around me, the forest was alight with beautiful lanterns, and the floor was bustling with family and friends dressed to perfection. This was my first ever ball, and I was having the time of my life. The highlight of the evening I'd like to say was Alex's kiss — but no, it was dancing with a dad I thought I'd never know.

Suddenly the hairs on the back of my neck stood up as I took in two things happening at once: Alex running like a lightning bolt in my direction, and Tallis on the balcony above transforming suddenly from man to wolfling and diving over the edge, Mica, Slater and Mylo following after him. They were huge and fast as they hit the floor running. Alex reached me first and threw me to the ground, severely winding me as my back hit the parquet floor. When I looked up, everything was a blur. Then Tallis flew over the top of me, so close I could almost feel his breath. I turned my head to one side and what I saw terrified me … another pack of wolves, not wolfling, but werewolf — half-wolf, half-man, as if only half turned. Their gangly bodies rippled with hairy muscle, their heads looking almost human yet with a long protruding jaw and deathly black, deep-set eyes, and razor-sharp teeth. They looked messy, unfinished, and they smelt like death.

I screamed, and Alex dragged me to my feet; hurried me towards the stairs. As we headed up, another pack of wolfling were running down towards the unfolding conflict. *Not my wolfling? Then whose?* I had hit my head, but was I seeing double? *Why would other wolflings be here, to protect who?* I turned back to the dance floor and watched as the new wolfling surrounded the Monsanto. Just in front of them was Tallis. He pounced on the back of a werewolf and pinned him by the throat; shook him savagely from side to side with great force. Slater snapped a branch from a tree with his gaping jaws and rammed it sideways through the stomach of a werewolf that was flying mid-air towards him. It fell on top of him, and the weight of the beast held Slater firmly to the ground. He howled, and Mylo came running, grabbing the back of the werewolf, dragging it off of Slater. It rolled to its back, its bloody guts spilling out onto the forest floor. Slater and Mylo howled in unison and dived into the woods behind, straight back into the fray.

My dad was on the floor, his hands grappling with the grotesque head of another large werewolf. It bled from the eyes as my dad dug his fingers into them. He bit into its neck, and blood spurted out as the werewolf's body went limp. As soon as he rolled from beneath, and the beast crawled away, another werewolf dived on top of him.

I felt myself being dragged forward, feeling dizzy but forcefully urged on. Every time I glanced back, I saw the Du Plessis and the wolfling in full battle with the savage werewolves. I was confused but angry and could feel myself losing control. I wanted to protect my dad, protect my own. I fought against Alex; turned and stood in a stance with my hands held out, pointing in the direction of the werewolves, trying to gain some perspective in my dizziness. Fire flew from my hands, and a huge bolt of flame hit the back of the werewolf straddling my dad, setting him alight and taking him off guard long enough for my dad to throw him off and clamber to his feet. My cousin Dominic stood behind him. He pulled out a long silver sabre and sliced the head off the werewolf in one smooth swipe. My dad ran into the woods towards another massive beast. Cousin Dominic grabbed hold of the other werewolf which had dragged its lame body across the floor. He snapped its neck and pulled its head off with his bare hands. He then turned and ran to the edge of the woods towards my dad. Suddenly a large wolf grabbed Cousin Dominic from behind. I threw another bolt of flame, but it hit a tree, bounced off and set fire to the trail of a beautiful ball gown worn by a Monsanto. She ran screaming through the crowd, setting others alight as she went. The wolf sunk its teeth into Cousin Dominic's neck, and I watched helplessly as my distorted vision sent my flames flying in every direction but his. Alex grabbed me by my dress and pulled me struggling up the stairs to the safety of the balcony.

'Leave it, Lily. It's not safe. There are enough of them to handle the pack.'

'No!' I screamed. 'I have to help.' I tried to release his grip, but he held me tight, and all the other Monsantos on the balcony surrounded me, blocking my path, keeping me captive. Panic was overtaking me.

'Let me go!' I screamed. 'I'll burn you up. I'll burn this place to the ground!'

'Calm down, Lily. Calm down,' shouted Emmanuelle.

I wanted to rip his throat out, and struggled against him.

'You'll kill us all!' he growled.

I looked through the crowd and over the edge of the balcony to the scene below, desperately searching for my dad; for Tallis. The forest was alight, and the werewolf and wolfling were assailing each other with all their might. But the werewolves were outnumbered as the Du Plessis fought alongside the wolfling. A large number of werewolves were either beheaded on the ground, badly injured, or running for the woods with the wolfling and Du Plessis in pursuit. I breathed deeply, trying to calm the rage within. Alex held on tightly to my fiery hands, and I could feel his burning flesh in mine — but he didn't let go.

'Lily, it's okay; try to control it. Don't let the rage get out of control. There's a time and a place for great power, and this is not it,' Emmanuelle said sternly.

I searched once more for Dad, and my eyes met his on the dance floor. He was okay. And Tallis, and the others? Yes, they were fine too — ruffled, cut and bleeding but alive. And the last of the werewolves were gone, scampering through the woods as fast as they could run. Bodies littered the floor: a few Monsanto, and one Du Plessis that I could clearly see. They had been caught in my misfired flames, and the smell of burning flesh hung in the air. My guilt overwhelmed me, guilt that my uncontrollable rage had hurt innocent people. Emmanuelle was right I could have killed them all.

Tallis came rushing up the steps, back in his human form and flew at Alex. 'Take your filthy hands off her!'

'Woah,' said Alex. 'She's okay; she's safe.'

'She'll never be safe around you,' he growled.

'I thought you were a wolfling, but I see there's a bit of green-eyed monster in there as well,' Alex said with a smirk.

Tallis moved in threateningly, but the Monsanto stood in his way, guarding Alex.

'Enough wolfling!' said Emmanuelle, pushing Tallis's chest. 'Remember your place. You are here to protect, Lily. We all are. Now come on, stop this!'

Then Dad was right there beside him. I released Alex's grip and ran to him. You could have cut the air between Tallis and Alex with a knife, and my dad patted Tallis on the back and said, 'Come on, lad, let's go get cleaned up. This is not the Monsanto's fault.'

He took me by the hand, and we made our way through the crowd and into the house, Alex and Emmanuelle following us.

'Sorry about Tallis,' my dad said. 'He just has Lily's best interests at heart — he can't help himself — you know what the wolfling are like.'

Emmanuelle nodded in agreement. Putting his arm around my dad's shoulder, they walked together into the drawing-room.

'We have to do something about this Lestrange lair. They want Lily dead. Sure, she was not hurt tonight because they were greatly outnumbered, but we need to minimise the future risk. Are you with me on this, Emmanuelle?'

'Totally,' said Emmanuelle. 'We'll keep Lily safe whatever it takes.'

My dad and Emmanuelle shook on this and Tallis hung his head shamefully. Alex looked at him with a smartass smirk, and for just a moment, I disliked him intensely. I took Tallis's hand in mine and stared stubbornly at Alex, saying nothing, but everything was in the look, and he glared at Tallis and left the room.

A commotion started up in the hallway and the big double doors burst open as a group carried a body hurriedly through and placed it onto the large dining table. It was Cousin Dominic, bleeding profusely from his neck. Blood poured from his ears, eyes and mouth, and I could sense his imminent death. Everyone fussed around him. My dad ran to his side, trying to reassure him that everything would be okay.

'I thought Vampires were indestructible,' I whispered to Tallis.

'Not totally,' said Tallis. 'There are wooden stakes, fire, sometimes the weakening effects of sunlight, the bite of a werewolf — all can be deadly to a vampire. Only you will have true immortality, Lily.'

I felt bad for Cousin Dominic, not sad though — just bad. I didn't know him well enough to feel any sympathy. And I didn't like him anyway, possibly because of his remark about Pippa. For a moment, as he took his last gasp of blood-ridden breath, I felt some remnant of the old Lily rise to the surface. I couldn't understand it. I so wanted to be devastated. This was my very own flesh and blood dying right before me, but I didn't feel anything for the horror I saw in his eyes. He knew his time was up, and he struggled to hang on, grabbing at my dad's jacket in his last moments of panic. He had died trying to help my dad, but in all reality, he had died for me, and yet I wasn't grateful. I wanted to be. So very much. But I can honestly say it was almost a relief for me to know that Pippa would now be safe. I smiled at this thought, and Tallis shot me a harsh look and shook his head disapprovingly.

The body count had been ten the night of the masquerade ball. Ten people dead. Nobody who meant anything to me. Even my Cousin Dominic's death had left my thoughts within hours. It did seem strange to me, however, that those killed by werewolves were either human or Du Plessis, and the only Monsantos that had met their end died by my hand. It was as if the werewolves had targeted my family and knew exactly who they were aiming for.

What were they trying to do? I wondered. *Were they trying to wipe them out to forge a path directly to me? Or did they simply not see the Monsantos as a threat?* I thought about this for days afterwards, but it made no sense to me. It didn't matter how I looked at it — the whole scene just seemed wrong in my head. And the Monsantos, yes, had kept me safe, but they wouldn't allow me to help my family. They were quite firm with me about controlling my rage, about leaving the Du Plessis to jump unaided into the fray.

When I thought back on the battle, and the few glimpses I got while being dragged to safety, it was *my* family who was targeted by the werewolves, and mainly them that fought the beasts off. Sure, the Monsanto was in the midst of it all, as were the strange wolfling team that appeared from nowhere. Some people were injured and even killed by the fire that shot from my hands and consumed them. But I couldn't frame one picture in my mind of a Monsanto or a Monsanto wolfling actually fighting or killing a werewolf. I think the Monsanto wolfling arrived just in time to protect the Monsanto, not to fight the enemy. I was angry but also afraid — shit scared in fact — that my dad trusted these people with my life. Yet I knew wholeheartedly that they couldn't be trusted with his.

I slept restlessly for some weeks after all this happened. The odd thing about that time was, I started having reoccurring nightmares about the ball, about my cousin Dominic's death. In my nightmare, I was reaching out to him, struggling to make my way through the crowd. It felt as if I were wearing concrete slippers. I was moving towards him but getting nowhere. The werewolf bit into his jugular then looked over at me, Cousin Dominic's blood dripping from its deformed jaws. Strips of Cousin Dominic's flesh hung from its jagged teeth and its black as death eyes stared at me in defiance. And still my heavy feet dragged slowly across the dance floor. Every time I woke from this nightmare, I could smell the rancid breath of the werewolf, as if he'd been right there in my room.

All day long, the vivid picture in my head of his haunting eyes and flesh-ridden teeth bore into my peacefulness, making each day unbearable and each night even worse. The strange thing was that as these nightmares became a part of my nightly life, and I started to feel bad about my reaction to my cousin Dominic's death. I had an urgent feeling that his death had to be avenged and that I should be the one to do it. Yes, revenge was very much on my mind. The more I thought about killing the beast that had killed my cousin, the less the nightmares bothered me. Until one night, I went to sleep, and they were no more.

They stopped, just like that.

I guessed it was all to do with my underlying guilt. Sometimes I'd feel extremely touched by an event, and sometimes I'd feel nothing in the worst of circumstances. I supposed my feelings were just trying me out for size, that maybe they were just growing in me, and that at some point they would no longer switch on and off but would be with me all the time. Like Marchella had said to me: my powers were linked to my emotions — the stronger the emotion, the stronger the outpouring of power — like when I'd thought about Pippa dying in the migraine territory incident at Olive's, obviously my anguish triggered my reaction. I dare to think what might have happened if she had actually died? Would I have left there that night? Or would I have stayed and hunted my grandad to the ends of the earth for revenge? The night Cousin Dominic died, I tried to feel how a normal person would feel at the death of a family member, but it just wouldn't come. I felt absolutely nothing, and I did feel bad about that now, wanting so much to feel for him, and yet there was nothing but a smile at the thought of Pippa's safety. Since that night, I had thought about his death often, and I felt so guilty … that I felt more for my cat than my cousin. Maybe this had triggered the nightmares. The nightmares only highlighted the fact that I couldn't help him, even though the urge was there deep inside. When the nightmares stopped, I saw it as a sign. I decided that if it were the last thing I did I'd find that werewolf and I'd kill it with my bare hands. I'd see him as dead as my cousin Dominic.

A FAVOUR FOR GOD

My eighteenth birthday was drawing nearer, and my powers were growing stronger. At the end of the school term, summer holidays began. I spent a lot of time hiding out in the cavern working on interesting spells and remedies, on things that Marchella had shown me. Sometimes they went wrong and I'd set things on fire. This scared me in the beginning, but as time went on, I realised the magic really was contained in the cavern. This was my safe place and, as long as nobody disturbed me here, they were safe too.

This day, I was trying a summoning spell. Nobody knew what I was up to, and Marchella would be mad and call me irresponsible if she found out. But I was determined to keep my word — even if only to myself. My dad had said I'd never kill anyone who didn't deserve it. The guy they found hanging in the back sheds deserved it. And the beast that had killed my cousin Dominic deserved it too. I knew I'd be putting myself in great danger — sure, my powers were getting stronger, and I wasn't immortal yet — yet it had to be done ... whatever the outcome. I owed it to Cousin Dominic.

Hanging on the back wall of the cavern was a silver sword. I lifted it down from its hook and placed it on the bench in front of me. I was reading Mum's grimoire, searching for information about werewolves. Apparently, the only way to end the life of one of these ugly, rancid creatures was to shoot it with a silver bullet or remove its head. The best way was to slice its head off with a silver sword. I couldn't imagine doing either of these things, not me personally. But from experience, I knew what I was capable of when out of my body — my conscience was not my own but that of the person I was inside. Whatever *they* were capable of, I would be capable of while inside them. I decided to summon with a spell the werewolf who had killed my cousin Dominic. I'd enter his body and have the creature slice its own head off with the silver sword. Having found a summoning spell, I gathered all the required ingredients needed. I set everything up around me and kept the silver sword close by. Performing the spell made me want to throw up, after all, there was always a chance it would go wrong and I'd be stuck in this cavern with a disgusting beast. I had to concentrate. I lit the candles, mixed the ingredients, spoke the spell out loud. Felt to the front of me, eyes closed, confirming the position of the sword. Then I opened my eyes.

Nothing.

There was nothing there. The cavern was empty except for me.

I frowned. *If I'm supposed to have the powers of a witch and the correct spell from Mum's grimoire then why didn't it work?* I went through the list of ingredients once more. *All correct.* I paced the cavern, wondering what the problem was, and how I could fix it. I couldn't ask Marchella for help: she would never allow me to do something so utterly stupid. I felt so incompetent. I hated failure, and I hated not understanding how this all worked. I was new to the craft, and I didn't know how to draw on my emotions to use in the spells, but I'd tried; I'd tried my best. I'd thought deeply about Cousin Dominic's death before starting. I'd thought about the werewolf attacking Pippa too, just to get the right measure of emotion. But it hadn't worked. I heaved a deep sigh.

It was quiet in the cavern, and cold, so I wandered through to the chamber and lit a fire in the large central hearth. The room soon glowed with an orangey tinge and warmed the air around me. The cold stonewalls drew in the heat of the flames as I sat for a long while reading Mum's diary entries in her grimoire. The more I read, the more I came to know her. I came across a page about the wolfling and read how they were created. Apparently, my mum's friend, a young girl called Sassy, worked in the morgue. Sassy was also into the craft and helped Mum find the bodies needed to create the team. They had to be extremely careful in their choice, the moral fibre of the deceased an essential factor: they couldn't have any history of murder or callousness in their past. And they had to have led a solitary life, having no family ties: at the least no family contact so the missing body wouldn't create too much of a stir. *John Does* would have been perfect candidates, but they were unusable due to the lack of life profiling. So Sassy would scour the files at the morgue at night for information on the deceased that were brought in. If their record was clear and they met the requirements, she would tag the large toe with a blue ribbon and make sure she was the last to leave. Then late at night my mum and her coven would visit the morgue and remove the body.

Lucky she only needed four. What a commotion the body-snatching would have caused. So this is what that diary entry was about, I realised, recalling the entry about the soldier that had died in action. *He must have been one of the team.*

My mum had used four Meta morphine rocks to create the wolfling. I read further.

Each body was buried below ground with the rock of choice placed on top of the heart; the ingredients for the wolfling creation spell surrounded the body. The rock then went through a process enduring high temperature and pressure created by the witches, the process changing the rock's form and transferring the qualities of the rock to the body, bringing it back to life, in the form of a wolfling. Each body was treated similarly.

As with any birth, the process was painful and hard work for the wolfling, who then had to find the strength to dig its way up and out of the earth, carrying the rock in its mouth, thus completing the process to survive. Forever after each wolfling was named after the rock that created it. *A rock that has the power to bring the dead back to life ...? Wow, how bloody interesting!* It was, however, a bit freaky because when I really thought about it, this meant that I had once kissed someone — Tallis to be exact — who'd been totally dead at one time!

Shuddering at the thought, I continued reading, then realised I was chuckling. *Maybe I have a penchant for kissing the dead … I also kissed Alex. And why do I find this so funny?*

I returned my focus to the notes in the grimoire. There were four names underlined in the book with a brief description beneath each.

> Meta morphine: Meaning: 'To change form.'
>
> Mylo: Derived from Mylonite's - beautiful quartz-like rocks.
>
> Slater: Derived from Slate — a foliate rock.
>
> Mica: Derived from Micas — a lamellar mineral rock.
>
> Tallis: Derived from Talisman — an object believed to contain certain magical properties, which will provide good luck for the possessor, and possibly offer protection from evil or harm. This

> Talisman over time has shown to protect beyond measure and also to bestow eternal life to the bearer under dire circumstances.
>
> Wolfling: Created to serve and protect. Has a large wolf-like physique. These creatures have a higher moralistic plane than any other human or supernatural being, and strong qualities of loyalty, empathy and love. Willing to die to save the protected.

It seemed strange that Tallis's description was so different from the rest. The Talisman must have been some kind of meta morphine rock, or the process could not have taken place. Yet my mum didn't name the rock, and Tallis was not named after it. *What does this mean? Is Tallis different somehow? Created the same but for a different purpose maybe? Do his qualities make him stronger, weaker, more moral or less than the others? He most certainly has all the qualities in the description. He is definitely programmed to serve and protect, and I most certainly am his greatest priority in life. But why is his description different?* I had no idea. I felt I would never get to the bottom of all the mysteries in my world … unless I could physically talk to my mum, which was of course impossible. All my conclusions would have to come from what my own mind made of her writings.

I placed the book back on its stand and laid back on the huge scatter cushions stacked on the chamber floor close to the fire, thinking deeply about all I'd just read. Before I knew it, I was waking up and checking my watch. A whole hour had passed. The heat must have made me dozy and I'd nodded off. Dinner would be an hour or so away so I started packing everything away. I left the fire burning safely in the grate; it would burn itself out eventually. I doused the lanterns, closed the door, and headed up and out of the cavern and back towards the house.

It was cooler up here in the woods and I breathed in the freshness of the air; brushed my fingers against the bark of trees as I walked along, dead leaves left over from many autumns crunching beneath my feet. I took a small path to the left, a short cut to the house, and there in the distance standing behind a tree I saw it — the werewolf that had killed Cousin Dominic. It snarled, slunk down and crept closer, and my heart lurched. I had summoned this beast, but thought it hadn't worked. And I wasn't expecting this.

Fear crept across my skin as it came closer, its ugly jaw protruding from its almost human face. Its black, deep-set, deathlike eyes stared me down. Its legs and arms looked slightly deformed as they dragged its gross, hairy body through the dead leaves. This was the most repulsive thing I'd ever seen, like an experiment gone wrong; bits and pieces from all different bodies slung together aimlessly, un-matching. Its form made no sense at all. Then it spoke.

'All alone out here, Lily?'

I gave no answer; watched as saliva dripped from its jaws with each word it spoke.

'Where are your people now? Tut tut … they should know better than to leave a precious gem alone,' he said. Then his cackled laughter filled the air around me.

He was taunting me as I edged backwards. As he came slowly closer, I almost stumbled on a branch and fell, and steadied myself on a tree for balance.

'Look at you,' he said, 'so scared, so vulnerable.' He smiled, though it was more a grimace, and a large glob of saliva flicked up onto his face. My stomach lurched again. His snout leaked and his eyes had crusty yellow pus at the corners. The smell of rotting flesh permeated the air. I tried to concentrate, to gather my composure in the face of this foul sight. I'd never been this close to something so disgusting. My skin crawled, and I retched from the stench.

'You know what's coming, Lily. I can see the fear. I can smell it. I'm going to rip you to shreds.' He laughed again, and I backed further away, terrified. This creature was pure evil. I could sense it so strongly — it was devil-created and, for a short moment, I craved the safety I'd felt as a kid in God's house.

I couldn't speak; was trying so hard to focus. I breathed in and out slowly. Purposefully. Tried to calm the fear so the rage could kick in. Then I remembered Mum's writings. *Fire's no good. It has to be the bullet or the sword. His head has to be removed. I have to get back to the cavern!*

I turned as if to run then had a thought. *Turn back and face it, Lily. You can handle this. Breathe deeply. Let yourself go.* I turned to see its haunches dip towards the ground. It was about to leap. I closed my eyes. Breathed calmly. My heartbeat slowed. Pulse dropped. And the next thing I knew I was inside the werewolf, landing on its front paws where I'd just stood.

I sensed its confusion.

In fact, I sensed a lot of things. I had only ever been inside a human form before, and this felt different ... uncomfortable because I was crouched down. I could also feel the evil within as if I were sinking into a muddy pool of depravity. I moved my mind into his as he struggled, as he suddenly realised what had happened. For just a few moments, I had his thoughts; saw what he had in mind for me; saw in his imagination myself after he'd ripped my body to pieces. It sickened me, and I shuddered inside him, almost losing my grip.

I had to act quickly, but he fought me all the way to the cavern. Strongly and relentlessly, he threw himself around, trying to shake me out. But I stayed stronger as I kept moving forward, kept my mind fixed on the goal and headed down to the cavern, dragging this unwilling torso with me. I couldn't pull the handle with his gnarled hand-like paws, only half changed and popping with sinew and muscle. So I leant his gangly limb on the handle. Luckily, I had forgotten to lock it, and the door burst open and the beast fell inside. Still resisting as I tried to move forward, he threw himself at the hard stone wall, then howled in pain. I didn't feel it, just kept firmly dragging him forward, towards the silver sword. At first, I felt the sudden shock that flashed through his mind when he saw it, as I made him reach determinedly out to grab the handle. I felt his lips curl back over his jutting jaw as he bared his full mouth of jagged teeth in terror. I went for the weapon, but his stupid gnarled clumps of half-human, half-wolf mutated paws found it impossible to hold it. It burned through his flesh as he touched it and it dropped to the floor. *Shit*! Desperately I struggled inside to make him retrieve it but every time I made him reach out to touch it, he screamed with pain, the silver burning his flesh.

Suddenly I felt dizzy. I was losing my grip on the situation. I'd never stayed in a body this long before and was suddenly scared and unsure of keeping a hold of his thoughts, of his body. He was more resilient, stronger than anyone I had entered before. And different, like his will wasn't totally mine. The others had been human. I wondered if this beast's supernatural power gave him an edge I hadn't expected. I started to panic as he threw himself around again, slamming his body against the wall again and again. If I lost my grip, my connection, what would happen? I'd be stuck in the cavern alone with this thing from hell, and it would most surely kill me! *So do something … Do it now!*

I could feel his strength overriding mine, and concentrated harder to bring my thoughts back into line. I breathed deeply. Refocused. Blocked out the fear. Reset the goal. Suddenly I felt it coming back — I was more in control again. *But what do I do now?* I couldn't pick up the sword to slice his head off, and I didn't have a silver bullet.

I could feel his evilness wrapping around my soul, and I wanted this over. I wanted to be out of this disgusting mess of a body, but the only way was to behead him … *there is no alternative!*

I concentrated harder. Dug my thoughts in deep, and relentlessly pressed on. I forced him to take hold of his bottom jaw with one gnarled hand, his claws digging into the flesh to get a proper hold. His jagged teeth pierced the skin as I made him pull down hard. I made the other hand grip the upper jaw and pull in the opposite direction, as hard as possible. His eyes bulged with the pain and an awful gargled scream emanated from his throat as saliva ran into a pool down the back of the tongue, making it hard for him to breath. I heard the cracking of the jaw as the bones broke on either side, ripping the top jaw from the bottom at the joints. The creature squirmed then squealed in agony. I felt his pain in his madly racing heartbeat, in his shaking limbs. With one more firm and fast whipping back of the upper jaw, the top part of the head came away from the bottom, ripping the flesh at the back of the neck. By his own hand, he tore the base of the brain from the top of the spinal cord, and I felt his head drop to the floor. His body slumped forward. His blood sprayed wildly in all directions, covering the area with specks of dark red as if I'd thrown a large glass of Shiraz at the wall. In short time, his heartbeat stopped and I felt his blood flow slowing. He slipped to the floor and lay slumped in a heap, his hand still resting on his dismembered head.

And me? … I was back standing in the woods.

I opened my eyes. I was exactly where I'd been standing when he was in mid-flight, about to attack.

Sprinting back to the cavern, I rushed inside and locked the door behind me. I had to hide the evidence; had to get rid of the stinking carcass. I dragged the body through to the chamber and dropped another log in the grate. The body was heavy, but I managed to heave it up and over the side of the metal bars onto the burning logs, its legs doubled over backwards as the flames set the hair alight. The skin began to swell, blister and pop in the heat. I ran back then and grabbed the head, slung it on top of the pile, then I crouched watching as the fire devoured the dismembered body.

While I watched, a log fell and dislodged the head from its space. It tumbled down the side of the grate; came to rest between two bars; stared directly at me with human eyes. It had transformed back to its former self, and now the rancid smell of death from burning the werewolf's corpse was replaced by the rather gross smell of burning human flesh. An hour later, all that was left were some charcoal black bones.

'One less Lestrange to deal with,' I said to myself and smiled. I had avenged my cousin Dominic, and I truly believed I'd done God a huge favour by removing this creature that could only have been created by the devil, from His earth.

A VERY DANGEROUS ASSOCIATION

One sunny afternoon a few weeks later, I sat out on the porch with Dad and Marchella, lazing in the hazy afternoon heat and enjoying my last few days of the holidays. The new school term would start soon and I happily realised this would be my last year of high school. I was also excited because, on achieving true immortality, I could maybe go off to college without bodyguards. Mylo had always been at school with me in England, and this first nine months in New Orleans Mica and Slater had both joined him as on-site school staff. While it was comforting to know they were around, I still craved the freedom of not having to watch my back.

The holidays had been wonderful. I'd spent heaps of time with my dad and the family, getting to know them, but also getting to know myself. With my newfound abilities and powers, my confidence had grown enormously and I had started to feel that there wasn't anything I couldn't handle. Marchella had helped me to gather knowledge about my strengths and weaknesses, to know what I was capable of, and how to control my emotions — which were linked to my powers — so they didn't take control of me. It felt strange knowing that I would soon be going back to school because, although I had already spent two terms there, I still didn't really know anyone. Well, I knew the names of a few who'd accepted me at first, but I hadn't connected with anyone, not like I had with Olive Briggs. Oh, how I missed that girl.

People had been friendly in the first few weeks of the first term, but when they found out I was living in the Monsanto townhouse this quickly changed. It seemed the legend of the Vampire Monsanto and Du Plessis clans, *and* the tales of the sealed loft, had even pervaded the high schools of New Orleans. So, terms one and two were spent pretty much on my own. I didn't mind though. I had occupied myself with reading and would often sit out under the Crepe Myrtle trees, enjoying the scent and the solitude.

Charlotte Rittal, the girl with the English accent, short blonde hair and baby blue eyes seemed just as lonely, and she would often join me. We'd sit and read together, but she'd never tried to speak to me, nor me to her. I was determined that this term I was going to make an effort to turn this into a friendship.

'Looking forward to school, Lily?' Dad asked with an enquiring look.

'Not really,' I sighed. 'I find it hard to make friends. The other students don't seem to like me.'

'Who could not like you?' said Marchella. 'You're as cute as a muffin.'

'Well, it seems most of Benjamin Franklin High actually.' I half-shrugged.

'Nonsense!' said Marchella. 'Do you want me to come in and sort those students out?'

'No, thanks. I can handle it myself. I'm not a child.'

The thought of Marchella coming into school to defend me made me smile. The bloodbath she would probably leave behind would do nothing but affirm the allegations of the vampire tales.

'She's almost an adult now, Mother. She'll be fine,' my dad said with a smile.

'Yes, Eli. But it's not fair for her to be outcast because of us. We should do something about it.'

'Please don't,' I beseeched her. 'Honestly, I can handle it, and the guys will be there if I have any major problems.'

Marchella stroked my hair and looked lovingly at me. Then she nodded and went back to her reading.

Monday came around too soon, and we were on our way to school, the guys and I in a large Black Range Rover four-wheel drive. We pulled up outside the campus on Leon C. Simon Drive and Mica dropped me off, with Mylo following closely behind me. Mica then went off to park the car. I wandered into the expansive foyer bang in the middle of which stood a large statue of Benjamin Franklin. Students milled around, but although they looked me up and down, not one of them met my eye. I headed for the lockers.

Once again, the hallway was full of excited students cramming stuff into their lockers, chatting with others about the holidays and boys, and stuff like that. Not one of them spoke to me. They gave me a wide birth, in fact, to the point I felt there was an invisible barrier around me, that they could see, but I couldn't. All of a sudden, I felt a tap on my shoulder and spun — Charlotte stood behind me.

'Do you mind? ... We're locker sharing this term,' she said, smiling as she reached past me to place her bag inside the locker.

'No ... no, that's fine,' I said. 'Want to walk to class?'

'Yeah, okay,' she said, and off we went, in silence, down the corridor towards homeroom.

Certainly not a chatterbox, this one, I thought. *This could be hard work.*

But I had no other option. After all, there was hardly a queue of people lining up to befriend me ... Lily Du Plessis, descendent of said evil vampires, and one-time resident of the Monsanto townhouse, which included one sealed loft, possibly containing one very depraved monster, if you could believe the gossip. In class we sat together, but not a word or a smile was exchanged until lunchtime when the bell rang. Charlotte said, 'See you under the Crepe Myrtle trees?' And I just nodded.

I sat alone in the dining hall, eating the contents of my tray, bored and staring at the black and white tiles on the checkered floor. Afterwards, I emptied my tray and headed out to the yard, scanning the area for Charlotte under the trees. She was there on the far righthand side, and I wandered over and plonked myself down.

'Lovely day,' I said, trying to spark a conversation. 'Not too hot, hey?' But Charlotte just nodded, stayed focused on her book.

I pulled my own book out and settled down to read. After a short while, I had the strange sensation I was being closely watched. I looked up from my book at Charlotte; she was staring at me.

'What?' I said, one eyebrow rising.

'There's something about you?' she said.

'Okay,' I said. 'Care to share?'

'Well, I can't put my finger on it, but you are definitely a strange one.'

'Oh no, not you as well,' I said, shoving my book in my bag and rising to my feet. 'Are you going to be just like the rest of these jerks here and judge me on stupid legends and tales of olde? I thought you might be different.'

'No,' said Charlotte. 'I'm not judging you, but those legends and tales are not stupid. You and I are one and the same in a way, Lily. You can't pull the wool over my eyes.'

'What? What do you mean?'

'Oh, come on, Lily! You can be honest with me. Are you going to deny that the supernatural exists when you very clearly live amongst them?' She laughed, and I backed away, unsure of how to react. I couldn't agree with her and then maybe find a mob waiting for me at the gate after school. But I couldn't deny it either because something about the way Charlotte spoke told me she knew exactly *who* and maybe *what* I was. I turned to walk away; walked briskly but she shouted after me.

'Don't walk away, Lily. Talk to me. All we have in this place is each other.'

I stopped and thought about her words, not looking back at her. But she was right, and really what did I have to lose? I couldn't lose her friendship because we didn't have one yet. *Maybe, just maybe, this is the beginning.* I went back and sat down. Charlotte ran her fingers through her cropped blonde hair. Her large baby blue eyes stared at me as I sat and took my book back out and placed it on the table.

'So ...' she said, 'you are obviously a vampire, being a Du Plessis and all?'

'Not totally. A bit of a mixture actually,' I said quietly.

'A mixture of what?' She looked a little confused.

'Half-vampire, half-witch,' I whispered, leaning closer.

'Oh, my Lord,' Charlotte said with a gasp.

'That bad, hey?

'No, not bad, well hopefully not. I'm a witch myself, but mortal of course.'

I looked at her and maybe looked as shocked as she was at that moment.

'Are you practising the craft?' I asked her.

'Well yeah, occasionally. I mean that's what witches do,' she said with a small laugh.

'Okay, well, good or bad stuff?'

'Good of course! Well … sometimes bad, but only when I feel threatened.'

'I've never met another witch,' I said. 'I mean, my mum was one, but she died in childbirth, so I never got to meet her.'

'And your dad's a Du Plessis vampire?'

'Yeah,' I said uncomfortably, shifting in my chair under her intense gaze.

'That means you are an Immortal! Wow! I know of the legend, but I never thought it would happen again, not in this day and age.'

'What? What do you mean … again?'

'Well, my great-grandma once told me a tale about another immortal child born in the 1820s; it was created by a Monsanto vampire and a voodoo queen.'

'You know of the Monsantos?' I asked.

'Yes of course … I'm a witch. It's my business to know who's who around these parts. I was actually quite relieved when you joined the school, and I learned you were a Du Plessis.'

'Why is that?'

'Because the Monsanto are the bad guys. And I wouldn't want to be in their company on a daily basis.'

'Okay, so you think the Du Plessis are the good guys then?'

'Well, as vampires go, they're a pretty decent bunch. Got quite good morals according to my mum.'

'Is she a witch too?'

'Yep. Anyway, the story goes that Anastasia Du Preez and Elijah Monsanto created an immortal, but because the mum was a voodoo queen, when it reached its seventeenth year its good emotions didn't kick in — because the mum didn't have any. Although it wasn't incredibly powerful due to its lack of good emotions, it definitely chose the wrong path. As it headed towards its eighteenth birthday, it got worse and worse. It became a destructive and dangerous force, killing everything in its path, even members of its own family, even its own dad. Emmanuelle Monsanto's dad, Elijah.'

'Woah! No shit. And then what happened?'

'Well, nobody is quite sure about the outcome? But it's not around today, so I guess the immortal hunters wiped it out before it reached immortality. It would have been a close one, though.'

'Well, that clears up a little something I've been wondering about.'

'What's that?' Charlotte said.

'Well, at the Monsanto ball, I saw a team of wolfling, and they are created to protect us immortals.'

'Yeah, I know. My mum's coven has helped a friend to create a team in the past.'

'I guess they must be the original team that were created for the immortal child in the 1820s. Is that possible?' I asked.

'Of course. The wolflings are timeless. I mean they can be killed, but they can also be brought back to life by a certain elixir, and also by the rock that created them. So yeah, you are probably right. I'd say they were the original team for the Monsanto immortal.'

'You sure know a lot. It's great to be able to discuss this stuff with someone. Sometimes I feel I could go batshit crazy with it all stuck inside my head.'

'Yeah, well, you need to be careful who you talk to, Lily. Be very careful. No one wants a repeat of the 1840s incident, and they are fearful of it happening again. If certain people learn of your existence, you could end up with the same fate as the Monsanto immortal.'

'Tell me about it,' I said, grimacing. 'I've been living undercover all my life, and here in New Orleans there's already been two attempts on my life. I have my wolfling team always close by, and actually the Monsanto have joined ranks with the Du Plessis to keep me safe. But I'm constantly under threat.'

'The Monsanto are not to be trusted, Lily. Not at all.'

'I think I've figured that much out for myself. But until I turn eighteen, which is only three months away now, it's best to act like I believe they're on my side.'

'You're probably right there. Also, another little tip: I'd keep your identity a secret from the covens. I know I belong to one, but I wouldn't trust them as far as I could throw them, not even my mum. She was coerced by a friend to make a wolfling team for an immortal kid some years ago. But the way she talked, she would have taken that kid's life in the blink of an eye, rather than risk another catastrophe like what happened back in the 1840s. Even if you have no intention of going off the rails — and actually I sense a really good side to you — my mum and her coven, and the other covens would rather see you dead.'

'So, more things to add to my worry list,' I said.

'Don't worry, Lily, I won't be telling anybody. This can be our little secret. I think you may just be capable of bringing the legend to pass without destroying the world and everything in it. I have a very good feeling about you.'

'Thanks. I do hope so,' I said. 'At least that's what I've promised my dad. My mum wanted me to use my abilities for the greater good, and that's just what I intend to do.'

'Well, we'll see,' said Charlotte. 'We'll see.'

The school bell rang as lunch break ended, and we went off to class together. It was biology and we were dissecting frogs. Some of the class members were retching and acting so silly about the procedure, stating how cruel and disgusting it was. I thought back to a few weeks before and the beheading incident with the Lestrange werewolf. It would have had some of these guys literally throwing up in the bushes, and I giggled at the thought. Charlotte giggled too, almost as though she'd read my mind. She couldn't, of course, but I'm sure that being a witch she would have dissected more than a few frogs in her lifetime to use in spells, so I guess she just got me; got my humour. It was nice to feel close to someone for once, and to top it all, it was a girl, a girl my own age, just like Olive.

This time in class Charlotte was bubbly and chatty and the time flew by. Before I knew it, the afternoon bell rang to go home and I almost felt sad leaving Charlotte, my new mate. I couldn't wait for school the next day.

Back on the plantation, I slipped into a nice hot bath then I headed down to the dining room for dinner. Marchella, my dad, and the team sat around the table with other family members discussing the fact that one of the Lestrange werewolves had gone missing without a trace. I sat with them eating my dinner, not saying a word. The rather intense and strange emotion of guilt ran through every fibre of my body, but I tried to keep quiet and act as nonchalant as possible.

They could never know what I'd done. Not because of the grotesque act itself, but because of the stupidity of my actions. It could have ended very differently, and I knew I'd never hear the end of it if the truth came out. After dinner, I pretended to be extremely tired after my long first day back at school and excused myself from the table. Back in my room, I lay on my bed cuddling Pippa and thinking about the day. I was so excited to have finally made a friend, one who understood me, who lived a similar life to me. We were different, and the humans somehow knew this; treated us like we didn't exist. This was very isolating for us, but I felt that together maybe we could live a semi-normal life.

The following day I walked into Benjamin Franklin High with a new sense of wonder. Everything felt different. Even the ignorance of students didn't bother me because I was no longer alone. I met Charlotte at the lockers and, this time, she didn't tap me on the shoulder; she hugged me like a long-lost friend. At lunchtime, we sat outside again under the Crepe Myrtle and talked instead of reading books.

'What kind of powers do you have, Charlotte?'

'Powers? Do you mean what kind of spells can I cast? Or what abilities I have?'

'I guess you'd call them abilities.'

'I'm pretty good in the craft and can cast a whole range of spells for all sorts of situations if needed. Us mortal witches often work with your dad's kind to help with certain situations they can't deal with themselves. So being useful to them, we have never really seen them as a threat. The werewolves are the worst kind of supernatural. They are as ugly on the inside as they are out. I've often had to use magic to deal with them. Wolfling are beautiful creatures. And I've never personally had a problem with one. But the werewolves are pure evil through and through.'

'I know that … learnt it firsthand … but what I mean is … do you have other abilities, like entering another body and forcing it to do your will? Or are you able to set stuff alight through anger?'

'I do have those abilities to a degree, but not to the degree that you would have them. Your vampire qualities would amplify your emotions, and it's the emotions that control the depth of the power.'

'I've heard that before. Marchella told me.'

'Marchella Du Plessis?'

'Yeah. She's my grandmother.'

'Oh, okay then. I guess that means either Caleb or Eli Du Plessis is your father?'

'That's right. Eli is my father. I don't know who Caleb is?'

'Bloody hell!' Charlotte suddenly went rigid. 'You are Lilith Montague's kid?'

'Yes, I am.'

'Wow, you're nothing like her. I've seen her picture so many times. I wouldn't have made the connection.'

'How have you seen pictures of my mother?'

'Because my mum's coven was your mum's coven ... before she left for England. She was the head of the Calibri coven and my mum's best friend. My mum was originally from England too. She and Lilith went to school and college together before they moved here. My mum must have helped her create your wolfling.'

'No way!'

'Hell, yeah!' Charlotte said, her eyes widening with surprise. 'I can't believe it. You are the immortal daughter of Lilith Montague. Gosh, I've heard this story my whole life, but I thought it was just another New Orleans tale.'

'Nope ... I'm for real,' I said with a hint of a smile.

'Obviously! But not many would know of your existence. My mum certainly doesn't. And the covens ... I guess they would think that the immortal hunters killed you long ago, which *is* generally what happens to every immortal child. You've done well to make it this far — you must have an awesome team behind you.'

'Shit, yeah,' was all I could think to say.

'Damn it to hell, Lily, I have formed myself a very dangerous association,' she said, staring at me with wide, fear-filled blue eyes.

Just then something hard hit me on the back of the head.

'Ouch!' I exclaimed, looking up. But it hadn't come from the tree. It had come from behind me. Briff had thrown an apple at my head.

He walked over to our table and glared at me.

'What happened to my uncle, scum bag?' he hissed in my ear.

'What? Who?' I said, scowling.

'Leave her alone, Lestrange, or you'll have me to deal with,' Charlotte said, standing up and leaning in towards him.

Lestrange? Briff is a Lestrange? Briff is a werewolf!

This hit me harder than the apple had.

'What ya gonna do, little witch? Do ya think you scare me?' he challenged Charlotte with a snort and shoved me against the tree.

'Carry on pushing, and you'll soon find out,' she warned, jumping up and over the table to put herself between Briff and me.

He backed off a bit, then snarled, 'Watch your back, Lily. I know where my uncle went the day he disappeared, and when I find out what happened to him, I'll do the same to you.' Then he stomped off across the yard, leaving me shaking — not out of fear — out of lack of control. I had nearly lost it, and it took everything I had in me to hold the anger in. I felt like I was going to implode, but there was no other way, the yard was full of lunching students, and I had to remain normal, act like a regular bullied student. I couldn't risk revealing my true self amongst all these haters.

Charlotte put her arm around me, 'Stay calm, Lily. There are other ways of dealing with scum like him.'

I nodded in agreement.

A LETTER TO LILITH

When I told Marchella and my dad about my new friendship with Charlotte, they were very accepting of it. This is not really what I really expected. But I guess it was easier for them to accept an outsider, who was at least a part of our world, than a human. I didn't think I'd ever be able to bring a human friend home. Not that I was ever likely to have one, considering their reaction to me at school so far. I didn't take it personally though because they weren't rejecting me because of me, exactly, but more out of fear that I was not what I appeared to be.

And, of course, they were right.

The only human friend I'd ever had was Olive and I hoped we'd always be friends. It was an easy friendship to have when I lived in England. Before I knew *who* and *what* I was. But I couldn't imagine being friends with Olive here. How difficult would it be explaining all this to her? And how hard would it be to protect her? I had enough trouble looking after myself, let alone looking after a human on a plantation full of bloodthirsty vampires. I could trust a majority of them, but there were a few who definitely suffered from bloodlust — even the human servants in the house steered well clear of them and wore a garlic-based perfume at all times, not that this would work but these southerners did love their old wive's tales.

Olive and I texted each other all the time — she was planning to visit me for my eighteenth birthday. I had suggested to my dad that while she was here in New Orleans, I would go and stay back at the Monsanto townhouse, in the French quarter with the team, just until she was gone. I couldn't say no to her visiting, but the closer it got to my birthday, the more I feared for Olive.

When the weekend came around, I invited Charlotte to stay. She couldn't tell her mum I existed, so she had to find an excuse to visit the plantation. Marchella said she would talk to Charlotte's mum, to suggest that she could do with some help setting up a herb garden, and that Charlotte would be ideal with her knowledge of herbs and their usefulness. Of course, mortal witches were always agreeable to helping vampires, because it assured their safety and survival in a town where the odds were not stacked in their favour. This little understanding had been going on between vampires and mortal witches for centuries. It gave the mortal witch protection that was invaluable to them. So, of course, the answer was yes. Charlotte's mum dropped her at the plantation gates early Friday evening. She arrived with a small suitcase and a batch of biscuits baked freshly for Marchella. What use could a vampire have for hot biscuits? Well, absolutely none. But it put the nosy neighbours' minds at rest when they could see human food being delivered to the house by human hand. Anything to quell the rumours, and anyway, the human staff and I appreciated the hot biscuits, so they didn't go to waste.

Charlotte and I spent a lot of time in my room the first day, and she absolutely adored Pippa who seemed to like her too.

'I think cats and witches have an undeniable affinity,' I said.

'I have a black cat called Maz,' said Charlotte. 'Do you know that if you are brought into contact with the correct cat — the cat that's supposed to be yours — you will form an unbreakable bond and the cat will become empathic towards you, sensing your feelings, your fears, anxieties, sadness, happiness — you name it the cat will feel it. This can come in very handy as a self-moderator. The cat also has the ability to sense danger and will tense up in certain situations, letting you know how you should react.'

'Funny you should say that because Pippa has reacted twice to alert me to things. Although she once slept right through an awful ordeal.'

'Well, the bond takes time to form. She won't be able to read you straight away. Sometimes it can take months.'

Charlotte stroked her softly, and Pippa purred loudly sounding like the distant rumbling of an avalanche pouring down a snowy mountainside. I brought out my mum's private box and showed Charlotte the contents. It may have been too early in our friendship to share such personal stuff but I so desperately wanted us to be close, and secrets were barriers to true friendship. So, in I dived feet first.

'Ask me any question, Charlotte,' I said with a smile.

'Was Briff right when he said that his uncle went missing here, Lily?'

Shit. I wasn't expecting that!

I looked towards the window and suddenly regretted my little *dare me to bare my soul* outburst.

'Well?' said Charlotte

'I guess,' I said uncomfortably.

'You guess … or you know?' she probed.

'I know, but I don't want to talk about it, okay? Let's just say he deserved what he got; he had it coming to him. He killed my cousin and revenge was fair.'

'Yeah,' said Charlotte, smiling and nodding knowingly. 'Sometimes revenge has the sweetest sting.'

I picked up the photos from the box and flicked through them.

Charlotte pointed to the one with my mum and a bunch of women.

'That's the Calibri Coven, Lily. Look, there's my mum Jane standing next to yours,' she said, pointing to the photo.

'I thought so. Well, when I first saw this photo, I thought it must be her coven. Quite strange to think our mums were so close, hey?'

'Yep, quite strange,' Charlotte said with a smile. 'And what's this letter then? Have you read it?'

'No, not yet. There's a poem in there too,' I said.

'I can't believe you haven't read it. Where's your curiosity, girl?'

'Read it if you must,' I said. 'But it's to my mum, not to me.'

'That's pretty obvious as it has her name on the envelope.'

Charlotte opened the letter and started to read.

'Out loud please,' I said, looking at her.

'Well surprise, surprise!' she said sarcastically. 'Looks like a certain someone had a little crush on your mum.'

I tried to grab the letter, suddenly interested, but Charlotte jumped up from the bed and walked briskly around the room reading it.

'Read it to me then,' I shouted, sprinting off the bed after her.

'Okay, okay. Sit down, Lily. Don't get ya knickers in a twist, girl.'

Then Charlotte read the contents of the letter.

Dear Lilith,

Your time spent here with me and my family has been most wonderful, and I would like you to know that I both honour and respect you and the path you have chosen, although you will be sourly missed. I would very much like for you to accept our family talisman for use on your journey. Take it as a token of our mutual respect and love for you.

Without your help, the Monsanto family would still be living under the curse of Anastasia Du Preez, and therefore we are forever indebted to you.

The Monsanto family talisman is a moonstone that is believed to contain certain magical properties, which would provide good luck for the possessor, and possibly offer protection from evil or harm. This Talisman over time has shown to protect beyond measure and also to bestow eternal life to the bearer under dire circumstances.

I offer you the use of this precious heirloom to use in your hour of need and will trust that when it has served its purpose, you will return it to me in the same good faith that it was given to you.

Return to us safely, Lilith Montague. Until then I will hold your memory in my heart.

With much love,

Emmanuelle Monsanto

Charlotte and I both fell silent and sat back down on the bed. Charlotte folded the letter and placed it back into its envelope, placing it back in the box.

'I don't understand,' said Charlotte. 'If your mum had the opportunity to save herself, to receive eternal life using the talisman, then why on earth didn't she use it? Why the hell did she die in childbirth?'

'I don't know?' I said, but in my head I was remembering the words I had read in my mum's grimoire, about the wolfling and how they were created. In the letter, the description of the talismans qualities was the same as those used to describe the talisman that created Tallis.

What had my mum done?

She had sacrificed her own life to create an eternal protector for me!

Tallis was the one she was talking about in her diary entry, the one that made no sense to me. He was the exemplary soldier. He was the other side of the coin.

'Do you think Emmanuelle loved your mother?' said Charlotte, interrupting my thoughts.

'No! No way! I mean ... maybe like a sister ... but not like my dad loved her.'

'How do you know?' said Charlotte. 'The letter was pretty intense.'

'Don't read something into it that's not there!' I snapped at her.

'Woah! I'm just pointing out the possibility that there may have been more to their relationship than meets the eye.'

'No. I think you're wrong. Emmanuelle Monsanto was just glad of her help and, as a gentleman, this was his way of saying thanks.'

'Never heard the word *Monsanto* and *Gentleman* used in the same sentence before,' Charlotte said.

'Enough, Charlotte!' I said.

'Just saying!' said Charlotte, squeezing the last word in.

The following morning Charlotte and I headed out to the cavern. I wanted to show her my mum's grimoire and get some tips on certain things. After all, I was pretty new to the craft and Charlotte had grown up in it. Charlotte loved the cavern. She wandered around touching everything in her path, incessantly talking. I liked Charlotte a lot, but she was so different from Olive. Olive never questioned, never probed: Charlotte didn't stop. I guess she was what you would call nosey and a little bit tactless, because she didn't think about whether her questions would piss me off; she just fired away. I found it quite annoying because she also had this way of extracting information. The way she looked at me, it was like she was pulling teeth, and most of the time I found myself telling her stuff that was really none of her business. Charlotte walked through to the chamber and around the edge of the walls, and then into the middle to the grate. She touched its metal edge and smiled knowingly at me, like she was seeing things past.

'What?' I said, feeling slightly intimidated.

'You burned that sucker up, didn't you, Lily?'

'Shit no! Come on. I want to show you something,' I said, trying to make her leave the chamber.

'Not until you tell me how?' she said stubbornly.

'What do you mean?' I squirmed.

'You know, Lily. Come on spill ... details, details, girl.'

'Damn you, Charlotte. How do you do that?' I said.

'Don't know?' she said with a smile. 'It's just the witchy way.'

'Okay ... well, I summoned the werewolf. Then I entered its body and beheaded it right here in the cavern. I burnt the remains ... didn't want to leave any evidence. Happy now?"

I walked off, and she followed.

'Well, I'll be damned, Lily. You must be incredibly powerful! To have entered a supernatural, that's unheard of.'

'Really?' I said, more interested in what she had to say now.

'Boy, oh boy, Lily, you'd have to be crazy to even try it. I can enter humans and force them to do my will, but even that's a struggle for me if they resist. But a supernatural ... no way ... no way on God's earth!'

'I'm telling the truth. That's exactly how it happened. It was difficult. In fact, at one point I was crapping myself ... thought I was losing my grip ... thought I was going to come out of his body before my time, and that he would gut me like a pig!'

Charlotte's eyes were wide with shock.

'I can't believe it. Little Lily Du Plessis getting one over on a supernatural. You're not even immortal yet — he could have killed you.'

'Yes, well he very nearly did. But in the end, I won. So, I don't want to talk about it anymore, okay? Nobody knows but you and me, and I'd like it to stay that way. If Marchella found out, she'd skin me alive.'

'Don't you worry, Lily. Your dirty little secrets are safe with me.'

I wanted to believe her; had to, in fact. I was worried that I hadn't known her long enough to feel safe trusting her. I guessed I'd find out in time.

'I want to do something for you, Lily. I can do it down here using your mum's stuff. You have everything I need. I just need your permission as it's your grimoire.'

'What do you want to do?' I asked.

'It's a protection spell, a really powerful one that will keep Briff Lestrange away from you. It will only protect you until he reaches full maturity but luckily his birthday is a whole month after yours, so by the time it wears off you'll be eighteen and immortal. You won't need the protection anymore.'

'Okay, that sounds good,' I said, suddenly feeling guilty — like maybe I was so wrong about her. She really did seem to care about me. She just had a nosy nature. I guess it couldn't be helped.

We gathered everything needed for the spell and searched through my mum's grimoire, then went to work.

'This will only protect you from Briff and the other young ones. Not the adult werewolves okay?'

'Okay, it's better than nothing.' I said, and then Charlotte cast the spell.

I didn't feel any different, but just like with the summoning spell, I assumed it had worked and would show its usefulness in time.

'Thanks, Charlotte,' I said, hugging her.

'That's okay, Lily. Can't let anything dreadful happen to my bestie,' she said and hugged me back.

Sometimes she could be so nice.

Monday came around too soon, and we were back at school. Although Monday didn't hold the same dread for me anymore, and I actually looked forward to being there. At lunchtime, Charlotte and I headed for the library. She had done a bit more probing, as was her way, and had managed to get even more information out of me, this time about my love life, or lack of one. I told her how I felt about Alex Monsanto and she was genuinely shocked.

'Woah! You're playing with fire there, Lily. Alex Monsanto is an absolute player. He's so well known as a lady's man, and I don't mean that as a compliment to him. He's a ruthless heartbreaker. I'd steer well clear of him if I were you.'

'Well, I am trying,' I said, 'but he's just so irresistible.' I giggled, and Charlotte giggled too, and punched me on the arm, a bit harder than I was expecting. She was such a tomboy.

'Let's see if we can find any information about what's in that sealed loft of theirs,' she said, changing the subject. 'Come on, we'll check the library archives, see what we can uncover.'

All afternoon we scrolled through pages and pages of French quarter history and came up with a big fat nothing — other than a tiny bit of information documenting that a vampire had been sealed into the Monsanto loft in 1842 by a coven of witches. They were supposedly working for a vampire family who wanted a particularly nasty vampire eternally sealed away. But this was speculative at best. It was also documented that this was just a legend, a tale of old created by superstition. So no solid evidence there. Charlotte and I were still none the wiser.

If it's a Monsanto in the loft, why would that be? Why would a Monsanto seal a Monsanto away? What if it's a Du Plessis sealed away in there? Surely Marchella knows the legend of the sealed loft; after all, she was around then, and so was Dad. I have to ask them.

The more I thought about it, the more it bugged me.

'You're going to stay at the Monsanto townhouse when your friend Olive is visiting, aren't you?' Charlotte said.

'Yes, I am. Why's that?'

'Well ... how about we take a look for ourselves ... see what's inside that loft. Whoever it is must be dead after all this time. Surely a vampire can't live without blood for that long, so I guess it would be safe to look. What do you think?'

I wasn't keen, but I did wonder what was up there.

'I guess it couldn't hurt to take a look.'

Charlotte smiled excitedly.

The end of school bell sounded, and Charlotte and I rushed back to the homeroom.

'See you tomorrow, Lily,' Charlotte shouted, disappearing up the hallway. Mylo stood by the lockers waiting for me but I realised I'd left my phone behind. The school was fast emptying as I rushed off towards the library, Mylo following me.

'Be quick; the guys are waiting.'

'Yeah, I'm hurrying,' I said, hurrying along the corridor and through the library doors. I grabbed my phone off the desk and headed back out just as the lights automatically turned off. I could hardly see where I was going. I pushed through the large swinging doors back out into the corridor and called Mylo.

'Here, Lily, this way. Come on, quickly.' I could hear him scuffling along in the darkness, then I saw another dark shadow enter the corridor but couldn't quite make out who it was. Then, with a look of sheer horror, I watched as the shadow jumped into midair, changing form and landing on Mylo before he had a chance to change himself. I froze to the spot and watched as Mylo lay on the floor bleeding and struggling to breathe. Then the thing turned to face me.

It came at me in the darkness, its onslaught so swift I hardly had time to react. It was almost on me when suddenly the thing hit something in front of me. It smashed into it with such force, it bounced off and hit the floor. Then it scrambled to its feet and charged again with all its strength, trying to penetrate this invisible barrier I seemed to be behind. Knowing it couldn't get to me, I stayed calm as it threw itself at me again and again, becoming more and more frustrated with each failed strike. Then the lights came on, and I could see the thing more clearly. It was a werewolf, and I watched it change quickly back to human form, back to Briff, and slip silently and speedily away through the fire exit doors.

From the other direction, Mica and Slater came running. It must have seemed odd to them that Mylo lay bleeding on the floor while I stood a good ten feet away doing absolutely nothing. This invisible wall had surrounded me as soon as Briff came near, but behind it, I couldn't move, couldn't help. Sure, I was safe but pretty bloody useless.

'What are you doing, Lily?' Mica shouted.

'I can't move,' I shouted back. 'Charlotte did a protection spell on me, and I'm stuck in this invisible bubble.'

I tried to move my feet, but they wouldn't budge. What could this mean? Only one thing — Briff was still nearby.

'There's a werewolf here, just behind that exit door,' I shouted.

Mica and Slater headed for the door. As they pounced through it, my force field seemed to fade away. When I'd shouted, Briff must've heard me. He must have made a run for it off the school grounds because as soon as Mica and Slater burst through the exit door, my invisible barrier completely disappeared. I could move again. I ran to Mylo and pretty soon the guys were back. We carried Mylo to the car and, within thirty minutes, we were safely back on the plantation. Mylo was a bit delirious but after a while started to make more sense.

'I thought you were done for,' I said, feeling concerned.

'Yeah, well I didn't see it coming, wasn't expecting that at all,' said Mylo.

'It's a nasty bite that one. You'll need the elixir within a few days or the infection will spread. A bite like that could be deadly,' said Slater.

'I'm not taking the elixir,' said Mylo.

'Don't be stupid, Mylo,' I said.

'It's the last one, Lily, so unless we can find a witch who knows how your mum made it, I guess I will be done for … just like you said.'

'But if there's one left, why not take it?' I said, confused.

Mylo looked at the guys, and then at my dad and Marchella. It was like they were all thinking the same thing but keeping me out of it. *Wow! This is a very old but very familiar feeling.*

'Oh no, you don't!' I said boldly, standing up. 'Tell me now. What the heck's going on? *Now*!'

'Calm down, Lily. It's difficult to explain. We don't want to upset you.'

'Oh, because telling me would upset me, but Mylo dying wouldn't? *Are you all batshit crazy?*

'We have to keep it for Tallis,' Dad said. 'We can't locate the meta morphine rocks that created the team. They were in your mum's possession when she left New Orleans for England. We searched her belongings after she died years ago, and they weren't among them.'

'Without your mum here, we don't know how to find the whereabouts of the rocks. We've survived all these years on the elixir your mum created, but we are on the last vile. We have a witch in Wisconsin, and one in New Berlin working on the formula but so far they haven't managed to get it right.'

'So, use it,' I said, 'We'll do a spell to locate the rocks. Charlotte can help me.'

'No,' said Mylo. 'I won't take it unless the rocks are located. Tallis is more important than me; he may need it at some point.'

'What do you mean?' I said, still confused.

'Tallis was created as your eternal protector, Lily. He's a different wolfling from the rest, and all our qualities are amplified in him. But we can't locate his rock either, so we need the last elixir to be able to recreate more, and as a standby to keep him safe, just in case.'

I loved Tallis with all my heart, but it seemed pretty screwed up to me to stand by and watch someone die when the elixir was available to save him.

'Don't you worry, Mylo. I'll find out where the rocks are, and if I can locate them, then will you take the elixir?'

'Of course, as long as you can guarantee Tallis's safety, I'll take it.'

I ran to the bed, hugged Mylo and ran from the room to call Charlotte. She had to help me, had to help me right now. There wasn't a moment to waste.

THE LILY I NEVER KNEW

Charlotte agreed to meet me at the cavern. She had told her mum that Marchella had some sick baby rabbits that needed ragwort for healing, as the ragwort in the herb garden had taken a turn for the worse.

'Hardly a life-or-death situation,' Charlotte's mum had said.

'It is kind of,' said Charlotte. 'If the ragwort isn't healthy enough to heal the rabbits, the rabbits will die, possibly in vast numbers, diluting the Du Plessis food supply … don't want them looking elsewhere for their food now, do we.'

'Well now, I hadn't thought of it that way,' Charlotte's mum replied, and within twenty minutes dropped Charlotte at the plantation gates again.

Down in the cavern, we gathered everything we needed, but something was missing.

'We need something from the guys. It sounds gross, but maybe a prick of blood from each finger. That way we can be sure to pinpoint their life force,' said Charlotte.

I rushed back to the house and up to Mylo's room, requesting the small amount of blood for the spell.

'Tallis has gone into town with your dad to get some advice from another witch about recreating the elixir. She was a friend of your mum's, so she may know how it was created. If you can wait a couple of hours, they'll be back,' Marchella said.

'No, I can't wait because Charlotte is on a timer — she has to go home soon.'

'Well, if you find one rock, you'll find them all. The wolflings are a team, a pack. Your mum would have kept the rocks together in one place, because it keeps the pack strong. It's the way of the wolfling to stay together. Locate one and you are bound to locate all four.'

'Of course!' I said.

'Yeah, but I'd rather not have my finger pricked in a house full of vampires,' Mylo protested.

Marchella laughed and said, 'Don't be a baby, Mylo. Besides, this is New Orleans ... we don't eat dogs here.' She pricked his finger and squeezed a small amount of blood into a tiny glass tube. Marchella licked her lips, and Mylo shuddered. I took the tube and ran back out through the woods to the cavern. Charlotte had set it all up ready for me, and as soon as she added Mylo's blood to the dish beneath the crystal ball, a very clear picture started to form inside the ball. I saw it — it was like zooming in on a Google map. First, I saw the world, then England, then London, and Blackheath. Then I saw my uncle's house, and an open door, then the big old fireplace in the lounge. Then the image came to rest in the crystal ball. It was a glass display case in the corner of the room and, as the picture zoomed in further, I could just about make out a few objects in the case. One in particular glowed like a burning piece of coal.

'What's that?' I asked.

'Mylo's rock, because it was his blood we used. The others will be there too in the same place.'

'You know where this is, don't you, Charlotte?'

'No idea, spill.'

'My uncle's house, where I grew up in England. Looks like I'm going on a journey.'

'That could be dangerous, Lily.'

'Don't see how actually, with my grandad and Briff being my main enemies right now, and both of them are right here in New Orleans. I should be quite safe there as long as we keep it a secret.'

'I don't know, Lily. Your dad may not like it.'

'Well, if he doesn't like it, he can come along. But I'm definitely going.'

'Are you absolutely sure?'

'Yeah, absolutely. I don't really have any option. I have to go get the rocks to keep my team safe, and to save Mylo.'

'It'll be risky.'

'But worth it,' I said with a thin smile.

I took a photo up close with my phone, so at least Mylo would be able to see his Mylonite rock glowing in the picture. Then he'd know the location spell was a success. Once the rocks were back safely with me and the wolfling, there'd be no need to create more elixir. I was feeling excited as Charlotte and I locked up and ran back to the house. My dad was back with Tallis, and Slater and Mica were in the room when I showed Mylo the photo. My dad didn't look pleased with my idea to go and retrieve the rocks, even though I suggested taking the team with me.

'Come along if you want to Dad, but I have to go.'

'It's just that it's so close to your birthday, Lily. Can't you wait till afterwards?'

'No, Dad. I think now is the best time. Look, Mylo needs to take the last elixir or he's going to die, and once it's gone, there is no more. The guys will be at risk until the rocks are here with them. It's for the best. Besides, my grandad and his men are here, you know that, so if we can do this secretively enough there'll be no threat to me over there. I can even see Olive. Maybe she can travel back with me. Please, Dad, *please*.'

'I guess it would be a better time to go than any other.' He sighed. 'And I guess if the team are with you, you'll be safe enough.'

'Yeah, and we'll be as quick as possible, I promise.'

'Okay, Lily, they are your wolfling … do what you must. I'll stay here and keep tabs on your grandad's movements … pre-warn you if he heads back to England.'

Dad put his arms around me and hugged me. Slater went to fetch the elixir, and Mylo drank it — the last of its kind — secure in the knowledge they were now a safe pack again, and soon their rocks would be back where they belong.

We waited a couple of days for Mylo to get back on his feet and prepared for the journey. Once he was feeling one hundred per cent, we were off to the airport, shrouded in secrecy. A day later, we arrived in England and made our way out into the mild weather towards Blackheath, a place I used to call home.

It felt surreal as we drove into the village, past the church, up and out the other side, past the music conservatory, turning left at the top into our road, and pretty soon drawing up outside the house.

I hadn't known 'nostalgia' before, but now I got it. It was like a yearning in your heart for things past. When I'd lived here, I didn't think I had any real attachment to the place, or the people in it. I loved Uncle Noah, but he'd died, and I was okay with that. I loved Olive, but if she'd died at any point in my childhood, I would have been okay with that too. Now, as a fully emotional seventeen-year-old coming back home, I felt different. A rush of emotions had hit me when we drove down the familiar roads, past familiar buildings. And now, as I looked up at the house, beyond the locked gates, my life flashed before my eyes. They say this happens before you die, but for me, maybe it had to happen before I could truly live.

Memories of me as a kid flicked through my mind like a rapidly page turning photo album — me laughing, running, reading, hiding, fighting with my uncle, feeling safe in this house. Feeling loved. I saw the familiar faces of Uncle Noah, Mica, Slater and Tallis. I recalled the deaths of Juliette and the robust burly man; the lady with the little white dog; Claire, who so desperately wanted to be a princess; the teacher in the gym, and all the other people who'd come my way and perished in my wake. I started to cry. It was so painful. So strange to me now, that these events felt so horrific and unnatural, when as a kid they meant nothing to me. I had been cruel and heartless, and flicking through my memories I hardly recognised the *me* I was then to the *me* I was now.

Tallis put his arm around me as I sobbed. I thought about my uncle, when I had found him slumped on his desk in a pool of blood. I hadn't flinched — hadn't even thought to say goodbye, and not out of fear but pure nonchalance. I just didn't care. I thought about all the years I'd spent with him and how he'd been like a dad to me. I owed him so much more than what he'd got in return, and I wished so badly right then that I could have shown him this side of me. Maybe then he would have loved me … could have loved me.

Tallis held me close as I shed tears for my uncle, although a year too late.

I couldn't believe a whole year had passed since I last laid eyes on this house. As we walked through the downstairs hallway, I could almost hear the childhood whispers of times gone by. It was eerily quiet, and dark inside with all the curtains drawn, masking the emptiness of the rooms. A year of silence had gathered in the atmosphere. I felt it falling heavily around me as we wandered through the rooms. The only sound was our footsteps on the creaking wooden floorboards as Mica and Slater began to push the heavy curtains back, allowing the sun to seep through the windows once more.

I walked through to the kitchen, stood in the doorway, remembering the laughter of Juliette as she baked, and Uncle Noah as he flirted with her. I saw myself sitting at the large table doing my homework, watching them both with a longing for a real family within me.

Then I wandered through to the drawing-room and stood looking through the huge French doors at the vast tree-lined garden. I used to lie there on a sunbed watching Tallis mow the lawn … before I knew *who* … before I knew *what* he really was. I had a sudden thought and a strange realisation: I had known Tallis for many years, yet he'd never changed. He had always been the same age. *Why hadn't I noticed that?* I guessed it was something a kid wouldn't really notice, especially the kind of indifferent kid I was. Details never mattered to me. The only person who I had actually seen grow with age was Olive, as she had grown up beside me. Not that I recall that happening with any great detail either, but my grandad, Mica, Slater and Tallis were the same to me now as they had been my whole life.

I turned and made my way upstairs past my uncle's study. I stopped there for a moment, and the vision returned, of his blood-soaked body slouched across the desk, eyes terrified. That was a memory I could do without. I flinched and moved on, looking out the window before climbing the next set of stairs. I remembered my grandad's car coming down the road the day I had to leave my life behind. And I felt a small amount of relief that he was still back in New Orleans, unaware of my trip to England.

I carried on past the third floor and up to the fourth, stopping outside my bedroom door. I turned and ran my hand across the nail marks that were embedded in the wooden balcony right at the point that Juliette had fallen. Just at that moment as I touched the marks, a vision came to me that scared the hell out of me. I froze to the spot reliving a scene that seemed to travel through to my senses as I ran my hand across the wood. I was lying in bed. A kid again. And in the darkness, someone was leaning over me. It was Juliette. I put my arms up to hug her around the neck then, in the glint of moonlight coming through a crack in the curtain, I saw the pure malice on her face. She placed her hands around my neck. I was frightened and shocked as I realised she wasn't there to tuck me in and kiss me goodnight, but to end my life. She increased her grip around my throat. I wanted to scream *stop!* but couldn't. I could hardly breathe.

'Sorry, Lily, but this has to be. It's sad but the world will be a better place without you,' she said coldly.

My wide, terrified eyes stared up at her in disbelief, then I blacked out.

Within a moment, I could see myself lying on the bed. I was inside Juliette. She was still strangling me. I concentrated hard on releasing her grip and moving her away from me. I walked towards the door. Juliette walked backwards. She struggled against me, not knowing what was going on. She started to panic as she backed out of the room, backed to the edge of the balcony. I turned around and looked over the edge, willing her to move closer. I put one leg over the side then the other, her body now on the opposite side of the balcony rails. She hung onto the wood for dear life, digging her nails in, trying to maintain a hold as I entered her mind.

'Just let go,' I said. 'Goodbye, Juliette … Juliette who I thought

I had loved … who I thought had loved me.'

I felt her fear as she heard these words, horrified that I was inside her. 'No, Lily, no … I'm sorry,' she said, shaking her head.

'Too late,' I said with a smile, letting go of the rail. Then she fell screaming to the base of the stairwell below.

I felt the impact as she hit the floor. Felt her skull crack. Saw the light go out in her eyes as a pool of blood spread out. Her beautiful blonde curly hair turned into a mass of dark-red, sticky locks. Back in my room, I closed my eyes and slept soundly, blocking out the devastation I was responsible for.

I gasped as I let go of the wooden balcony, and the vision stopped. I stood there shocked, shaking, then the truth hit me. This was not just some sick vision — this was a childhood memory. I had killed Juliette.

Feeling faint, I turned the handle to my room and went inside. I lay on the bed looking up at the paintings on the ceiling; breathed in, breathed out trying to control my emotional state, trying to calm my loudly beating heart.

Is this a new ability? How has it come about all of a sudden? Is this a one-off, or will I forever be able to touch objects and see things from my past?

I didn't like it — not one bit. This was not a power I wanted, and it was one I certainly didn't need. All of a sudden I was scared. If I had no recollection of the Juliette incident until today when I touched the balcony, maybe there were other things, horrific things, I had done and not remembered. I felt sick and dizzy, closed my eyes and lay for a little while longer trying to push these thoughts from my head. Half an hour passed, and I had calmed down enough. I sat up and moved to the edge of the bed, looking at all the stuff I'd left behind: my mum's vinyl's; my books; the doll; the pram and the teddies. I had a little pleasant thought just then that maybe my new ability would not always show me bad stuff. What if some of it was good? And what if it were not just my own memories but also other people's that I could see? I reached out and picked up Tilly, one of my mum's old bears and pulled it close. My mind immediately fogged over with the same intense feeling I'd felt standing at the balcony's edge with my hand on the wooden banister.

Then the vision came.

I could see the back of a woman with long, strawberry blonde hair standing outside a shop called *Pockets*. Just behind her was a sign on the corner of the road that said *Greenwich Village*. She walked into the shop and an old-fashioned bell tinkled as the door closed behind her. She wandered around turning things over in her hand, picking them up, putting them down. Then she picked up a bear, an antique-looking bear wearing a pale green shawl with a beautiful brooch pinning it closed. As she turned towards the counter to pay, I saw her face — it was my mum. Then I saw her pregnant form, her hand rubbing her tummy in soft circular motions.

'You like?' she said, looking down at her bump, and I swear I saw a little movement just to the left of her hand. Suddenly the vision shifted, and I saw myself inside the womb. Peaceful, floating, staring at the bear as though it were right there inside of her with me. My little waxen face smiled. My little hand stretched out as if to touch it, and I could see my tiny heart beating with joy.

She turned to the shop assistant. 'I'll take this bear, please. The baby seems to like it.'

The shop assistant smiled back. 'Would you like it wrapped, madam?'

'No need,' said my mum. 'Baby's already seen it.'

The shop assistant gave her an odd look and slipped the bear into a bag. My mum took her receipt and headed out into the street, stopping only to pop on her French beret to guard against the windy weather. She patted her tummy gently ... then the vision stopped.

Wow! I hadn't expected that, seeing my mum in the flesh, pregnant with me; seeing myself tiny in the womb ... *that was really weird!*

My head spun with excitement, and also, quite understandably, a little of being freaked out. I sat in silence thinking about the vision, quite in awe of what my new ability had shown me. *So, this wasn't my mum's bear, she had bought it, especially for me.* I hugged the bear closer to me. It had always been my favourite and now I knew why. I'd chosen it before I was even born. That was a wonderful experience: seeing my mum for the first time in actual form rather than just in photographs. While a little strange and overwhelming, it was much more enjoyable than the vision of Juliette I'd just had. There were sure to be many items I could touch that would show me nice memories of the past, of my mum, of Uncle Noah, and of living here in this house. But I wasn't certain how many items would hold bad memories, that would show me things I simply didn't want to see. I decided then and there not to touch anything else for the next two days, just in case.

I did, however, pack up a few treasured bits I didn't have time to take with me in my rushed escape last year. I'd send them to New Orleans, where I'd have the freedom to touch them and enjoy the visions in the safety of a home with less history of violent or horrific events. I was more than happy to wait. I made my way back downstairs where Mica had ordered in some pizza. I joined them in the kitchen as evening fell across the garden. The full moon shone brightly in through the window, casting a beautiful shadow across the table where we sat.

'I think an early night is in order, after all that travelling,' said Mica, and the rest of us just nodded.

I looked at them all sitting there stuffing themselves with pizza and a thought came to mind *These guys knew the truth! They knew the truth about Juliette; the truth about the ten-year-old me. But they loved me anyway.*

An hour later, we headed off to our rooms. I lay on my blue checkered quilt staring at the ceiling. My mum's tomb was right there in the painting amongst all the other three-storey tombs, and beside hers was a large grey wolf with startling blue eyes. Tallis was guarding her deathbed, and I thought deeply about how Mum had created him to be with me. I wanted to touch the paintings ... to see if Mum was the artist, but I was too scared of what I'd see. I tossed and turned for a couple of hours, dreaming about Juliette and her lovely smile, then about Juliette's look of pure malice. I woke with a start! Then I couldn't sleep.

I was unhappy and uncomfortable now in this room, in this house, and craved my beautiful room at the plantation, or even at the Monsanto townhouse, where my mum had been at her happiest. For the first time, I felt her emotions fully and freely in this house, and it hurt. The room filled me with a sense of impending doom, and sadness, and right there in the middle of the night I realised why I felt this way. My mum had spent her last days in this room. These were possibly her paintings, and I'd been born, just as she had died, on this very bed. I jumped up, grabbed my robe and rushed from the room, to leave a ghost behind. Next thing I knew I was knocking on Tallis's door. I heard his footsteps then he opened it a crack and peered at me in the darkness, his eyes sleepy, his hair a mess.

'Lily?' he said, puzzled.

'I can't be alone. That room is full of bad memories — it's too much for me,' I said, pushing past him to enter the room. He stayed by the door, not closing it … probably wondering what to do next. So I walked back and pushed it closed, then leant against him, my head on his chest. It felt like the longest time that he just stood there not moving, then he nuzzled his chin into my hair and wrapped his arms around me.

'You have the bed, Lily,' he whispered. 'I'll grab the sofa.'

'No … I need you to hold me. I don't want to be alone, Tallis,' I searched his face for his response as we stood silently in the dark.

'Okay, Lily, but no funny stuff, okay?' he said seriously. He took my hand and led me to the side of the bed.

'Tallis!' I said, a little shocked at his presumption that I was trying to lure him down a crooked path.

He smiled that beautiful lopsided smile and pulled me closer. Wrapping his arms securely around me, we snuggled up under the covers. In his embrace, I had all the comfort and safety I craved, and before I knew it I had fallen into a deep sleep.

Tallis made all my bad dreams go away.

Early next morning I woke to the familiar sound of birds tweeting in an English garden. I moved Tallis's arm from around my waist and slipped out of bed, trying not to disturb him. I left the room, closing the door behind me, first checking the hallway for signs of life. It wouldn't be good to be seen leaving Tallis's bedroom, even though it'd been purely innocent, I didn't know what the guys would make of it.

As I made my way down the stairs, I heard voices in the lounge room. As I poked my head around the doorway, I noticed Mica and Slater standing over in the corner, beside the display cabinet I'd seen in Charlotte's location spell. The lid was up, and Slater was gathering items into a small wooden box.

'Check the whole house,' he said, 'and all the other cabinets. It has to be here somewhere.'

'But they're supposed to be together,' said Mica. 'I don't understand?'

'Don't understand what?' I said, coming in on the conversation.

'Oh Lily, good morning. Sleep well?' Slater asked.

'Yeah, thanks. Really good,' I said with a smile, feeling a little guilty, although I didn't know why?

'We have a bit of a problem,' said Mica.

'What's that then?'

'Only three rocks here, Lily.' They both stared sadly into the box as I drew closer.

'Three?' I said, 'But I thought they were all supposed to be together?'

'Yes, well, that's what we were expecting, but one is missing.'

'Which one?'

Mica and Slater fell silent. I looked over the edge of the box.

'Well?' I asked.

'Tallis's rock is not here.'

We all stood there in silence. I didn't know what to say next as a flurry of thoughts rushed through my mind. I had a vision of Mylo drinking the last elixir.

'Let's check all the other cabinets,' said Slater. 'It's bound to be here somewhere.'

'Well, what are we looking for exactly?' I said.

'A moonstone,' said Mica. 'It's white, of course, but kind of opaque with little pale blue veins running through it. It's about the size of a walnut but flatter.'

'Really? I thought it would be large. Like the other three rocks.'

'No, not the moonstone. It's a talisman and can be worn as a piece of jewellery like a necklace or a ring,' said Slater.

'Okay, so we're not just looking for a rock. Maybe a small box with it in or a piece of jewellery,' Mica reiterated.

'We can't tell Mylo about this, not unless we find it,' I said. 'He'd feel so bad having used the last of the elixir.'

'True,' said Mica. 'And Tallis ... What do we tell him if we can't find it? We've come so far, and for what?' he said, shaking his head.

'Well, at least we have the rocks for the three of you, so it was worth coming all this way,' I said. But inside I felt slightly sick that Tallis's rock was not with the others. My beautiful Tallis, totally unprotected, with no elixir and no moonstone. His life would be hanging in the balance until we could either find his life force or recreate the formula.

We spent the next hour searching through all the display cabinets for anything that resembled the moonstone; we searched through drawers and boxes and any place that might hold a hidden gem. But at the end of our relentless search, we came up with nothing!

'I'm going to call your father, Lily ... and tell him to go through all of your mother's belongings again. It has to be there. If it's not here, where else can it be?' Mica said.

'Yes, well let's get Charlotte working on the elixir too. She needs to go through all the old paperwork that was used at the time to see if she can find the formula,' Slater added.

Mica left the room and went to call my dad while Slater called Charlotte, with such urgency in both their voices it broke my heart. Tallis slept on upstairs unaware of the turmoil we were in. I sat in the big bay window looking out at the tree-lined front garden, a second sense of impending doom and sadness creeping over me. Someone was going to have to tell Tallis what was going on and I didn't like the thought of seeing the look on his face when he heard the news. A knock at the door broke my train of thought.

There, standing in the hallway with Mica, was Olive, bags and all. I jumped up so excited to see her familiar smile and we rushed forward and slung our arms around each other.

'Oh, Lily, it's so great to see you,' she beamed.

'You too,' I said, and we hugged for a bit longer.

Mica and Olive's mum stood chatting in the hallway, and Slater moved the suitcase and backpack to the side so he could shut the door.

'Let's have some tea,' Slater said, so we headed through to the kitchen, and Mylo put the kettle on.

'How's life been treating you, Lily?' Olive's mum asked.

'Great,' I said. 'Never been happier. You're going to love New Orleans, Olive.'

'I'm so glad she'll be travelling with you instead of going alone. I was so worried about her making the trip on her own,' Olive's mum said, stroking her daughter's arm.

Olive looked embarrassed. 'Mum, I'm not a baby! Me and Lily turn eighteen soon.'

'Yes, well even so, you're still my baby no matter how old you're going to be.'

'Don't worry, Mrs Briggs. She'll be fine. We'll look after her,' said Mica with a wide, reassuring smile.

Olive's mum nodded. 'I'm sure you will,' she said. 'I'm sure she'll be fine.'

If only she knew the dangers that lay ahead of us in New Orleans, I'm not sure she'd have been so confidant in letting 'her baby' go. But I could hardly tell her that I was now living amongst about thirty vampires; that a werewolf pack was dogging my heels; that my new best friend was a mortal witch, and that we'd be staying in an old vampire townhouse containing a sealed loft with God only knew what inside it. So, I just smiled and carried on drinking my tea.

'Wow, this is a big house, Lily. And look at that garden — it's more like a park,' said Olive's mum in awe.

'Like a tour? 'I said.

'Yes please,' said Olive's mum.

We finished our tea and wandered from room to room, me throwing in one of my 'uneventful' childhood memories every now and then to break the silence. We ended up in my room at the very top of the house. Olive's mum looked out the window, looked left then right, and looked up and down the road.

'Beautiful view from up here,' she said, then she glanced at the ceiling 'Well! ... they're scary paintings,' she said. 'Did you sleep in here as a child with those above you?'

'Yep, but I don't find them scary, it's actually a scene from a real place where I live now in New Orleans.'

'Minus all the scary creatures hopefully,' she said with a slight laugh. I laughed back. *If only you knew the truth, Mrs Briggs ... if only you knew.*

Night fell and Olive's mum left us with a lot of hugs and a tearful goodbye.

'Come home safe,' she said, hugging Olive tightly.

'Don't worry, Mum, I will,' said Olive, hugging her back. Then she was gone.

'Pizza again,' said Mica. 'Is that okay? We don't have the stock to cook anything up.'

'Fine by me,' said Olive.

We slept well that night after long chats about the year that had passed. I decided I'd tell Olive some of what to expect in New Orleans, but not tonight, not until we reached the French quarter — just in case she changed her mind. She'd seen what happened in her kitchen and knew what I was capable of. She knew my uncle had died under mysterious circumstances, but this didn't seem to bother her and didn't seem to affect our friendship. I was so happy that she would be with me for my eighteenth birthday and I didn't want to risk anything changing her mind. So, I kept quiet. But I knew I'd have to tell her sooner rather than later, for her safety. She really had to know the whole truth.

The following morning when we rose, the suitcases were already in the hallway. The guys and I had tiny little cases, but Olive looked like she had an elephant in hers. She must've packed everything but the kitchen sink, but I guessed that if she was staying for six weeks, she'd need a lot of stuff. I left her in my room and headed down the stairs.

Tallis stood in the hallway looking rather subdued, so I figured the guys had filled him in on the missing moonstone. I put my arms around him and hugged him for a long time, letting him know that I knew, and that I couldn't bear to lose him. He wrapped his arms around me and hugged me back, kissing the top of my head as I lay against his chest. His heartbeat thudded near my ear, and there was no better place in the world than right here in Tallis's arms. No better feeling. I felt he had finally come to the same conclusion, as he no longer held back with his affection. He had finally caved in.

'We'll be leaving here in half an hour,' Mica shouted from the kitchen. 'Lily, make sure your package is ready to send home. We can drop it at the post office in the village on the way.'

I looked up at Tallis's handsome face and said 'Thanks, Tallis,' as I pulled away.

'Thanks for what?'

'For loving me.'

'My pleasure,' he replied, and there was that amazing grin

again.

There was just one thing I had to do before we left — not something I particularly wanted to do, but it had to be done, for my peace of mind. I stood outside my uncle's study staring at his desk and remembered my grandad's words as clearly as if it were yesterday.

'She killed my daughter, and now she's killed my son. I want her dead.'

I jolted suddenly, hearing his fist banging on the table. Even though I was only remembering, it still filled me with fear. I walked slowly towards the desk, then almost turned on my heels to walk away.

No! Do it Lily, or you'll always wonder …

I forced myself to move back towards the desk, to move around to the side to where Uncle Noah last sat. I sat down in his big leather chair and, with a feeling of great trepidation, I placed my hands on the desk in front of me. This was where he was slumped in a pool of blood. I ran my hand smoothly over the leather-topped desk; closed my eyes. I could feel all the little nicks and scratches that had been etched in by all his hard work over the years while waiting … waiting for what I thought was to come. I fought my conscience, wanting to remove my hand before the vision came. But I held it there, running it slowly back and forth. I had to know … I just had to. I squirmed inside, felt sick, expecting the worst. But there was nothing — nothing but a short vision of Uncle Noah writing at his desk deep in thought, tapping furiously at his keypad, stopping only momentarily to scribble notes on a pad before continuing to type. Not even a flicker of remembrance that had anything to do with the old Lily Du Plessis, and there I had it — my answer. Someone had ended my uncle's life … but it hadn't been me.

TO SEE YOU BURN

We'd been back in New Orleans French quarter for two whole weeks and I still hadn't told Olive anything substantial about my new life, nothing about the people in it, nor the danger I faced. I wasn't quite sure how? When we'd arrived at the townhouse all my stuff was back in place as if this is where I'd been all the time. Olive loved the house, the people, and the aromas that were just so New Orleans.

'I could live here, Lily. This place is amazing,' she'd said to me after only a day.

'Yeah, but there's more to this place than meets the eye,' I said.

'Really, in what way?' She looked at me, puzzled.

'Well, there's a lot to tell you, but I just don't know how,' I said quietly.

'Mmm … I think we've been down this road before. Who's dead this time?' she replied with a giggle.

'Yeah, true … no dead bodies. I just don't know where to start.'

'How about at the beginning,' she said. 'But of course, only if you want to. If you feel I need to be kept in the dark that's fine with me, as long as it doesn't affect my safety. I mean I kind of know what you're capable of Lily … is that what you want to talk about?'

'That … and other stuff,' I said awkwardly. 'It's probably safer if you know the truth.'

'Okay … well go for it,' said Olive, giving me her full attention.

'Well, I'm going try to sum it up, so it doesn't get too confusing, okay?'

'Okay,' she said, smiling. I wondered if she would still be smiling when I was done explaining.

'Well, basically here in New Orleans you're going hear a lot of tales about things such as vampires, witches and werewolves.'

'Okay,' she said seriously, but a nervous giggle escaped her.

'Well, they're all true. No bullshit,' I said, looking directly into her eyes and waiting for a reaction.

She didn't reply.

'My mum, who died when I was born, was a mortal witch. My dad is a vampire, and I have a whole family here in New Orleans … all vampires.' I said this as plainly as I could. 'There are werewolves here too, and they're after me. But I'm pretty well protected by the wolflings, and there's a spell around me that protects me from a guy called Briff Lestrange, who I go to school with.'

The silence was deafening so I carried on. Olive shifted uncomfortably on the bed, but still said nothing.

'I have these powers … I can set things alight, as you know. And I can enter a body and make it do what I want. I can cast spells, and when I was in England recently, a new talent came to the surface. I can touch things and see the past.'

I had never known Olive to be so quiet, but I guess it was a lot to take in.

'Oh, and also, I am supposed to fulfil a prophecy. Legend says that I will create a new race of supernaturals and unite the existing factions … once I become immortal, on my eighteenth birthday. And Tallis, the hot gardener I'm always talking about … well he was created for me as my eternal protector. He's a wolfling.'

Olive still wasn't talking, but her mouth was open so wide I felt I could throw a Malteser up in the air and she'd catch it without any effort at all.

'Oh, and my other best friend, Charlotte … she's a mortal witch too. She's amazing, you'll love her, honestly.'

Breaking her silence, Olive spoke at last, 'Anything else?'

'Nope. That's about it,' I said. 'Well, except for the loft.'

'The loft?' Her right eyebrow rose.

'Yeah. The loft in this house has been sealed since 1842 and, well, we're not quite sure what's up there, but we think it's a bad Monsanto vampire. A dead one of course.'

'Of course,' said Olive with a little scowl.

Then an uncomfortable silence filled the space between us, like she didn't know what to say next. But that was Olive. If I were with Charlotte, she would have dissected every word I'd said by now. I guess that was the difference in personalities. I guess that's why I loved Olive so much. She was not at all judgmental, and I supposed she was just processing all the information before putting her two cents worth in.

'Lily,' she said suddenly, with an understanding little smile. 'I don't know how much of this is true, and unless I see some of these things for myself, I guess I'll never know the real truth, but as your very best friend I'm just going to say *I believe in you* … if nothing else. I'll be here for you as I always have been, and I'll never judge you.'

I wasn't quite sure how to take that. I mean, what *was* she actually saying? Did she think me crazy or something? Did she think I'd just made all of that shit up?

I felt a little offended, then thought about the reality of the situation. She was just a mere human living a normal human life. What I had just told her would seem to be straight out of a novel or movie. I guess I couldn't expect too much too soon. In time she would come to know the truth as little bit by little bit I introduced her to my supernatural world.

It was nearly the end of August. My birthday was only one month away, and pretty soon we'd be attending the end of year formal. On Monday morning, the postman delivered the mail, as usual, and amongst the pile was an envelope addressed to me — a beautiful gold leaf envelope with the Monsanto family seal on the back, set in black wax. My first letter here in the French quarter and, even though it was obvious who it was from, I was a little excited. Tallis had brought it to my room and handed it to me. He looked anxious and seemed not to want to hand it over, when I tugged at it when offered it, he kept a firm grasp.

'Tallis,' I said, 'stop being an ass.'

He let go, and I sat on the bed and opened it.

It was an invitation to the school formal. In the most beautiful curly handwriting, it said:

> Dear Lily, I would be honoured if you were to accept my invitation to escort you to the Benjamin Franklin High school formal. Please advise whether you would be open to my sincere longing to share this event with such a rare beauty.
>
> Yours respectfully
>
> Alex Monsanto

Now I had a dilemma on my hands. The invite was enticing, but I really wanted to go to the formal with Tallis. Although Tallis hadn't asked me yet.

I had also invited Olive, but I needed a partner for her. Tallis still stood in the doorway, waiting expectantly.

'You know what this is?' I said to him.

Yeah, of course, he said looking slightly disappointed.

'Well, the problem I have, Tallis … is … if I say no to this invitation, I won't have a partner for the formal.'

'Well, you know I want to take you.'

He had said the words I was waiting to hear.

'And I would love you to take me, but that leaves me with a bigger problem.'

'What's that?' Then he looked across at Olive sitting by the window and seemed to get it. He nodded at me understandingly.

'I need a partner for Olive, and I can hardly offer her as a partner to Alex, even though I'd prefer to go with you. Can you imagine the danger I'd be putting her in if I sent her to the formal with Alex. She is after all only human?'

'So … you want me to partner Olive?'

'Well it makes sense, don't you think?'

'Yeah, I guess so. I can't stand the thought of Alex having his hands all over you though.'

'I swear I'll behave, Tallis. I won't let him get too close. You'll be there to watch me,' I said convincingly.

'Okay, but I'm only doing this for you, Lily, and for Olive. He's not your first choice?'

'Definitely not! He's just an alternative that solves our little problem,' I said, glancing over at Olive.

'Fine,' Tallis said. 'But he had better keep his hands to himself, or I'll be dancing on his jugular.'

'Fine,' I said, and jumping up from the bed I hugged him. He could be so lovely sometimes, being the gentle soul that he was.

That night at dinner, I gave my RSVP to Mica to deliver to the Monsanto household, and Olive and I talked about what we were going to wear. Mica said he would get Elisabeth to bring a selection of dresses from the plantation for Olive and me to try on, as she and I were the same size. This seemed the perfect option. *Olive's dark auburn curly hair, chestnut eyes and pale complexion would suit a nice blue.* So I asked Mica to bring a nice selection of colours, not just the dark colours that suited me.

'Done,' he said. 'I'll go tomorrow.'

'Thanks, Mica,' I said, gleaming with happiness.

The following afternoon Mica turned up with a car full of stunning gowns. Olive and I hurriedly carried them up to my room and threw them on the bed with excitement.

'Wow, Lily, these are amazing. Look at the detail in them — they must be so expensive.'

'Yeah, they belonged to my mum,' I said, feeling slightly proud and a little nostalgic at the same time.

For the rest of the day, we dressed up in all of the beautiful dresses, checking ourselves out in the full-length mirror. There were so many to choose from, it was extremely hard to choose. Olive, being slightly top-heavy, chose an amazing teal blue number. The gown was fitted at the waist but flowed out from the hip slightly with a beautiful deeper teal floral design down one side of the gown. The overlapping front was beautiful and not too revealing with a tiny upturned collar at the neck that framed her long, thin, white neck perfectly. *That will surely tease a few ravenous vampires, especially Alex.* I smiled.

I chose a slim-fitting, full-length black dress. It was almost plain except for a fine entwined twig-like pattern around the bottom. It swept down almost to the waistline revealing my back, with only a small tie at the neck to secure the fabric in front. With my smaller bust, it looked perfectly stylish. I had a pair of black patent leather high heels that gained me a few extra inches, so I didn't look shorter than Olive. When we stood together fully dressed looking in the mirror, I thought we looked stunning.

On the day before the formal Charlotte arrived at the townhouse, dress in tow, as she wanted my opinion. She'd chosen a shorter 50's style baby blue dress that matched her eyes, with powder blue heels and a set of navy-blue pearls, with earrings to match, and a little navy-blue leather clutch. She tried it all on for me.

'Wow, you look so lovely,' I said. 'The style of dress really suits your short hair too.'

'Yeah, you look so cute,' said Olive.

'Well, cute's not exactly what I was hoping for,' said Charlotte looking a little disappointed.

'Well, hot too,' I said quickly.

'Oh yeah, hot ... definitely hot,' said Olive, shooting me a look with eyebrows raised as Charlotte looked at herself in the mirror and smiled smugly.

Then Olive and I tried our dresses on for Charlotte.

'What do you think?' I said, smiling.

'Yeah, it's okay. Not really you though — a bit grown up, hey?' she said, glowering at me. 'And Olive, I'd be careful wearing blue with that wild colour hair if I were you. What do you think?'

'Oh, I'm quite happy with my choice, thanks,' said Olive confidently.

I wasn't too sure about my choice now I thought about it. I checked myself in the mirror. Maybe she was right about the dress. I mean I didn't want to go to the formal looking like an old maid. It felt so great on me earlier, but now I felt uncomfortable and just like Charlotte had said, 'a bit too grown-up'. I wondered how old my mum was when she wore it. I caught her looking at me in the mirror's reflection: it was a look of pure jealousy, which took me by surprise. But as I turned to look at her, she gave the biggest smile ever and said, 'Maybe save that one a few years till you're much older, hey?' I just smiled back. 'Anyway, I have to go now. Mum's waiting for me on the corner. See you tomorrow night, girls.' And with that, she was gone.

'Nice friend you have there, Lily,' Olive said after she'd gone. 'That bitch should have green eyes, not blue.'

'Green eyes?'

'She's totally jealous of you! Can't you see it? You look amazing in that dress and she can't handle it. Her comments were totally out of order. Look at yourself, Lily. You look perfect!'

I looked once more in the mirror, a little sceptically, but perhaps Olive was right. I mean, the black really suited me, and it showed off my body perfectly, and the drape at the back was very … sexy. Plus, I knew I could totally trust Olive's opinion as there wasn't an ounce of jealousy in her. I guess I couldn't be quite so sure about Charlotte's remarks being fair.

'I do look good in this, not too grown up, hey?'

'No not at all. Honestly,' said Olive, 'you look absolutely beautiful.'

She smiled at me with those big, honest chestnut eyes, and I knew it was the truth.

It was ten to seven the following evening when the big white limo drew up outside our house. Alex knocked on the door as I rushed to get my shoes on. Olive and I giggled like a pair of silly kids and made our way downstairs, both feeling a little self-conscious in our beautiful gowns. Elisabeth had stopped by to do our hair and makeup, me with bright red lipstick, Olive with glossy coral. Mica was first to the door and standing outside in a gorgeous maroon suit with black trim, black shirt and black tie, stood Alex holding a beautiful corsage. I'd never seen anything like it. It was a bracelet of three black roses on a black satin band. *Who knew there were black roses? I certainly didn't.* He stepped inside;

watched me with total admiration in his eyes as I came down the stairs.

'Oh my, Lily, you take my breath away,' he whispered as he placed the band around my wrist.

Tallis walked through from the kitchen and handed Olive a beautiful white rose corsage, which she tied around her wrist with Mica's help. Tallis nodded at Alex, acknowledging him, but there was no smile only a slight clenching of the jaw, an all too familiar trait of Tallis's. Alex nodded back with a huge smile, I guess because he felt he'd won the prize. Then we headed out to the car, slipped into the back and headed off to the ball.

It wasn't exactly a comfortable journey, and I'm not talking about the plush white leather seating. Alex and Tallis were silent the whole ride and Olive and I hardly spoke as the atmosphere was so tense. At the other end, we alighted and entered the large hall, which was packed with students, all seemingly dressed to kill. Alex went off to get me a drink, and Tallis followed him to get one for Olive. We mingled with the crowd, dancing to the band as everyone began to dance and enjoy the night. Olive and I stayed close even though we knew Alex and Tallis were unlikely to be talking. I knew that staying close to me would suit Tallis, as he was desperate to keep an eye on Alex and me. I watched the door waiting for Charlotte, and to my surprise, she came alone. She searched the floor for me and, when our eyes met, she came rushing over and dramatically swung her arms around me, as if we hadn't seen each other only yesterday.

'Oh,' she said, looking down at my dress, 'you decided not to take my advice?'

'Well it was too late in the day to find something else,' I lied.

'Okay, well I guess it will do … shame though,' she said with a slightly solemn look.

Olive, overhearing her snide remark, made a disgusting face behind her back that almost made me laugh, so I just smiled, tightly.

Tallis and Alex returned with our drinks and Alex slipped his arm around me. Tallis seemed to be keeping a slight distance between him and Olive and I hoped she didn't feel awkward about it. Although, best friend or not, I don't think I would have been very pleased had he slipped his arm around her waist, as Alex had mine.

'Charlotte?' said Alex, 'I didn't think you'd show.'

'Can't miss the end of school formal, Alex, even if your partner ditches you for a prettier girl,' she said sarcastically.

I wondered who she was talking about, but I hadn't known her long enough to know if she had a love interest. Just then a tall, curly-haired, not bad looking guy, wandered over to Charlotte. He seemed very nervous.

'Want to dance, Charlotte?' he asked bravely.

'Awe that's so sweet of you,' she said, 'but do I look like the type who would dance with a loser?' Then she flounced off in a huff, leaving him standing dejected and red-faced.

'Bitter piece of work that one,' said Alex, watching her go, and I nodded in agreement.

'You never know, Alex, he could be the one who dumped her. She might be upset, and he may have deserved that.'

'Ahh, Lily, your propensity to always see the good in people astounds me.'

'Not always,' I remarked smartly. 'I quite often see the bad in you.'

He smiled wickedly and laughed out loud.

I watched Charlotte standing alone by the bar and felt sorry for her. Still, I had to admit that the bitchy side of Charlotte certainly seemed to be scratching the surface a lot lately. Across the room, I could see Briff standing with his friends, giving me a nasty stare, but he didn't faze me. I was here with the wolfling, and I also had the added benefit of Charlotte's protection spell so felt quietly confident that, if he attacked, the barrier would appear to protect me. I felt even more confident knowing that he knew that too. After the incident outside the library, how could he not, so I just smiled sweetly at him and danced on with Alex. This seemed to wind him up, and he glared at me through the crowd. But I wasn't going to let him spoil my night. I turned away and ignored him showing only my backless dress, which seemed to impress his friends if not him because I heard a few loud wolf whistles in the distance.

'Causing quite a stir in that little number,' said Alex with a proud smile.

'Thanks, Alex,' I said.

'You look beautiful,' said Tallis.

'Keep your comments for your own date,' Alex responded, glaring at Tallis, and then he spun me softly around so Tallis couldn't look at me anymore.

Towards the end of the night, I had to visit the Lady's Room. Olive came with me and, as we came back out into the hallway, Briff was standing there.

'Look at you, all up yourself,' he snarled. But I knew he couldn't touch me, so I just carried on walking. 'Bet you feel all special dancing with that Monsanto vampire creep, hey? Bet you don't know what his agenda is.'

'Well I'm sure I can work that out for myself,' I said. 'And if you're saying he's after my body, you're probably right, but that doesn't mean he'll be getting it.'

'Your body,' he said, laughing. 'He wants more than that, Lily.

He wants your family dead. Who do you think tipped us off about the Monsanto masquerade ball? How do you think we knew the Du Plessis would be there? He wants you all right. He wants you all to himself, and when he helps us wipe out your entire family, he'll be your only option, sad little vampire girl. Personally, I don't see what the attraction is?' And with that, he smirked and walked off back towards the dance floor.

And I just stood there, so shocked I couldn't move. I stared at Olive, my eyes wide with disbelief.

'Briff?' she said.

'Yeah,' I nodded.

'Could just be stirring trouble, Lily. Think carefully before you do anything crazy.'

I stood a moment longer, unsure how to feel. I felt foolish and oh-so pissed off. I had to leave, now, before my fury took over and got the better of me. I couldn't lose it. Not here. Not in front of all these humans. I breathed heavily, and Olive looked really worried, like she was remembering the incident in her kitchen.

'Maybe we'd better leave,' she said quietly. 'Perhaps now would be a good time.'

We walked back out onto the dance floor. Alex smiled at me and I brushed past him, ignoring him as best I could. I couldn't face him now — couldn't have it out with him. It was way too dangerous as I could feel the familiar symptoms of rage — my hands heating up — my blood boiling inside like a volcano about to erupt. I grabbed Tallis's arm and dragged him across the room and out the main doors, across the front grass and down to the road. Olive followed as quickly as her feet would carry her.

'What's going on, Lily?' Tallis asked, frowning. 'What's wrong?'

Breathe in. Breath out. Breath in ... breath out ... Calm the storm. Just breathe.

I couldn't speak so Olive spoke for me. 'Briff, that's what happened,' she said.

'That bastard!' Tallis shouted and tried to march off towards the hall. I rushed after him stopping him sharply. All I could think was that there was no elixir, no moonstone, and I simply couldn't allow him to fight for me.

'No, Tallis, not Briff. Alex!' I said, but I couldn't explain anymore. 'I just need to get away. Please ... *please*,' I pleaded with him.

Then I saw Mica running from the left and Slater drew up in front of the school in his car.

'Lily?' Mica shouted. 'What happened? We didn't see anything,'

'Nothing happened,' said Olive. 'It was just something that was said. Come on, let's get her home!'

We jumped in the car and Tallis held me close trying to calm me. It seemed to work, as if his inner peace transferred through to me as our skin touched. Or maybe it was just getting away from Alex that helped. I don't know what it was, but the rage subsided and the threat was gone. When we arrived home, there were, of course, twenty questions, which Olive answered as best she could because I didn't want to talk about it. I just wanted to sleep. I wanted the night to be over. One thing I knew for sure, my little dalliance with Alex Monsanto was over. I never wanted to see his face again, without wanting to watch it burn and turn to ash.

THESE FOOLISH THINGS

The following morning, my mood was no better. I was so angry at what I had already surmised. The Monsanto's friendship was completely false. My dad was right, they didn't want to hurt me, but they wanted me to join their ranks. They wanted my powers for their own use, and it seemed like they would do anything possible to secure my allegiance. Maybe Emmanuelle was to blame. Maybe he was trying to set me up with Alex. Maybe he was desperate to bring me into the fold. *And Alex … is he just using me? Are his affections in any way real?*

I thought back to the kiss the night of the masquerade ball. It had felt so real. I was sure his feelings for me were undeniably true that night, but now I wasn't so sure. Charlotte had warned me about him; she'd told me he was a player — warned me to stay away. She obviously knew something I didn't — more than she was letting on. I remembered the flirtatious look he had given the other woman on the dance floor when he was dancing with me, and suddenly I felt like a complete idiot. Well, he wouldn't be getting a second chance. I wrote a note in my diary under the date of the formal, to remind me not to be such a fool in future. Alex was right about me. I did have a propensity to always see the good in people, even if it wasn't there. A willingness to forgive also ran through my veins like golden thread, but I knew this was something I could never forgive, no matter what. Alex had played with my heart for the first and last time.

With this in mind, my mood started to lift. I hopped out of bed. Olive and I went down to breakfast, the smell of freshly cooked French toast wafting up the stairwell tempting our taste buds.

'I'm starving, aren't you?' said Olive.

'Sure am,' I said.

'Feeling better this morning?'

'Yeah, I'm getting there.' I smiled weakly.

'You really scared me last night. I thought you were going to burn the bloody school down.'

'Nah, I'm learning to control my outbursts, and as much as I hate math, I have no intention of destroying my school,' I said with a laugh.

'Good.' She smiled back.

We sat and ate until we were full, and Mica asked, 'What are you young ladies up to today then?'

'Don't know yet? But I'm sure we'll find something to occupy us,' I replied.

'Well, Charlotte called early this morning to see how you were. She's coming over to stay for a couple of days. She kind of invited herself and I wasn't able to say no. She's very persistent that one.'

'Damn!' Olive said, exasperated.

'Oh, she's not so bad, a little bit up and down but she does have her good points,' I said.

'Well, I've been here a couple of weeks and I've yet to see any,' said Olive.

Mica laughed. 'Teenagers!' He threw his hands in the air.

A few hours later, Charlotte arrived, carrying a weekend bag. She didn't even knock, just walked right in. That was Charlotte for you.

It was a beautiful sunny day, and we put our bikinis on and lay out in the garden on towels, catching some rays. Mica made us some amazing iced lemonade, and we covered ourselves in sun lotion and lay there like strips of bacon sizzling in the afternoon sunshine.

'So, what happened last night?' Charlotte finally asked.

'Oh, just something Briff said to me. I'm over it now,' I replied.

'Thank God,' said Olive.

'Alex was really upset when you left, you know,' Charlotte said.

'I don't want to talk about Alex,' I said firmly.

'Why? Has he done something wrong?' Charlotte pried.

'Let's just say you were right about him, Charlotte. I should've listened to you when you told me to steer clear of him.'

'Well, what did he do?' she pressed the point again.

Olive looked at me as if to say, 'Does she ever give up?' and I gave her a look back that said 'No, she's relentless'. Olive sighed.

'Briff told me that Alex set my family up at the masquerade ball. He said the Monsanto's want to wipe them out, that Alex wants me all for himself.'

'Surely not,' said Charlotte, looking shocked. 'Alex may be a player, Lily, but I don't believe Briff. He's just trying to cause trouble I bet.'

'I don't know, but I think he was telling the truth. Anyway, I can't trust Alex now and I don't want anything to do with him.'

Charlotte smiled. It seemed a strange reaction to what I had just said, a little out of context.

'He'll be heartbroken, Lily. He really has a thing for you.' It was then I realised what she was thinking — *finally the player gets played*. It was his heart on the line now, not some vulnerable teenage girls, and I totally got her out of context smile.

'If you see him around you can tell him from me that I know what he did, and that I don't want to see him again … ever!'

'Message received loud and clear,' she said and smiled again — a wicked little smile that made her eyes twinkle.

After tea that night, we were up in my room and for the first time Olive and Charlotte seemed to be getting along. They sat chatting about Olive's home and family, which seemed to really interest Charlotte. Usually with her, you couldn't get a word in edgeways, but she sat listening quietly. But then Olive did know how to tell a good tale, and her life was so mad and interesting who wouldn't be enthralled.

'You should've brought your twin brother with you, Olive. He sounds like hot stuff, and we could do with some new testosterone around these parts.'

That was what had caught Charlotte's interest, the thought of fresh relationship material. *Was she boy mad?* This made me smile.

'Frankie is adorable,' I said. 'You'll have to bring him over, Olive. We'll introduce him to you one day, Charlotte.' She nodded eagerly.

'Let's watch *10 Things I Hate About You*, it's my favourite movie,' I said.

'Okay,' said Olive. 'But we'll have to get our pjs on, and have you got any face packs?'

'Bound to have, I'll check in the bathroom.'

'Well, if we're going to watch that old movie, we'd better do it right,' Olive said.

'Better steal some of Slater's ciggies then, if we're really going to do it right,' said Charlotte.

'Oh, I so had the hots for Heath Ledger,' said Olive.

'I sure did too,' I said dreamily.

'Ugh! No,' said Charlotte screwing her nose up.

Charlotte skipped off downstairs to pinch some cigarettes and

I searched through the bathroom cabinets for face packs while Olive set up the Blu-ray ready for the movie.

'This is more like it. This is what we should be doing at our age. Not fighting with boys and putting our hearts out there to be trampled,' Charlotte said, coming back into the room.

'Well, I guess that depends on your choice of boy,' I said. 'They're not all Alex's out there. Some of them are just like Tallis.'

'Yeah, you're absolutely right there,' said Olive.

'Well, I don't seem to have much luck with boys. Sometimes I forget to turn my douche bag radar on. Looks like I'll have to get me a Tallis,' said Charlotte.

Olive and I frowned at her.

'What?' Charlotte said innocently. Then we all giggled and snuck out onto the balcony for our first taste of tobacco.

Charlotte seemed to be a pro at it and she sat there smoking, looking rather grown up while Olive and I spluttered and coughed and tried to look cool.

'Oh, I don't think this is for me,' I said. 'It actually tastes disgusting!'

'Don't be a baby,' Charlotte quipped back. 'It tastes alright once you've had a few.'

'Yeah,' said Olive. 'I guess it's alright?'

We smoked a few more then we went back inside and put out our pjs and put face masks on. Boy, we sure looked crazy, but were having a good time. Charlotte clicked 'Play' and we sat watching the movie for the rest of the night until our faces had gone as hard as rock. With all the giggling our masks cracked, and we looked like ancient mummies.

'Let's make a pact,' I said. 'Let's never let anything spoil this friendship. Let's vow to be friends forever, to be there for each other even when boys come along. Let's never fight over them.

Let's always be true to each other.'

'Done,' said Olive.

'Oh, I don't know ... The boy thing is pushing it a bit too far, don't you think? I mean, love should always come first,' said Charlotte.

Olive and I looked at her, shocked.

'Joking!' she said, 'I'm just joking.'

But Olive and I looked at her with eyebrows hiked, not so sure.

Later that night when the movie finished, we cleaned our faces as quietly as possible as the house was dark and silent, so we figured the guys had gone to bed.

'You know what we were talking about in the library before the holidays?' Charlotte said.

'No? Refresh my memory,' I said.

'We were talking about having a look at what's in the loft, remember?'

'Oh yeah, I do remember, but I'm not so keen now, what with Olive here and all. I mean, she is human. What if it's something bad up there?'

'We know what it is, Lily. We did the research, remember — it's just a dead Monsanto vampire. Dead vampires can't hurt anyone.'

'If it's dead what's the point in looking?' I said, trying my hardest to find an excuse *not* to unseal the loft. But Charlotte persisted as always.

'What do you think, Olive? Wouldn't you like to see a vampire? A dead one of course.'

'Mmm, I don't know,' Olive said, looking a little nervous. 'What if it comes to life?'

'Olive, don't be stupid. It's been sealed in there since 1842. Do you really think there'll be anything but pointy teeth and bones up there?' Charlotte rolled her eyes.

'Okay,' I said, relenting because Charlotte certainly didn't seem as though she was going to give up.

'I tell you what,' said Charlotte, 'if it makes it safer for Olive, I'll do a protection spell over her so the vampire can't touch her. We'll mask her body odour, so she'll smell like rotting fish — just in case.'

'But you said you were sure it was dead,' Olive said.

'Yeah, it will be — but just to be on the safe side,' Charlotte replied flippantly.

'Okay,' said Olive.

So back in the room, Charlotte unpacked her bag. Seems like she had everything she needed in there — she had come prepared. *How sly! She knew she would talk us into it. When she wants something, she's relentless!*

Charlotte gathered her bits and sat them in front of Olive.

'How do you know it will work?' Olive said, looking perplexed.

'Oh, it'll definitely work,' said Charlotte. 'I'm good at this protection stuff — just ask Lily.' She looked over at me for confirmation. And I had to agree, because so far, she'd succeeded in protecting me from Briff. I nodded calmly at Olive and then Charlotte cast her spell. Then she gathered a few jars containing herbs and other strange things, plus a little black book, and we headed out into the hallway, through the door to the stairwell and up to the landing underneath the loft hatch. The chain hung from the hatch, bound tightly around and around, connecting link by solid link with no visible lock. Charlotte spread everything out directly underneath the hatch. She unfolded and laid out a cloth with a pentacle in the middle. At each point was a tiny emblem, and in the middle, she placed a bowl. On each corner, she poured either a powder, or laid a small bunch of herbs in place, then into the bowl she placed a dead frog and a rose — a black rose.

'Where did you get the black rose?' I asked suddenly,

remembering the black rose corsage Alex had given me.

'They come from a place called Halfeti in Turkey, the only place in the world where they grow naturally. They have very strong binding powers, and if one was used to seal this loft, it will unseal it too, if I can reverse the binding spell.'

I felt sick all of a sudden and wondered whether Alex was using the black rose corsage to bind me to him in some way. I shuddered at the thought.

'What's wrong?' Olive said.

'Oh nothing. It's just that Alex gave me a black rose corsage for the formal. It's still in my room.'

'Sneaky git,' said Charlotte. 'Get rid of it as soon as possible or he'll use it to his advantage, I can promise you that.'

'I will,' I said, 'for sure.'

Then Charlotte began. She started chanting, and swaying back and forth. Olive giggled and I nudged her. This was just a game to her. I could see she didn't believe there was any real truth to this whole witchcraft thing. But then what proof did she have that Charlotte was actually a witch, Briff, a werewolf, Tallis, a wolfling, or Alex, a vampire, when in front of her they hid their true selves so cleverly? For Olive, I guess this was like telling ghost stories in the dark on school camp, scary but generally all make-believe. Charlotte finished up but the chain didn't budge. She tugged at it, but it just bound itself even more tightly around the loft handles.

'Argh!! What did I do wrong?' she said, checking the cloth below, re-reading the unbinding spell from the little black book. She sat looking angry and confused. 'I don't get it,' she said. 'I did everything just as it says. I used all the correct ingredients. Do you know how hard it is to come across a black rose?' She shook her head in dismay.

'Not really,' I said. 'There are three down in my room if you need more.'

'Yeah, well, let me tell you, they are like gold dust. So, Alex would have gone well out of his way to acquire them. Just shows you how much he wants to be with you,' snapped Charlotte, then she gathered her stuff and sauntered off down to my room. *Sulking.* I don't know whether she was sulking because the spell hadn't worked or because Alex had bought me black roses. *Maybe she has a little crush on him, Just maybe.*

'Maybe the spell will work,' I said, trying to cheer her up. 'I mean, look at the summoning spell I did. It took a whole day to work.'

She smiled at this, as if there were some chance I might actually be right.

'We'll see,' she said.

'Let's get some sleep then, hey?' Olive suggested.

'Yes, let's,' I agreed.

'Okay, so where shall I bunk?' Charlotte said. 'No room for three in this bed.'

'There's a spare room up the hall, if that's okay?' I said.

'Fine by me,' said Charlotte. 'Point me in the right direction.'

I showed her to the room down the hall, on the other side of the bathroom, and when she was all settled in, I went back to my own room.

'You don't really believe in all that stuff she did ... do you?' Olive asked.

'Oh, Olive, if only you knew ... if only,' I said, smiling at her.

At this point, there was no point in trying to persuade her that the supernatural existed. But I was sure that at some point she would find out for herself.

We awoke early on Sunday morning and headed out with the team for brunch. It was such a lovely sunny day, and the eggs

Creole were cooked up simply perfect. In the background, one of my favourite songs was playing, *These Foolish Things*. A bit of an old classic and one I recognised from my mum's vinyl collection. It reminded me of my bedroom in England. But it also made me think deeply about being screwed over by someone you love. Sitting in the alfresco area, I suddenly noticed a figure walking towards me. It was Alex, and before I knew it, he was standing right beside me. I looked down at my napkin trying to avoid looking up at him. It was so hard. I felt so drawn to him, but I considered that it might have something to do with the black rose corsage, so adamantly kept my eyes averted and refused to acknowledge him.

'Lily,' he said sharply, 'follow me. I want to talk to you.' This said with authority, commanding me to do as he wanted. It was so strange because I had to fight the urge to do as he said. It was a real internal struggle of mind over matter, but I sat, trying to make myself smaller, less visible, and ignored him.

'Lily, I mean it!' he barked.

'Can't you see she's not interested,' Charlotte quipped. 'Go find some other chick to play with why don't you?'

He glared at her and moved closer to the table. I edged my chair in closer to Tallis, and he moved his chair over slightly and put his arm around me.

'I see how it is,' said Alex glaring at Tallis.

'If you see correctly then you'll know there's *nothing* here for you, Alex,' Charlotte spurned him. He turned on her and bared his fangs, his beautiful green eyes glazing over until they were almost hauntingly black, pulsating veins of fierce red blood on the surface of his usually beautiful porcelain face. These effects disappeared in almost an instant as he realised he'd lost control in public, and quickly regained his composure. Olive froze, a look of absolute horror marring her face. But it was also a look of stark realisation that at least one of the myths I'd told her was true.

'Shut your mouth, Charlotte,' Alex menaced, then Mica and Slater stood up, warning him with their stance.

'Come on, enough now, Alex. We're just out for a peaceful Sunday brunch. Don't want any trouble now do we, not in such a public place,' said Mica with a friendly smile.

'Whatever!' Alex muttered as he turned to leave. 'But you haven't seen the last of me, Lily Du Plessis.' He glared at me with those startling green eyes, and for the first time I looked up and bravely said, 'I sincerely hope you're wrong.'

He stood looking suddenly lost, and I almost felt sorry for him. *Stupid, stupid me, what on earth is wrong with me?*

Our eyes met momentarily, but he never said another word, simply turned away from me with a bitter look on his face and stormed off into the Sunday morning market crowds. Once the danger had left, Tallis removed his arm from my shoulders, but I didn't move my chair. I felt so safe with Tallis, so comfortable.

It was quite funny really because Charlotte, being the flirtatious creature she was, spent the whole of brunch flirting madly with Tallis. She batted her eyelashes and talked herself up, as if she were really something special — a prize catch — trying desperately to impress him, right in front of me, without any regard for my feelings. Olive couldn't believe it, and I could read the anger in her eyes. But it didn't bother me. I knew full well Tallis only had eyes for me, and even in 'that' he showed restraint. He was no pushover when it came to girls, and being created perfectly for me made him as loyal as the day was long. He basically ignored all of Charlotte's advances and at one point even suggested out loud and quite boldly that she remove her hand from his leg. She was touching him under the table. She flushed bright red when he brought this to everyone's attention.

When brunch was over, we made our way back home, Charlotte sulking all the way and Olive still savouring the moment that Tallis had exposed her. I knew Charlotte was an odd creature, but there was still something about her I liked. I couldn't shake the feeling that somewhere deep down she was a decent human being, although she was also a mortal witch with powers of course. Something must have happened in her life for her to turn out this way … *We all carry baggage. Maybe Charlotte's is a little bit heavier than ours.*

RED DRAGONS AND INK

My birthday was just over a week away and I was excited. Emmanuelle Monsanto had offered to hold my eighteenth birthday at his house in his beautiful ballroom but, as stunning as it was, I declined, gracefully saying I just wanted a quiet family affair. I guess this would have offended him, but I didn't care. For all I knew he could have been planning to set my family up for another fall. Plus, I absolutely had to steer clear of Alex. I couldn't trust myself around him and did not want to put myself in a position where I could give in to his charms.

For some reason, we didn't see a lot of Charlotte that week. Maybe she felt deflated after her attempt at wooing Tallis had failed, but she seemed to be keeping her distance. I called my dad and suggested we have my birthday at the plantation. He was so happy with my choice and made me a promise that Olive would be safe. He would talk to the whole family and make sure they fully understood that Olive was totally out of bounds. Anyway, I told him in no uncertain terms there'd be nobody 'midnight snacking' on my best friend or they'd have me to deal with, so he'd better be firm about it.

'I promise, Lily,' he said with a laugh. 'I was a bit worried that you would accept Emmanuelle's invitation then I'm not sure I could have promised you anything. But the Du Plessis have been trying to control their lust for human blood since the day they were born.

Why do you think we breed rabbits?'

I giggled and smiled.

'Okay, I'll trust you. But if something bad happens to her I can't be held responsible for my actions, okay?'

'Okay darling. But don't you worry. We'll all be on our best behaviour. If anyone spoils your eighteenth birthday, I'll kill them myself.'

'Thanks, Dad,' I said lovingly.

'Anything for you, Lily,' he replied.

My birthday was now just a few days away! Soon I would be eighteen. And my best friend in the world, Olive, would be there to share it with me. I would be surrounded by my family — a family I had longed for my whole life — and to top it all, Tallis and I were now officially an item. Although we had secretly been seeing each other for some time, I couldn't wait to tell my dad and Marchella the news. I knew they'd approve. They couldn't possibly find anything about Tallis to dislike. They were sure to love him as much as I did. He certainly had Olive's stamp of approval and that meant a whole lot to me. I loved him so much that I sometimes felt that, although he'd been created for me, I might have been created for him.

Olive and I had a rather busy week, and I was constantly on the phone to Marchella, making sure all the arrangements were coming together.

'Lily, darling,' she said, 'what colour scheme would you like? What colour dress are you wearing? Help me out here. I want everything to be perfect.'

'Well, actually I'm wearing a short cream satin dress so you can pretty much go with any colour theme you like. I have grey crocodile leather high heels and a clutch to match. I wanted to keep it simple. After all, it's just going to be a family affair.'

'Oh, but, Lily, you only turn eighteen once, and for you, it's a most important day. The day you reach your immortality. Did you not invite the Monsantos?'

'No, Marchella! I don't want them there. I only want close friends and family I can trust.'

'Okay,' she sighed. 'But I have ordered a massive cake.'

'Really?'

'Oh, indulge me, Lily. This is the last birthday you'll ever have.'

'What do you mean?' I asked.

'When you turn immortal on your eighteenth, you'll remain that age forever. Immortals never pass their eighteenth year.'

'Oh,' I said, a bit surprised by this news. 'Well, I guess I could mentally note the years as they pass by, so I'll always kind of know exactly how old I am.'

'Yes, you could do that. But trust me, when you get into the hundreds you'll stop counting, or you'll start to feel really ancient.'

I said goodbye and put the phone down. Then I had a dreadful thought. Olive would grow old and die and I would still be eighteen. Sure, all my family would live this eternal life with me if they were careful enough, and hopefully Tallis too, but even that I couldn't be sure of. If only we could recreate the elixir, or eventually locate his moonstone, I would be able to relax, knowing he would always be by my side. But Olive … there was no hope for her. She was merely human, and I wondered whether the years that would come between us would change the dynamics of our close friendship. I couldn't imagine not having Olive to turn to, and as I thought about her dying, a lump appeared in my throat and my eyes welled with tears. Becoming Immortal was certainly going to have its drawbacks. Living through the lives' and deaths of people I loved would be the worst part of it, and I wondered if I would ever get to a point in my life where I would beg for the grave myself.

On the morning of my birthday, I woke feeling vibrant and more alive than ever. The sunlight seemed brighter, and the simplest of things seemed so much more beautiful to me. Even the breeze from my open window felt like silk brushing across my skin, bringing my senses fully to life. I turned over, expecting to see Olive lying next to me, but the bed was empty. Fully awake now, I stared at the open window — the window that was firmly closed last night. It was now wide open, and Olive was gone! I swung out of bed feeling sick and rushed out to the balcony with newly acquired speed, searching for Olive. She was nowhere. Alex immediately came to mind and terror filled me. *Has he taken Olive to spite me? What can I do? What if he turns her, or worse, kills her?* I trembled with fear. Then anger replaced it. I vowed I would find her and kill Alex, *even though he's already dead.* I spun around and rushed back into the room, my temper rising. And ran bang splat straight into Olive. She stood there with her fiery red hair a ball of mess, tired eyes and a shocked expression.

'Woah,' she said. 'Feet on fire?'

I wrapped my arms around her, so relieved. 'Almost,' I said, still hugging her. I could have cried I was so happy.

'What's that for?' she said with a giggle. 'Missed me while I was peeing, did you?'

'Oh, you don't know the half of it,' I said, mustering a smile.

'Anyway, Happy Birthday, Lily,' she said, hugging me tighter. 'If the tales you've been filling me with are true, you are now truly immortal. You made it! Now go forth and procreate.'

'Procreate?' I said.

'Yes, doesn't the legend say you're going to start a new race?' She smiled then laughed, tussled my hair and jumped on the bed.

Reaching over to her drawer, she pulled something out.

'This is for the birthday girl,' she said, handing a card and a small present to me.

'Awww, thanks, Olive.' I opened the card. On the front it said: 'To my beautiful sister', and inside a beautiful rhyme about sister's being inseparable. It made me want to cry. I opened the present and inside was a small box. Inside the box was a silver chain with half of a heart with the word *Forever* engraved on it.

'I have the other half,' Olive said, showing me her necklace. On her half was engraved the word *Friends*.

'It's beautiful. Thank you, Olive,' I said, putting the necklace on. I ran my hand over the writing ... *Forever. If only* ...

At breakfast, the guys had made an enormous effort. They had laid on a massive spread with all the usual fried breakfast stuff but also amazing homemade pancakes with strawberry jam and cream as well. I was one spoilt birthday girl. Mica and Slater gave me a present between them. It was a framed picture of the plantation house with my family all standing out the front. It was my first family photo with all the Du Plessis together. At the bottom of the frame, a quote said in beautiful script, *Home is where the heart is*. I simply loved it. Tallis handed me his present. When I opened it there was an old vinyl record, *Frankie Valli and the Four Seasons*, and tucked inside two tickets to a show, *Jersey Boys,* plus two flight tickets to New York.

'Wow, Tallis!'

'Thought you'd like to see the show. It's one of my favourites, and I know you appreciate the old stuff,' he said with a smile. I leant across the table and kissed him on the lips, raising a few eyebrows and making him blush slightly. 'Thanks, Tallis. It's a fantastic present, but New York?' I said excitedly.

'Yeah, the place where we first kissed,' he said with his cute lopsided grin, blushing slightly again.

I just smiled, remembering.

'Oh, really?' said Mica. 'Kept that one a bit quiet, didn't ya, hey?' He nudged Tallis playfully with his elbow.

'Well,' said Slater, 'if it's meant to be, it's meant to be.'

I smiled at Tallis as his alluring blue eyes met mine. Then we all tucked into my wonderful birthday breakfast. There was a loud knock at the door and Slater went to open it. It was my dad and Marchella. They walked through to the kitchen, Marchella carrying a huge box, which she placed on the kitchen bench.

'Happy birthday, darling,' she said, hugging me, slightly less like an ironing board now she'd become accustomed to my hugs.

'For you,' she said, pointing to the huge, coffin-like box on the kitchen bench.

'I hope it isn't meant for me to sleep in,' I joked.

'No darling. Don't be silly. It's not big enough for you.' Obviously, her sense of humour hadn't quite caught up with her hugging skills.

Then my dad hugged me and handed me a small black box tied with a red ribbon. Inside was a silver and ruby signet ring. On the head of the ring lay a sleeping dragon, curled completely around the outside of the inset ruby, as if guarding it with its life.

'Woah! That's stunning,' I said.

'It's our family emblem from the Order of the Red Dragon,' said Marchella. 'And something that will become a family heirloom with time.'

'Vlad Tepes Dracula himself once wore one of these rings. It denotes our family's bloodline. See, I wear one myself,' Dad said, flashing his gold ring at me. It had the same dragon curled around the top like mine, but his ring was all gold with a black onyx inset. I liked my one the most. With the dragon set on the ruby back stone, it was stunningly beautiful.

'Thanks, Dad. It fits perfectly,' I said, slipping it onto my finger.

'A perfect gift for a perfect girl,' he said, smiling.

'And I guess this is Olive?' Marchella said, gesturing towards her.

'Yes, my *best* friend in all the world,' I said boldly, stressing her importance to me.

'Pleased to meet you, Olive. You smell nice,' Marchella said, holding out her hand.

I shot her a look, but her eyes didn't meet mine — they were glued on Olive.

'Likewise,' said Olive, shaking it.

'Yes, it's lovely to finally meet you, Olive. We've heard so much about you,' my dad said, subtly moving in-between them.

'All good I hope?' Olive responded.

'All exceptionally good.' Dad smiled.

Then they joined us at the table. The guys and Olive and I tucked in, and Marchella and my dad just sat chatting. Olive offered Marchella a plate of pancakes.

She just laughed.

'Oh sorry ... I forgot you don't eat,' Olive said awkwardly.

'Oh, we eat,' said Marchella with a slight smile. 'But the only thing in this kitchen our kind would be interested in is out of bounds.'

I shot Marchella a surprised look, and Olive laughed thinking Marchella was joking. Little did she know that humour simply wasn't Marchella's thing.

'Forgive us, Olive,' my dad said. 'We are not used to spending solid time around new humans. You smell quite delightful, and there's only so many rabbits one can consume before it becomes tiresome.' I shot him a look of disbelief and frowned deeply.

'That's okay,' said Olive. 'I guess it can't be helped.'

'We'll be leaving now,' said Marchella. 'Oh, by the way, your uncle is joining us for your birthday, Lily. He's been away at Yale but he's coming to your party, especially to meet you.'

'My uncle? I didn't know I had another uncle.'

'My brother Caleb,' my dad said. 'He's a bit younger than me; he stopped ageing at twenty-three.'

'Yes, and he's totally gorgeous, isn't he, Eli?' Marchella said softly.

'Mother, you do exaggerate,' said my father. 'Nobody's more gorgeous than me, other than Lily, of course,' he said, smiling sweetly at me.

They left the house after hugging me, but thankfully seemed to keep a safe distance from Olive, just as they had promised.

'See you tonight, darling. I hope you like your present,' Marchella said.

'I'm sure I will. You have such good taste.'

I waved goodbye then Olive and I headed up to my room, dragging the huge box up the stairs between us. In my room, I opened it and inside was a black dress, short but ruffled at the knee with layers of tulle underneath. Fitted at the top with thin straps and tiny Swarovski crystals sewn into the bust, it was stunning. Underneath was another smaller box with a pair of patent black leather, red-bottomed stilettos with heels so sharp they could be used as a weapon.

'Wow! They are the coolest shoes I've ever laid eyes on,' said Olive.

'They're fantastic!' I said, trying them on.

'Try them with the dress,' said Olive.

I did, and when I looked in the mirror, I felt amazing. Marchella knew just what suited me, and this, I had to admit, was much more appropriate an outfit for my eighteenth. My very last birthday!

'Can I wear the cream satin dress you were originally going to wear then?' Olive asked.

'Of course,' I said. 'It'll look lovely on you.'

'Thanks,' said Olive, beaming.

I changed back into my track pants and we lounged around on the bed chatting.

'Let's sit out on the balcony and get a bit of sun on our legs,' Olive suggested.

'Sure, why not?' We grabbed our coffees and went to sit outside. On the little table at the end, I noticed something that wasn't there that morning. A single rose. But not a red one this time, a black one with a red bow around it and a little note that said:

> 'You have it all wrong, please forgive me. Happy 18th ImmortaLily'

I felt a pang of sadness at his words, but not sad enough, and now he had given me a nickname too ... ImmortaLily. *How weird, although quite appropriate,* I thought. I held the note and the rose for a moment then threw the rose over the balcony. There'd be no more black roses binding me to him. Not if I could help it. I'd guessed he'd keep trying to worm his way back in, but little did he know that I now knew the power of the black rose — there was no way I was going to be sucked in by his charms again. I was with Tallis now. He was a one-girl guy, just like it should be, and I was determined to remain loyal to him.

'Got a real thing about those black roses, haven't you, Lily?' Olive said, looking a little disturbed that I'd just chucked it over the balcony with abandon.

'Yep, they're not my favourite, because now they remind me of Alex.'

'Fair enough.' She glanced over the balcony just in time to see the rose crushed beneath the wheels of a passing car.

All of a sudden, I remembered the most important thing. *The parcel from my mum!* I jumped up, scaring the crap out of Olive and ran to my bed. Scrambling underneath to pull up the floorboard, I pulled out the tin and the package.

'I'd totally forgotten about this, Olive,' I said excitedly.

'What is it?'

'Oh, don't worry about the tin, that just holds a small fortune. It's the parcel that's important. My Uncle Noah gave it to me just before he died. He told me not to open it until today.'

'And you did as you were told? How did you manage that? I'm always sneaking a peek at Christmas presents before Christmas day. I can't help it. But you've had this for a year and not even sneaked a peak?'

'Well, to be honest, I did try a little while ago, but it wouldn't let me open it. Sounds strange but it's true. It just kept wrapping itself back up.'

'That's crazy! Well, try again now.'

'Yeah, it should work ... it is my birthday after all.'

I pulled the parcel close to me and peeled the wrapping gently, waiting to see if it would close up again. But no, I could peel back the layers, and did one after the other until I came to the contents. It was a wooden box, and on the lid, a red crest encased in silver, engraved into the wood. There was a circle within a circle and a sword running through the middle with a red dragon either side of the sword facing one another, their wings splayed out on either side. Within the rim of the circle at the top, it said *Ordo Dracul,* and at the bottom *Transylvania.* A small coat of arms in the middle of the sword between the two dragons displayed the letter D. I looked down at my ring, remembering my dad's words about the Order of the Red Dragon. *This must be our family crest!* I thought, running my hand over the top of it. I opened the lid and inside was a letter and a small glass bottle filled with what looked like black paint. *A strange gift*, I thought, holding it up to the light. It moved fluidly — *thinner than paint*. The lid of the bottle was sealed tightly with red wax. I placed the bottle back in the box and opened the letter.

My dearest Lily,

If you are reading this letter, then congratulations are in order. You have made it to your eighteenth birthday, and therefore you are now truly 'Immortal.' Everything I had hoped and wished for you can now come to pass.

The glass bottle within the box is a gift from me for your birthday. It contains an ink mixed with my blood and, when used, this will impart all of my wisdom of the craft into you, filling you with my life learned knowledge and experience of magic.

There is an address on the back of this envelope for you to visit. A dear friend of ours will be expecting you there, and he will use the ink for your half-sleeve.

Along with all the good morals, let's hope there's a little bit of rebel in you somewhere, and that a tattoo doesn't offend you too greatly, as magic is a powerful tool. Without it, the covens will be able to seal you away. They cannot kill you but sealing away can be just as long term as death itself. With my magical abilities inside you, this cannot happen. My imparted wisdom and your immortality will make you stronger than any coven you may come up against.

In case you have made it this far but lost most of those around you, I will fill you in as best as I can on the details of your existence and the reason for it. You were created Lily, created by your dad and I to fulfil a prophecy. As an immortal, you will be a most powerful being, with few enemies and possibly no other that can match your powers.

With your uncle's upbringing, your dad's goodness, and my strong emotions in you, I believe you would have grown into a most wondrous creature, fair and moral with a strong sense of right and wrong. This can be put to good use in the pursuit of a perfect world.

So many supernaturals abuse the powers they are given, and there is constant war between most factions. Century by century there is more devastation caused by wickedness in one form or another, and a new stronger race would solve all of these problems.

There will still be those supernaturals who oppose the change and the restrictions that will be placed upon them, but the killing of innocents has to stop, and the fighting has to cease. You could be the bringer of eternal peace, and there will be none strong enough to go against your will.

Whatever you want in life, Lily, you will be

blessed with, and with all the resources available to you, you will be more than capable of changing this world for the better, for supernaturals and humans alike. And this dearest, Lily, is my dying wish.

I have created a partner for you. He will be an eternal protector, and you will feel such a great connection to him that you will never be found wanting in Love. I don't suppose any young adult would be happy to have their partner chosen for them and so I will leave you to find out who this true love is for yourself, as if it were your very own choice. By now you may already have found where your heart lies.

Many will come against you in your time on earth, Lily, and I can only hope my dear brother, and in turn the Du Plessis family, will have instilled in you an unbreakable spirit, a love for this earth and all things on it, a love for all people, both human and ours, and a strong sense of self-identity that will carry you through any situation.

I hope for you, Lily, that the sun will always shine on your life, that peace will follow wherever you go. I hope that you will come to know the deepness of true love, the kind your dad and I shared.

I wish for you to know the beauty of respect throughout your eternal life, and that your internal arrow always guides you along the right path.

I loved you before you were born, Lily, and I love you still. Even in death, I know my spirit will *always be with you, and I wish you the very best of everything in life.*

With eternal love,

Your devoted mother x

I turned the envelope over, checking the address on the back. I was tearful, but Olive didn't pry. She didn't even ask me what was in the letter. Charlotte would have pried it out of my hands! I handed Olive the letter and she handed me a tissue. Nothing was said, just a quiet understanding between two inseparable friends.

'Well I guess we now have a plan for what to do today,' said Olive, smiling softly at me. 'Are you okay, Lily?' She leaned in closer, putting her arms around me, and her head against mine.

'Yeah, I'll be fine. I guess I should have expected there would be a letter or something from my mum, as that *was* who the parcel was from,' I replied, sniffing a bit.

'It's a lovely letter, Lily. Beautiful. Something you can keep forever.'

Oh, I was beginning to know the true meaning of *forever,* and I wasn't sure I liked it one bit.

'We can't do the tattoo today,' I said. 'I have the party tonight and everyone will see it.'

'Well, eventually everyone's going to see it anyway,' Olive noted.

'Yeah, but not tonight. I mean, I don't even know what it's going to look like. Will I get to choose the design I wonder? Do you think they'll keep it light like Tallis's sleeve?'

'Surely you can't say it's something you've never considered doing ... having a cool tattoo?'

'No, I haven't really. Uncle Noah didn't like tattoos. And anyway, if I was going to have anything at all it would probably have been a small butterfly or something on my ankle, not half a bloody sleeve! That's the kind of things guys have, but not girls, surely?'

'You'd be surprised,' said Olive.

'Well, I guess I have no choice in the matter, so we'll have to go there on Monday and get it done.'

'I might be daring and get one myself while we are there.'

'Really! Won't your mum go nuts?'

'Probably, but she's not here, is she? And I'm eighteen myself next Friday so she can't really say anything.'

'Okay,' I said. 'But when you get home next week don't blame it on me.'

'It's not the only thing that she's going to be mad about,' Olive said.

'Why? What else is there?'

'I've decided I'm moving to New Orleans!'

It took a moment to register, then all I could do was scream and scream and jump up and down. Within minutes my bedroom door burst open and in pounced four extremely large, growling wolfling, all baring teeth, hair bristling on their back, ready to rip to pieces the intruder who had caused me to scream so hysterically.

Olive fainted on the spot.

TWO BECOME ONE

When we arrived at the plantation that night Olive was understandably a little nervous, she now knew for sure that my seemingly outrageous tales were true. She had seen Alex's transformation and the bearing of his fangs and had felt the full force of four very intimidating, angry wolfling. She had read my mum's letter to me, and therefore no further proof was needed of my supernatural lifestyle or Charlotte's claim to be a witch.

'I'm a little bit scared that I'm willingly walking into a dangerous situation,' Olive admitted warily.

'And I'm a little bit immortal … in actual fact, totally immortal so you don't have a thing to worry about,' I reassured her. 'If anyone hurts you, they'll burn in hell. Trust me.'

She gave me a weak smile as we pulled to a stop outside the house.

As we entered the hallway, I immediately noticed the effort to which Marchella had gone to prepare for the party. The banister of the stairs was entwined with white Lilies and everywhere I looked the house seemed filled with them. The place smelled heavenly - although the scent was a bit overpowering. I thought it just might have been Marchella's very clever way of masking Olive's very own heavenly scent from the army of vampires that seemed to have turned up to celebrate my birthday. Every room was filled to the brim and almost overflowing with stunning well-dressed people. Most I recognised as Du Plessis, but quite a few I had never met before. I scanned the rooms as I passed, double-checking that no Monsanto had been invited because, although I had strongly expressed that they were not welcome, I wasn't totally sure Marchella and my dad had taken me seriously. After all, I had also stated that I wanted a small family affair, and they obviously hadn't listened to that!

'Stay close to me, Olive,' I said.

'Don't you worry,' she said, frowning. 'I intend to be glued to your hip.'

We made our way into the busy dining room where the table was laid out with very little human food, but many jugs of red wine and a fine array of crystal wine glasses. At least I hoped it was red wine. Once again, I noticed Lilies everywhere and the beautiful, though pungent, aroma filled the air. Nobody seemed to look twice at Olive, even when they spoke to me to wish me a happy birthday and to congratulate me on reaching my immortality. I was very happy about this. Then I saw Dad and Marchella standing over by the fireplace mantle and I dragged Olive across the room to join them.

'Lily, darling,' Dad said, kissing me on the cheek. 'Happy birthday, my sweet girl. Have you enjoyed your day?'

'It was pretty awesome, thanks, Dad,' I replied, smiling.

'You look adorable in that dress, Lily,' Marchella cut in.

'Thanks so much. I love the shoes,' I said, tipping my shoe on its edge to reveal the sharp heel.

'They look a bit dangerous,' Dad worried.

'Compared to what?' I said glancing at the myriad of vampires surrounding us.

He laughed and Marchella smiled proudly.

'Don't you worry, Lily. Orders have been issued and your friend will be totally safe tonight.'

'I like the word *tonight,* but the word *forever* would please me more,' Olive uttered beside me. I noticed her hands were shaking, as if she was cold. I put my arm around her and leant my head against hers.

'It's okay, honestly. I won't let anything happen to you. I'd die for you.'

At this, she perked up a bit, looked a little more confident, and her smile came back.

'What a beautiful smile you have,' said a voice from behind my dad. It was a young, extremely handsome man, with dark cropped hair and honey-brown eyes. His voice was like silk.

'Ahh, Caleb ... I'd like you to meet Lily, my daughter, your niece,' Dad said.

So, this is my uncle Caleb. It seemed odd to have an uncle who was so close to my age. But weirder things had happened - much weirder.

'It's lovely to finally meet you, Lily, and congratulations on reaching your immortality,' he said holding my hand and kissing the back of it. 'And who is this gorgeous creature?' he said, staring at Olive.

'She's out of bounds,' I said rather loudly, and aggressively.

'Strange name that *out-of-bounds,'* he said with a laugh, and Dad and Marchella laughed too.

'Don't over-react, Lily,' my dad chided me. 'I told you she'd be safe here and I meant it.'

'Totally,' said Caleb, smiling at Olive.

I thought Olive would be scared but she smiled back, and her eyes met his and they held for a long time. *Uh-oh. I've seen this kind of behaviour before. I believe the term is Smitten.*

'Care to dance?' Caleb asked.

'The name's Olive,' she said introducing herself, and placing her hand on his, 'and yes, I'd love to.'

She let go of me and followed him into the dance space a few yards from me but still I felt uneasy and stared after her.

'Don't worry, Lily. He's an absolute gentleman,' said my dad. 'He's been living alone in the human world for years now and nobody he knows has any idea of his vampire origins. He behaves just like them, and other than the one time here at the plantation when he had to fight to survive, he has never taken human blood, or another human life.'

At this news, I relaxed. I could let Olive have some fun knowing Uncle Caleb was a good guy.

'Okay,' I said. 'But I'm not letting her out of my sight.'

'Fine, Lily, fine. Then I suggest you make an old man very happy and dance with me.'

'Of course, I'd love to.' And we strolled onto the dance floor.

Mmm, that's weird. My best friend and my uncle. Not that I minded because I didn't really know him, but I did wonder how this would all pan out, him being a vampire and all. I watched them as I danced with Dad and it seemed Caleb was sweeping my best friend off her feet!

And I was totally enjoying my party. Everyone was having a lovely time and they all seemed so friendly, even the strangers amongst us who had travelled in from out of town to attend. I had my first taste of champagne, which went slightly to my head after the second glass, and I stood by the human food snacking on crisps and bits, trying to soak up the alcohol and get my head straight. It was strange because, although Caleb and Olive were a good ten feet away, I could hear their conversation as if they were right next to me, and I didn't even have to concentrate or listen really hard. *Mmm, maybe alcohol has brought out another talent*

I didn't know I had.

'You promise you'll be back?' I heard him say.

'Definitely, as soon as I can. I guess my parents won't be that happy, but I love it here and Lily means so much to me.'

'It's great that my niece has a friend like you. Great for her and ... great for me,' he said with a flirtatious grin.

Olive smiled coyly and moved in closer.

'But aren't you going back to Yale after the party?' she said.

'Yes, I leave next week but I'm finishing up at the end of the year, so I'll be back here too.'

'Cool,' she said. 'Maybe we'll be back at the same time?'

'I hope so, Olive. I really do.'

I looked away from them, glancing across the room to my dad who was standing even further away, but I could also hear his conversation.

'I'm so proud of Lily - look at her, mother. She is so beautiful and such a lovely girl. Noah certainly raised her well. Her mother would be so happy with how she's turned out, don't you think?'

'Absolutely,' Marchella agreed.

I could feel my head swelling from the compliments, or maybe I was imagining it because of the champagne ... oh, I didn't know ... but it sure felt strange. I looked around the room. If I looked at too many people at once and tried to listen, it got a bit confusing, but if I just looked where I was interested, I could block out everything else and hear clearly. *Oh my god I'm so drunk, I'm imagining this surely.* A giggle escaped, and moments later Tallis was beside me.

'I hope you're taking it easy with that champagne, Lily. You want to have your wits about you,' he said.

'Tell me about it. Who'd have thought a few glasses could make anyone feel this way. I'm pretty woozy ... won't be touching any more of the stuff, don't you worry,' I said leaning unsteadily against him.

'Dance with me, Lily?'

'Certainly,' I said, my words slurring slightly. I hoped this wasn't going to take too long to wear off as I felt pretty vulnerable and a little bit silly as I struggled to keep my balance. Sensing this, Tallis held me tightly, half supporting me; he smiled and held me close as we danced. I felt as light as a feather one moment and as heavy as a rock the next. It was an odd feeling and all I really wanted to do was sit in a corner and go to sleep.

Thankfully the night was nearly over, and people started to leave. Marchella cut the cake and handed it out to all the guests. She was right: it was huge, and although the neighbours would see people leaving with little cake boxes; it seemed a shame they were all going to end up uneaten and thrown in a bin somewhere. Well, I was going to stuff my face with the biggest slice, and I was sure Olive would too. We love cake but also, I knew this would make Marchella very happy after the lengths she'd gone to making sure I had the perfect eighteenth birthday. My very last. *I might just decide to have an eighteenth birthday party every year to re-celebrate* I thought, because I'd had such a wonderful time. The house slowly emptied and all that were left were my close family members, and the wolfling. 'Let's stay here tonight,' I said to Tallis, 'and go home tomorrow, yeah?'

'Okay, for sure, if that's what you want.'

I stood on tippy-toes and kissed him. 'You are what I want, Tallis, always and forever.'

He kissed me back. 'Happy to hear that, but now I think it's bedtime for you, madam. You need to sleep this off.'

I giggled and he chuckled back, knowing I wasn't quite with it. He helped me to my room. 'I'm going to sit out here and keep watch tonight, Lily, as your guard is down and I'll make sure the others are patrolling the perimeter of the house just in case we have unwanted visitors.'

'But I'm immortal, Tallis. Nothing can hurt me now.'

'I don't know about that. It's your powers that will keep you safe, Lily, and at this precise moment I believe they are pickled in a few glasses of champagne.'

Just then Caleb and Olive turned up. He had walked her to my room. My dad was right - he was such a gentleman. Tallis kissed me good night and Olive helped me into my pyjamas and managed to tuck me in even though my body felt like it had turned into a mass of jelly, like boneless chicken. I didn't like the effect alcohol had on me and promised not to drink again.

'Never drinking again, Olive, never, ever, ever, ever again,' I said with slurred words and blurry vision. I think Olive realised it was the champagne talking because she just tucked me in tighter and said, 'Sleep tight, lovely ImmortaLily. Tomorrow is another day.'

She had used Alex's nickname for me, and it reverberated in my head as I drifted off to sleep, sadly now as I thought of him, which of course I would never have done if sober. I slept like a log and the following morning woke around 10 a.m. with a raving headache. Olive was gone but Pippa was snuggled up beside me purring very loudly. I was glad the guys had brought her here rather than leaving her alone at the townhouse. It wouldn't have been the same without Pippa here to snuggle up with on my birthday. On the table beside me were two tablets, a glass of water and a little note.

> Good morning Lily. Take these two tablets for your hangover. I have gone to breakfast with Caleb, hope you don't mind. And don't stress, I'm not going to be the breakfast ha-ha ... Think I'm in love.

Olive x

I didn't mind at all that Olive had left me, because it meant more time in bed to nurse my sore head. Plus, I was absolutely confident she was in safe hands with Uncle Caleb. I took the tablets and slept for most of the morning. When I woke up Tallis was sitting on the end of the bed.

'Hey, sleepy head, how're you feeling?' he said.

'Fine. Checking up on me, are you?' I replied with a smile.

'I'm always checking you out and you know it,' he said, moving closer.

'Lay with me a while,' I whispered.

I moved over and Tallis lay down next to me, wrapping his arm around me.

'You know I got a present from my mum for my birthday and it was a vile of ink?'

'What's it for?'

'I need to have a tattoo apparently. Half a sleeve to seal a spell, that will impart my mother's wisdom of the craft into me. What do you think of that?'

'Pretty cool, I guess. It will make you more powerful for sure. What do you think?'

'Mmm, not too keen. I hope it's nice, not some ugly skull and crossbones thing,' I laughed.

'I'm sure it will be fine, Lily.'

'I like your tattoo, Tallis.'

'Yeah, well your mum drew my tattoo. She said it was what she saw in me.'

'I wonder if she drew mine?'

'Most likely. She was an amazing artist.'

I traced my hand up his arm, touching the artwork, artwork my mum had drawn. Right at the top near the shoulder was a spirit sitting at a drum kit, drumming, its wings spread out and wrapped around the top of his arm.

'Do you play drums, Tallis?'

'Yes, and guitar.'

'Really? How come I don't know this about you?'

'I guess it's not something I talk about much. I mean it was something I did before - you know.'

'Before?'

'Before I died.' He looked sad, as if suddenly remembering something far off, something painful.

I knew this about him. I knew he had died and been brought back to life by my mum, forever changed. But still it shocked me, hearing it from his very own lips.

'Oh yeah, I forgot,' I lied.

'It's okay. Your mum did a good thing. I'd rather be here with you than dead beneath the ground forever.'

I cuddled up to him, stroked his arm and ran my hand up to his hair, pushing it to the side so I could see his eyes. He looked so solemn and I wondered whether he was struggling with those memories from the past. I kissed him and he kissed me back, first gently and then more passionately. I felt his tears on my face and decided right then that our new memories would one day push the old memories so far to the back of his mind that this new life would be all that mattered. And the only tears he would ever shed again would be for us, for our happiness.

On that warm and sunny afternoon, in my dimly lit room, with only a few rays of sunlight peeking through the curtains I gave myself to Tallis completely. We became lost in each other, two bodies that moved as one; our heartbeats and our heavy breathing was the only noise to be heard in the silence of our passionate embrace. I didn't know what this experience would have been like before my eighteenth birthday but in my immortal state I could not have wanted more. This vibrant, all engulfing feeling was as close to heaven as I could ever imagine being. His kisses soft against my skin made me tingle with sheer ecstasy. My back arched at his touch as he ran his hand the length of my thigh and up and across my belly, discovering me, discovering the unknown. I touched him back, softly running my fingers across his lower back as he moaned with pleasure. He kissed my neck and touched my mouth with his fingers tracing the outline of my lips. I pulled at his hair bringing him in close, bringing his lips up to reach mine as we melted into one another. The tips of my small breasts brushed against his firm chest sending shock waves of pleasure through me, making my toes curl and the hairs on the back of my neck stand up. I felt alive, more alive than ever before. Even in the dimly lit room as I studied his face and his form, every tiny mark and wrinkle, every crease stood out like the finest veins on a leaf. I felt like I was exploring every facet of the man I loved in more detail than was humanly possible. His scent stirred me and sank into my skin as our bodies slid against one another.

So, this is what I've been saving myself for. So, this is true love.

Then suddenly he quietly whispered, 'Marry me, Lily.' He looked into my eyes, his damp fringe hanging down. 'I want to spend my life with you, always.'

'Absolutely,' I whispered back. Tears fell softly on my cheeks, and I saw his eyes brimming with tears of happiness as I wrapped my arms around him. He laid his head on my bare breast, stroked my skin gently with his fingers as we lay in the silence, exhausted, elated, and totally in love.

UNCHAINED

That night at dinner I sat close to Tallis, feeling a new sense of oneness with him. My mum would be happy that I was feeling this way; that my heart was feeling the love she had wanted me to feel, the love she had felt with my dad; that the one she had created for me was the only one I wanted to spend my life with. She was right, far from arranged ... if I could have chosen for myself, Tallis would have been my only choice. Tallis was the one. He would always be the one. My dad and Marchella were looking at me as if they understood there was something different about me. I had gone to bed a girl and come down to dinner a woman.

Halfway through dinner, Tallis stood up and tapped his fork on the table to gain everybody's attention. Their idle chatter filtered into silence and they all looked up at him expectantly. Tallis looked extremely nervous as he shifted from one foot to the other, one hand in his pocket the other wiping his brow as he sighed heavily.

'Sir,' he said, looking down at my dad, 'I would like to ask for your daughter's hand in marriage.' He shifted again from foot to foot; wiped his brow and looked quite terrified as no one uttered a word.

Dad looked at me — a very serious look — and my stomach lurched inside. 'Is this what you want, Lily? Is this what will make you happy?'

'Yeah, this is what I want. Tallis makes me very happy. He's the only one who can,' I said quietly but with conviction.

He stood up suddenly, startling Tallis and making him step back; he almost knocked over his chair. 'Well, I guess congratulations are in order, young man. If Lily is happy with your proposal, then I am more than happy to accept it. Welcome to the family, Tallis.' My dad smiled for the first time in what seemed like forever and I could see the look of relief on Tallis's face as if only moments before he had thought him capable of ripping his head off. My dad shook his hand and drew him in for a hug. Everybody stood up and shook his hand and congratulated him and in turn congratulated me. It was smiles all round and I felt a lightness in my heart that I hoped would stay forever. Everybody sat down again, except Tallis. Instead, he knelt on one knee in front of my chair and pulled out a velvet ring box.

'Lily, would you please do me the honour of becoming my wife?' He looked lovingly into my eyes and handed me the open box. Inside it was a beautiful engagement ring. It was a plain gold band with the largest solitaire diamond I had ever seen. So simple and yet so magnificent at the same time.

'Yes ... yes!' I said, tears welling in my eyes again, then he slipped the ring from the box and placed it on my wedding finger. I stood up and he gently kissed my lips.

'Forever, Lily,' he whispered.

'Forever,' I whispered back.

Everybody clapped and cheered, and Olive couldn't help but cry.

'You can't get married without me here, Lily. You'll have to wait till I get back,' said Olive.

'Of course,' I replied. 'I can't have a wedding without my best friend.'

Marchella looked elated and the look on her face said she was already in planning mode. Oh, how I loved that look.

After dinner, Dad took me aside. 'Are you sure you want this, Lily? You're so young … don't you think it's a bit rushed?'

'Dad,' I said, 'I'm immortal. I will always be this young. Eighteen forever right. So, what difference will it make if I wait, one year, two? I'll still be eighteen — I'll still be too young in your eyes. He's the one Mum created for me. You should be happy with my choice.'

'Yes, I am — it's just that I've only just got you back and now another man is stealing you away already. It hardly seems fair,' he said sadly.

'He's not stealing me away, Dad, he's joining us,' I said with a reassuring smile. 'Be happy for me. He really is what I want more than anything in the world.'

He smiled and hugged me closely. 'Joining us, you say?' he said with a crooked little smile. 'I like the sound of that.'

I stared across the room to where Tallis stood talking to Olive. She stroked his arm and he laughed at something she said. I could have listened in, but I didn't — I didn't want to abuse my powers to spy. Besides these were two of the most wonderful people on earth and I was so happy to be sharing life's journey with them. Tallis noticed me looking and smiled at me. It was a lovely feeling to know he was all mine, forever — he was my one true love, my safety net, my protector, and seemingly perfect for me in every way.

The following day when Olive and I woke, she was bounding around the room with excitement. 'Tattoo day today, Lily,' she said happily. 'And I guess we have to go back to the townhouse?' she added, pouting and looking a little disappointed.

'We can stay if you like — you obviously feel safe here,' I said.

'I'm just so hooked on Caleb. I don't know what I'm going to do in England for six whole weeks. I'm going to miss him so much — and you, of course.'

'Of course,' I said, mocking her slightly.

'Oh, Lily, you know I love you to bits, but I can't help the way I feel about him.'

'It's okay, Olive. I feel the same about Tallis. We can have each other and still have our men.' I smiled an honest smile and meant it. 'I don't see Caleb as a threat to our friendship, actually I see him as a drawcard for keeping you here with me. As long as he doesn't break your heart, because then I might have to kill him, and I don't think my dad or Marchella would be very happy about that.'

Olive laughed. She knew I was only joking. Me? … I wasn't so sure.

We dressed and went down for breakfast, and after we ate, Dad drove us to the address on the back of the envelope in my mum's parcel. I showed Dad the letter and asked him about the tattoo.

'Your mum drew it for you, Lily. Her works are simply beautiful. I wouldn't be worried because it's bound to be perfect for you.'

We arrived at the address and, as surely as my mum had said, I was expected.

'Hi, Lily. I'm Marlon,' said a huge, tattooed, bearded creature with a bull-ring through his nose. He was rather scary and intimidating but when we followed him into his house and through to a back parlour, he picked up a tiny white dog and straightened the bow on its head as he carried on talking.

'This is Moses. Moses meet Lily,' he said, handing me the little fluffy ball.

'He's my precious Papillon,' said Marlon.

'Nice,' I said, stroking the dog and sitting down nervously.

'You have the ink with you?'

'Sure do,' I said, handing him the glass bottle.

'You're going to love this. I watched your mum draw it. It's beautiful.'

'Yeah, I hope so, but I'm terrified of needles,' I squirmed.

'You won't feel a thing. You are no normal girl, Lily. It will take time but there'll be no pain for you because you are so powerful.'

I felt suddenly relieved.

'Want to see what's in here then?' he said, peeling the wax from the lid.

'I guess so,' I said, feeling slightly nauseous.

He sat me in a chair and placed a sheet over me, leaving my left arm on top, little Moses in my lap, and Olive by my side, holding my other hand. Dad stood behind Marlon, looking over his shoulder. He readied the ink in the gun and placed the needle close to my skin at the shoulder.

'I thought you said no needle, Marlon?' I queried.

'Trust me,' he said with a huge, bearded grin.

Then he touched my upper arm with the needle. I felt nothing but a slight pleasant tingle as he carefully started to follow a line that appeared. It flowed very slowly down from my shoulder and out around my arm, with another line running in the opposite direction. The needle followed first one line then Marlon removed it and started on another. The lines began to appear all over, running the length of my upper arm from shoulder to elbow, wrapping around the sides and disappearing under my arm and around. It was very faint but as the ink began to fill the lines and the shaded areas filled themselves in, I began to see what it was. At the crease of my arm, roots entwined around and stretched out, the trunk of a graceful tree reached up and around the length of my bicep to my shoulder, sprouting branches at the top with tiny red buds and leaves that spread up and around the top part of my arm. A full moon at the top of the tree to the left, half-obscured by tree branches. And amidst the tangled roots at the bottom lay a sleeping red dragon, its wing wrapping around the bottom of the tree. Just above it at the base of the tree a beautiful grey wolf sat keeping watch, and etched into the bark, halfway up the trunk of the tree was a pentagram. The tattoo was pale and extremely beautiful, light grey, with only a hint of colour in the red dragon and the tiny red buds amongst the leaves. Not at all what I had feared. It almost came to life, as each tiny detail was carefully etched with ink. Three hours later and it was finished. The tingling sensation still remained but there was no pain, no blood, not what I had expected at all. It was as though someone had simply wrapped a priceless artwork around my arm, and it had molded itself perfectly to my skin, like a gracefully painted porcelain vase.

'The tree of eternal life,' announced Marlon proudly. 'The tiny red buds and the dragon represent your vampire ancestry, the moon and wolfling your eternal protection, and the pentacle represents your witch powers, your mum's ancestry. The tree itself depicts your eternal immortality. Amazing, isn't it?"

'Yeah, it is,' I said warmly. 'I love it. I was so worried it would look gross but it's so light and pretty.' I smiled at Olive and she squeezed my hand.

I stood up and walked to the mirror, checking out the design. I never thought I'd hear myself say this — 'But it actually suits me'.

'It looks good, Dad, doesn't it?'

'It's wonderful, and being only half a sleeve, it can easily be covered if needed,' he said, smiling at me.

'My turn,' said Olive.

'What would you like?' said Marlon.

'Just a small one on my wrist. I think the peace symbol with a Lily entwined around it. It will remind me of my mum and you, the two most important people in my life,' she said, smiling at me.

'Great choice,' I said.

Olive sat in the chair and Marlon started to draw freehand on her wrist. A beautiful lily with a peace symbol engraved over the top of it, then he filled the ink gun and began his work.

'Shit!' said Olive. 'That kills.'

'It won't take long,' said Marlon. 'I'll draw in small bursts so you can handle the pain. It will sting but will relieve instantly when I remove the needle. He started and stopped, taking his time, with Olive cursing through the whole twenty-minute ordeal. I had never heard her swear so much and I giggled as I watched her screwed up face. She squirmed with the pain, breathing heavily in and out, biting down on her lip and telling herself not to be a baby. And then it was done.

'So not fair,' said Olive. 'That absolutely killed me, and you didn't feel a thing. A whole half sleeve with no pain, and I was bloody tortured for this little thing.'

'Well, it was your choice. I didn't force you,' I said, laughing at her.

'I know, I know,' she said, checking it out in the mirror. 'But it's cool, hey?'

'No pain, no gain,' said Marlon.

'Yes, it looks good, Olive,' I said and gave her a big hug.

'One of the downfalls to being human I guess,' said Olive. 'Feeling pain.'

'Yes, well that could all change with time, and yet ... another painful choice you'll have to make,' said Dad.

Olive and I both looked at him confused, then Olive looked worried as if she suddenly realised what he'd meant by that. *Would she end up with Caleb? And if she did would she one day choose to be turned?* In my heart I kind of hoped so, because then we really could be friends forever, but it wasn't an issue I was ever going to influence her on. Giving up a human life for this existence by choice would be an extremely hard decision, and painful, as my dad said. Not just in the realm of actual pain, as in the process of 'turning', but in the pain of leaving everything and everyone behind to start a whole new existence.

'Stranger things have been done for love,' said Olive, looking rather sad all of a sudden.

'Well, it's not something you have to think about now,' I said boldly, hating to see her upset, and even more so hating to see her torn, because she loved her family dearly. But I had a feeling she had fallen so hard for Caleb that she already knew what her eventual fate would be.

Just then Dad's phone rang, breaking the awkward atmosphere with a jolt.

Olive picked up Moses and sniffed his fur. 'Mmm, so like Smith,' she said. 'Maybe Mum will let me bring him with me.'

'She's going to be so mad that you're coming back,' I said.

'She's going to be even madder about this,' said Olive, looking down at her tattoo. She giggled softly and we both made a fuss of Moses until Dad was off the phone.

'Thank you so much, Marlon,' I said as we were leaving.

'Anything for you, Lily. Your mum was a gem. Come back anytime, okay?'

'Sure, Marlon,' I said, giving him a big hug even though my arms didn't fit a quarter of the way around his barrel of a body. He was indeed a gentle giant.

Back in the car, Dad seemed rather quiet, and a worried expression had crossed his face.

'What's wrong, Dad?'

'Nothing to worry your pretty little head about,' he replied.

'Well, what then?'.

'Mica called. He went to collect some stuff for you guys at the townhouse, so you can stay at the plantation until Olive leaves on Friday, but there's been a break-in, well ... more of a breakout really.'

'Break out? What do you mean?'

'We'll stop there on the way home, and I'll explain'.

We drove swiftly to the townhouse and when we arrived the team were all there, plus a few Du Plessis, including Caleb and Marchella. We parked the car and went inside. There were no signs of a break-in, or break out, whatever my dad had said, but I followed him through the hallway and up the stairs to my room. At the end of the hallway, the door to the loft stairwell was open and a few people stood around.

'This way, come see,' said Caleb, gesturing to my dad. We followed him up the stairs, and to my surprise and utter shock, the loft hatch was open, the hefty chain lying on the floor beneath it. Caleb pulled the ladder down and my dad climbed up. Olive and I followed closely behind. Inside the loft was dark and musty, and cobwebs hung everywhere. In the middle of the floor stood a large pewter coffin, its lid open, its black velvet interior reeking of antiquity. The coffin was completely empty, no remnant of dust or bone, no sign of the remains of anything that had once lived. Just an empty space. On the floor, a dried-up, long-stemmed black rose with petals so old and crusty a simple breath would have disintegrated it in seconds.

'This loft has been sealed since 1842,' Dad said.

'What was sealed in here?' Caleb asked.

'Well, speculation says a Monsanto vampire, but if that legend had any truth to it the remains would definitely still be here,' he replied with a frown.

'Then what?' Caleb queried again.

'No idea. But whatever it is was sealed into the coffin with this long-stemmed black rose, so it must be of vampire origin — there must be some truth to the tale.'

'Well, maybe the tale is true. Maybe someone broke in and stole the remains,' Caleb said, shrugging his shoulders.

I looked at Olive, and a sudden rush of guilt hit me, remembering the spell we had cast just a short time ago to unseal the loft. It had taken its time, but the spell had obviously worked, and I now felt two things — glad that it hadn't worked at the time or who knows what our fate would have been, and dreadfully guilty that we were responsible for releasing an unknown entity onto the streets of New Orleans. I didn't quite have the guts to tell my dad what we'd done. And searched Olive's face for any clue as to what we should do next.

'Why would anyone want to do that? What good is a dead vampire to anyone?' Olive said, joining in on my dad and Caleb's conversation.

'I don't know — it's all a mystery. But just in case we are not dealing with a vampire and instead some terrible fiend, we had better lock up this house and move you girls to the plantation where you'll be safe.' Caleb smiled at Olive and took her hand in his.

I couldn't believe it. Here we stood, in a deserted loft with a million cobwebs, an empty coffin, with a huge possibility that whatever had been in it was roaming the streets of New Orleans looking for prey, and my Uncle Caleb was still trying to woo the socks off of my best friend!

'Good idea — a great idea in fact,' Dad said, scratching his chin and looking worried. 'Let's lock up and go, guys. But take some pictures with your phone first, Caleb, just so we don't have to come back. Someone sealed whatever it is away up here … we just need to find out who that was, so we can find out what it is?'

'Okay. Well, where do we start?' said Caleb.

'With the Monsanto's of course. It's their loft.'

We grabbed all of our stuff, locked up the townhouse and headed back to the plantation. Yesterday I would have been pretty scared not knowing what had been released from the loft, but today I felt confident that, whatever it was, it would be no match for me. Not that I knew what my true capabilities were yet. But turning eighteen and becoming immortal made me feel indestructible, like nothing on earth could hurt me or the ones I loved. I felt this so deeply, it helped me to remain calm and peaceful. If the time came and this thing was the fear I had to face — the fear I had been waiting for all my life — the fear Uncle Noah had talked about constantly, then so be it. I would face it head on and summon all the power I held within to use against it. The only thing I would ever have to truly fear would be another immortal, and as I was the only one, it seemed quite obvious to me that whatever was on the loose, already had its days numbered.

A MONSTER AMONG US

When we pulled up at the house, Charlotte was sitting on the steps patiently waiting. She sat cross-legged in the sun, her baseball cap tilted over her eyes, a book in her hand and she didn't even look up. I was mad at her. She hadn't turned up for my party, and she hadn't so much as called to wish me happy birthday. *Some friend she is!* I hopped out of the car and walked straight past her, ignoring her.

'Hey, Lily,' she called as I passed her by, 'I have a present for you. Sorry I couldn't come to your party. I was so sick, throwing up and everything. Happy birthday ...' She smiled, holding out a present for me.

I wanted to carry on walking but if she'd been sick, I guess she couldn't help it. I mean, whoever calls to wish someone a happy birthday with their head stuck down a toilet?

Olive looked at me as if to say '*You're a gullible fool*. She shook her head and carried on past me into the house. I took the present and invited Charlotte in, but she didn't budge, just stayed on the steps.

'How come you're staying here?' she asked. 'I thought it wasn't safe for the ginger nut.'

'Enough of that, Charlotte. There's no need to be rude. Olive's done nothing to you.'

'Oh, I'm joking ... don't take me seriously. Anyway, she can't hear me from in there.'

'Just be nice, Charlotte, *if* you're at all capable, and if not, I suggest you piss off home.'

She smiled sweetly and said 'Okay, okay. Don't get ya knickers in a twist. Open your present.' She jiggled up and down with excitement and I sat down on the steps next to her and pulled the wrapping off the present. It was an old manuscript bound together with a leather spine but no cover, front or back.

'What is it?' I said.

'One of the Calibri coven's greatest works.'

I looked at her, confused.

'The elixir for the wolfling, Lily. It has the formula in it,' she said excitedly.

'Really!' I squealed.

'Really,' she squealed back. 'I've been searching for it since you went to England and I finally came up trumps … couldn't believe it. I went through boxes and boxes and piles and piles of stuff. I thought it was never going to end. But I believe this is the one, this is what you need. I know you have the rocks now, but you should always have a backup.'

I couldn't help myself. As angry as I was, I slung my arms around her in sheer happiness.

'Do you know what this means, Charlotte? Tallis will now be safe. His moonstone is missing. We searched everywhere and still haven't found it. But now we have the formula. Thank you, Charlotte … thank you so much.'

'Woah!' she said, looking shocked. 'You can't find his moonstone? Are you joking?'

'No. It's been missing for years and the location spell you did only found the other three rocks. Tallis's moonstone was not with them. But it's okay now we have this. I mean, it will give us more time to find it.'

'Well that all sounds good but what if I'm wrong? What if it's not the correct formula? I can't be 100% sure.' She looked suddenly worried, and also a little guilty as if she'd been playing me along about the formula to get back in my good books. *Could it be possible? Could she be that shallow?*

'Well, we'll give it to a friend of my dad's who knew my mum well, and we'll see what she comes up with, hey,' I said, trying to sound excited, but now doubt had set in.

'Yeah, well I hope it works, I mean, I'd hate for anything to happen to your precious Tallis.' She tried to sound sincere, but her lip turned up at the edge slightly as if she were trying to suppress a smile.

'I think you should go, Charlotte,' I said quietly.

'Why?' she asked.

'Because there's something about you I just don't like. It's as simple as that.'

'Oh, thanks,' she said, looking shocked. 'I come here bearing gifts and you insult me!'

She stood up, propped her hands on her hips, and glared at me. 'You don't want to make an enemy of me, Lily,' she said boldly.

'Oh really,' I said calmly. 'And why is that?' I also stood so we were eye-to-eye and stared at her forcefully.

'I know too many of your secrets,' she snarled.

'Go tell them to the world then Charlotte. It's what I expect from you anyway.'

'Maybe I will,' she said.

'Feel free,' I snapped back. 'But don't forget what I became two days ago. I'm an immortal child that has reached its immortality. You can't mess with me now. Nobody can.' I smiled confidently.

'My kind have sealed your kind away before,' she hissed at me.

'I doubt that very much. I'm apparently one of a kind. But if you did, well maybe that's because they didn't have one of these,' I said, shoving my immortal sleeve up at her face. Her eyes narrowed and her jaw set as she stared at me, then she stormed off down the driveway occasionally glaring back at me.

'You're such a bitch, Charlotte,' I shouted after her. 'I thought you had more sense than to get on my bad side.' Then I went indoors and slammed the door behind me.

It was the first time in my life I'd had an argument with anyone. It felt good yet somewhere deep inside I felt ashamed. I felt like she didn't really deserve it. She couldn't help how she was any more than I could help being so forgiving. But this Immortal sleeve, the ink that contained the blood from my mum, that had seeped into my very being, seemed to bring with it a kind of arrogance, an attitude that wasn't there before and I wasn't sure I liked it one bit. Plus, as nasty as she could be, Charlotte was not a friend I wanted to lose. She was my only ally in the French quarter, and she had helped me in many ways — ways in which I was sure she would help me again. But I wasn't ready now to call after her, to make amends. Not today. There were more important things to worry about.

Inside the house, I handed the tattered old manuscript to Marchella.

'Take a look at this, Marchella, it may hold the formula for the elixir. Of course, it might be a red herring so let's not get our hopes up. Charlotte can't always be trusted.'

'Well, it's worth checking out, you never know,' said Marchella, 'we'll send Mica into town with it later and get it looked at.'

'It's like grasping at straws,' I said sadly. 'It's the worst feeling knowing there's no elixir and no rock for Tallis.'

'It'll turn up, I'm sure of it,' said Marchella, stroking my hair and trying to reassure me.

'Why don't you give Charlotte some of Tallis's blood and ask her to try another location spell?' my dad suggested.

'Mmm, well at the moment we're not talking. We just had a bit of a quarrel on the front porch and she stormed off. So that's not really an option right now.'

'Oh, that's a shame. Did she say something bad?'

'Yeah, you could say that. But it's more about her — you know — there's something not quite right in her, there's an underlying nastiness that I just can't handle.'

'Takes all sorts to make a world, Lily.'

'Oh, don't I know it.' I said, frowning.

Dad's phone rang, and he looked serious and disappeared from the room. When he came back, he leant thoughtfully against the fireplace. I could see his worried frown as he stared blankly at me, as if not seeing me, his thoughts so deep.

'What's up, Dad?' I asked.

'Emmanuel Monsanto has called a meeting at his house, tomorrow at 9am. We are all requested to attend. There will be other clans there, so I suggest Olive stays here with Marchella.'

'What's it about?'

'He heard about the unsealing of the loft. He won't discuss it over the phone, but I think he knows what was released. He seems to be quite panicked about it. Must be some deranged vampire for him to be kicking up such a fuss. Anyway, we'll find out tomorrow,' he said solemnly.

The following morning my dad, Caleb and I left for the Monsanto mansion. Emmanuelle welcomed us with open arms. I don't know why it was, but although I was angry at him for possibly being the instigator in the set up at the masquerade ball, it was incredibly hard to dislike him. There seemed to be an affinity between us that was undeniable. I guess I was feeling what my mum had felt for him. When he gently touched my arm, my anger seemed to melt away, and *forgiving* Lily rose to the surface. He led us through to the huge ballroom where a large table had been set up to accommodate all the other clans. There were so many of them, chatting and shaking hands like they hadn't met in years. Emmanuelle asked everyone to be seated. I checked the room and noticed that Alex was not among the crowd of faces. Maybe he stayed away because my dad and I were going to be there. Anyway, his absence made me feel better. Emmanuelle stood at the head of the table and everyone turned to him, waiting for the meeting to begin.

'I extend a very warm welcome to everyone here,' said Emmanuelle. 'Thank you all for coming. Some of you know the reason I've called this meeting and the rest of you may well be alarmed. But it is imperative that you all hear what I have to say.'

A few shifted in their seats, but an eerie silence fell upon the room as they waited for him to continue.

'I guess, for those of you that don't know our history, it would be best for me to fill you in on the background of this dire situation we now find ourselves in.

'In the early 1820s, my father Elijah, who some of you knew well, married the voodoo queen Anastasia Du Preez; she gave birth to a son — my brother, Fabian Monsanto. He was, of course, an immortal child, and well-protected — he grew up amongst us. We saw the signs all through childhood of his evil intent, but my father Elijah had every faith that when he neared his immortality and his emotions kicked in, he would change for the better. Many of us tried to make Elijah see the error of his thinking, and there were regular meetings to discuss Fabian's progress as he got older, but my father would never see the sense in our warnings. As

Fabian reached his seventeenth year no change came, there were no emotions evolving other than hatred, anger and bitterness. We all put this down to the fact his mother — the voodoo queen, Anastasia Du Preez, had a very dark soul.'

There was a stirring at the table and a lot of uncomfortable glances, as people exchanged looks of shock and worried expressions, as if they knew where the conversation was going.

'As he grew in age he grew in power and started to abuse those powers. A few of you here have felt the force of that firsthand, with Fabian attacking the clans and wiping out some of the best of us in order to gain full control for himself.'

Some nodded in agreement; some whispered around the table but still nobody spoke.

'As Fabian drew close to his eighteenth birthday, my father finally came to realise he had been protecting a monster, and that indeed Fabian was capable of wiping us all from existence. My father realised that this was Fabian's one and only goal as the evil in him grew to uncontrollable proportions. We had another meeting and some of us, who are here now, persuaded my father to join us in ridding the world of this monstrosity. My father was obviously disturbed by our request, but he agreed to compromise. He decided not to give Fabian his ink for his immortal sleeve, enabling the witches to seal him away.'

Some gasped; and sat stunned by the revelation. Then one of them stood up.

'Emmanuel, may I speak?' said an elderly man.

'Yes, of course, you may, Cousin Edward,' said Emmanuel.

'As one of the oldest amongst us, I'd like to say that I can recall that meeting very well. I remember your father, at the time, also agreed to allow the immortal child hunters to take Fabian out. It almost broke Uncle Elijah, but he always had the best interest of the clans at heart. Even when he made this awful decision about his own son. I remember the immortal child hunters came in droves and Fabian destroyed them all. Our only weapon against him was the ink, and once we had destroyed it, we felt at peace. There was a glimmer of hope for us all. Your father was a good man, Emmanuel, and I think I can speak for us all when I say we all had the greatest respect for him.'

'Thank you, Cousin Edward, that means a lot. The problem is that Fabian *did* make it to his eighteenth birthday. We tried everything to wipe him out. The more devastation and havoc he caused, the more we tried, but we were unsuccessful. When he reached his immortality, we knew we had been defeated and that there was absolutely no way of killing him.' Emmanuel looked down at the table, and I could tell he was feeling the defeat as if it were only yesterday.

'Elijah was killed by the hands of his own son — Fabian slaughtered my father in cold blood. The day he died, I knew there was no hope for mankind, or for our own kind. If Fabian could kill his own father, what hope did the rest of us have of surviving his wrath?'

Sadness reflected on many faces in the room, and I realised Elijah Monsanto had been held in high esteem.

'It took some time, as many of you know, but eventually I found a way to deal with him. We came across an ancient prophecy that told of a powerful spell that could be used in our favour. We had to find a black rose and a powerful moonstone. With the help of the Calibri coven, I fought the Primeval wolf for the moonstone that eventually sealed Fabian away. That beast almost killed me, but he was turned to stone, ridding the supernatural world of one of the most dangerous monsters of our time. He was a tyrannical leader, and although the werewolf clans have always had the power to release him, none ever dared. Not one of them wanted to release his cruelty back on themselves and the world.

'Using the moonstone, and with the help of a supernatural army, the Calibri coven was finally able to seal Fabian away in 1842. He was drawn into a deathlike sleep from the spell, then the binding power of the black rose and the magical properties of the moonstone were used to seal the loft at the Monsanto townhouse. Until recently, his name had not passed my lips, no thought of him had crossed my mind. But now we are faced with this dire situation. Fabian has been released.'

I gasped! There was another immortal on the loose, and one with a soul as black as the devil himself. My dad sensed my anxiety and put his arm around me.

'What I don't understand is, how?' Emmanuel said, looking confused. 'The moonstone that was used to seal him away must have been used to reverse the binding. I gave that moonstone to Lilith Montague before Lily was born and it was never returned. As far as I know, the moonstone went missing years ago, because when Lilith's body and belongings were returned to New Orleans, the moonstone was nowhere to be found. So how can it have been used to unseal the loft?'

For just a moment, even though we were in the middle of a dreadful revelation, I had a strong feeling of relief. That the moonstone had been used to unseal the loft meant it was here somewhere — here in New Orleans, in the hands of someone. None of us could possibly know who. But it gave me a flicker of hope for Tallis. What I should have been feeling was horror at the devastation that Fabian's release could cause, but all I could think about was Tallis. He would be safe as long as we could one day get our hands on the moonstone. And, of course, I had a slight sense of relief, from the guilt of thinking I had helped to release my fiercest opponent. Because obviously the spell Charlotte had performed would have been useless without the moonstone. Knowing that made me feel a whole lot better. Besides, finding the moonstone was really my only problem, as far as I was concerned. I had only just become immortal and with less than a year's training on how to reach my true potential, there was no way I was going to get involved in this. Or put my life on the line for a room full of strangers. No way!

'But who would be responsible for releasing such an evil entity into our world?' Cousin Edward asked.

'Well, there is an unsolvable puzzle,' said Emmanuelle. 'Who indeed would do such a horrific and stupid thing? Even the Lestrange lair wouldn't be that idiotic. When Fabian was among us, he wanted to wipe out all of our kind — all supernaturals. Why would anyone think it would be any different now? I don't believe I know of any living being, supernatural or not that would release such an atrocity.'

'So, what do you hope to achieve from this meeting?' My dad said, suddenly rising to his feet.

'We have a huge dilemma, Eli, because we don't know the location of the moonstone. Fabian doesn't have an immortal sleeve, so we still have an advantage over him, but the sealing spell won't work without the moonstone. Our only option is …' Emmanuel looked directly at me.

'No, absolutely not!' my dad shouted. 'Lily has only just reached her immortality. She's not strong enough yet. She still has a long way to go before she could handle an ancient power like that.'

'She is the only way. Only an immortal can kill an immortal,' Emmanuel said.

'No. I won't allow it,' shouted my dad.

'It's Lily's decision,' said Emmanuel, looking at me, 'and you won't be leaving here until we have it,' he threatened.

All eyes were now on me. The hairs on the back of my neck prickled as I realised we were unlikely to leave here without a fight if I didn't tell them what they wanted to hear. I had to protect my dad at any cost. And we had to get out of here.

'*No*!' my dad roared, dragging me out of my seat. 'We can't put her in danger. I won't do it. I won't let her make a decision that will end her life.' He tried to pull me to the door but Emmanuelle and a few others stood in his way. A few of the crowd moved in and surrounded us. *I knew it — saw it coming a mile off.* There could be only one way out of here, and that was to pretend to concede.

'Hang on!' I shouted. 'Isn't this one of the reasons you and mum created me? If I'm supposed to achieve what the legend says and form a new race, a peaceful new world. Surely I'll have to face this danger?'

'Yes, but not now, Lily! Not yet!' he said, putting his arm protectively around me.

'Dad, Marchella told me that our powers are controlled by our emotions. If Fabian was evil because of his lack of emotion, then his powers won't be as strong as mine.'

'Maybe ... maybe so, but I will not allow you to take the risk. You need time to grow, for your powers to develop. What if he kills you, Lily?'

'What if he kills us all?' I said, looking around the room at all the faces. 'How can I form a new race, and bring peace to our world, if there is nobody left?'

He fell silent.

'I made a promise to you, Dad. That I would use my powers for good. That I would try to accomplish my mum's wish — to see peace in this world of ours, and I fully intend to make her proud.

But to do this, I will have to defend what is mine. If we roll over and let Fabian have free reign, he will destroy us all. He will destroy this world you love so much. I can't allow that.'

I looked into his eyes, trying to connect with something deep inside, a greater cause, not just a dad's desperate need to protect his precious daughter. He stood silently looking at me, sad, unspeaking.

'Please, Dad, please understand that this is what I was born for — to protect you all. I'm sure I can defeat him. Yes, I could fail, and he could kill me, and indeed all of us. But if I don't at least try, that will happen anyway. Can't you see that?'

Tears had filled his eyes. He wrapped his arms around me. 'You, Lily, are everything your mum wanted you to be. She would be so proud,' he said, placing a kiss on my forehead.

This filled me with guilt. He had believed my words, just like the rest of them. I so wanted to make him and Mum proud … but more so, I wanted to live. I hadn't had much of a childhood, not that I could remember anyway, and this year had been so amazing: I'd learned so much, gained so much, found my family, and fallen in love. Turning eighteen was such a milestone for me, one I thought I would never reach. And when I thought about what it had taken to get here, there was absolutely no way I was going to let it all slip through my fingers, not for anything, not for anyone … especially not a bunch of warring clans who couldn't give a stuff about me or my family. I would find a way to survive this Fabian Monsanto situation without having to fight him. I didn't know how; it would take some thought. But for now, all I could think about was surviving this meeting; getting me and my dad out of here.

'So … how do we find Fabian?' I asked Emmanuel.

'No need,' said Emmanuel. 'He will find you.'

YOU CAN CALL ME BETH

The clans seemed all at once relieved, and many smiled. My dad, however, was solemn. I knew he worried deeply about my abilities and whether they were strong enough to see me through this treacherous path he knew I was about to walk. I felt the same but didn't let it show. I didn't feel ready, not in strength or ability, and I certainly wasn't ready to lose everything, including my life. But, if there was any truth to the legend of the immortal child, I should not turn away from my responsibilities, even though I might die trying.

I had spent most of the past year learning about the role I would one day have to play, learning how to hone my abilities, control my powers, and let my emotions flow freely. I had the best teachers: Marchella, Dad and the wolfling. They had taught me all I needed to know about the legend and my part in it … the bringer of peace, uniter of all clans. It had seemed a steep request when I first learned who I was and what I was born to do. But, in my time in New Orleans, I had realised what Uncle had been protecting me from and preparing me for. I had seen so much, learned so much, killed … well, not so much … but knew I was capable of killing anyone to protect myself. My powers had grown immeasurably and my abilities to control them with it. To fulfil my mum's wishes, I had to be willing to follow my destiny.

But I wasn't willing.

The way I saw it, I had three choices: face the evil, fight and possibly die; or not fight and die anyway, which meant I'd be taking the whole supernatural world down with me; or find another way to defeat this monster without losing everything. Option three seemed the most logical, if it was possible.

Deep within my soul, I knew that doing the right thing by all — which included the supernaturals — would stand me in good stead as a leader … provided the outcome of the battle was in my favour. I was destined to be the ruler of this world and bring peace to my kind, but it was a position I had to earn. I couldn't just walk in and take over — I had to go through the fire first — I had to earn the respect of the clans' elders, the covens, and the lairs. For them to accept me, I needed to show them I was prepared to die for them. To earn their respect, I had to show them the deepest respect by putting *their* lives', *their* safety, before my own. This is what had been drummed into me for almost a year. And I didn't know if I could do it. I felt precariously torn between wanting to do what was right for the clans and what was right for me, between what my parents wanted *from* me and what I wanted *for* me.

And would they, if I fought this battle, treasure me above all others and allow me to lead them into a peaceful new world?

When the chatter in the room became loud and bustling once more, Emmanuelle led my dad away to a private corner. I stood listening to all the chatter but didn't focus on any particular conversation, my mind wandering elsewhere. I could hear familiar voices in the distance, outside the room. I strained to listen above all the noise, but it was difficult. Edward was standing beside me talking, but although I could see his lips moving, I couldn't focus on his words.

'Excuse me, Edward, I need to use the bathroom. Please let my dad know I won't be long.' I smiled and walked away as he looked awkwardly around for someone else to talk to. I felt as though I'd been rude, but it couldn't be helped, I couldn't stop my thoughts from wandering into the hall.

Outside in the hallway, I walked to the right and passed by many beautiful marble statues, paintings of people from times gone by, and a large spectacularly ornate mirror. I stopped outside a door to the left, and as I came close enough and was about to turn the handle, I heard the familiar voices again. It was Alex, definitely, and the other person ... Charlotte. *Charlotte?* My mind swam with confusion. *Why is she here at the Monsanto's, and with Alex of all people?* I leant gently against the door, focusing on the whispers within until they became audible.

'It's a dreadful thing we've done, Alex. I know Lily and I have our issues, but I never wanted to hurt her,' Charlotte said sincerely. I smiled, yet wondered what she was talking about?

'Yeah, right,' said Alex, 'and you decide to feel this way now when the deed is already done. What use is that? You've been sleeping with me since before she arrived in New Orleans and the whole time she's been here, so what do you really care?'

Suddenly everything started to make sense — Charlotte's behaviour — her jealousy. I had an overwhelming feeling of pity for her. She was in love with Alex. She always had been, and I had turned up on the scene and become an object of fascination for him. *He* was the guy who had jilted her at the ball — for me. Her warnings about staying away from him were to protect what she thought was hers — the tales of him being a heart breaker, all true. But hers had been the most recent heart broken. I felt terrible and although I wanted to stay and listen, I felt I was once more intruding on what was hers. He meant nothing to me. But at least now I knew the truth and the sad thing was she was still defending me; not wanting to hurt me, after all I'd done. I felt terrible and quickly slipped away, not wanting to hear anymore. I knew now that I had to contact her to make amends; to apologise for how I'd treated her that day at the plantation; to explain that I didn't care for Alex, and that I knew about them.

Then I had a thought. *No, I can't do that. I can't let on that I know the truth ... that I've been listening to their private conversation, even if it is about me. I'll just have to say sorry and accept her for what she is, without her knowing that I know. That'll be the best way to handle it.*

I made my way back along the corridor and slipped into the ballroom, mingled amongst the guests and all their incessant chatter. My thoughts though were still with Charlotte and her poor wounded heart.

The adults in the room bustled around me, agitated yet excited. Dad was still in a heated debate with Emmanuelle, and Edward had honed-in on me again, drawn like a moth to a flame. I wanted to leave; to get away. I tried to catch Dad's eye, but he was too wrapped up in his intense discussion. I longed to be back at the plantation with Olive. She was leaving here in two days and I felt like I was wasting time. Edward was mumbling on about me being the saviour of the supernatural world, and people all around us nodded in agreement. I felt smothered, claustrophobic, slightly faint. Then from across the room, Dad noticed me, took in my pale demeanour and swiftly came to my rescue, as if he'd read my thoughts.

'Come, Lily, we're leaving. We are just wasting our time here.'

He seemed angry, hostile even — not towards me — but I could see he wasn't pleased with the outcome of his chat with Emmanuelle.

'They have spent their existence spoiling the lives of others, fighting between themselves, causing havoc amongst their own kind and humans alike. Fabian is their problem, not ours! They should deal with the mess they have made! But no … who do they turn to? My daughter, whose sheltered life has not prepared her for the bloodshed to come!' he shouted.

Banging doors, we left the Monsanto household and clambered into the car. He drove extremely fast and erratically out of the gates and all the way home. Two weeks before I would have told him to slow down. I would have been worried for my life, but now I just pulled my seatbelt tightly round me and relied on my immortality. Putting my two cents in would only make things worse at this stage — he was far too angry to reason with.

I realised as we drove that, when they'd created me to fulfil the prophecy of forming a peaceful supernatural world, they were only thinking about the outcome — they hadn't considered the amount of danger involved in me actually fulfilling my obligations. I could see Dad's point. I'd just turned eighteen and had only just begun to harness my powers. New abilities were arising in me as time passed, adding more complications. As if being a teenager wasn't stressful enough on its own!

Over the past few months, my flame-throwing skills had become more accurate … thankfully: there'd be no unintentional burn-ups from now on. I'd learned how to stay in a body without losing my grip, although I wasn't sure this would work on another immortal. I'd begun working on spells — freezing spells, weather spells and a few others. I could hover momentarily and was working on maintaining some height, but I still struggled, maybe because I wasn't too confident at it. Marchella said I didn't practise enough, and I often relied on Charlotte for the simplest of things. At this point, I preferred my emotional power over magic. My anger occasionally made me feel like I could defeat anything, but sometimes I felt like everything hadn't quite kicked into place yet, like something was lacking. When I really raged, I felt like I would implode, or explode, depending on the situation. But I didn't feel as powerful as the legend portrayed me being. I felt like I'd learnt so much and yet still felt so inadequate. Maybe I hadn't reached my true potential or if there was more to come, I hoped with all my heart there was, and if there was, what would it take to trigger it?

Fabian, on the other hand, might not have the emotional power I had, but he would be excellent in the craft — and if it was his mother's magic, it was dark magic. I worried about this constantly because voodoo magic was so powerful. And he would surely play dirty. I didn't think I could expect him to act like a gentleman simply because he looked and spoke like one. No, he was a contrary creature indeed — beautiful to look at yet evil to the core. And though I wasn't sure what his capabilities were, I was sure his depravity would be his primary weapon. He had been eighteen for nearly two centuries, so his powers would be fully functional, and more than likely he could use them to maximum effect. *Very unlike me*. Nevertheless, there was really no point in arguing with Dad over this. It was something I had to work out on my own. I had promised Emmanuelle and the clans that I would deal with this monstrosity, and that's exactly what I had to do. *Somehow*.

Then a thought crossed my mind. 'Dad, do you think the guy who released Fabian could possibly be Grandad? He's here in New Orleans. If the moonstone went to England with my mum, maybe Grandad stole it when she died. Maybe he released whatever was in the loft in the hope it would wipe me out as all his attempts to kill me so far have failed.'

'Maybe. It's a crazy enough notion to be true, and he's crazy enough to do it.'

'Then we just need to find Grandad and we find the moonstone. We can use it to seal Fabian away again. If we can get the covens to help, a battle could be avoided.'

'That's a good plan, Lily. I'll get a search team together immediately to track your grandfather down. And if I find out that Theo Montague was indeed responsible for releasing this beast … why … I'll kill him with my bare hands!'

I hoped I was right. I hoped with all my heart it was Grandad. I couldn't think of anyone who would want me dead more than he did. If we could find him, we would find the moonstone. Fabian could be eliminated, and Tallis would be safe once more.

Friday came around too soon and we were on our way to the airport to drop Olive off. I knew she would be back, and the thought filled me with happiness, but deep inside, I wondered whether there would be anything left for her to come back to. If I was right about Grandad, our chances were good. But if I were wrong … the possibility of my annihilation was highly likely — entirely probable. I didn't tell Olive the details of the meeting. I didn't want her to stress while she was away. So I told her we weren't sure what had been released, but suspected my grandad of unsealing the loft using the Monsanto moonstone, and that we would be tracking him down while she was in England.

'Best of luck,' she said, giving me a massive hug before boarding the plane. 'See you in six weeks, Lily. Take care.'

Back on the plantation, Marchella busily compiled lists of things to do for my wedding, which had been set for one week after Olive's return. Tallis was happy, and oblivious to my worries about the future. He had every faith that whatever came my way I would be able to deal with because, now I was immortal, I was basically invincible. Depressed over the situation, Dad overly controlled me, and my time. He knew Fabian was coming, he just didn't know when. The pressure of waiting and wondering pulled him down and cracks began to show in his usually vibrant, charming personality. I wanted to take his pain away; wanted to tell him I wouldn't fight to protect Emmanuel and the clans, but this wasn't possible.

When we arrived back at the plantation, I asked him to walk with me, and we wandered through the woods in awkward silence.

'How are you feeling, Lily?'

'My wedding is seven weeks away, and I really need to concentrate on that. We must go on as normal. We don't know when Fabian will come, but I'm ready, Dad,' I lied, needing him to stop worrying. Coping with my own anxieties was hard enough without worrying about his levels of anxiety. 'I know I can defeat him. You need to believe in me ...'

'Oh, Lily, of course, I believe in you! I'm just worried for your safety.'

'Well, for now, let's just put our fears on hold. Coming up against Fabian is inevitable if we can't find Grandad, or if I'm wrong about him possessing the moonstone, but moping around won't help anything. We both need to be mentally and physically prepared, so let's stop worrying. Have a little faith. It will take us a long way.'

I smiled at him and leant into him for a hug.

'I can't lose you, Lily, not now. You are all I have left of Lilith, and I will go to any lengths to protect you.'

'You won't have to. I promise, we've got this. I have the whole range of Mum's emotions, and Fabian only has anger. We will win

... just you wait and see.' I tried so hard to hide my doubt and deceit when I spoke these words.

He stared at the ground and nodded soberly. Then he looked up and shook his head, smiling at me. 'We've got this,' he said. Stepping closer, he wrapped his arms around me, leant his forehead against mine momentarily. Then he pulled away again and stood staring at me for a long time. It was a look of sheer adoration. Finally, he said, 'Come on, girl, we've got a wedding to plan.'

We wandered back through the woods and up to the house along the winding path between the trees. As we walked, I imagined the old-fashioned lanterns that would hang there on my wedding day. I imagined the rows of trestle tables covered in lace tablecloths; chairs with beautiful ivory bows; tabletops filled with candles and teapots and vases that would overflow with pretty blush red and cream peonies. I looked over to the edge of the wood by the lake where a large white gazebo stood and imagined it covered in flowers. Tallis would wear a black suit and an ivory waistcoat and cravat, and I would wear my mum's wedding dress, passed down to me from Marchella, who had kept it wrapped carefully ... especially for me. My heart felt light and, as I imagined Tallis's beautiful face, butterflies rose in my stomach. They flittered and fluttered for all they were worth. It was such a wonderful feeling. *So much love*. Thinking about Tallis always kept bad thoughts at bay. His love made me feel almost invincible because I was certain it would last forever.

The next day, I did something I hadn't done since I was an emotionless child. I went to church. I sat in the old wooden pews and prayed. I prayed for the strength to come up with a plan to defeat the enemy. I prayed for the safety of my family and loved ones. I prayed for a miracle.

Outside, after the service, I wandered through the graveyard in the sunshine. It was quiet and peaceful, and I stopped to rest under the shade of a big old oak tree. My nostrils filled with the scent of times past … of moss on stone; aged bark; warm earth and damp grass. It was so nice to be alone. I pulled a book from my bag and leant back against the tree to read. No one would miss me this morning. The family would assume I was off in the cavern practising some magical monster-defeating spell. I was going to enjoy the peace and solitude while I could. I longed for time alone, time I was never allowed unless I was on the plantation. It felt good, and kind of grown-up, to be out here on my own without the watchful eyes of my dad, Marchella and the others.

Suddenly a gust of wind blew up and rustled the leaves on the ground around me, whipping the pages of my book into disarray. I lost my page and my concentration. Then my book flew from my hands. My hair flew madly across my face in the wild breeze, and when I wiped it away and looked up from my book, there in front of me was a young man. He was tall, dark and handsome, a typical prince charming stereotype.

He smiled and knelt down to pick up my book, his dark curls brushing his temples, coming to rest in tangled waves, unkempt and almost savage as if he had just walked across the windy moors of England. My heart fluttered slightly because the situation was almost romantic, even though he was a complete stranger. It was like a scene from a movie. But also, because his smile was close to dangerous — and I realised how vulnerable I was, sitting under a big old oak tree, alone, with a complete unknown kneeling before me.

'Ahh, an admirer of the Bronte sisters I note. A girl with extremely fine taste.' He smiled again as he handed me the book and flashed his super-white teeth. Normal teeth, I noted, no pointy incisors. My heartbeat calmed. Humans rarely talked to me, especially once they knew my last name, so this was a rare pleasure — to be this close to a stranger, who seemed unbothered and almost confident in approaching me.

'Nothing quite like a good book,' I replied. 'Were you in the service this morning? I didn't see you.'

'No, no. Churches, God — and all that is holy — totally not my calling. I was just passing through. Searching for directions actually.'

'Oh, okay. Well I'll see if I can help you. Where are you trying to find?'

'I'm looking for an old plantation around these parts, owned by the Du Plessis family. Would you know of them, or indeed the way to the property?'

Immediately the hairs stood up on the back of my neck. And I was glad I was wearing a long-sleeved dress as I could feel the goosebumps rising on my arms. I was quite sure at first sight that this was just some harmless human due to the lack of pointy teeth. But if he didn't know these parts, he was obviously an out-of-towner. *So why is he interested in a plantation full of vampires?* Well, I wasn't about to reveal my true identity to him or reveal the location of my precious family to a complete stranger, whose agenda I couldn't be sure of. 'No, sorry,' I said. 'I mean I've heard the name before, and I do believe they are around these parts somewhere, but I have no idea where. People at school tend to avoid anyone with the name Du Plessis for some strange reason,' Then I laughed, trying to hide my nervousness.

'Oh, so you are a local?' he said. 'What school do you go to?'

'Benjamin Franklin High,' I said, forcing a smile.

'Would you perchance know if a young lady by the name of Lily Du Plessis attends your school?'

'Once again, I've heard the name, but nobody mixes with the Du Plessis. Must be a bad lot,' I said innocently.

'Well, if you do happen to bump into her, please send her my regards, won't you.'

'Sure will,' I said with a huge, false smile. 'And who shall I say sends his regards?'

'Fabian. Fabian Monsanto.'

I think I physically trembled, but with the gusty wind around me and the flapping pages of my book, I don't think he noticed.

'Okay, I'll be sure to pass that message on if ever I see her. It was nice to meet you, Fabian,' I said, pushing away from the tree. 'I must go now because I'm having brunch with a friend.'

He put his hand out to grasp mine, and I realised he was staring at my ruby ring, the one with the dragon curled around the stone.

'What an exquisite ring,' he said.

'Yes, pretty isn't it? I found it here in the grass last Sunday.' My voice trembled, even though I tried to sound convincing. My heart pounded as I walked away, and I didn't look back. And while I walked, my legs trembling, I could feel his eyes boring into my back.

'By the way, young lady, what is your name?' he shouted after me.

I turned to face him, thankful there was now a good few yards between us.

'Elisabeth,' I shouted back, 'But you can call me Beth.'

'See you again, Beth. See you again soon,' he shouted. Then he stood there watching me until I was a dot in the distance.

TO DREAM OF HIM

Back at the plantation I headed for my room, or rather, the bathroom because I felt physically sick. I had just had a full-on conversation with someone I was going to have to kill or be killed by. Thoughts scurried through my head so fast that they were almost obscure as individual thoughts. I couldn't make any sense of anything, except the jabbing insistence of how stupid I was to go out alone. *What would have happened if I'd introduced myself to him first?*

Did he really believe I was Beth after seeing my ring?

Why did he watch me so long when I walked away?

Did he follow me home?

Have I put my family in danger?

How can I tell them what happened without getting into trouble?

Was he playing with me all along?

Does he know my true identity, after all?

Is he just biding his time, sizing me up, checking out the competition?

So many thoughts, so many questions merging into a blur ... my stomach lurched. Just as worrying was that nobody seemed to notice I'd been absent half the day. Marchella commented at dinner about the time I spent in the cavern being valuable to me, and Dad asked if I had learnt anything new, and whether I thought my skills were increasing with time.

Actually, I had gained a new ability since Olive had left. Which was quite exciting. When I slept, I dreamt of familiar people, and sometimes I would dream of a situation they were in, such as Olive going out to lunch with her brother and discussing her trip to New Orleans. In one dream, Olive told Frankie all the basics, without revealing the supernatural side of the town she loved so much. But even with those details left out, he seemed enthralled and talked excitedly about visiting someday soon. This dream seemed vivid, almost as though I were within inches of them as it happened. I could almost feel their breath as they exhaled and, when they touched, it sent a slight shiver through me as if I were almost a part of them.

Almost a week had passed since this dream. Since then, I had spoken to Olive and asked her about England and her time with the family. During one call, she had described the scene of my dream almost word for word: the lunch with her brother and everything that was said. I realised then that these were not dreams but some weird connection to familiar people I thought about. When I slept, my body or mind had been entering an astral plane that spanned across time and space. This essentially meant I could be in this place and elsewhere at the same time — standing beside certain people, listening in on their conversations. In those moments, when I was possibly pure soul, I could hear their words. When they held hands, I could feel them touching and how it made them feel. It was magical.

Dad looked over at me waiting for a response to his question. 'Lily, honey, did you hear me?' He smiled subtly.

'Well actually, Dad, yes. I didn't think I could have a more intense ability than touching an object and seeing the past. But recently I find that when I go to sleep, I can enter someone else's presence wherever they are, and listen to their conversations. I can even feel them to a degree. I dreamt that Olive had lunch with her brother in a small café in Blackheath, but then when I spoke to her, she repeated word for word everything they'd said, and I realised it wasn't a dream, but an actual interaction of minds while I was sleeping. It was amazing!'

'That particular talent could come in very handy,' said Marchella. 'Why don't you try thinking about someone other than Olive, maybe Charlotte, tonight. See if you can discern her current attitude. We could do with her help you know.'

'Smart thinking, Marchella. I guess that way she would soon know if the path was open for her to hold out the olive branch,' Dad said. Then he stood abruptly, almost knocking over his chair. 'Fabian!' he blurted out, his eyes wide with excitement.

'Fabian, where?' I shouted, bolting up from my seat, almost believing that the dreadful moment had arrived.

'Dream about Fabian! Think about him in your sleep and listen in on his conversations. What a weapon you would have, Lily, if you could utilise it in this way. Do you think it's possible?'

Indeed, I wondered if this would be possible. I had dreamt of those close to me but not about a complete stranger. However, I did have the benefit of knowing what he looked like. I'd been in his company only that morning. His gentlemanly accent resounded in my ears as I remembered his words from the graveyard.

'I can try, for sure. It would give us an amazing advantage if we knew his plans. We could be prepared.'

'Yes, yes!' he said. 'Give it a try, Lily.'

'I will tonight,' I said, beaming back at him.

'Mmm … it might be difficult with you not knowing his whereabouts and what he looks like … it could be impossible,' said

Marchella solemnly.

'Don't be so negative, Mother. She has to try.'

I decided to risk my dad's wrath and come clean about my visit to church. He would be really annoyed, but I figured it was best to tell the truth.

'Well … actually, Dad, I have something to tell you. Now don't be mad.'

I sat down again, hoping he would too, but instead he walked around the table and stood beside me, waiting patiently. My lip trembled slightly when I spoke.

'I have met Fabian.'

'What!' he bellowed.

'Let me explain,' I said, raising my voice. 'I wasn't in the cavern this morning.'

He backed away, absolute disappointment crossing his face, then it mixed with worry and he cocked his head with intrigue. He started pacing, his jaw clenching as he waited for me to continue.

'I went to church.'

Both looked at me oddly. Fell quiet. Stared at me.

Dad grunted slightly.

Marchella shifted uncomfortably in her chair.

'Anyway,' I said, breaking the awkward silence, 'after the service I was reading in the graveyard when a young guy approached me and asked me a few questions. I didn't feel threatened. He was an absolute gentleman — dressed well with lovely manners — had a beautiful old worldly accent. He seemed really nice, not intimidating at all and we talked for a while. Then he asked me the location of our plantation; asked whether or not I personally knew the Du Plessis, and that's when alarm bells went off.'

'Oh, my goodness!' Marchella gasped, putting her hand to her mouth.

'Yeah … and then he asked me to give Lily Du Plessis his regards. I asked, 'who should I say was asking after her?' and he told me his name — Fabian Monsanto!'

My dad looked shocked.

Marchella couldn't speak; her eyes were wide with horror.

'It could have been the end of you today, Lily. What if …' He shook his head.

'I know, right. But I think I fooled him. There was a moment when he took my hand and saw my ring and commented on it. That was bat shit scary, but I just said I'd found it in the grass the week before and he seemed to accept that.'

'He knows!' my dad said. 'I bet he was playing a game, Lily. He would know full well the location of this plantation.'

'I thought about that too,' I said. 'He did stand watching me for a long time, and it did make me wonder. But he could have started something then and there, me all alone without any help. I could have been easy pickings. But no … he let me walk away. He either hasn't got a clue or he's biding his time.'

They both looked at me quietly, worry on their faces but didn't say anything.

'Anyway, I now know what he looks like, what he sounds like. And tonight, I will see if it's possible to dream of him.'

'Okay, Lily, but please promise me you won't go anywhere alone from now on. His coming may be imminent and we all need to be on our guard … promise me.' My dad glared at me, instilling his point.

'I promise, Dad.'

Later that day I walked to the gate to get the post, Elisabeth skipping alongside me, humming a tune. As I lifted the latch to retrieve the letters inside, a strange shudder ran through my arm and the hairs on the back of my neck stood up. Fabian's smile stretched broadly across my mind. I knew in that moment, that he had stood where I now stood, touching the post box, possibly watching me from afar. So, this was my reality. Strange because I always thought the fear I would eventually face would be somehow monstrously terrifying. It was hard to feel that way about such a good-looking guy, with such lovely manners, and a heartwarming smile. But deep inside, I knew I couldn't let my guard down because no matter how I felt, this threat was real, and he would be coming for me sooner or later. This would be a fight to the death for one of us.

I also knew without a doubt that he would try to kill anyone in his path to get to me. My family had become so precious to me, this thought scared and angered me. But anger was good. Any emotion out of control would increase my powers and my chances of winning the battle. I just couldn't bear the thought of Tallis getting hurt. He was so vulnerable right now without the moonstone or the elixir. I would have to devise a plan to keep him safe when the time came.

Slowly walking back to the house, I wondered how this would be possible. Then came the lightbulb moment. *The Cellar*! Dad had talked about a cellar with metal walls in the basement of the house where they had imprisoned my mum all those years ago. *Perfect!* I would just have to enlist the help of some of the stronger young men in the family, as I didn't suppose he'd go willingly. It would have to be a trap and, while I knew he would be mad at me, it had to be done. I couldn't risk losing him. I'd rather die than live without him.

That night in bed, I slept restlessly, trying to picture Charlotte's face. After a while, my perseverance worked, and I was transported to a time when she was standing in the kitchen. She was alone. I watched her walking around deep in thought, tapping what looked like a pen against her brow, occasionally chewing the end of it. She took a seat at the table and began to write. I stood closer, leant over her shoulder to see the words. It was a letter to me! It seemed to be an apology for doing me wrong. The writing was fuzzy, hard to make out, but bits of it floated off the page at me

> *'Alex persuaded me' ... 'The love I feel for him makes me his puppet' ... 'Can't believe it's gone this far' ... 'Sorry may never be enough ...'*

I couldn't make the words stay still. Couldn't make any sense of the total content, but one thing was clear: she was finding fault in Alex and apologising for her behaviour. That was good enough for me. It paved the way for me to make amends with her, and that's exactly what I wanted.

Pippa had wrapped herself around my head and, feeling slightly claustrophobic, I woke from my dream. Pulling her to one side, I snuggled down into my pillow once more. This time with a clear vision of Fabian in my head. This was a hard one. I thought and thought about him, but other than the memory of him standing in the graveyard, nothing came to me. He stood by the tree I had been leaning against and softly touched the bark. I looked to where I had been standing, but the space was empty. So no, this was not a memory. This was actually happening. Behind him, I saw another figure, more of a shadow than a form and I couldn't make out the features. Another man maybe, as tall as Fabian, his shadow large. But when Fabian looked in his direction and talked to him, there came no audible answer — that I could hear.

'I'm going out of town for a short while, I'll be back in a month or two,' Fabian said.

The shadow moved and Fabian's arm went up as if to protest.

'I have important matters to attend to. There is no hurry, the sure demise of the young lady will happen in good time. We may as well let her enjoy her last few months on earth in peace. Soon all of this will be mine.'

He smiled that endearing smile as he spoke in his impeccable gentleman's accent, waving his hand in the air to dramatise his last words.

The shadow lunged at him, caught him off guard. He tripped and fell, but no sooner had the looming shadow pounced than Fabian was back on his feet and had a vice-like grip around the shadow's neck. I was still unable to make out who it was? I wondered why he suddenly attacked Fabian. *Is this person he's first talking to, and battling with, someone I know, someone on my side?*

Fabian shouted at the shadow. 'I'll wipe you all from the face of the earth. Do you think you stand a chance against me? All of you, do you hear? If I can't have her, then she must die. The balance of power will shift too uncomfortably in her favour if I allow her to live. It's as simple as that. Don't try to fight me on this, you fool.'

He let go of his grip, and the shadow jumped back, away from him, gasping for air. Fabian stood up, squared his shoulders, and straightened his jacket. He wiped his dark unruly curls back into place, looking like a gentleman again. He patted the shadow on the back and said, 'Listen, we know not the outcome thus far. The young lady may very well have the intelligence to succumb to my charms rather than lose her life in battle. There could yet be a very amicable ending to this situation we find ourselves in.'

The shadow's head dropped solemnly — he knew he was

beaten.

'You released me, you fool. What were you expecting? ... that I'd hand over my rightful kingdom to her and that pathetic wolfling? I will rid her of the fool she loves, you may not have a care in the world on that matter, but never cross me, do you hear me? Never cross me!'

He turned once more towards the tree and knelt down before it, touching the ground at its base where I had stood last Sunday. 'Pretty little thing — certainly a face to revere,' he said with a smile. 'Shame about that.'

Then he stood and walked away, leaving the shadow to loom over the patch of grass. I believe I saw a tear fall to the ground beneath him. And woke with a start. The dream and every word came back to me as clear as a cloudless sky. My first thought was that I was safe for now. He was going out of town and had mentioned that I had a few months, a couple at least. This would give me more time to prepare, more time to get Charlotte back on side — more time to find the elixir formula or the moonstone. *It's time to marry the man I love in peace, with no threat hanging over me.*

But, as the rest of the conversation came flooding to my mind, I realised this was not as clear-cut as it seemed. Fabian had a notion that I could possibly be his ... that I would choose him over death. The absurdity of that shocked me. He didn't want to kill me unless he had to. He wanted me to be with him, but that was never going to happen, not in a million years. Tallis was the only one for me and if I had to die to prove that, I would, willingly. Not that I intended to give up easily, of course, I'd summon every ounce of power to win the battle. *But who is the shadow? Why did he release Fabian? And why is he sad for me?*

It was so confusing. If only I could have seen who the shadow was or even heard his voice. It could have been anyone, but it was quite obviously someone who knew me. I discounted anyone really close, not my own family surely, not a Monsanto, though maybe. Not Alex, for sure, because he loved me whether I liked it or not. Maybe Briff Lestrange, in revenge for his uncle, I shuddered at the thought. One thing I knew for sure was that, with my new ability to spy in my sleep, I would be keeping a close eye on Fabian over the next few weeks, getting to know his ways, his weaknesses and strengths, and the exact time of his coming, so I could be fully prepared and able to warn the others. I could also make plans to keep Tallis safe. This brought me some amount of relief. But for now, my life would go on as normal. Or as normal as was possible in my chaotic supernatural world!

A TRAITOR IN OUR MIDST

Marchella and I wandered through the markets flanked heavily by the wolfling, in human form of course and slightly disinterested in our little shopping spree, which was all about lace and flowers. Still, their presence was comforting, and Marchella and I spent a wonderful couple of hours scouring the markets for time-worn lace tablecloths, old teapots, cups and saucers, and vases for all the table flowers. My wedding theme was going to be 'old-fashioned' — kind of 'shabby chic' because I wanted to wear Mum's wedding gown, which was in that style. It was packed in a box and passed down to me by Marchella. When I opened the box, I fell in love with it. It was a beautiful Vera Wang, light ivory, A-line macrame lace gown, paired with a light ivory split away lace skirt with corset details and elbow-length sleeves — so elegant, yet so 'high tea in the garden'. It would go perfectly with the blush red and cream peonies Marchella had ordered for the bouquets and table vases. I originally wanted pink, but Marchella said, 'Oh no, my dear, red is so in fashion this year.' *Isn't it in fashion every year when you are a vampire?* I thought, but I let her have her way. It was great fun shopping for the last bits, and overwhelming to know that come this Saturday I would become the wife of Tallis Summers — although I had already decided to keep my own surname and just add his on the end: Mrs Lily Du-Plessis-Summers. It had a nice ring to it.

Fabian was constantly in the back of my mind, but I saw no plans in my dreams for his immediate return. All the hard work I'd been doing to perfect my magic and increase my powers in his absence seemed to be paying off. I felt proud of myself for learning so much in such a short time. Marchella had been by my side every step of the way, guiding me, pushing me — even occasionally losing her temper with me when I wanted to give up and sleep. So, I forged on, and up until two days ago, I'd been living on four hours sleep a night, which was incredibly draining. Last night I'd slept like a log — felt almost comatose — and when I woke up this morning, I felt as though I'd been kissed by a prince and awoken from a hundred-year sleep. Tallis took my hand as we made our way out into the street. I leant up on tippy-toes to kiss him and thought about how wonderful he was in every way, as he held me lightly about the waist as his lips brushed mine.

'We better finish up shopping now — Olive arrives at four,' Tallis said as we headed along the street towards the waiting vehicle. Olive had been gone six weeks already and the time had flown by. I'd been so busy looking for the moonstone, and any other possible escape from my impending doom, but also being forced by Dad, Marchella and the wolfling to get ready for the possible impending battle with Fabian that I hadn't had a minute to miss her. Happiness filled my insides to bursting ... to know she'd be arriving today and staying forever. Well, forever in human terms at least. And that was enough for me, for now.

We drove back to the plantation, and Tallis helped me to empty the boot of all our purchases. He then lay on the porch for an afternoon nap while Marchella and I made our way through to the kitchen with as much stuff as we could carry.

Later that night, as Olive and I lay out on the roof beneath my window underneath the stars, we discussed every detail of every minute we'd spent apart. I was glad my Uncle Caleb was away for the weekend because it meant I had Olive all to myself, at least for a couple of days.

'I can't believe you're going to be a married woman this time next week,' squealed Olive, squeezing my arms.

'I know,' I said. 'I'm kind of scared and excited all rolled into one. I keep thinking how young I am to be doing this. But then I keep thinking — whatever — I'm always going to be this young,' I giggled nervously, and Olive squeezed me even tighter.

'My mum was so happy to hear the news. She was so unhappy about me coming to live here. But she was so happy for you that she couldn't keep the sad act up for long. Anyway, I promised I'd visit sometimes, and I'm sure she'll come here too, although it probably wouldn't be a great idea to bring her to the plantation.'

'No, not at all,' I replied. 'But with the potential danger of the loft at the townhouse lifted we could always take her there.'

'Yeah, what's up with that? Have you heard anything more about what was released?'

'Oh yeah! It's another immortal — Fabian Monsanto — and he's after me. I don't know who released him, but I know it wasn't us because there was an important element missing from Charlotte's spell. Whoever released him used the moonstone, the one used to create Tallis. We all thought it was just a vampire that was sealed in the loft, but it was way worse. An evil entity. An almost emotionless immortal, who's hell-bent on ruining my life. I can tell you that much,' I frowned.

'Oh, Lily, no ...' Olive gasped.

'It's the truth, I swear it. I've been keeping track of him in my dreams, so I'll know when he's coming for me.'

'What are you going to do?'

'Well, I've been preparing. Marchella has been helping me to unleash my powers and to control them effectively. We've been at it for weeks now. You know my powers are linked to my emotions. So, I've just been learning how to trigger them — to think of something that makes me mad or sad. It's quite hard when I have nothing to be mad or sad about right now, but I'm sure my time will come.'

I stared dreamily out of the window thinking about my perfect life and wondering how I'd ever muster enough emotional rage to outwit Fabian. Everyone was counting on me, and that pressure was so hard to handle, but I didn't want to download to Olive, not when she'd just decided to move here. I didn't want her to know it might all be for nothing.

'Do you still have the backup of the Monsantos? Or are they on his side?'

'They didn't release him. They're as freaked out as the rest of us. They are on my side, totally. The most likely suspect is my grandad, but we haven't been able to find him.'

'Don't look so worried, Lily. You have an army of vampires surrounding you, and I really don't think they will let Fabian get anywhere near you.'

'Well, that's just it. All of their combined strength means nothing against a force like Fabian. Rather than protecting me, they are all looking at me to protect them.'

'Well, that's not so ridiculous either. I'm sure your mum knew what she was doing when she created you. She must have known about the other immortal surely. She must have known you would be able to defeat him?'

I hadn't thought of that. I'd been feeling angry at her for weeks now; angry that she had created me for this. *What kind of mother creates a child to fight a war? So selfish!* She wanted to unite the clans, to bring peace, but not at her own cost, at mine!

But maybe Olive is right. If Mum was working for the Monsanto, I'm sure she'd have learnt about the legend of the other immortal, before she made me. So, she must have been confident I'd be more powerful than him.

'Maybe, but as far as I know, nobody knew except the Monsanto elders. He's a terrible evil, and he's been around a very long time, so unless I fine-tune my emotions, I'm not at all sure what will happen when I come face to face with him.'

'Well, I believe in you, Lily. Your ability to love wholeheartedly is proof of the strength of your emotions. If he's as evil as they say, I doubt he has the ability to control himself fully, if at all. He probably has the emotional capacity of a fly.'

'Let's hope so,' I said with a twisted smile. 'Let's really hope so'. *But let's also hope we can locate the moonstone and seal him away again, so I don't have to lose my life trying to save a bunch of people I hardly know'.*

The following day Olive and I spent almost the whole day in the cavern. I showed her a few tricks, some of what I had become capable of. It was so funny to see her shocked expression jump to the surface so freely and so often, as though she really couldn't believe her eyes.

'I really have to consider what to do to protect Tallis when the time arrives,' I said sadly. 'He's going to be so pissed off at me, but I think the cellar is the only way.'

'Better the cellar than the grave,' said Olive.

'True,' I said, 'very true.'

We were at the back of the cavern near the fire pit, where last I had seen a head roll in the grate and watched those human eyes sizzle and pop in the intense heat. I wasn't about to reveal any details of that event to poor Olive, and yet a shadow of guilt fell over me that there had to be secrets between us.

'Let's talk to Caleb when he's back tomorrow. We'll ask him to arrange a group of willing family members to help with a plan we can use at the last minute. When you know Fabian is on his way, they can just spring into action and lock Tallis away in the cellar until the danger passes.'

Yeah, that's a good plan. But Tallis mustn't get wind of it. He'd totally lose his shit!'

'Absolutely! I can't imagine him going gracefully,' she said with a suppressed giggle.

'He'll fight them to the death to protect me. So, they are bound to have a struggle on their hands. Maybe we should see if Caleb could possibly organise a tranquilliser gun, just to put him out for a short while. It may be the kindest thing to do.'

'Great idea,' said Olive. 'Not that Tallis will consider it kind, but I get where you're coming from.'

'You always do,' I said with a huge smile.

'Still no sign of your grandad then?' Olive asked next.

'So far, no. My dad's men have enquired everywhere but with no luck. He has at every turn throughout my life just waited for an opportunity to pounce, and now, when we need him to appear, he's vanished without a trace.'

'Maybe he's already on his way back to England. If he thinks Fabian will succeed in killing you, perhaps he thinks he's no longer needed here.'

'Maybe,' I nodded. 'We have a team going to England too, to see if they can track him down. Finding the moonstone is our only defense against Fabian, and our only hope for Tallis.'

Olive sat quietly, staring at me.

'What?' I said, noting the strange look on her face.

'You dreamt of me when I was in England, yeah? And you dreamt of Fabian to track his moves?' she said excitedly.

'Yes ... oh, yes! Olive, you're a genius!'

To find my grandad all I had to do was dream of him, and soon the moonstone would be mine!

That night I tossed and turned in my sleep, one leg out of the covers and then back in as thoughts of monsters under my bed ran riot. Who would have thought an adult would still have those childish thoughts in slumber? But it was a regular occurrence for me and often woke me from my sleep. I sat up and flicked on my lamp, wanting to head for the bathroom, but too fearful of placing my feet on the floorboards, afraid of something grabbing my ankles.

Don't be so stupid, Lily! You're immortal. You have nothing to fear but another immortal, and there's hardly likely to be one under the bed. I chuckled inwardly at this notion and quickly hopped out of bed and ran to the bathroom. Climbing back into bed five minutes later, I quickly checked under the bed beforehand ... just in case. Nothing there except a few discarded socks and an odd slipper, so I snuggled up under the covers. I tried to drift back to sleep with thoughts of another kind of monster — my grandad — and as sleep overtook me, I found myself standing on the deck of a boat, at the edge of a circular table. And right there in front of me sat my grandad and three of his men. He held a fishing rod and carefully applied a maggot to the end of a hook. I looked around to get my bearings; tried to fathom exactly where we were. But all around me were just unfamiliar marshes and a murky river running farther than the eye could see. This could possibly be the Louisiana swampland but I couldn't be sure. It could just as well be some river in England, and in a sleeping state, I was unable to judge the weather conditions. There was no hot or cold. I looked for clues in the sky, but when I looked out past the vision of Grandad everything began to blur. I brought my focus back to him and the others at the table.

'So, what's the plan after today?' the big bald guy to the left of my grandad asked.

'I haven't decided,' Grandad said. 'We can't get anywhere near the plantation. And since our last visit resulted in Stan's hanging, I don't think it's a good idea to get too close to Lily and those crazy bloodsuckers. Anyway, I don't see the point. I've failed. She's eighteen now and we are totally defenseless against her. We've wasted so many opportunities over the years. I cannot believe she's still breathing. But there you go, guys ... our job is over. So, home it is I guess, and we'll just keep our ear to the ground for news of any newly born immortal children. Until that happens, I guess it's back to the normal daily grind.'

'Makes me sick that she got off scot-free. No repercussions for her over the death of poor Lilith and dear old Noah,' said the bald guy. The other two just nodded.

'You guys didn't even know my son and daughter so what the hell are you on about? Don't make it personal. This was my war, not yours. I may have lost, but someday she'll get what's coming to her. Good always triumphs over evil.'

This last sentence made me shudder.

My grandad really thought he was a good guy doing the right thing by trying to get rid of me, and he really saw me as evil. This was not how I saw myself. I may be immortal, but I certainly wasn't evil! In *my* eyes, my grandad was the bad guy. But 'bad guy' though he was, he was obviously not the bad guy who released Fabian from the loft. Otherwise, I was sure the conversation would have gone more along the lines: '*We'll leave the crazy gentleman to rip Lily's heart out, and go back to England safe in the knowledge that we did our bit to avenge poor Lilith and Noah'.* But no, this was a defeated man. My grandad was miserable — failure was written all over his face. I guess it didn't matter that I would wake without the slightest idea of where he was because obviously, he had no idea about Fabian's release. Therefore, he would not have the moonstone. I felt a raging disappointment creep over me, mingled with sadness that turned to despair when I thought about Tallis and the uncertainty of what our future would hold.

When I woke the next day, Olive was sitting at the end of my bed, smiling broadly, expectant. How I would have loved to give her the news she waited for. But no. Instead, I burst into tears as the clarity of the dream forced itself back into my head, and out poured the disappointment from my mouth. Olive hugged me as I cried, and Pippa wrangled her way in between us and tried to nudge a belly rub out of my hand. *Jealous little feline.*

'We need to get our thinking caps on,' said Olive. 'We have to work out who the traitor is. It has to be someone in New Orleans — someone who wants you dead. Surely there can't be too many people out there that despise you. I mean, you're so lovely — it can't be personal. It has to be someone very depraved, like ...' Olive looked deep in thought then she suddenly shouted, 'Charlotte! What about Charlotte?'

'Oh, Olive, that's just ridiculous. She's a bit warped yes, and perhaps suffers from a bit of jealousy when it comes to me, because of Alex. But I don't think she's depraved.'

'Okay, well what about Alex?'

'No, not Alex. Alex loves me. That I know for sure. And I don't believe he'd ever hurt me. He'd wipe out my family without a second thought, but I don't believe he'd want me dead.'

'Well, what about his dad, the old guy?'

'Well, no. I don't think *he* would be idiotic enough to release something that would not only kill me but the entire supernatural community. And he was a good friend of my mum, and he has sworn to protect me.' I scratched my chin, deep in thought.

'Briff?' said Olive.

'Briff ... yes. Briff is a huge possibility. He would love to see me dead. But how on earth would he have got a hold of a moonstone that's been lost in England for eighteen years? It just doesn't make sense.'

'Well, out of everyone in this supernatural circle, he seems the most likely suspect. I mean he definitely seems to have a score to settle, although I don't know why?'

A flush of guilt heated my cheeks at this innocent comment, but I still couldn't tell her about my murderous behaviour, I just couldn't, so I nodded.

It did make sense though for two reasons. Firstly, Briff wanted his revenge on me because of the death of his uncle, and secondly, because the moonstone had originally belonged to the Primeval wolf. I'd heard the story from Emmanuelle. The ancients and the elders of the werewolf clans knew the story too. *But does Briff know the whole story? Does he think he can gain favour amongst the clans by returning the moonstone to its rightful owner?*

'You could be right, Olive, but it may not be about settling a score. You see, there's a story about the moonstone and how the Monsanto came to possess it.'

'Tell me,' said Olive. 'I want to know.'

'Well, far back in the early 1820s Elijah Monsanto, Emmanuelle's dad, married a voodoo queen called Anastasia Du Preez and they created Fabian. When he reached maturity, his dad and many others realised he was pure evil, but his dad Elijah couldn't bring himself to kill him and the immortal child hunters failed at every turn.'

'Mmm ... tough choice for a parent. So, what did he do instead?'

'Elijah withheld the ink for his tattoo so he didn't receive his mother's magical powers of the dark craft. They allowed the witches to destroy it. Then Fabian killed his dad for revenge.'

'No! He killed his own dad. Surely not!' Olive's jaw dropped open.

'Yeah, I'm afraid so, and Emmanuelle vowed to avenge his dad.'

'Good on him!' said Olive, nodding seriously.

'There was an ancient prophecy that told of a spell to seal an immortal away. Without the ink, there could be no immortal sleeve, leaving Fabian vulnerable to the witches. But the prophecy foretold that there also needed to be a black rose for binding and a moonstone containing great power for use in the sealing spell.'

'And this is the moonstone we're searching for?'

'Yes. The witch's coven, and Emmanuelle formed a plan. Together they confronted the Primeval wolf. Emmanuelle fought almost to the death to obtain the moonstone and, using their combined powers, the witches cast a spell as he battled for his life. Just as the Primeval wolf was about to strike a fatal blow, he turned to stone right before their eyes, saving Emmanuelle's life. The coven retrieved the moonstone and used it to seal Fabian away.'

'Oh, thank goodness!' said Olive.

'A black rose was flown in from Turkey, and a supernatural army was formed to bring Fabian to his knees, and finally to the loft where he was successfully sealed away. He had wreaked so much havoc and destruction on the human and supernatural worlds and had brought death to the best of many clans, all were happy to see him finally put into a death-like sleep.'

'Wow! But didn't that cause the werewolves to rise up and fight to retrieve the moonstone?' Olive said, frowning.

'No, not at all. You see, under the reign of the Primeval wolf, the werewolves lived a suppressed and miserable life. They were often tortured, and they all lived in fear of him. When he was turned to stone, they all enjoyed a new kind of freedom. They elected a new leader who was fair and just in their eyes, and their old leader was left in stone. It would have been possible for any one of the elders to ask for the moonstone back to release him, but not one of them was willing to bring his reign of tyranny back on their people. So, the moonstone remained with the Monsanto family with the blessing of the elder werewolves. It had been in Emmanuelle's possession right up until he handed it to my mum just before my birth. She took it to England and created Tallis with it. No one knows what became of it after that.'

'Maybe it's not Briff then, because surely he would know the history of the Primeval wolf and only a fool would go against the elders.'

'Who's to say he's not a fool?'

'So, what do we do now? How do we find out if he has the moonstone?'

'I don't know. We could enlist Charlotte's help, but I would have to make amends first. And I'm not totally sure we will have enough time.'

'Why?'

'Because I dreamt of Fabian last night and he is making plans to return. I don't know exactly when. But I feel our time is definitely running out.'

SAVING LILY DU PLESSIS

Late on Sunday Caleb returned. Olive's face flushed and her eyes sparkled when he walked into the room. I had to agree that Uncle Caleb sure had a wonderful way about him. I could certainly imagine him having many admirers, but the way he looked at my best friend was as though it was the first time he had ever laid eyes on a woman. When all the greetings and welcome homes were done, I sat with my dad, Caleb and Olive devising a plan to keep Tallis safe — without his knowledge of course. Dad gave Caleb the key to the cellar for safekeeping, and we drew up a list of guys who would help to secure Tallis in the cellar when the time came.

'There's no way he'll go easily,' Dad said. 'It's in the breeding, Lily. Even if we explain the dangers, he won't listen. It's like these wolflings are on autopilot, programmed so they cannot be averted by any means. He would gladly die for you and we are going to need a lot of force to take him down.'

'But is the cellar secure enough?' Caleb asked.

'Yes, most certainly. If we can get him in there, he will be safe,' Dad assured him.

'Have you seen the size of him when he turns?' Olive said, wide eyed. 'He's huge.'

'Yes, well there's strength in numbers. We'll just have to make sure there are enough of us at hand to complete the task,' said

Caleb.

I was quiet, listening but feeling terrible discussing all this behind Tallis's back, the man I was about to marry, who loved me more than life itself. But there was no other way to keep him safe. He'd never agree to being locked away while I went into battle against Fabian. Bloody hell no! I sincerely hoped the cellar would hold him because he would tear it apart to escape if he could, protecting me so hardwired into him. It was his only mission in life — to keep me safe — to save me. Well, now it was my turn to save him.

While everyone around me plotted, planned and strategised, getting ready for the onslaught of terror to come, I lived on the hope that our efforts to find the moonstone would be fruitful; that the battle would be avoided. I prayed constantly that all these meetings turned out to be a waste of time, that Tallis and everyone, me included, would be safe from this fiend. I had seen what he was capable of: he was a warped individual, and it wouldn't be a fair fight. And for that reason, I was frightened. But everyone was counting on me, so much so I felt I would buckle under the pressure. I had to please everyone — including my mum- but guilt seeped deeply through me, knowing she would be disappointed in me — not for going into battle and losing, but for not wanting to bear this responsibility at all.

'Right. All plans are in place,' said Caleb. 'You just have to say the word, Lily, and we'll spring into action.'

'Thanks, Caleb, Dad ... Thank you both.'

Olive squeezed my hand tightly. 'It'll be okay, Lily, just you wait and see. Caleb has a tranquilliser gun ready just in case. He won't use it unless there's a real problem, but it's a good back up.'

So it was all sorted. And as bad as I felt keeping the truth from Tallis, there was some relief knowing he would be safe when the time came.

'Okay, well now we have to discuss what we are going to do about Briff. How can we find out if he has the moonstone?' said Olive.

'I've dreamt about him, and other than having a close shave with him stripping off and getting in the shower right in front of me — which was quite an assault on the senses — he is a man of few words. So far, he hasn't revealed anything about his possible involvement in releasing Fabian. All he seems to do is eat and sleep.'

'I guess Charlotte is our only avenue there then. You'll have to contact her and see if she can help locate the moonstone. That way, whether it is Briff who has it or someone else, she could lead us straight to its location,' said Olive.

'Okay. Well, I guess it's time to make the call,' I said hesitantly.

Swallowing my pride and apologising to get back on her good side was going to be difficult, but I knew it had to be done. I desperately needed her help to find the moonstone - but she would be doing much more than that. She could inadvertently be saving my life. Who would have thought Charlotte capable of such a heroic act ... not that she'd have any knowledge of it. Agonising momentarily, I dialled Charlotte's number.

She picked up immediately, which was a good sign. If she was really mad, she could have ignored my call.

'Hi, Charlotte. It's Lily here.'

'Hi, Lily,'

'I'm calling to say sorry for losing it that day at the plantation.'

'When you called me a bitch?' she said confidently.

'Yes, when I called you a ... a bitch,' I said awkwardly.

'Okay. Well, apology accepted, because I guess you were right,' she said as simply as that.

'Well, do you want to catch up?' I said quietly.

'Yeah, sure,' she said calmly.

'When?'

'Whenever.'

An awkward silence ensued, then, after a few seconds, she said, 'I can pop over if you like. I'm not doing anything tomorrow. What do you think?'

'Yeah, that'd be lovely,' I said, relieved that she'd made the decision.

'Okay then, see you tomorrow around twelve.'

'Twelve sounds good.'

'See you then.'

'Bye, Charlotte.'

'Bye, Lily.'

'Well, that was slightly uncomfortable. I guess it will take a little while to get back to normal. But it will be worth it to have her back on side,' I said to Dad, and he nodded in agreement.

'You know the old saying: *keep your friends close and your enemies closer*,' said Caleb.

'Shit, yeah,' I nodded. 'I can do that, no problem.'

When Charlotte turned up the following day, I handed her an invitation to my wedding. It was the best olive branch I could think of given the circumstances. When she opened it, her sour face suddenly melted into one of the most genuine smiles I'd ever seen her wear. She immediately hugged me, breaking down the wall between us instantly. Olive had gone out with Caleb for the day to give me some time alone with Charlotte, Charlotte not good at sharing at the best of times. But today I knew she would want to be alone with me.

'It's good to see you, Lily. It's been so long.'

'Sure has. I'm truly sorry for what I said.'

'I deserved it. I *was* actually being a bitch.'

'No, you weren't. Not really.'

'Oh, you don't know the half of it. I was jealous of you, Lily.'

'Jealous? But why?'

'Oh, you know how it goes … new girl comes to town — she's prettier, funnier, more popular,' she smiled weakly.

'Charlotte, I'm so sorry. I didn't know you felt that way. I value your friendship, you know.'

I wasn't lying because, until recently at the Monsanto's, I had no idea how Charlotte felt, or that she was head over heels for Alex. I totally got it now and this revelation excused anything awful she'd ever said or done to me.

'Don't say that. You make me feel bad. I've been a terrible friend. If I were you, I'd never talk to me again.'

'Don't be so hard on yourself. We all have our dark side. It's over now, so let's just put it behind us.'

'But …' she said, almost in a whisper, 'you don't know what I've done.'

Ah, but I did know. She just didn't know I knew, and I wasn't about to let on that I knew the truth about her and Alex. 'It doesn't matter,' I said. 'Honestly, I'd rather not know. If you are really sorry for whatever it is then let's just wipe the slate clean.'

'But I really need to tell you.'

'I really don't want to know, Charlotte. Can we leave it at that please?' I said.

'Okay, but if you find out for yourself one day, you can't hold it against me, because I was willing to come clean.'

I didn't want to humiliate her. I already knew the truth, so why should she feel so bad about her actions when it was Alex that had played us both? He didn't matter to me, so her sleeping with him didn't matter to me. I really just felt sad at how he had treated her and wondered whether she was still allowing him to walk all over her. Love has the strangest effect on people.

'I swear I'll forgive whatever it is. Okay? Can we change the subject now?'

'Okay, have it your way,' she said, looking at the floor. 'Maybe I could do something for you that would make me feel better about what I've done. Even though you don't want to know what it is. Is there anything you need that maybe I can help with?'

'Funny you should say that,' I said with a wry smile.

'Anything,' said Charlotte.

'Maybe you could do a little spell for me, a location spell. I simply don't have the time myself, what with planning the wedding and all.'

I didn't want to give her any real details on exactly why we were looking for the moonstone, and I certainly didn't want her to know about Fabian. But I needed her help to locate it so I had to come up with something quickly.

'Remember when I called you a bitch?'

'Sure do, like it was yesterday,' she said.

'Well, I was just mad because I felt you were dangling a red herring in front of me, giving me that book and suggesting the elixir formula was in it, even though you were acting like it probably wasn't.'

'I know. It was really mean of me, but I wasn't lying. I really thought it might be the formula for the elixir. I just couldn't be 100% sure. But then you were going on about Tallis, and I felt so jealous that you had a love like that. You see, I want a love like that, and what I actually have is so far from the fairytale it makes me crazy sometimes.'

'It's okay. I understand. But I'm still left with a dilemma because, as it turns out, it wasn't the correct formula. I still don't know the location of Tallis's moonstone. If we draw a little blood from him, do you think you could try a location spell for me?'

'Yeah, of course I can.'

'Great!'

'Well, let's get to it,' said Charlotte. 'The sooner I do something spectacularly nice for you, the better I will feel about myself.'

I laughed when Charlotte said this because I seriously thought she was trying to be funny. But she didn't laugh with me; just stood up, picked up her bag and headed for the door with me following close behind. We found Tallis and Mylo sitting in the kitchen going over their wedding speeches. The look on their faces when I walked in was as if I'd walked in on them plotting to murder the queen. They were being so secretive, fell silent, then folded their papers in half so I couldn't see the writing.

'It's okay. We'll be gone in a minute. I just want some of your blood,' I said, looking at Tallis.

'What, my heart is not enough for you?' he said with a cheeky grin. He stuck his finger out ready for the pin I held ready. I took what I needed then kissed him on the lips and headed off to the cavern — me with an expectant heart, and Charlotte with a hidden agenda that would rid herself of her guilty conscience.

Once we were in the confines of the cavern, we opened Mum's grimoire and gathered everything we needed for the spell. I was hopeful the answer to my prayers could really be this simple, but half an hour later I felt deflated. The crystal ball misted over as the spell was performed, but though we waited patiently no vision appeared. In fact, the mist just thickened and turned a murky grey.

'I don't know what's wrong,' Charlotte said. 'I get a strong feeling that Tallis's moonstone is here in New Orleans and not in England as you suspected. Its energy is too strong to be that far away. But other than that, I can't tell you where it is. It's trying to show itself, but something or someone is stopping it. It's hidden. Maybe locked away in something, maybe a metal box of some kind. Objects are hard to locate if they are encased in anything made of metal, silver, or gold even. Wherever it is or whoever has it, we are not going to find it with a location spell, they've made damn sure of that!'

'You mean whoever has it is hiding it?'

'I'd say it's a huge possibility. I'd say whoever has it doesn't want anyone to know.'

'Why do you think that?'

'Because this moonstone has a force that feels trapped. It's like it knows it's in the wrong hands. If it was lost, buried somewhere or laying forgotten in some cupboard, it wouldn't be emitting such a strange vibe. It's like a beacon out at sea in the pitch-black desperately flashing its little light, eager for someone to find it.'

'Isn't that a bit strange?'

'Not at all. If this moonstone created Tallis, it will only settle when it's back in his possession. What I don't understand is why someone would be hiding it? I mean, what use would it be to anyone other than Tallis?' She wasn't prying this time she was genuinely confused. However, I wasn't about to go jumping in feet first again trusting her with the details of my private life, especially as I now knew she had a strong connection to Alex. He wasn't in the meeting, so I doubted he knew anything about the situation, but I felt the less people who knew, the better. I didn't want anyone involved that didn't need to be. Fabian had talked to me in the church graveyard, and he could very well be talking to people all over town, trying to gain information about me and my family. I didn't want anyone tipping the enemy off, accidentally or otherwise. Charlotte was waiting for a reply, but I kept my silence, just sat staring at the crystal ball wishing it had more to tell. One thing I now knew for sure was that a battle was inevitable. We were not going to be able to find the moonstone in time, if at all, and Fabian would be coming for me. Sooner or later, he would be coming.

'So, the wedding is next Saturday?' said Charlotte.

'Yes.'

'You don't seem all that excited.'

'Oh, I am. I just have other stuff on my mind,' I said sadly.

'Is it the age thing? I mean you are a bit young to be settling down with someone.'

'I'm always going to be this young, remember? I'm immortal.'

'Oh yeah, sorry. I forgot. Another thing to be jealous of: I'm going to grow old and decrepit and you are always going to look this gorgeous!'

'I'm afraid so,' I said.

'Ugh, it's not fair. I hate you.' Charlotte stamped her foot, but she smiled, and I knew she was pulling my leg. 'Thanks for the invite. After everything that's happened, it means a lot to me.'

'No problem, Charlotte. It wouldn't be the same without you there.'

'If there's anything I can do to help, you know, on the day, setting up or anything? Just let me know. I'm happy to help.'

Charlotte never ceased to surprise me. She had proven she could be absolutely awful occasionally. But there was something about her that always made me want to forgive.

When she finally went home, it was quite late.

Olive drew up in the car with Caleb just as Charlotte's mum hooted her horn at the gates. It had been a long day and I was tired but in no mood to sleep without Tallis. I kept thinking about the moonstone, or lack of it, and what this could possibly mean for him if it were never found. I couldn't always keep him out of harm's way; there were bound to be times I would come up against enemies, and I didn't know how I would stop Tallis trying to protect me. This thought scared me. To tell Tallis to save himself and not to worry about me would be like telling a fish not to swim. The danger would always be there. The risk of Tallis losing his life would always be hanging over me. I couldn't bear the thought of living without him. I wanted to spend forever with him, and forever was exactly what I had ahead of me.

I started thinking about the people I loved — Tallis, Olive ... Charlotte. People who I felt life would mean nothing without. This included my dad, Marchella and even young Elisabeth. Two on my mental list were human, but even the supernaturals in my life suddenly felt easily expendable, like they could be wiped from the face of the earth at any time. It seemed an impossible task for me to keep everyone safe all of the time, regardless of my abilities, my strengths, and my immortality. It was impossible to be with all of my loved ones every minute of every day. Of course, there would be times when any one of them could find themselves in trouble without me by their side and I struggled with this thought.

Suddenly forever seemed like a very, very, very long time. And I was heading into an eternity of loneliness.

I wandered through the house searching for Tallis, found him asleep on the couch out on the porch. I sat on the porch swing, watched him sleeping and was overwhelmed by my feelings for him. A lump rose in my throat, and tears welled in my eyes. I sat there and wept as Tallis slept on unaware. When he stirred and he sat up, he noticed me sitting in the dark, puffy-eyed.

'What's up, Princess?' he said, his brow creasing with worry.

'Just contemplating what forever really means,' I said wistfully.

'Well, to me, forever means a lifetime of loving you. How lucky does that make me?' he said with a smile. He patted the seat beside him and I moved across the porch and settled by his side, snuggled into him for comfort. There was no place I'd rather be than in his arms. I felt so safe. He was so calm and soothing on the soul, and as usual, he made all the sadness disappear. I fell asleep in his arms, thinking about Fabian and how long it would be until he came to unravel all of this loveliness; drifted into a dream that quickly became a nightmare. I was standing in a dark room, in a strange house. I moved slowly forward unable to see ahead of me. Suddenly I tripped over something and, as I fell, I put out my hands to break my fall and landed in something wet and sticky. I quickly rose to my feet, the pungent aroma of blood wafting from my hands to my nose as I wiped the wetness on my jacket. Shocked and scared, I carried on walking, through to the next room. I could see better in this space as the light from the tall windows made everything more visible. And gasped! Bodies were strewn across the room, blood splattered in all directions, on most surfaces. In a bowl on a little round wooden table was a pile of … hands. I looked at the bodies and down at where the hands should be, and I was right. I wanted to vomit. *Why would someone remove their hands?* As I looked at the women's faces, I realised they were familiar to me — I had seen them somewhere before — not all, but some. I thought back carefully to where I had seen them. My mum's box — the one my dad had given me — came to mind. Yes, that was it, the photo of her and her coven. At least a handful of these women were in that picture. I didn't recognise the others, but they were most likely from other covens. Then it struck me. The covens had helped to seal Fabian away — he had exacted revenge on these women, making sure it could never happen again. My nightmare showed me his deadly handiwork, and his reason for taking time away before dealing with me.

Still reeling from this sight and still startled by the evilness of this deed, I move on, out of this room and along a corridor. I came to a doorway where a slip of light shone out into the hall through a crack in the almost-closed door. I could just see through the minimal opening another open doorway into a room on the left side. Not wanting to open the door and alert anyone to my presence, I made my way further along the corridor and turned right into the next hallway, to find the open doorway. I came upon it, could see the walls inside lined with bookshelves, and a large mahogany, leather-topped desk sat in the middle of the room. Fabian sat at the desk in a high-backed, studded, leather chair, writing with a quilled pen and ink like they did in the olden days. He was most certainly stuck in the past and, as I watched him, I wondered how he would cope in this modern age. I noticed then that his hands and clothes were covered in blood.

Our eyes met briefly, which happened on occasion, but it never fazed me. This time however, it gave me a strange feeling in the pit of my stomach, maybe because of the carnage I had just witnessed, and now knowing who the perpetrator was. It was as if I was actually there and he could physically see me.

My goosebumps rose.

As unnerved as I was, I tried to remain calm, knowing it was just my imagination. I had done this on many occasions. This time was no different. I couldn't see what he was writing, but when he'd finished, he tore a page from the journal in front of him, stood and came around the front of the desk, laid the piece of paper on the corner closest to me. Then he turned and walked towards the other door to leave. I moved to the corner of the desk and read the page. It was a short letter to the covens with instructions at the bottom to send it to the people on the list. Maybe instructions to himself. The letter stated that he had greatly diluted the coven members and that he would be coming after the rest of them next, in restitution for his time spent locked away rotting in the loft. He said he figured it only fair that, given all the life he had missed out on, they should now miss out on theirs, and slaughtering every witch in New Orleans would be his next step.

I shuddered at his words and let out a little sigh. I looked up only to realise he had stopped in his tracks and had turned back to face me, his eyes staring straight into mine. This time he held my gaze and I struggled to hold my composure — his look was so chilling. Then he spoke. 'I'm coming for you now, Lily.'

In that instant, he was across the room and in front of me, his hand around my throat. Staring at me, he squeezed the breath from me, and enjoyed the horror in my eyes as I struggled. My eyes bulged with the pressure of his grip.

Suddenly I woke up, choking and coughing, holding my neck and trying to take a breath. Tears streamed down my face and disbelief ran rampant through my brain. I made it from my bedroom to my bathroom on shaky legs, desperate for some water, and when I looked in the mirror, there were bruises forming where he'd grabbed me. This was the first time ever that I'd woken from a dream or nightmare in a different location to where I'd fallen asleep. I should have woken up in Tallis's arms.

Confused, I couldn't work out why. But one thing I knew for certain … this had not been a nightmare — this was real. He had been able to see me, and he had probably had that ability every time I had dreamt of him. I shivered, realising that he'd probably seen me at every visit, but never let on, like a cat playing with a mouse, watching and waiting until the time was right to pounce.

RAGE

It was the day of my wedding and the surrounding woods were undergoing a beautiful transformation. My family wandered around beneath the great oaks, arranging tables and chairs ready for the many guests who would arrive in the late afternoon. The tables were being adorned with beautiful lace tablecloths and all sorts of collected china. And a dance floor was being laid out by the gazebo, which had been patiently threaded through with beautiful flowers. Large white lanterns hung from the trees and more were being hung as the morning stretched into afternoon.

A week had passed since my frightening encounter with Fabian and I hadn't told a soul, figuring it could wait — thankfully the bruising had gone almost as quickly as it had appeared. I could now not bear the thought of spending another minute not married to Tallis and I wasn't going to let the memory of that night disturb my happiness today. The Monsanto were already arriving in droves, as were most of the other clans. I hadn't wanted them at the wedding but Dad had insisted that the correct protocol would be followed on this occasion. While my dad looked young, he was old school in his ways sometimes. Anyway, with Briff holding first place as the possible traitor, I couldn't be sure anymore if he'd been telling the truth about Alex and the ball. Besides, I couldn't possibly be the instigator of future peace between the clans if I held a grudge against the closest clan to us.

They had sworn their allegiance to me, and I had to believe they would be true to their word if we were to move forward.

Afternoon drew nearer and it was time to dress in my mum's gown. Elisabeth had applied my makeup and was busily seeing to my hair. Marchella hung the dress on the curtain rail by the window where the sun shone through — it hit the lace at such an angle it spread the shadow of its pattern on the wall. *So pretty.* When Elisabeth finished, I stood up and walked to the window, stood slightly behind the curtain so I could see, but not be seen. In the distance to the left of the barn, cars drew up and parked, the many guests then walking the path behind the barn, disappearing around its side to wander beneath the lantern-filled branches of the oaks that stretched out towards the Mississippi. Butterflies stirred in my stomach and my head throbbed slightly with the excitement. I hoped it wouldn't turn into a full-on headache and asked Elisabeth to pass me a couple of Tylenols and a glass of water just in case. Marchella helped me slip into my wedding gown. I breathed in, feeling slightly giddy as she buttoned up the dress at the back, and Elisabeth spread the train out behind me. The sleeves rested gently on my upper arms. Marchella handed me a small box and I took it with a trembling hand.

'Nervous, baby?' Marchella asked.

'Just a bit,' I said.

'One more hour and it will all be over.' She smiled, and I smiled back.

I couldn't believe I was feeling this way. I had been so excited right up until today and now as the moment drew closer- I was having — not doubts — but an underlying fear that this was my last day as a single girl — that somehow after today everything would be totally different. I loved Tallis with all my heart; he was the one I wanted to spend my '*forever*' with so there were no doubts that this was a wrong decision. I just had this nagging sensation inside me that made me feel giddy and nauseous … but I couldn't pinpoint what it was.

'Damn it. I have to sit a moment,' I said to Marchella, wiping my hand across my brow.

'Do sit, child, and stay calm now. What you're feeling is completely natural. Last-minute nerves, that's all it is,' she said, wrapping an arm around me. 'And stop touching your face, you'll ruin Elisabeth's beautiful makeup,' she teased.

I opened the tiny box she had given me :inside was a pair of beautiful droplet pearl earrings.

'Something old,' said Marchella. 'Ridiculously old in fact. I wore them at *my* wedding a few centuries ago.' She helped me to put them on and then handed me a small mirror.

'Oh my, thanks, Marchella. They are just perfect.' I smiled, and the butterflies settled but seconds later they were fluttering rampantly again.

'Damn these butterflies! Leave me alone why don't you?' I shouted.

Feeling like I was going to throw up, I stood and headed for the open window. Suddenly the butterflies felt like they were no longer in my stomach but rising to my throat and the tickling sensation made me cough and cough. I reached for the windowsill and poked my head out to gasp fresh air. Marchella patted me on the back and Elisabeth tried to shove a glass of water into my hand. My eyes watered and I could hardly breathe.

As I opened my mouth to take a breath, a bunch of pretty little blue butterflies came pouring out from within. They flew into the beautiful afternoon breeze, which swept them up and away. One more cough, and one last tiny little blue butterfly fluttered out. It sat there on my hand for almost a minute before the breeze caught it. I looked on, shocked, as did Elisabeth. But Marchella just turned me around, opened my mouth to check there were no more butterflies, took the water from Elisabeth and passed it to me. Then she carried on as if nothing had happened. Elisabeth stood staring at me and I sat down to take a sip of water and pull myself together.

'What the hell was that?' I said when I could finally speak.

'Nerves settled now?' Marchella asked.

I thought about it for a second and Marchella was right, the nerves had settled. The nausea had faded away, and the butterflies … well they were no longer fluttering. At least not in my stomach anymore.

'Yeah,' I breathed deeply. 'I'm feeling fine now.'

'Good,' said Marchella, 'because it's time to head downstairs. … don't want to be late now, do we? Come on … come on.'

Elisabeth still looked slightly worried, but I suddenly felt awesome. So off we went, out into the hall and down the stairs to where Olive and Caleb waited with my bouquet. Olive looked tearful when she saw me.

'Don't you dare cry, Olive,' I warned. 'You'll start me off and I'll ruin my makeup.'

'Sorry, it's just … well … you look incredible in that dress.'

Marchella was trying to push us along, urging us out the back door towards the woods and the beginning of the aisle where my dad was waiting for me. Caleb and Olive went ahead of me — the Best Man and Maid of Honour — followed by six little vampire bridesmaids. They looked so cute: my heart melted at the sight of them. Then went the youngest of the Du Plessis family, three-year-old twins — Nat, the pageboy in his tiny suit, shirt and bow tie, carrying the ring cushion, and Bea, in a tiny version of the bridesmaid dress, carrying a basket of petals,

As they walked down the aisle ahead of Dad and I, they threw handfuls of petals out onto the ground. I watched the little ones as I walked, holding Dad's arm firmly as I was worried about tripping in my heels on the uneven forest floor. Then I caught a glimpse of Tallis looking back at me. His eyes followed me down the aisle and a look of absolute joy crossed his face. He looked so handsome in his suit. From where I stood, the scene was so pretty, and with Tallis in it I felt as though I were gazing on a painting, a work of art. A masterpiece. Then we stood face to face and my dad handed me over to him and stepped back. The way they both looked at me, I couldn't tell at that moment which one loved me more.

Tallis led me to the beautiful flower-covered gazebo, guided me up a couple of steps and stopped in front of our local church pastor, who smiled welcomingly. The crowd's rowdy chatter diminished as they sat and fell into silence. And the vows began.

In the front row, Marchella dabbed her eyes with a hanky, and next to her Dad sat looking so proud. The Monsanto's sat in the row behind them, to the left, and, as I scanned the guests, I noted Alex was missing. I scanned all the rows and came to rest at the back where, to my surprise, was Charlotte. And sitting next to her was a very sad-looking Alex. *So, he came after all.* It must have been hard for him to receive the invitation, hard for him to watch me marry someone else when he so obviously thought I was the one for him. I brought myself back to the moment and smiled at Tallis as he spoke beautiful words of love to me. Then it was my turn.

I had especially prepared a beautiful verse that I began to read. Tallis watched me adoringly and I swear his eyes misted over as I finished the last line of verse. We were so wrapped up in each other at that moment that we may as well have been alone. The crowds of onlookers, the pastor, even Dad and Marchella disappeared into a haze of fuzziness. I only had eyes for Tallis, and he for me. Then the pastor spoke, breaking the spell, and we were surrounded once more.

'Do you, Tallis Summers, take Lily Du Plessis to be your lawful wedded wife, to love and to cherish, to have and to hold, as long as you both shall live?' the pastor boomed so that even those at the back could hear.

'I do,' said Tallis without wavering. He held my hand gently and smiled that beautiful smile.

'And do you, Lily Du Plessis, take Tallis Summers to be your lawful wedded husband, to love and to cherish, to have and to hold, as long as you both shall live?'

As he spoke these words a strange feeling came over me. A weird coldness spread up my spine, and my hands began to tingle. A sharp pricking sensation, like a million tiny needles, shot through my brain interrupting my thoughts, the feeling so overwhelming I almost passed out. My hands shot up to hold my head, and Tallis rushed forward to grab me as I almost collapsed.

'Lily, what's wrong?' he shouted. But I couldn't speak, the pain was so intense. I could see Dad and Marchella rushing towards the gazebo. The guests all rose to their feet and scrambling from their seats towards the front.

'He's coming,' I whispered.

'What?' Tallis said.

'He's coming,' I shouted. 'Fabian's coming!'

Sudden and utter chaos overtook the peaceful setting as everyone struggled to move out of the pews into the aisle. Some climbed over the seats. Chairs were knocked over and women screamed, trying to get to the toddlers, who were crying because of the commotion.

The little bridesmaids were shuffled quickly away towards the safety of the house. Tallis hung on tightly to me as we moved down onto the forest floor. Suddenly a group of men grabbed him and dragged him from my arms. The look in his eyes meant trouble as his pupils enlarged and his muscles started to pulsate, the change taking place as the men strained to hold him. Then Caleb dashed through the crowd and the next thing I knew a small arrow jutted out of Tallis's neck. He stared at me in disbelief and confusion before his legs gave way beneath him. His struggling ceased as his eyes slid shut. I started crying — it was so hard to see that look on his face as he realised what was happening, and knowing he could do nothing to save himself, or me.

'Quickly, take him to the cellar. There's no time to waste. Everyone here needs to leave. Find safety. Maybe the cavern,' I shouted. All I could think about was the safety of everyone there. I had to get the area cleared.

'We are not leaving you here alone — no way!' my dad yelled.

'Please, Dad,' I begged. 'Let me do this ... please! I can't stand to see any of you hurt.'

'Not your choice!' Dad shook his head, and a crowd of others surrounded him. Du Plessis and Monsanto nodded their heads in agreement. The men carried Tallis off to the safety of the cellar, which gave me a small sense of relief. But not much. There were far too many of my loved ones that were refusing to leave me, and I felt like I had no control.

I started to shake with anger. 'Everybody, *LEAVE*!' I screamed at those around me.

Then, in the distance, I saw him coming through the trees, alone.

And fear gripped me.

It was no longer a fear for myself but for those around me. I ran through the crowd, pushing them out of the way, and shouting, but they stood firm. Others scattered in all directions, toppling over tables, the pretty floral teapots smashing on the ground. They headed for the house, for the safety of the trees, scooping up small children as they ran from the path of the monster.

He was now only twenty feet from me. My brow started to tingle, and my sweaty palms began to emanate flames. Rushing towards him, I threw flames in his direction. Dad, Caleb and Emmanuelle overtook me and flew at Fabian, biting his neck and his arms, trying to constrain him in any way they could, to stop him moving forward. He hit out at them with terrible blows, sent them flying far into the trees. A group of Monsanto's attacked from the left. But he fought back, hurling punches and kicking, but so far he'd not used any of the greater skills at his disposal. I knew why. These attacks were nothing to him, these vampire's pure fodder. He was saving it all up for me.

I heard a snap and turned as Edward Monsanto's head flew across my shoulder, blood everywhere. He had survived one battle with Fabian in the past, only to be taken out by him after all. And still Fabian fought on, dispensing with each attack as it came upon him.

My dad, Caleb and Emmanuelle moved with the speed of bullets. As quickly as he fought them off, and sent them flying, they were on their feet and straight back at him, relentless. All to no avail. Onward he marched at a dreadful pace, removing anyone and anything in his path. Then he stood before me, his brown curls wet and stuck to his forehead.

I could now see his constraint showing. Noticed his hands dripping. His jaw tensed as if he was holding in a hurricane. The fireballs I'd thrown at him had bounced off, as if a force field protected him. The forest was alight, and the lanterns, most of them, hung like tiny burning bushes through the trees. He stared at me, and I held his gaze, not knowing what would come next and how I would stop him. Mica, Slater and Mylo now flanked me, growling, baring their teeth, ready to pounce at him.

Then he said the strangest thing.

'Marry me, Lily.'

That was all he said.

Angry, I hurled a ball of flame at him. Up close, it penetrated whatever cover he had in place and set his jacket alight, yet he didn't flinch.

'Your efforts to hurt me are futile. We are one and the same and yet so different, you and I. Imagine a new race with our bloodlines, Lily.'

'Never! I'd rather die!' I screamed.

'So be it,' he said calmly, with a smile. The wolfling leapt, knocking him off balance, and I ran from the fray. I had lost sight of Emmanuelle and my dad. I was so scared for them. They had fought long and hard, and in all the commotion, I didn't see anything after the flying decapitated head. I hoped they were alive, or at least revivable. I turned back. Saw Fabian fighting the team as they tore at his legs and arms. Slater had a firm grip, Fabian's head in his mouth, but Fabian reached up and with both hands he grabbed a hold of Slater and flung him far into the forest. I heard him howl as his back hit the trunk of a tree and he went silent.

Quickly I scanned the forest, searching for Dad, Caleb, Emmanuelle. Caleb was in the distance out cold on the ground, but I couldn't see the others. I turned again to see Fabian snapping Mylo's neck, letting him fall to the ground, limp. *They have their rocks. They'll be okay. They have their rocks.*

I turned again, ran a little farther, still looking for familiar faces. Then suddenly from behind Fabian lunged at me. He threw me off balance, winding me, and as I went to straighten, I felt something … like a bolt of lightning had hit me in the side of the head. I chanted a freezing spell trying to buy some time, but he punched me again before I could finish. I went flying into a tree stump. Intense pain ripped through me and I realised I must have broken something. I staggered to my feet, tried to drag myself away, tried to get the spell out as quickly as I could but he was on me again. This time he knocked me to the ground and held his fists above my head ready to smash my skull. In the distance, I could see Mica's body lying curled up on the floor, as if he were sleeping. But I knew it wasn't so. In the opposite direction, I saw Caleb coming to. As he stood and looked across at me, I caught his eye. Then he looked at something past me. I couldn't see what it was because my head was pinned to the ground. He was the only one in my line of vision and I heard him scream '*No!*' as he rushed in my direction. All of a sudden Fabian's grip loosened and he fell forward with a thud, his head hitting mine as he fell. I turned my head quickly, and there behind us with a whacking great tree branch stood Olive.

'No, Olive,' I shouted. 'No, get out of here!'

But she kept on hitting him. In one foul swoop, Fabian twisted around under the weight of the branch and grabbed hold of it; he pulled Olive towards him, without letting go of me. Tears streamed down her face. Then Fabian let go of me and grabbed her around the neck. I heard her gasp as I scrambled to my feet. What happened in those next moments felt like much longer, as if I were watching it all in slow motion — Caleb running towards us — Olive's beautiful face draining of all its colour as Fabian squeezed tighter — me scrambling to my feet as Olive fell to the ground. As Fabian turned around, I swung at him with all my might, sent him hurtling towards the trees. Caleb was now beside Olive, wailing 'No, no, Olive, no!' He cradled her in his arms. I jumped across them and headed in Fabian's direction to keep him from them. He rose to his feet and shot through the woods, grabbing hold of me and throwing me up into the trees. My back hit a thick branch, which sent me hurtling towards the ground. When I hit the ground, he was waiting.

'You've got one last chance to give me the answer I'm looking for,' he said, dragging me up onto my feet.

My voice quavered. I was losing. Olive was possibly dead. Caleb was distraught. I didn't know if Dad was alive; whether Emmanuelle had left me to die, or died himself … Right now, I no longer cared … about anything. I figured dying would take all the pain away.

'I said *Never!* And I meant it. You are a monstrosity. I'll never marry you, so kill me now.'

He smirked with disappointment then I felt his fist hit my face. 'Not right now,' he said, smiling, 'I'm having too much fun.'

My head spun. I couldn't think straight. Couldn't see straight. But my anger was bursting at the seams. I closed my eyes and the pain shifted through me like little jolts of electricity. My hands were on fire, but I had no energy to use them. I wanted to run, but my feet felt detached. Another swift blow crunched into my upper body.

I'm going to die … we are all going to die. Where is my power? Where is it? I've failed. I've lost it all.

All these thoughts ran through my mind, and in the distance, I heard a voice shouting. The words were obscure, but the voice was so familiar. Then I felt an ice-cold shiver go through me, a sharp, stinging feeling slicing right into me. I looked up to see a long thin blade being pulled from me. It wasn't real for it faded as soon as it was withdrawn. But it had the same effect as a real sword and blood started to pour from my side. I fell to my knees on the ground, losing sensation in my legs as they shook with the pain. And the voice: it was coming closer now. Fabian was no longer standing over me. I slumped down and rolled onto my side — eyes closed.

It's Tallis's voice I can hear. I must be so close to death now. I'm hallucinating. He's not here. He's locked away, He's safe … he's safe.

I was losing consciousness. Imagining Tallis was with me. One last time. *The voice — so loud — so clear — so near. Shouting.* I opened my eyes and looked towards the direction of the voice, hoping to see a vision of the man I loved — a piece of him to take to heaven with me. What I saw made my stomach turn over, and bile rose in my throat. It was no vision. Tallis was there right in front of me. He was wolfling, snarling, growling, baring his huge fangs. I watched as his paws left the ground close to my head. He pounced at Fabian who was now laughing like a jackal. I pulled myself up to a sitting position, reached out for the nearest object to steady myself on. Pulled myself up slowly so I was standing, unsteadily as it was.

How did Tallis get here? Why isn't he in the cellar? Who released him? Who would do such a thing?

I felt sick; felt I could actually vomit. I felt weak, beaten and scared — scared for me and scared for Tallis. I felt so useless. All that training … what was it for? Fabian was a powerhouse. What had made me think I stood a chance against him? Even in my angriest state, I couldn't draw on the powers within me to their fullest extent. I was a three at best, and Fabian was a ten.

As my vision settled, the pain subsided. And the bleeding seemed to stop. I could almost feel the healing process, as if the deep cut was starting to close itself. The giddiness slowly reduced, and I felt the power building up inside once more. But I still felt defeated. One more round with Fabian and I was certain he would kill me. Right now, I just wanted to help Tallis. If I could just pull myself together enough to repeat that spell, perhaps I could freeze Fabian momentarily, distract him for a short while so Tallis could get to safety. *Who are you kidding? Tallis isn't going anywhere. He won't ever leave my side unless forced to.*

Shifting quickly to the left, I ducked as Fabian's body flew past me. Two seconds later Tallis in huge wolfling form thrashed through the leaves, grabbing Fabian by the neck and shaking him like a little ragdoll. He seemed to have the upper hand, but I knew only an immortal could kill an immortal. So Tallis's tactics, while they may hold Fabian at bay for a while, were little more than a distraction from the end game. That game was one I would have to play. And it was a game I was unlikely to win.

Tallis and Fabian were struggling on the forest floor, thrashing around, bashing against trees. I tried to gather my strength, to pull something magically out of my bag of tricks. But worrying about Tallis distracted me. I couldn't think straight while thinking about Tallis. He had Fabian in his grip, his sharp teeth biting down to the bone. Sprays of blood splattered the surrounding area. Fabian looked worn down but, although Tallis was massive and strong, Fabian was stronger. I started reciting the words to the freezing spell as I walked briskly towards them. My hands were now back to the usual torch-like limbs of earlier, and I started to throw flames at Fabian, trying my best to miss Tallis. I threw one bolt of fire, which was so strong it snapped a tree in two, and I had to scream at the top of my lungs, 'Tallis, move!' before it fell and trapped him. The falling tree was barely inches above him when something I wasn't expecting happened — the tree flew up in the air. I flicked my hand and the tree levitated above him, giving him time to shift quickly from beneath it. I flicked again, and the tree flew towards Fabian, knocking him to the floor just as he was rising to his feet. I pointed my hands at anything nearby that could move, sent a barrage of broken trees, stumps, branches, even rocks in his direction. One small branch struck him in the eye and came out through the back of his skull. Now he clearly looked like the monster he was.

With one hand, he pulled at the protruding branch at the back of his head, screamed as it went through, taking his eyeball with it. In the other hand, he held a long, spiked branch, pointing it in Tallis's direction as Tallis flew mid-air towards him.

'No!' I screamed, rushing forward. But too late. Tallis landed on the spiked branch which tore through his fur and flesh, severing his spine as it passed through. The crack of his bone breaking filled the air.

'Argh! Tallis screamed. His eyes searched for mine in desperation. He found me, and our eyes locked on each other. His lips moved and I concentrated to hear what he said as I rushed forward.

'I love you, Lily. I'm sorry I failed you,' he whispered.

Fabian brought his other hand around and swiftly snapped Tallis's neck as he squirmed on the branch. His body writhed, then suddenly fell limp. He hung there dripping with blood and Fabian howled in triumph.

'No … no!' I screamed. *'NO!'* My world crumbled around me. My heart beat so fast I thought it would burst with the pain. Shaking violently, I fell to my knees, screaming. Sheer horror rushed through me like a torrent. And then the tears came. Fabian tossed Tallis at my feet. Lifeless. Beautiful. Dead.

'There now, Lily. There'll be no half-breeds running my

kingdom. You have no choice now. Join me or die. Only I can be King. Only I can rule this kingdom. Be my Queen. Don't make me kill you.' He spoke softly now as he came towards me, slowly, putting his hand out.

'No good can come from the reign of a fool.' I whispered through my tears, my head down.

But something was happening inside me. Something I'd never felt before. A power so intense I thought I would explode. The sky darkened above us. The forest around us fell into an eerie blackness as if night had suddenly fallen. The only light to see by was the burning of the trees and lanterns around us.

Fabian looked up as the starless black sky started to pop and crack, as if gas were escaping and trying to ignite.

I leant my head against Tallis as his wolfling form slowly turned back to human form, turned back to the man I had loved beyond all reason — to the man who, today, should have become my husband. Tears poured down my face as I held him in my arms, as I kissed his beautiful face, knowing this was the last time I would be able to touch him, to feel him close to me. I clung to his lifeless form, as yet warm but so still. I ran my hand through his hair, touched his soft cheek. His eyes stared up at me with the same desperation I had seen only moments before when he'd said his final words. I shook as I leant against him. Remembering. One hand on his heart now, the other hand closing his eyelids as my tears fell on his lips, which no longer held even the trace of a whisper.

Standing, I felt a tremendous rage burning inside me, like I had been infused with the power of an atomic bomb. And for the first time, Fabian looked at me and took a step back. No fast retreat, just a tentative backward step as I moved fearlessly forward. My emotions in full explosive mode, power streamed out of me like never before. Not only my hands, but my arms, my body, were all suddenly alight, engulfed in a ball of fire. Sparks shot out in every direction. I couldn't stop crying. Crying for Tallis. And I realised … *love* was my emotional strength.

My love for Tallis and my deep sense of loss brought about a crescendo of emotional power that even the heavens in all their glory couldn't surpass. I walked staunchly towards Fabian, and he backed away. Then, in a surprise move, he flew at me, but my reflexes were lightning fast as I grabbed him by the throat. Lifted him easily into the air. Threw him far across the woods. He hit the trunk of a burning tree. I sent shockwaves of fireballs at him relentlessly, one after the other, setting him alight, burning him up without a moment's relief — no chance for him to gather himself, to gather his strength.

I ran at him, screaming at the top of my lungs, and the sky above me opened up. The cracks screeched as the fabric of the sky tore and stretched open. Rain poured down in torrents. The more I cried, the heavier it rained. The more I screamed, the louder the crackling and popping came from above. Thunder rolled, and lightning bolts shot down through the pitch blackness. Then the rain turned to fire and poured down all around us, burning everything up in its path.

I was completely out of control.

I no longer had any way of stopping.

I was no longer even thinking.

My mind in an irrational mess, the only message coming through was death … death of my beloved — an eye for an eye — death of Fabian Monsanto. In that blind rage, I knew no boundaries. He rose to his feet with great difficulty and, by the stern concentration on his face, I could see he was trying to fill himself up, trying to recharge his power. He shouted in a language that could only be the devil's as he dragged himself towards me. Within seconds I had him by the throat again.

'You can burn me up, Lily, but you can't kill me. I'm invincible! You belong with me. We belong together. This world is ours ... ours, I tell you.' His gargled reasonings, his desperate pleas squeaked from his throat as I squeezed tighter. I looked upon his monstrous face as it caught alight, watched as his dark curly hair sizzled and burnt. What was left of his gorgeous features started to melt, his one good eye warping and drooping with the intensity of heat. 'You can't kill me!' he squealed. A small laugh escaped as if he really believed his own words.

'You killed the man I love. He's gone forever,' I whispered venomously.

'I did you a favour,' he said, squirming in my grip, his feet a metre off the ground. 'You'll thank me one day when we are together.'

'Can the dead receive thanks?' I whispered, then smiled wickedly.

'You won't kill me, Lily. You can't. I'm immortal! I'm fireproof!' he replied loudly, and confidently.

I released my grip and, for a fleeting moment, I saw relief on his burning features, as if he thought I had finally seen the light. I grabbed him again and shoved him up against the tree trunk, stared straight into his eyes so I could all at once capture his look of agonising terror. I shoved my hand through the flesh of his chest, crushing his ribs on the way through. I could hear the muscles tearing. His warm blood poured down my arm, and his pulsating heart throbbed in my hand. I concentrated hard on releasing the power I held within. The sky crackled so loudly, and the burning rain beat down so fast we were ankle-deep in flaming water. Nevertheless, I squeezed even tighter, heartbeat after heartbeat pounding against the palm of my hand.

'Let's see if you are fireproof on the inside?' I said calmly, and with those words I looked skyward, summoned all the power flowing through me into his rapidly racing heart. Fire rushed from the outside of me to the inside, through my body and up my arm, releasing all at once from my hand. The fire infiltrated every vein and artery within his pumping organ. He struggled, kicked, screamed, then with one swift heartbeat I felt first his heart then his insides explode. I looked down at that final moment to see his body — his outer shell and inner being- shatter with the intensity of an exploding bomb. A million tiny pieces scattered everywhere with such force there was not a scrap of Fabian left standing before me.

There was just an empty space ... as empty as my broken heart.

EPILOGUE

If I'd known the pain emotion would bring, I would have begged beyond all reason to remain emotionless, like I'd been as a child. I had, in growing, glimpsed the meaning of true happiness and felt the lightness of a swallow on the wing, lifted by the breeze to higher places, places that were out of reach of mere mortals. To have found all that I had ever craved and then to have lost it, seemed an outrageous fate, one that had seen hell rain down, without mercy, on all my kind. I wanted to run far away, to the ends of the earth, ravaging everything in my path, crushing every mortal and immortal alike. My nerve endings were raw, and the blood that pulsed through my veins seemed to stop short of my heart. I would never be able to calm the storm within again. Someone should have told me that reaching my Immortality would come at a hefty price. I would gladly have taken a bullet before that day ... before my new world fell apart.

https://www.facebook.com/ImmortaLily

Watch out for Book Two in the Immortal Hearts Trilogy

ImmortaLily Rage

Coming soon!

ABOUT THE AUTHORS

Georgia Beyers was born in London, England, and has been living in Australia since 1989. She is married with three grown-up children, three grandchildren, four foster children, and a dog called Charlie Bear; she loves books, chocolate and cats; hates sharks, cottage cheese and the cold. Georgia writes both middle-grade books and young adult books. In her spare time, she enjoys reading, travelling, spending time with her family, especially her children and grandchildren, and writing about herself in third person - Haha.

Jak Collins was born in Perth, Western Australia in 1992. He married his soul mate and best friend. He has one incredible, beautiful little girl called Emerson. He is highly creative and runs a successful Perth based photography business — JWC.IMAGE - where he gets to shoot some of the most beautiful models in WA, on some of the most pristine beaches in the world. He spent two years at The Acting Corps in Los Angeles and is the co-author of the Young Adult urban fantasy — Immortal Hearts Trilogy. In his spare time, he likes to ride his motorcycle, go free diving, hang out with photography associates and friends, and enjoy family life.

www.ingramcontent.com/pod-product-compliance
Lightning Source LLC
Chambersburg PA
CBHW030352310726
48979CB00001B/276

* 9 7 8 1 9 2 2 3 4 3 7 2 7 *